FATAL RECALL

Also by Deforest Day

A COLD KILLING
AUGUST ICE

FATAL RECALL

DEFOREST DAY

Carroll & Graf Publishers, Inc.
New York

First Carroll & Graf edition 1991

Carroll & Graf Publishers, Inc.
260 Fifth Avenue
New York, N.Y. 10001

Library of Congress Cataloging-in-Publication Data

Day, Deforest.
Fatal recall / by Deforest Day. — 1st Carroll & Graf ed.
p. cm.
ISBN 0-88184-681-3 : $18.95
I. Title.
PS3554.A959F38 1991
813'.54—dc20 91-14224
CIP

Manufactured in the United States of America

Dedicated to the memory of
Margaret C. Day
Mother, Mentor, Muse

Acknowledgments:
Thanks are due to both Robert Dunkelberger, for clues to unfamiliar life-styles, and Robert Mariano, for inside information on official Washington, a world that is always arcane and often clandestine. Any errors of fact are solely the author's.

Thanks also to Margaret Norton, an editor whose wise and sensitive guidance brought this novel to realization.

Special thanks to my agent, Janet Wilkens Manus; her experience and knowledge of the publishing world, coupled with her steadfast faith, helped me over the rough moments.

Prologue

Shortly before his death Lieutenant General Harmon Kilgallen, USA, Ret. is sitting at the large walnut partner's desk in the den of his northern Virginia farmhouse, a modest rural dwelling when compared to the far grander homes of his neighbors. The General's neighbors are named Harriman and Mellon, Duke, Defoe, and Dillon; people whose fortunes predate the present century and whose antecedents predate the Constitution.

At the time of his death, General Kilgallen is working on his memoirs, a pleasant enough task to occupy the twilight years of a long and illustrious life and career, and one generally considered harmless. The chapter in question, however, wherein Harmon Kilgallen, a colonel when the events took place, recounts how he was wounded in action and returned to the States for rest and recuperation, will prove to be anything but harmless. And the General's frame of mind, as he sits at the big desk, its broad surface littered with notes and manila folders and stacks of history books—drab in their faded blue and gray and maroon buckram bindings, the gold-stamped titles faint from years of handling in the War College library—is anything but pleasant. He is puzzled, and not a little annoyed. The mutters and murmurs, not fully formed into words, that escape his lips betray his emotions. An eight-by-ten envelope, with the General's name and road, town and zip code typed on a label bearing the return address of the National Archives and "Photographs: Do Not Bend" stamped in red across its front, lies between his hands. His slender, slightly arthritic fingers sort and resort the several dozen photographs, as though by the mere act of noisily shuffling the glossy black-and-white prints the images can be modified to meet the preconception the General brought to the task of studying the pictures.

He is therefore not pleased when he hears a sound at the French doors that open onto the brick terrace overlooking his rolling fields and looks up to see what the interruption is.

The right-hand French door, the one with the exterior handle, opens and the General's visitor enters, the muffled click of the latch signaling the closing of the door behind him. If an autopsy were to be performed, it could be later calculated, by those who employ the formulas of forensic medicine, that it is some time after four in the afternoon. The General's den is at the rear of the house, facing west, so his caller must be backlit by the afternoon sunlight that streams through the doors; a dark silhouette with a walking stick or cane that he repeatedly taps on the floor, playing a nervous tattoo as each contemplates the other.

"What?" the General says, no doubt shading his eyes with his hand, *"Ah, it's you, is it?"* The tone of the General's voice can be categorized as irascible, even angry. He is not happy to see the visitor, but his appearance is not altogether unexpected. This from a single word; not even a word, really, just a sound. "Oh, it's you" would denote a slight element of surprise, whereas "Ah, it's you" indicates a certain expectancy. Nevertheless, the overall tone of the General's voice definitely carries a hint of annoyance above his usual irritability.

The General's caller says something in response from across the room, but the voice is far away and the words are indistinguishable. It is a mature male voice with a sureness that transcends its incomprehensibility.

There are several Oriental rugs in the General's den, a five-by-seven Sarouk between the dark leather sofa and the fireplace, and a longer, narrower runner leading into the hallway and the interior of the house, but the path from the doors to the desk is bare and highly polished oak, and the visitor's footsteps click on the floor with the hard sound of leather soles and heels as he crosses the room. It is an infrequently heard sound in this day of the Adidas and the Nike and the rubber-heeled street shoe. The General's chair squeaks and its casters rumble on the floor as he shoves it back and rises. *"What the devil d'you—"* he says.

There is a sharp, puzzling sound, then an "uhhh," and the General noisily falls to the floor, bringing first the chair with him, then books and papers from the desk. Perhaps he has caught his foot in the chair as he stands and has lost his balance. The leather heels click again, fade; there are sounds from the far end of the room; the footsteps return. A rich, mechanical sound—precision machined metallic parts against each other as though the tumblers of an expensive lock are being worked—is followed by a sudden, deafening noise, so short and yet so overwhelming that it is unintelligible.

The deep, ball-bearing rumble of a steel filing cabinet drawer being opened, then closed, is repeated, followed by the sounds of the surface of the desk being quickly cleared. The noise of these activities is followed, in turn, by the crackle of flames. Ten minutes later the French doors are opened and quietly closed again. The sound of the fire continues for another seventeen minutes.

ONE

Chase Defoe, Captain, USN, Ret. awoke and lay naked on, under, and among a cloud of futon, stared up through the skylight above his head and contemplated the enormity of the silent universe. The thought of a time-space continuum and the even more abstract concept of infinity were among the scant few creations of the human mind that could bring him to his metaphoric knees.

The stars were dying in a pale-blue sky tinged with pink at the horizon as the radio clicked on several seconds after six, and the Morning Edition theme music faded to Bob Edwards saying, "This is NPR, National Public Radio."

Defoe rolled off the elevated sleeping platform, a slightly raised area delineated by the hard straw of three tatami, a pair parallel, the third perpendicular, and fluffed the futons into a semblance of order—easier, after all, than making a bed—then walked to the opposite end of the room and stood under the shower while the NPR reporters brought him up to date.

Defoe's bedroom had a twelve-foot ceiling at its center, and sloped to nothing at the eaves. The large skylight was centered in the south side of the slate-shingled roof, so that he could look both up and out from his bed—up at the clouds or sun or stars, out at the patchwork quilt of the Pennsylvania farmland; four-, five-, ten-acre fields bounded and defined by rod-wide hedgerows. The size of the field was determined by the abundance of rocks the early settlers found beneath the forest floor after they had cleared the timber. With only an oak sled and a team of oxen to pull it, the pioneers did not drag their loads of stones too far before piling them in orderly rows, rows that soon sprouted with black locust and white oak, volunteer seedlings of sumac, and the occasional osage orange, the last a stunted, smooth-skinned tree that yields globular green fruit christened "monkey brains" by the local children who fling them at passing cars and each other with youthful abandon. The other trees serve no less a purpose; the black locust, a legume, takes nitrogen from the air and passes it to the soil through root nodules—anachronistic perhaps in the era of chemical fertilizers, but it grows to a diameter of eight inches in less than ten years and yields a fence post that lasts for more than thirty. A hundred years ago the white oak was cut to length and stripped of bark, then split and rived into billets that were further peeled and woven into stout baskets, trugs, and lugs to haul potatoes and onions from the fields. Today, those same containers—the survivors—have found their way into museums and the collections of the rural cognoscenti, while the offspring of the oaks still provide hot, clean fire for the airtight stoves of their commuting owners. Sumac, a weak and weedy useless thing, yields a cluster of dry, red seeds that looks like maiden grapes withered on the vine. Steeped in water, they offer both a tart beverage and a pinkish dye, each appreciated by the natives of the area centuries before the Hypermart provided packaged Rit and powdered lemonade. And even the unloved osage offered a wood for spoons and bowls, a color for the artist's palette, and a name for an indigenous nation. All this, and more, Defoe learned as he discovered the heritage of colonial Pennsylvania.

The fields delineated by these shrubby boundaries were planted with corn, alfalfa, rye, and winter wheat, the colors and crops dependent on the rotational whims of the neighboring farmers and the progress of the seasons.

Closer to the eaves, Defoe could look down at the foundation of the old stone farmhouse a hundred feet away, now a crumbling ruin covered with Virginia creeper just starting to show its pale new growth in the early spring. Defoe had lived there, in the house, alone, before the fire. He'd lost the house and everything in it, and after the last volunteer fire company had folded their hoses, stowed their pikes, and driven back out the narrow farm lane, he'd sat on the whitewashed stone wall that surrounded the loafing yard of the old bank barn and considered the smoldering remains of his house, decided the fire had been just another rite of purification, the second one.

The first had come five years earlier, in southern California, in the desert, uncounted hours east of San Diego. He drove there nonstop in the old Jaguar sedan, with nothing but five gallons of water, his .38 revolver, and the demons. Four days later, he returned to San Diego with just the Jag. Then he resigned his commission, signed the necessary papers his wife's lawyer had prepared, and headed east again, this time not stopping until he reached Pennsylvania.

The old farmhouse and bank barn, tucked away at the end of a quarter-mile dirt lane, had been the perfect hideout while he rebuilt his life.

Defoe lathered his short, salt-and-pepper hair with shampoo. His ears were filled with a mixture of soap and rinse water and he didn't hear the report of General Kilgallen's death. The shower stall was formed by three large sheets of plate-glass mirror that he had gotten cheap from a salvage yard and he used them now, both to shave his whiskers and appraise himself. At five seven, Defoe was shorter than most, but broad-shouldered and slim-hipped and, he thought as he studied eyes that were gray or blue depending upon the color of the sky or the shade of his suit, not bad for a man recently returned from a twenty-fifth college reunion.

He slipped on his warm-up suit and Reeboks, picked up the two-suiter he had packed the night before, killed the radio, and went downstairs, his quick steps clattering on the metal treads. He stopped at the main floor just long enough to put a kettle of water on the stove, then went back to the spiral stairs and took them to the bottom level of the old bank barn.

The cast-iron staircase had been his single folly, his only extravagance when he had converted the barn to a dwelling after the fire. The stairs had come from a lighthouse on the Outer Banks and now formed an ornate double helix that rose forty feet to the top of the barn.

The middle level of the structure, where teams of horses had once stamped impatiently on the three-inch planks that formed the floor while men unloaded hay with forks and sweat, was now the living area, one large room, thirty feet square and fifteen to the ceiling. A simple kitchen was tucked into the northwest corner, and the south wall was storefront glass, flooding the interior with warmth and light. A large Oriental rug in muted earth tones occupied much of the floor and a comfortable leather sofa faced the view. That was the extent of the furnishings. A decorator had once come into the building and stood, taking in the whitewashed bricks of the west wall, the honey hues of the rough plank floor, the view, and pronounced it the most perfect, exquisite example of minimalism he had ever encountered. Defoe shrugged and said, "Right." He considered it simply a space in which he could define himself without competition from the clutter of civilization. Possessions can be a curse.

At the bottom level, the part that was below ground on the north side, he unlocked a heavy steel fire door in a concrete block room he had constructed at one end of the barn. The fluorescent light flickered and caught, and Defoe slid into the office chair behind the gray steel desk. He opened the briefcase that sat on its surface, checked that the tools of his trade were inside, then turned his attention to the fax machine that was connected to both the telephone and the computer. Satisfied that there was nothing that demanded his attention, he locked the door and took his briefcase back upstairs, put it by the door with his suitcase.

He poured boiling water into a small stoneware teapot and filled an infuser with Earl Grey, then emptied the pot, dropped in the tea ball, and refilled it with the remainder of the boiling water. Earl Grey is a large-leaf tea and needs five or six minutes of steeping. He put two slices of bread under the broiler and got an orange from the refrigerator while the tea brewed and the bread toasted. He cut the orange in half, then extracted its juice and poured it into a glass, spread honey on the toast, poured tea into a cup, put it all on the kitchen counter, hooked a stool under his rump with his foot, and turned on the small clock radio. It was seven and Bob Edwards was back with the second hour of Morning Edition. This time Defoe heard about the death of General Kilgallen.

He turned off the radio and finished his breakfast in silence, then picked up the cordless telephone and walked to the south side of the barn, looked out across the fields at the March sunrise burning the dew from last year's corn stubble. He punched up the number from memory, having only to hesitate for a moment to get the area code right.

In Defoe's briefcase there was a fat leather-bound five-by-seven loose-leaf notebook containing the names, numbers, and vital statistics of nearly a thousand people, but he didn't need it for this call. He'd known the number since he was six or seven; used it as a kid, young man, then less and less as the years progressed, until now it was a twice yearly ritual at best —Christmas and Mother's Day.

"Hello?"

"Hello, Dad."

"Chase."

"Sorry to call so early, but I assumed you'd be up."

"Yes."

"I just heard about the General, on the radio. They said it was an accident. He was cleaning a gun that he thought was empty? Seems suspiciously euphemistic. Sounds like suicide to me."

"Damn right!" Defoe's father snorted. "Put the barrel of a side-by-side in his mouth and pulled the trigger. Twelve bore. Of course it was suicide. Harmon was a fine shot, always hit what he was aiming at."

"Do they have any idea of why he did it?"

There was a pause before the older man answered. "He'd been depressed lately. His doctor said he was in good enough health, for his age, except for some talk of this damn Alzheimer's nonsense. Seems to be a lot of it going around; every time you pick up a paper or look at the news somebody else has caught a dose."

"I think you're confusing it with AIDS."

"Queer's cancer? Don't be ridiculous."

Defoe sighed. "Alzheimer's is a degenerative disease; I don't think you catch it so much as it just develops. It's part of growing old, Dad. You remember Grandmother, how forgetful she was at the end."

"Hah. My mother was always forgetful."

"Speaking of mothers, could I talk to mine?"

Defoe the father put the telephone down without comment and Defoe the son watched a flock of starlings settle onto the corn stubble to glean the kernels missed by the combine the previous fall. The neighbor who rented the field would be plowing it under any day now, and planting a new crop.

The widening rift had finally become an uncrossable gulf when Defoe had resigned his commission just a few years shy of twenty. He could have hung on, retired honorably, barely forty and with a good pension, gone on to a second career. Defoe's father had made his disgust at his son's decision very evident. "Damned candy-assed wimp," he'd called his son. "You set a course, then goddamn it, you see it through to its conclusion. I told you it was stupid fifteen years ago, staying in the Navy after your ROTC obligation was fulfilled. You could be cresting in the State Department now, if you'd listened to me. Instead, you were off playing cowboys and red Indians with your cloak-and-dagger foolishness."

Defoe had needed, at the time, sympathy and understanding, not a lecture on Spartan values and lost opportunities.

George Philip Clinton Defoe had graduated from Yale at twenty and come into his grandfather's trust fund at twenty-one. He had taken the hundred thousand dollars and used it over the next half century to both build a fortune and assure himself a place in the power structure of the federal government.

When a Republican administration moved into 1600 Pennsylvania Avenue, the elder Defoe soon found himself a slot—if never quite at Cabinet level, always one not far removed. During Democratic days, he contented himself with increasing his fortune and influence behind the scenes. Now, at seventy-eight, he had nearly ten million dollars and knew everybody worth knowing.

The cynicism with which he led his life affected his son, and the sore that developed during prep school and college finally erupted when, after graduation, the young ensign had chosen the assignment offered in Naval intelligence rather than the position his father had arranged over at State.

His career had started with the capture of the intelligence ship *Pueblo* by the North Koreans, and then continued with fifteen years of covert work in Naval Intelligence rather than behind-the-scenes diplomacy in the State Department. Then Andy died and he chucked it all, realizing that the one was no more meaningful than the other.

"Hello, darling. Does it take a tragedy to have you call?"

"Hello, Mother. I see that Dad is tip-top. How have you been?"

"Oh, as well as can be expected, for a postmenopausal woman living with your father. I gather you're calling about Harmon Kilgallen."

"Yes. I just heard about it on the radio. Dad says he killed himself. How's Kit taking it? I assume you've seen her."

Defoe's mother cleared her throat. "Yes. That is, I've spoken to her on the telephone. Your father, of course, took charge of everything, went over there right away. I really think he's rather enjoying it, Chase. All the activity, I mean."

"He always was the puppeteer."

Mary Defoe laughed, a throaty chuckle. "Yes. Anyway, as I was saying, I spoke to Kit; she called here, as a matter of fact. Naturally, she was a wreck, but she's a strong girl, she'll come through. Her daughter was the one who found him. The child has been doing some typing for the General, apparently she stopped in after her job and found . . . him. She telephoned her mother and Kit called us, asked your father what she should do."

"When is the funeral? I really should come down; for Kit's sake, if nothing else."

"The funeral? I don't know that plans have been made yet. What?" Defoe could hear his father's voice in the background. "They are burying him on Thursday, your father says. At Arlington, of course."

"Thursday. I have to go up to Boston today, supposed to be a three-day trip, but I can shorten things a bit and drive straight down to Washington Wednesday night."

"You'll stay here, of course, darling."

"I don't know, Mother—"

"Don't be ridiculous. I'll have Anna make up your bed and air out the room. We'll have a lovely visit, even if I have to lock your father in the garage to get it." Her voice faded as she turned to address her husband. "I will, too! He's your only son, Philip, and you'll be civil when he's here or Chase and I will both check into a hotel and leave you here with Anna and Butterfield for company."

Defoe laughed, said, "All right, Mother, I promise I'll stay there. See you sometime Wednesday evening, probably late. I'll want to wait until the morning traffic thins out before leaving Boston."

He took his bags out to the car and fired the engine, relieved when it caught. The Jaguar, a MK II Saloon, was approaching its third decade and even when new, the typically British machine had been peckish in the damp. But it had a powerful engine and lots of leather and walnut inside and had been a steal when Defoe had bought it, slightly used, from a dealership in northern California. It was the right-hand drive that set the price; the car had been brought over by an English film star, then sold for plane fare home after his Hollywood career failed to materialize.

Defoe blipped the accelerator, slipped into first, and drove to Boston.

TWO

Defoe took the Capital Beltway, 495, and skirted Washington, dropped down on Fairfax County from the northwest. It was nearly ten when he downshifted into first at the top of the long driveway and killed the engine in front of the three-car garage, but one of the overhead doors was up and a shaft of yellow light was shining out onto the black macadam.

A tall, broad-shouldered old man walked outside and grinned as he recognized Defoe, wiped his right hand with a rag before offering it to the younger man. "Your momma tol' me you was coming down," he said, shaking hands. "How you been, son? I see you still driving that English car."

Defoe turned and glanced at his Jag, touched the warm hood. "Yep, still have it. Stick with a good thing, I guess, is as good advice as any. Hello, Butterfield, how are you?"

John Butterfield had been with the family for nearly half a century. He'd taught the young Defoe to ride a bicycle on this driveway, taught him to drive a car over the country roads it led to, taught him how to counterpunch—done a lot of things that are a father's job.

"I'm good, doing good." He smiled and bobbed his head and waved the rag in the direction of the garage. "Just shining up your daddy's car for tomorrow." He shook his head. "Terrible thing, about the General. Terrible."

Defoe got his bags out of the car. "Yes. I have a lot of fond memories of General Kilgallen. I learned a thing or two from him, Butterfield, had some good times over there." He turned and looked across the low hood of the Jaguar into the night. It was warm for March, and humid, the way Virginia can be in the spring.

Butterfield chuckled and said, "I know you did," winking when Defoe turned back to him.

Defoe felt his ears redden. He'd been seventeen and the General's daughter, Katherine Kilgallen, had been sixteen, and they had taken care of each other's virginity problem that July, then spent most of August enrolled in a crash course on sexual experimentation before returning to their separate preparatory schools. Not much got past Butterfield. Defoe remembered that he had been the one who had admonished him to be careful if he couldn't be good, and then had showed him how.

"Nothing wrong with your memory, either, Butterfield." He smiled at the old man, added, "Talk to you later. Time to go in and face the old boy." He picked up his bags and walked toward the familiar entry beneath the Federal portico. Trimmed yews and boxwood framed and softened the formal entrance to the house, and the gentle light from a pair of copper carriage lamps illuminated the three broad brick steps that marked the transition from driveway to dwelling.

It seemed strange to ring the bell and wait. He had a key, of course, but God knew where it was. Probably melted and buried under the rubble of the old farmhouse. He'd visited his parents only once since the fire, for his father's seventy-fifth birthday celebration, but that had been held in one of the hotels in town. More convenient for the President and the rest of the movers and shakers who had attended the occasion.

The door opened and Anna said, "Hello, Mr. Defoe," and stood aside for him to enter. "Your mother and father are in the library. Have you had your dinner?"

"Hello, Anna. Yes, I stopped for a bite a couple of hours ago."

"Well, then, let me take your bags up to your room and you go right in and say hello to your family."

"Don't be silly, Anna," he replied. "I can carry my own luggage upstairs. Go to bed or whatever it is that you do at this time of night." She smiled, and shook her head, headed for the kitchen.

Defoe put his suitcase and the crocodile briefcase on the green-and-white marble floor in front of the hall table, glanced at his reflection in the gilded mirror above it. His mother's patrician tastes reflected her husband's, and she had decorated the large Federal house almost entirely with furniture from its time. He took a breath and opened the pair of well-buffed mahogany doors to the library.

The same worn silk Tabriz greeted him, its colors and patterns faded to a muted mixture that, in the dim lighting, brought to mind the dried and crumbled leaves of autumn. Bookshelves, filled from floor to ceiling with the rich maroons and blues of calfskin and the duller tones of linen bindings, covered every inch of wall not given over to windows. Enough sun penetrated the translucent curtains during the daylight hours to give the room and its contents a painterly atmosphere, but after dark the volumes absorbed much of the light falling upon them from the pair of floor lamps on either side of the fireplace, and the brass student lamp centered on the long library table that dominated the center of the room did little to alleviate the gloom.

A sofa, upholstered in damask silk, was backed up to the table and faced the fireplace. Mary Maxwell Defoe sat in the center of the sofa, her back to her son. A warm pool of light from the lamp behind her fell over her shoulder and illuminated the book on her lap. Her husband, George Philip Clinton Defoe, sat in a matching armchair placed at a right angle to the sofa and nearer the fireplace. He was reading *The New York Times* and folded the top of it down as his son came across the room.

"Ah. The prodigal returns," he said, and noisily closed the paper, put it on the oval Sheraton table between his chair and the sofa. "You look like a damn hippie or yuppie or whatever they're calling them now." He waved his hand at Defoe's warm-up suit and running shoes. "I trust you're not planning on wearing that getup to the funeral."

"No, Dad. I have a couple of suits with me, don't worry. It's just that I find a ten-hour drive more comfortable without a coat and tie." Defoe looked at his father, dressed in his customary dark three-piece suit, shod in gleaming Oxfords, and then raised his eyes to the portrait above the mantel. Timothy Daniel Defoe, B. Hartford, 1735, D. New London, 1810. He smiled, remembering the antecedent catechism drilled into him by his father. Old Tim had been a New England shipping magnate; made his pile in slaves and rum. The portrait was one of the last that Copley had painted before leaving for Europe in 1774. There was another, by Benjamin West, in the National Gallery. His father had inherited the prominent nose and high forehead, he decided, looking once more at the man beneath the painting. *But then, I guess I have it, too,* he thought. Someone had once remarked that, in profile, Defoe was a dead ringer for the man on the nickel.

"Hello, darling," his mother said, and laid her book facedown on the sofa beside her, turned her cheek to receive his kiss. "Have you had anything to eat?"

Defoe contemplated a smart remark about turning to Judaism in her old age, then thought better of it and said instead, "Yes, I stopped in Delaware. You're looking well." Mary Defoe was sixty-eight, ten years younger than her husband, but could have passed for a woman in her fifties with the clear skin and auburn hair that was her Scottish heritage.

"What were you doing in Boston, dear?" she asked.

"Talking to one of the high-tech outfits about their security system. They're building a new plant and want to get it right the second time around. I think I got the contract to design it."

"Chase Defoe, a burglar alarm salesman." George Defoe gave a snort that exploded from his nostrils like a truck venting its air brakes.

"That's about it, Dad." Defoe smiled, knowing it would annoy him. "Chain-link fences, dawn-to-dusk lights, junkyard dogs." He didn't mention the more sophisticated and larger part of his business—computer security and communications interception. Electronic bugging and its prevention was a billion-dollar business, and Defoe was one of the best, having learned all there was to know in the Navy. Among other things, he had directed the team responsible for sweeping foreign embassies and had discovered and then helped dissect the unholy embarrassment that was to have been the new Moscow facility. But he had passed the need to impress his father, done that years before, in college, when he realized it couldn't be done. Like so many fathers, George Defoe had wanted to clone himself, and when his only son had taken a diverging path, he had used sarcasm at every opportunity to belittle his achievements. His marriage to a California girl—below, according to the senior Defoe, the family's station—had done nothing to improve their relationship. And the divorce that followed a dozen years later only solidified the father's conviction that his son could do nothing right.

"Stop fighting this instant!" Defoe's mother looked crossly at both of them. "Chase, go over and shake your father's hand. George Philip, stand up, get up out of that chair."

Defoe grinned and walked the two steps to his father, who rose, stiff and grumbling, but who nevertheless looked his son in the eye as he offered him a firm grip. "Hello, Chase. Welcome home." He gestured with his chin toward a butler's tray that held several crystal decanters, a silver pitcher, and half-a-dozen glasses. "Fix yourself a drink. And might as well make me a short bourbon and water while you're at it."

Defoe went over and picked up the decanter with the little silver collar identifying its contents as bourbon and poured a splash into one of the old-fashioned glasses. He turned and asked over his shoulder, "Mother?"

"No, thank you, nothing for me."

Defoe poured water over the bourbon, then fixed himself a Scotch. "It was a shock to hear about the General on the radio" he said, standing with his back to the fireplace so he could see both of his parents. "You said on the phone, Dad, that he'd been diagnosed as having Alzheimer's. How long had they known?"

"How the devil should I know? I wasn't the old fool's doctor."

Defoe looked at his mother, puzzled by his father's response, but she was looking down at her hands, folded in her lap. General Kilgallen had been a neighbor since Defoe was an infant, and he remembered his father and the General hunting the countryside and fishing the Chesapeake together, remembered going along with them since his tenth birthday. "I thought you two were great pals, Dad. You have a falling out?"

"Huh!" George Defoe swallowed the remainder of his drink. "That old fool," he said again, stood, and put his empty glass on the newspaper beside his chair. "I'm going to bed. Long day tomorrow, with the damn funeral and all." He gave his wife a stiff little nod, followed by the slightest inclination of his torso—residual politeness ingrained seventy years earlier by a governess—and left the room.

"What was that all about, Mother?"

Defoe sat next to her and took a sip of his Scotch. She still avoided his eyes, picked up her book instead, and said, "Oh, you know your father, dear. And Harmon *was* getting a bit peculiar." She looked at him then and smiled, put her hand on his thigh, gave it a maternal pat. "Just old age, Chase. Don't give it more attention than it deserves. How long can you stay with us?"

Defoe noticed the deft change of subject. "Couple of days, anyway. While I'm down here I want to say hello to a few friends. One of my college roommates is in the Justice Department now. You remember Doug Winston, don't you?"

"Doug? Yes, I think so. He was the boy from Connecticut. Well, it will be nice to see your friends, of course, but don't short us during your stay. Neither of us are getting any younger, you know." She hesitated before adding, "The next time you come down it may be to plant one of us."

"Oh, Mother! You and Dad are going to live forever. You're both too busy to die, and you know it."

She stood up, used the dust jacket to mark her place in the novel, and put it on the table behind the sofa. "Yes, of course you're right, dear. It's just that Harmon's death has made us all more aware of our mortality. Well, it's late for us senior citizens—God, I hate that phrase—and I think I'll follow your father off to bed." She put her arm around her son and kissed his cheek, then walked softly across the room. Defoe watched her enter the hall and start up the wide staircase, smiled as she hesitated a few steps up and waved to him.

He poured another measure of Scotch in his glass and sat with it, contemplating the cold fireplace.

THREE

Thursday greeted Defoe with a brief flash of panic as he awoke, disoriented by the unfamiliar bed, blankets, and subtle background sounds of the house. Then he eased his tensed muscles, relaxed, sank back into the mattress and considered his surroundings. He'd spent the better part of twelve years, the nights, at least, in this room, before his parents had shipped him off to the prep school in New England that was his father's alma mater. And then summers, spring and Christmas breaks as well, until college provided other, more interesting diversions. Bermuda one spring, he recalled, and he'd skied in Utah with a classmate over the Christmas of his junior year. He felt a pressure in his loins and thought of Katherine Kilgallen and the summer between prep school and college. He smiled. True, he'd slept most nights in this bed alone, but not before loping in the moonlight across the fields from her house and silently stealing up to his room at one or two in the morning. He lifted the covers and looked down, grinned at the iron-hard erection that stared back at him. "Get up, Defoe," he said aloud, "and pee before you give away the whole plantation."

By the time he'd crossed the cold floor to his bathroom his faithful companion had dropped ninety degrees and he was able to direct an accurate stream into the toilet.

He turned on the shower, stepped into the big clawfoot bathtub, and pulled the curtain around him. The bathroom had been modernized sometime after indoor plumbing had been introduced to the building, but well before the Second World War. However, the boiler in the basement was a more recent addition to the house, and Defoe, tired and aching from a long drive, luxuriated under the abundant hot water that flowed from the brass shower head.

Anna served him scrambled eggs and coffee in the dining room. He glanced quickly at the *Times,* reassured himself that the world still existed, and abandoned the paper for a second cup of coffee and the view of the Virginia countryside through the bay window. He turned as his mother came into the dining room.

"Good morning, darling," she said. "Did you sleep well?"

"Yes, thank you." She wore her robe, a quilted blue affair that reached her ankles, and her hair was up in curlers. Defoe checked his watch. A few minutes before seven. "Dad not up yet?"

"Oh; I, ah, don't know." Mary Defoe poured herself a cup of coffee from the silver pot on the sideboard and turned to Anna as the domestic came through the door from the kitchen. "Nothing for me, Anna, I'll wait until Mr. Defoe comes down." She sat at the opposite end of the long mahogany table from her son and sipped her coffee, hot and black. "Your father has moved into the guest room, Chase. His back has been bothering him lately, and he thinks it might be our mattress." She looked up and caught her son's eyes. "Too soft, he says."

"Ah. Could be. I sleep on tatami at my place. Those Japanese straw mats? Seems to have worked for them for several millennia, and I find it suitable . . . Well, what time is the funeral?"

"Eight? I think that's what your father said. I know we're supposed to be out of here no later than seven-thirty."

"Bright and early, eh? You said on the phone that he was being buried at Arlington. I suppose it will be a Full Honors ceremony—caisson, a band, and all that."

"Oh, I don't know. Your father has handled all the details for Kit. He's rather taken charge."

"He would. What's her new husband think about it?" Defoe poured himself another cup of coffee. "Dad taking over, I mean."

"Jack? I have no idea. Dad said he was out of town when it happened."

"He's some sort of government lawyer, isn't he?"

"No, I believe he's in private practice. You've never met him?"

"No, Mother, I haven't seen Kit in over ten years. Not since Quinn died." Defoe sipped his coffee and looked across the table at his mother. "And the time before that was at her mother's funeral. We seem to only meet when death takes center stage . . . Ah, good morning, Dad."

Mary Defoe turned as her husband entered the room. He nodded to his wife, looked at his son. "Ah, you *do* own a suit. And you even managed to find a black necktie. I guess we can sit together at the chapel after all." He took his seat at the head of the table and pulled his napkin from the ivory ring beside his place setting.

Defoe looked down at the sleeve of his suit, a deep charcoal worsted with a faint maroon stripe. He'd had it made in London a dozen years earlier, when he'd been there doing the embassy. The necktie was standard Navy issue, black wool. "Yes, my Bond Street banker's suit. Left the bowler and brolly home, though, thought that they would be a bit much."

"Don't be an ass. Anna! Where's my breakfast?" George Defoe looked at his watch, a slim gold Patek Philip. "We've got to get out of here by seven-thirty; I've got this thing laid on for eight. Best get it over with before the damned tourists start to invade the cemetery." He picked up his knife and fork and began to work on the sausage and eggs that Anna put before him. "Hadn't you better get dressed, Mary?" He poured cream into his coffee, spooned in sugar.

"Just a glass of juice and a piece of toast for me, please, Anna," Mary Defoe said. "I've plenty of time to get dressed, dear. Have you ever known me to be late or to hold you up, in the forty-eight years we've been married?"

"Don't remind me how long we've been married, not today, of all times. Do you think I might be able to see my newspaper, Chase?"

Defoe stood up and carried the *Times* to his father's end of the table, clamped his jaws shut, determined not to let the sarcasm trigger a response. He'd learned long ago that crossing verbal swords with his father was a useless exercise. "Think I'll make a weather check, Mother. I'll meet you two at the car." He left his parents silently consuming their meal and went outside.

The big Mercedes, gleaming black, stood in front of the house, and Butterfield, in a matching suit, leaned against the post and rail fence that surrounded the close-clipped pasture.

"Seems strange, not seeing a couple of horses out there."

Butterfield turned, said, "Yes, it does. Got to be where they was a part of the place. Good morning, Mr. Chase."

"Morning, Butterfield. I guess it makes your life a little easier, though. Not having to muck out stalls, clean tack."

The old man turned and looked at the barn a hundred feet beyond the garage. "Oh, I don't know. I kind of enjoyed fussin' with the animals." He chuckled. "And now I got to mow the fields, instead of lettin' the horses do it. Besides, it was kind of nice, watching your momma ride, jumping over them fences and all. You still got a horse up there in Pennsylvania?"

Defoe shook his head. "No, I got rid of him, after my place burned down." He looked at Butterfield and smiled. "Had to; I moved into his house!" He turned back to the empty pasture, recalled the hours he'd spent there learning to ride and jump as well as his mother. "I hadn't hunted for a couple of seasons before that, anyway. Always off somewhere on business. Besides, it is getting so built up there that we can't really support a decent hunt anymore. The newcomers to the country don't much tolerate forty hounds and as many fools on horseback thundering through their backyards." He laughed. "The peasants don't seem to tug their forelocks the way they used to, Butterfield."

"Yeah. And that ain't necessarily a good thing. The old days, people knew how to behave."

Knew their place, you mean, Butterfield, Defoe thought. *Easy for you to say, with your sinecure here. You didn't have to deal with the realities of being a second-class citizen every day, not as long as you worked for my father. But maybe you did, on a subtler and more painful level. You certainly know as well as I do, after all these years, my father's feelings toward your race.* Instead he said, aloud, "The world changes, and we must change with it. Here comes my

mother and father. I guess it's time to bury General Kilgallen."

They crossed Chain Bridge Road and picked up 66 East toward Arlington. Defoe rode in front with Butterfield, left the spacious rear of the car to his silent parents. "What's HOV?" he asked as the chauffeur accelerated into morning traffic.

"High Occupancy Vehicles. Got to have three or more people in the car, certain times of day, to use this route. Been awhile since you was down here, huh?"

"Been awhile." Defoe watched the landscape slide past. "I don't think ninety percent of these buildings were here last time I was."

"Yes." Butterfield turned his head enough to direct his voice to the rear of the car. "We going to the Fort Meyer entrance, Mr. Defoe?"

George Defoe leaned forward. "No, get on the Jeff Davis, take it to Memorial Bridge. The cortege is forming up there."

Butterfield could have asked if the senior Defoe meant the W. Wilson Memorial Bridge or the G. Mason Memorial Bridge or the T. Roosevelt Memorial Bridge, all spanning the river within a couple of miles of each other, but he had driven his employer to the Arlington National Cemetery enough times and waited through enough funerals to know that Mr. Defoe meant the Arlington Memorial Bridge—the one that leaped across the Potomac to the traffic circle surrounding the Lincoln Memorial. Every bridge, building, and monument in Washington larger than a fireplug has Memorial as its middle name, Defoe thought, watching the river flow past. It's a place where the representatives of the people come together, make the laws and divide the spoils among themselves. And devote themselves nearly full time to getting reelected. If they manage to do that often enough, and avoid the Justice Department sting operations that lie, hidden like leg-hold traps, in the District of Columbia, their final reward is a federal edifice named in their memory. Defoe was jarred from his cynical musings by the rough cobblestones of Memorial Drive, a broad expanse of roadway that ended at Memorial Gate.

A man in a dark suit with a walkie-talkie at his ear held up his palm to their car. "General Kilgallen," Butterfield said as the man leaned close to the driver's window. The man gestured to his right and they took their place at the end of the line of cars.

Several minutes later they moved slowly forward, turned onto Schley Drive at the gate, wound their way steadily uphill, rose above the JFK gravesite and its eternal flame on their left, and proceeded to the Fort Meyer Chapel.

Defoe watched Katherine Kilgallen Brill and her husband and daughter get out of the black limousine that stopped behind the hearse. Six enlisted men from the Third Infantry, dressed in Class A uniform, removed the casket from the back of the hearse and, in muffled cadence, marched it into the chapel. The Army chaplain met them at the entrance, made the sign of the cross with his right hand, and said, holding a Book of Common Prayer against his breast with his left, "I am the resurrection and the life, saith the Lord; he that believeth in me, though he were dead, yet shall he live: and whosoever liveth and believeth in me, shall never die."

I guess, Defoe thought, *that he's done this often enough to have the whole thing committed to memory.*

"We brought nothing into this world, and it is certain we can carry nothing out. The Lord gave, and the Lord hath taken away; blessed be the name of the Lord." Again the chaplain made the sign of the cross, then turned, entered the chapel.

The Defoes followed the chaplain, the casket, and the rest of the processional inside.

One by one the mourners dipped in genuflection, ritually passing from secular to ecclesiastic as they took their places behind the family of the featured player. The Defoes sat in the second pew on the left side of the chapel. The three members of the General's family occupied the first pew to the right of the center aisle, and the half dozen pews behind and on either side were filled with friends and former colleagues of the dead man. Lots of uniforms, Defoe noted, and lots of white hair. All deep in contemplating their own mortality. *Better, at least, than the last time Katherine and I were at a funeral.* That had been to bury her husband, Delaney Quinn. Quinn had been a close friend and college classmate of Defoe; he'd introduced him to Kit the year Defoe had asked her to his senior prom. He smiled at the memory. Quinn, virgin-shy and dateless, had been infatuated, had, he later told Defoe, "screwed his courage to the sticking point," and stolen her away. Not that Defoe had put up much of a fight; Kit had been a last-minute replacement for his own steady girlfriend at the time, a girl who had come down with mono the week before the prom. He'd never told Kit she'd been his second choice, but she wouldn't have cared. Because, before two weeks had passed, she was obliviously in love with Quinn and started making weekend pilgrimages from Poughkeepsie to New Haven that didn't stop until Delaney graduated and married her that June.

The chaplain did his liturgical business at the altar, then turned to the congregation and began his litany.

Defoe wondered if Kit regretted leaving college in her junior year to marry Quinn, then realized that she might very well have gone back to get her degree while her husband was in Vietnam. He didn't know; he'd attended their wedding, been an usher at the union of his friend and his first lover, but lost touch with both of them as his career took him off to another life.

"Thou turnest man to destruction; again thou sayest, Come again, ye children of men." The chaplain's voice was soothing, a monotone that urged one's concentration elsewhere, and Defoe obliged, watched Kit from her rear quarter. He and Quinn had next met at their fifth reunion; Defoe was by then a lieutenant, Delaney had put the war behind him, and Kit had given birth to their daughter, had the two-year-old child with them. Defoe smiled at the image of the three Quinns, all dressed in college colors; Delaney in a blue blazer and white slacks, wearing, God help us, a straw boater. Kit had on a blue skirt and a white blouse, reversing her husband's color scheme, and the little girl was dressed in white tights and a blue jumper, had a straw hat with long blue ribbons trailing down behind. Her golden hair she'd gotten from her father; Kit's was raven's-wing black. Black Irish, General Kilgallen often called himself. Kit's eyes were dark and always seemed to be amused by some private thought; they sparkled like her wit. Samantha, the child, had her father's eyes. Defoe remembered they'd been a china blue—still were, he realized as he noticed with a start that she had turned and was watching him watch her mother.

Samantha Quinn wore her hair in an asymmetrical shingle cut that was very current and a bit too dramatic for Defoe's taste. The ear he could see had been pierced three times; she wore a large gold hoop and a pair of studs in the lobe. *Thank God there's nothing in her nose,* he thought, and then said to himself, "You're getting old, Defoe." Samantha looked at his parents in the pew beside him and recognition dawned. She released a slight smile across the few yards that separated them, a smile that hinted at some hidden amusement, before she turned her attention back to the man who stood before her grandfather's casket.

"For a thousand years in thy sight are but as yesterday; seeing that is past as a watch in the night.

"Glory be to the Father, and to the Son, and to the Holy Ghost; As it was in the beginning, is now, and ever shall be, world without end. Amen."

The fifty or so people in the chapel answered with a chorus of Amens of their own and shuffled in their seats, welcoming the chance to participate and shift position on the hard pews. The chaplain opened his prayer book and launched into the Lesson, taken, he told them, from the fifteenth chapter of the first Epistle of St. Paul to the Corinthians.

"Now is Christ risen from the dead," he said, "and become the first-fruits of them that slept." Defoe didn't have the faintest idea of what that meant, and reached for a Book of Common Prayer in the rack before him.

He thumbed past specific prayers that ran from Advent to All Saint's Day, past the order for Holy Communion and Baptism of Children, until he came to Burial of the Dead. "Here is to be noted," he read, "that the Office ensuing is not to be used for any unbaptized adults, any who die excommunicate, or who have laid violent hands upon themselves." He raised his eyebrows at that. As near as he could tell, putting the business end of a shotgun into one's mouth and then pulling the trigger could be considered laying violent hands upon oneself. He guessed that his father had had some hand in categorizing the General's death as accidental, at least as far as the media and the church were concerned. Be interesting to find out if the Fairfax County coroner concurred with the accidental death theory. Probably did; George Defoe's reach far surpassed local government. He found his place in the prayer book and followed the chaplain's words through the reading of the optimistically Christian conviction that the dead shall rise, closed the book, and returned it to its rack as the cleric intoned "Therefore, my beloved brethren, be ye steadfast, unmovable, always abounding in the work of the Lord; forasmuch as ye know that your labour is not in vain in the Lord."

The processional was reversed from its entrance into the chapel and all waited outside as the body-bearers loaded the flag-draped casket into the hearse for the descent to the gravesite. Defoe looked out through the windshield at the six-hundred-acre hillside cemetery across the Potomac from Washington. Two hundred thousand veterans lay beneath the small white headstones aligned with mathematical precision in the dozens of plots separated by macadam roadways named MacArthur, Marshall, and Eisenhower. Even in death the military adheres to order. General Harmon Kilgallen's final resting place had been designated in Section Two, alongside other field grade officers who had shared his wars. Admirals Halsey and Leahy, Generals Chennault and Bradley. Phil Sheridan was there, too, the Union calvary commander. A graduate of the West Point class of 1853, he'd whipped J.E.B. Stuart and chased Robert E. Lee all over Virginia, finally cut off his retreat at Appomattox and forced the Confederate leader's surrender. It's ironic, Defoe thought, passing Sheridan's grave on his way to Kilgallen's, that Philip Sheridan's final resting place is here. Arlington plantation had belonged to George Washington Parke Custis, and he had willed it to his daughter Mary, who, in 1831, married a young Army officer named Robert E. Lee. They lived there for thirty years before, in 1861, Lee resigned his commission rather than bear arms against his native Virginia. Federal troops crossed the river, occupied Arlington House and made it into the headquarters of the Army of the Potomac, and a year later the government levied a property tax of ninety-two dollars and seven cents on the plantation. Mary

Lee, the owner of the estate, sent a proxy to pay the tax, but the government claimed that the tax had to be paid by the title holder and confiscated the plantation. The victors write a lot more than the history books.

Defoe noticed that Samantha Quinn had detached herself from the burial procession, had moved apart, carrying a large black nylon bag over her shoulder. He watched as she took out a .35 mm camera with a motor drive and a long lens and began to photograph the burial.

He turned his attention to his more immediate surroundings, watched as the body-bearers deposited their load at the gravesite, then stood rock-still over the coffin that rested above the open grave, holding the flag taut in their white-gloved hands.

The chaplain moved to the grave, his white surplice a stark contrast to the black of the gathered mourners. "In the midst of life we are in death: of whom may we seek for succor, but of thee, O Lord, who for our sins art justly displeased?

"Yet, O Lord God most holy, O Lord most mighty, O holy and most merciful Saviour, deliver us not into the bitter pains of eternal death." The chaplain turned to the General's daughter and nodded once. Katherine stooped, supported by her husband at her elbow, and picked up a small handful of earth from the open grave, let it fall from her black glove onto the coffin.

"Forasmuch as it hath pleased Almighty God, in his wise providence, to take out of this world the soul of our deceased brother, we therefore commit his body to the ground; earth to earth, ashes to ashes, dust to dust: looking for the general resurrection in the last day, and the life of the world to come, through our Lord Jesus Christ."

The chaplain closed his prayer book and lowered his head. "Please join me in the Lord's Prayer. Our Father, who art in heaven, Hallowed be thy Name."

Defoe bowed his head and listened to the murmur of the voices surrounding him, heard some clear and loud, others a mumble, heard at some more private, inner level his own voice as it whispered ". . . and forgive us our trespasses as we forgive those who trespass against us; And lead us not into temptation; But deliver us from evil."

Defoe looked up, saw the chaplain make the sign of the cross over the casket as he said, "The grace of our Lord Jesus Christ, and the love of God, and the fellowship of the Holy Ghost, be with us all evermore. Amen." The mechanical sounds of seven rifle bolts blended with the sharp but unintelligible commands of the firing-party leader. Three volleys echoed over the hills above the Potomac and the bugler began to play taps as the body-bearers folded the flag they had held so still.

Defoe felt the hairs rise on the back of his neck as the bugle notes died, and a tear sprang unbidden in the corner of his eye as the soldier presented the folded triangle of red, white, and blue wool to Kit, saluted, and executed an about face. He noticed a lot of nose-blowing among the men and women dabbing at their eyes as he said to his mother, "I can't think of anything much more impressive than a military funeral, can you?"

She smiled, squeezed his arm, but said nothing, knowing an answer really wasn't expected.

"Still," Defoe said, turning to his father, "I expected to see Full Honors. Surely three stars rated the six horses and a caisson, the band, fife and drums."

"Hmph. The old fool was lucky to get Modified Honors; been up to me I'd have plumped for a No Honors burial. Drop the old bastard in the hole and cover him up."

"George!" Mary Defoe reached out and pinched the loose skin of her husband's wrist, hard. "Hold your tongue. Remember where you are!"

"Uh; yes, of course." He coughed, looked at his son. "Just that it's not done; suicide, y'know. Bad form, laying on Full Honors, when everybody knows that he shot himself." He looked around as the funeral party began to break up, individuals stopping for a brief word with the family before heading for their cars. He plucked at his son's sleeve. "There, Kit's shed the lot, except for Senator Kinship. Come on, let's go and do our duties to her and get on home. Mary, come along!"

The three Defoes passed the grave and approached the General's daughter and her family. "Hello, Billy," George

Defoe said, clapping Senator Kinship on the back. "Thought we'd find you here."

He waved his hand at John Brill, said, "Hello, Jack, how's our girl holding up?" and turned to Kit, who smiled wanly as she offered her cheek to Mary Defoe. Kit was several inches taller than the older woman, stood almost at eye level with her son. She wore a black suit, Chanel cut from wool knit, and a black lace head scarf that paid lip service to the antiquated Christian concept of feminine decorum.

"Aunt Mary, Uncle George. As well as can be expected." She switched her attention to Defoe, said, "Chase. Thank you for coming. It would have meant a lot to Dad."

Defoe stepped forward, between her and his mother, and took her gloved hand in both of his. "Hi," he said, and they touched cheeks, then locked eyes for a moment before she turned to her husband.

"Jack, this is Chase Defoe. I know you've heard me talk about him, but I don't think you two have ever met."

Brill shifted the black pistol grip cane to his left hand and offered his right to Defoe. "Howd'yado. No, we haven't met; I know your dad, of course." He turned to the senior Defoe. "Thanks for all you've done for the family these last few days. All the running around, dealing with the details. This damned knee has slowed me up." He then said to Defoe, "I slipped on the ice a few weeks back, busted my kneecap. Your father has made things go very smoothly through this trying time." He had very white, very even teeth, expensive work by a very good dentist. He was six inches taller than Defoe and ten years older, but fit, stayed in shape with swimming in the summer and racquetball in the winter. The tan was the real thing, acquired under the St. Thomas sun.

"Dad's good at that," Defoe answered, releasing the other man's hand as he turned back to Kit. "Was that Sammy? Taking the pictures? I haven't seen her since she was . . . what? About ten, I guess." He looked around for Kit's daughter, saw her talking to a man in a black suit standing beside the hearse.

Kit put her hand on her chest. "Yes, I guess it *has* been that long. We haven't seen you since Dee's funeral." She paused, let out a sigh, shook her head. "Hard to believe it's been twelve years, isn't it, Chase? Are you staying down for a while? A few days? We'd love to have you for dinner some night, wouldn't we, Jack."

"Sure, certainly. Let's get together after we've all recovered a bit. Give us a day or two . . . Sammy!" He called to his stepdaughter, then turned back to the Defoes. "I didn't much like her breaking away to take pictures of all this, but she insisted. Something to do with her grandfather's book." He shook his head. "I don't know what she has in mind . . ."

"Book?" Defoe asked.

"Sammy was helping Dad with this writing project. His memoirs," Kit said. "She majored in journalism in college, but history is really her first love. She was transcribing Dad's notes, and then the two of them were going to work together on the book." Kit turned and watched her daughter sling her camera bag over her shoulder and stalk toward them, the motor drive camera still around her neck, ready to shoot anyone who offered an attractive target. She wore a short black skirt and black stockings, had a tight black turtleneck above them that showed off her youthful figure. Got her mother's body, Defoe thought, even if she did get her eyes and hair from Quinn.

"Sam's working as a photojournalist," Kit continued. "Free lance, although she does ninety percent of her work for *Women's Wear Daily.*"

"Washington's a major fascination of theirs for some reason," Brill explained.

"Because it's where the power is, Daddy," Samantha Quinn said as she joined the group. "New York and Washington. Power and money. That's what women's fashion is all about, anyway. See and be seen. Hi; you're Chase Defoe." She stuck out her hand and took his, then stepped into him and kissed him, briefly on the mouth, leaving the taste of lipstick. "Mother's told us *all* about you."

Defoe threw his eyebrows up and smiled, turned to Kit, who said, "No, Mother hasn't, either. Chase is an old friend, and an even older boyfriend. You both know that." She turned to her husband for confirmation.

"Old enough to have dunked her pigtails in the inkwell,"

Defoe said. "Your mother was just telling us that you and General Kilgallen were writing a book."

"Uh huh. Grampy and I were working on next year's Pulitzer for biography. Which makes me wonder why he did it. Shot himself, I mean." She looked at Kit. "Oh, don't start; getting all weepy and wimpy on us. Everybody knows what he did, Mother, there's no sense in pretending he didn't. Only I can't understand *why.*" She turned to Senator Kinship. "I mean, we were making great progress, plowing through those piles of notes and diaries and books he'd scouted up from the libraries." She shrugged, slid the bag off her shoulder, and eased it onto the dormant sod. "Then, all of a sudden, Pfft! And he burned all his papers; what was the point of that? I've still got the carbons at my place. Everybody says it was Alzheimer's, that he was depressed, but that's a crock. I saw him almost every day; well, couple times a week, anyway, and hell, I'd have noticed if he were depressed, right?"

Brill chuckled, moved closer to his stepdaughter and put his arm around her shoulder, squeezed. "Sweet bird of youth. Doesn't understand quite yet the strange things that can happen to an old man's mind." He winked at the men. "Keeps *me* young, anyway, right, little girl?"

"Oh, phoo, Daddy," Samantha said, hugging him back briefly; then she bent, unzipped her bag, and stuffed the camera inside, pulled out a large manila envelope to do it. She fished out a pair of dark glasses and put them on, waved the envelope at the group. "Mr. Dandrea, that creepy undertaker guy, just gave me this; Grampy's personal stuff. Said there was a mix up, back at the funeral home. Somebody was supposed to see that we got it the other day. His glasses and wedding ring; whatever he had on him. Kind of tacky, handing it to me here, huh?" She offered it to her mother. "I guess you ought to have it, Mother. *Your* duty, after all."

Kit took the envelope, looked at it without the reality of its existence registering. "Yes. I suppose I'll have to come to some decision, about everything of his." She looked up, added, "His personal effects, I mean." She turned to her husband. "Jack, isn't a whole bunch of it mentioned in his will? The mementos, things from his career."

"Yes, sure. It's been a while since I've gone over it, but yes, you're right. There's a long list of bequests. War trophies to old war cronies. Half of them probably dead by now. The will hasn't been updated for some time." He looked at the Defoes. "I tried to get him to go over it with me annually, make the usual adjustments, but as you can imagine, I got nowhere with the idea." He shook his head and patted his wife's arm. "We'll look into the disposition of the personal items when I put it to probate. Nice to have seen you again, George, Mrs. Defoe, Senator. And nice to have finally met you, Chase. If you'll excuse us, I think we'd better be going. Been rough sledding, these last few days. I think my girls need a little time alone."

"Certainly," Senator Kinship said. "We understand." He reached inside his coat and handed Kit a sheet of Senate stationery. "Katherine, I want you to have this. It's the statement I'm going to read into the Congressional Record later today. Just a few words about your father, the high points of his long and illustrious career. He was a good soldier and a fine friend. We'll all miss him."

Kit's eyes filled, as they had many times over the past few days, and she hugged him, said a quiet "Thank you, Senator" before turning and walking slowly with her daughter and husband toward the waiting limousine.

"Well, young man, what have you been up to these years since I last saw you? At your dad's birthday bash, wasn't it? Where Reagan told that awful shaggy dog story about George here and the foreign exchange student from the Sorbonne, and got the French all wrong."

Senator William Henry Kinship turned to the younger Defoe and peered down at him over the top of his tortoiseshell glasses.

Defoe smiled at the memory and looked at the senator. He still wore bow ties—even at the funerals of senior military men—and rumpled suits, and affected the shaggy appearance of a tenured professor. He had, in fact, never advanced past the level of instructor, due to a world war that cut short his career as an art historian. He'd been three years behind George Defoe, had graduated in 1935, gotten his MFA a year later, and then joined the history department at Yale. "Much the same as last we met, Senator. Designing security systems, then monitoring them, seeing that they are doing what they are supposed to do."

"Selling burglar alarms, Billy. Studied philosophy under Paul Weiss and the classics with Tom Bergin so he could sell burglar alarms." The senior Defoe glared at his son. "State Department's one of the few places outside a university where he could have put that education to some use, but would he listen to me? Hell no. Opts for a career playing at James Bond."

Senator Kinship chuckled, winked at Defoe. "Well, George, look at the brighter side of it. At least he didn't end up at The Campus. You know Langley is still, after all these years, referred to as the 'Yale Alumni Society?' inside." He turned back to the younger Defoe. "I sit on the Senate Intelligence Committee, son, and like to think that I have my finger on the pulse of the clandestine world. Fascinating business, Chase; I can see the appeal it would have for a bright fellow like you." He turned to Mary Defoe, abruptly changing the subject and keeping those around him off balance and a half step behind, a technique that had served him well in his years in the Senate. "Mary, lovely Mary. How have you been?" The senator ran his hand through the rampant shock of white hair that crowned his massive head. "It was a sad day for the bachelors of the world when you turned your back on them for George here." He reached out and took her hand, continued to speak in the soft, rolling cadence that he'd refined in the lecture halls at Yale a half century earlier. "Run away with me, Mary; come with me to some sunny place. We'll lie on the beach and forget about the rest of the world."

"Oh, Billy, don't be a tease," Mary Defoe said, an anxious note in her voice as she pulled her hand away and glanced at her husband. George Defoe had a cold glint in his eyes and his lips were white. She seemed, then, to come to some inner decision and suddenly turned back to the senator, put her hand on his arm. "Come back to the house for coffee and some of Anna's pastries instead, and you can tell me more about this sunshine. We could use some warmth around here; it's been a long winter."

Senator Kinship laughed, said, "Done! Let me make a few calls, push my schedule back an hour, and I'll be there." He turned to her husband, said in a more serious voice, "There's a couple of things I wanted to have a word with you about, George, and I suppose this morning is as good a time as any." He touched his old friend's arm, nodded to Mary and her son, and walked off toward the few cars that still remained along Grant Drive, his heavy hickory cane digging into the soft turf.

"The cane's a new touch," Defoe said, watching the massive man pick his way through the white headstones toward his car. "Next it'll be a cape. 'We'll drink no wine before it's time.' "

"Hip joint; they put a new one in last year," his father said, stepping briskly in the direction of the Mercedes. "Some of us wear better than others."

FOUR

Once again Defoe chose to ride in front with Butterfield, listened with half an ear to his parents in the backseat. His mother called home, told Anna that Senator Kinship would be having coffee with the family in half an hour, then went into a long lament with her husband about what a shame it was that the senator's wife had died the previous year, after a long illness. Defoe tuned out the tale of death, a subject of seemingly inexhaustible delight for the aging, and thought instead of his own mortality.

The year before someone had christened his twenty-fifth class reunion as "Halftime," designating it as the midpoint of their lives. Halfway to where? he wondered, staring at the Potomac as it headed toward the bay. Halfway to ninety? I doubt that many of us, even with the wonders of modern medicine, will make it that far. Halfway, maybe, along in our careers. If so, then I have some catching up to do with others in my class. Halfway, he finally decided, to his fiftieth reunion, when he could go back, a seventy-plus codger, and cackle with other senescent classmates over the members of the group who hadn't lasted that long. *"Vita Brevis,"* he murmured, loud enough for Butterfield to glance over at him.

"You say something, Mr. Chase?"

"No; I was just thinking that there's nothing like a funeral to make you take stock of your own life, see where you are."

"Yessir. And see if you're ready to go." The old man paused, then gave a chuckle. "You better be, 'cause the good Lord don't take to no 'wait a minute, come back next week.' "

"Yes, right. Except I don't think anybody is ever really ready, Butterfield."

The chauffeur turned off the secondary road and headed up the long driveway toward the house. "You say that now, you what? In your forties." He looked over at Defoe and smiled. "You get to be my age, you'll find out that you're a whole lot more ready. Better be, anyways, because you a whole lot closer, whether you ready or not!" He stopped in front of the house, got out, and opened the rear door for his employers.

Mary Defoe stopped at the front of the car, looked at her son, still sitting in the front seat. She tapped on the window. "Chase, darling. Aren't you coming inside?"

He looked up at her, slid the window down. "Oh, yes, sure. I was just wool-gathering. Be along in a moment, Mother." He smiled, and sat straighter as Butterfield put the car in gear and circled, headed into the garage.

Defoe got out, slammed the door, walked over, and looked at the car in the center bay. A two-year-old Audi. "This yours, Butterfield?"

"Huh, you got to be kidding. Your daddy is good to me, but not that good. No, that's your momma's car. Said she was tired of having me drive her ever' place, and she bought that little thing. Kind of sporty, ain't it?"

"Sure is." Defoe walked to the back of the garage, looked at the workbench that ran across the building. He remembered the big old machinist's vise, had tightened its jaws on a thousand different projects. He ran his hand over the scarred, oil-stained planks that were the surface of the workbench. Tools were suspended above it on nails driven into the wall. Beneath the bench the shelves held dozens of wooden and cardboard boxes, filled with cast-off memories of the Defoe family. "What's going on, Butterfield? With my parents, I mean."

"Going on?" Butterfield got out a pack of Marlboros, shook a cigarette out of the red and white box. "I don't know what you mean."

"Sure you do. You've been around them longer than I have. Something's eating at them; I picked it up last night, when I first got here, and a couple more times today. I don't know what it is, but something's not right. Mom was always pretty close to you, on account of the horses. She hasn't said anything?"

Butterfield fired his cigarette with a kitchen match that he struck with his thumbnail. He turned toward Defoe, his face lost in a cloud of smoke as he said, "Nuh-uh. She ain't said nothin' to me, son. Probably just the General's death got them upset. Like I said, you get to be our age, death a whole lot closer when he calls for someone else."

"Maybe." Defoe poked at the boxes under the bench, idly pulled them out, examined their contents. One was filled with lawn games; a set of quoits, warped badminton racquets, and two-thirds of a croquet set. Another yielded a pup tent, a mildewed sleeping bag, and a Boy Scout mess kit and canteen.

"Lord," Defoe said, looking into a big wooden chest, "is this boat stuff still around?" He pulled out a taffrail log, the linen line on the bronze screw still sound. A Very pistol and a disintegrating pasteboard box of flares was in a canvas sail bag, along with a marlin spike in a leather sheath, a couple of monkey's fists, and a ship's compass, mounted in gimbals. He took the compass out, watched it orient itself toward north. "It must be close to forty years since Dad had the boat. I remember sailing the Chesapeake with him, but just barely. I couldn't have been more than five, maybe six." He put the compass back in the sail bag. "Funny what people keep, isn't it? Not a Chinaman's chance that he'll ever get another boat, but here this gear sits, just in case."

Butterfield came over, looked down at the nautical equipment under the workbench. "Oh, I don't know as he's keeping it in case he gets a longing for another boat so much as he's just holding onto a memory." He nodded toward the camping gear. "I don't think your daddy's planning on sleeping outside, neither, but your Scout gear's still here. Kind of like a scrapbook, if you know what I mean."

"Sure. All this junk can get in the way of living, though. That's why I'm not terribly upset about my fire." Defoe looked up at the sound of tires on macadam coming through the open garage door. "I guess that's Senator Kinship. I'd better go have a cup of coffee with him and my parents. Talk to you later, Butterfield.'' He smiled at the old man. ''Over a couple of beers.''

Defoe found his parents and their guest in the morning room, at the back of the house. The room had lots of glass and overlooked Mary Defoe's flower garden, and in season it was difficult to discern the dividing line between indoors and out. In March, however, the demarkation was obvious. Outside the roses were dormant, the trees bare, and the only sign of life was the first tentative green leaves of the crocus plantings pushing up from their beds against the house. Inside it was a different season altogether. The floor, unglazed pavers laid in a herringbone pattern, was sprayed each morning with the garden hose now neatly coiled beneath its bib so that the bricks slowly gave back the moisture to the air, giving the room a soft, chiaroscuro look that echoed the Monet above the sideboard in the adjoining dining room. Mary Defoe had filled the space with luxurious greenery; potted palms, ficus, and philodendrons in large moss-incrusted tubs stood beneath hanging baskets of ferns, fuchsias, and spider plants, the whole giving the sun filled-room a jungle atmosphere.

A wicker sofa and a pair of matching armchairs, painted white and upholstered in a bright floral print, were grouped around a glass-topped coffee table that held a silver service, cups, saucers, and a basket of scones wrapped in a linen napkin. The Defoes sat across from each other in the separate chairs; Senator Kinship occupied one end of the sofa and busied himself with applying raspberry jam to a scone.

''I always loved this room, Mary,'' he said, putting half of the flaky pastry in his mouth. ''How I envy you, being able to sit here and watch the seasons pass. Hello, Chase. Better grab one of these before I eat them all. I was just telling your mother that if she won't run off with me, maybe I'll steal your cook.''

Defoe gave the remark its obligatory laugh and poured himself a cup of coffee, then sat beside the senator, balancing the cup and saucer on his knee.

''Butterfield was showing me your new car, Mother. Getting pretty sporty in your golden years, aren't you?''

''Yes, isn't it the cat's meow? I don't like driving that big old thing of your father's, and I hated having to ask Butterfield to take me every place I want to go, so I bought myself a car to call my own."

"Dangerous, if you ask me," George Defoe offered. "Little car like that's no protection in an accident." He leaned forward to the table, put his blue-and-white Wedgwood cup on its saucer, looked at Senator Kinship. "You mentioned wanting to talk to me about something, back at Arlington, Billy. Anything we can discuss in front of these civilians?"

The senator looked at him over the tops of his glasses, smiled. "Oh, my, yes; nothing ulterior in my motives, George, you know that. Just a little political maneuvering I wanted to chat about. Boring, but hardly secret."

Defoe sipped his coffee, said, "Sub rosa's not part of your vocabulary, right, Senator Kinship?" He turned to his father, added, "He probably doesn't even know what it means."

The senator laughed softly, leaned toward Defoe, and patted him on the knee. "Bright young man you have here, George. Chase, if you ever decide to involve yourself with politics, I could use you on my staff."

George Defoe snorted, said, "That'll be the day. Mister High-and-mighty here has a pretty low opinion of politicians. Thinks every deal you cut in the Senate cloakroom should be put to a referendum."

"No I don't, Dad. I realize that quid pro quo is the fuel that runs the government, and I don't object to it. What bothers me is the hypocrisy of the whole thing. Politicians uttering platitudes and pieties for the folks back home at the same time they are looking out for their own interests here."

Mary Defoe stood up, smoothed her skirt. "If you men are going to argue politics, I'm leaving. No, no, don't get up, Billy. I want to get out of this suit, anyway. You go right ahead with your fight. See Anna in the kitchen if you need a cold compress or some ice cubes for your bloody noses!"

Senator Kinship said, after she had left the room, "What I wanted to bring up with you, George, was the appropriations bill before my committee that I mentioned to you the other day. I wanted to ask you to put out some feelers, get a reaction from the intelligence community. Back channel stuff. I don't want the bill coming before the full Senate if there's going to be a great hue and cry raised over this rider Senator

Bickley is championing." The senator poured more coffee into his cup and leaned back, settling into the soft cushions. "A few of your famous telephone calls can get me a quicker, and probably more accurate, reading on this than all the official flailings by our staff."

Defoe smiled, thought "government of, by, and for the people," but said nothing, concentrated instead on looking for an excuse to drop out of the conversation and leave the room. Anna brought it to him a few moments later.

"Excuse me, sir," she said from the doorway, "there's a telephone call for Mr. Chase."

"Who is it, Anna?" Defoe asked, standing, wondering who knew that he was here.

"Miss Kilgallen; I mean Mrs. Quinn." She fluttered her hands at her apron and said, "That's not right, either, is it? I can't remember her new husband's name. She just said, 'It's Kit, Anna,' and asked to speak to you."

Defoe raised his eyebrows, said, "I'll take it in the library, Dad," and followed Anna from the morning room.

"Hi, Kit," he said, picking up the receiver and slouching onto the sofa. "What's up?" He looked up into the eyes of his ancestor over the fireplace and listened to the anxious voice on the telephone.

"Chase, we—Sammy and I—are over at Dad's. Do you think you could come over for a few minutes?"

"Sure. What's the problem? You sound upset."

"Yes, I know; I guess I am. Nothing's *wrong,* it's just that we've found something . . . Well, I can't really explain it over the telephone, you'll have to hear it for yourself."

"Okay, I'll be right over. See you in a bit." He broke the connection and cocked his head, like the old RCA Victor dog, hearing his master's voice. Then he shrugged, went back to the morning room. "That was Kit. She and her daughter are over at the General's. Said they found something, want me to take a look at it, so that's where I'll be."

"Jesus! That old fool, reaching from beyond the grave to make more trouble." George Defoe looked at the senator. "I thought we'd heard the last from Harmon when we planted him this morning."

Defoe left the two men discussing the third, a man Defoe

had thought until that morning was a close friend of his father's. He stopped in the hallway and took one of the blackthorn walking sticks out of the big Chinese porcelain umbrella stand beside the door. It was nearly two miles by automobile from the Defoe front door to the General's, but less than a thousand yards cross country, and the morning was warming rapidly under the spring sun. He climbed the whitewashed fence and headed across the pasture, swinging the stick as he made his way toward the Kilgallen property on the other side of the beechwood copse that straddled the boundary line.

It was a trip he'd made often enough, he thought, both afoot and ahorse. He smiled, coming out the wooded area and spying the old carriage house, its upper loft the scene of his introduction to the carnal world. "Ah, Kit," he said softly. "The soft, sweet flesh of youth. Long gone, but still palpable in the memory."

He rapped at the glass of the French doors with his stick, then tried the handle, found it locked. He looked around the side of the house, saw a tan car parked in the driveway, then turned his attention back to the doors as they opened.

"Chase! We were looking for you out front. You walked over?"

"Yes, figured it was just as quick as driving." He looked at Sammy, coming through the doorway from the kitchen, a can of diet soda in her hand. "Hello, Sammy. What's the mystery you two have come up with?"

"Hi, Chase," Samantha said, sprawling on the sofa, her skirt riding up over her thighs as she displayed her long legs and most of the black panty hose that covered them. "Mom and I decided to stop here on the way back from the cemetery and drop off that envelope. So everything of Grampy's was in one place."

"Jack drove Sammy's car back home; he's got to get ready for a business trip, and we came here in the Volvo," Kit explained, going to her father's desk. The manila envelope was centered on its dark surface, and Kit touched it lightly with her fingertips. "I opened this up, to put the things where they belonged." She picked it up and peered inside, as though confirming the contents of the envelope. "Dad's eyeglasses, his wallet, class ring from West Point. A handful of pens and pencils, some blank three-by-five cards. The . . . the things he had on him when he . . . Anyway, this was in his jacket, the inside pocket, Sammy says. Where he carried it, I mean." Kit looked at her daughter for help.

Samantha got up, crossed to the desk and picked up the little recorder, not much bigger than a pack of cigarettes. "Grampy used this for his dictation," she said, pushing a button and ejecting a microcassette. "There's this switch here; you can set it so it's voice activated—it starts up automatically when you talk."

"Sure," Defoe said. "I have one very similar. I use it when I'm driving, make notes to myself."

"Yes. Well, Grampy had trouble writing, with his arthritis? So he'd use this. Set it on auto pilot, stick it in his coat, and then dictate. And I'd stop by a couple of times a week, pick up the cassettes, and transcribe them." Samantha paused, looked around the room, looked at the fireplace. "We had a couple of hundred pages, I guess." She shook her head. "And they say he burned them, there, in the fireplace, before he . . . shot himself." She looked back at Defoe, and her eyes flashed. "Except I don't think he did. Shoot himself, I mean—"

Kit interrupted. "Samantha, dear, I know something seems strange, but you can't jump to the conclusion—"

"Mother! Damn it, Grampy wouldn't *do* that! I know, I was working, I was like really close with him. You . . . you didn't see him from one month to the next, how would *you* know how he was doing, what he felt?"

Defoe said, "Wait a minute, I think I'm missing something here. What's his dictation machine got to do with this?"

"Oh," Samantha said. "I thought Mom told you, on the phone. See, I wondered, since Grampy didn't write a note or anything, if maybe he left something on the tape, saying why he'd done it, I mean. Shot himself. So I played it, a little while ago." She raised the soda can to her lips, took a swallow. "Play it for Chase, Mom. See what *he* thinks."

Kit hesitated, then handed the machine to her daughter. "You do it, dear, you're more familiar with how it works than I am."

Samantha gave her mother a look that oozed contempt, put her soda on the desk, and pressed the button to rewind the cassette, then switched it to play and put the recorder beside the can of cola.

There were mutters and murmurs, not fully formed into words, and the crisp sounds of papers against each other. "He is sitting here, at the desk," Samantha said, pointing to the office chair. "It's where he always worked."

They listened to the flat, tinny sounds coming from the little speaker as the tape slowly wound from reel to reel.

The right-hand French door, the one with the exterior handle, opens and someone enters, the muffled click of the latch signaling the closing of the door behind them. The tapping of a stick on the floor plays a nervous tattoo.

"What?" the General says. *"Ah, it's you, is it?"* The tone of the General's voice can be categorized as irascible, even angry. He is not happy to see the visitor, but his appearance is not altogether unexpected. This from a single word; not even a word, really, just a sound. "Oh, it's you" would denote a slight element of surprise, whereas "Ah, it's you" indicates a certain expectancy. Nevertheless, the overall tone of the General's voice definitely carries a hint of annoyance above his usual irritability.

Kit starts to say something, but her daughter puts up her hand, silencing her.

The General's caller says something in response from across the room, but the voice is far away and the words are indistinguishable. It is a mature male voice with a sureness that transcends its incomprehensibility.

Defoe listens to the hard sound of leather soles and heels as the visitor crosses the room. It is an infrequently heard sound in this day of the Adidas and the Nike and the rubber-heeled street shoe. The General's chair squeaks and its casters rumble on the floor as he shoves it back and rises. *"What the devil d'you—"* he says.

There is a sharp, puzzling sound, then an *"uhhh,"* and the General noisily falls to the floor, bringing first the chair with him, then books and papers from the desk. Perhaps he has caught his foot in the chair as he stands, and has lost his balance. The leather heels click again, fade; there are sounds from the far end of the room; the footsteps return. A rich, mechanical sound, precision machined metallic parts against each other as though the tumblers of an expensive lock are being worked, is followed by a sudden, deafening noise, so short and yet so overwhelming that it is unintelligible.

Defoe looks up from the recorder into the puzzled eyes of the two women.

The deep, ball-bearing rumble of a steel filing cabinet drawer being opened, then closed, is repeated, followed by the sounds of the surface of the desk being quickly cleared. The noise of these activities is followed in turn by the crackle of flames. The French doors are opened and quietly closed again. The sound of the fire continues for another seventeen minutes. Long before then, Samantha leans over the machine and pushes the stop button.

"That real loud sound, Chase," Sammy said, finishing her soda, "I think it was the gun going off." She rewound the cassette, found the spot, and played it again. "And after, that's when the papers are burning. I mean, you can hear that plain enough, right there in the fireplace, right?" She put the recorder back on the desk. "So Grampy couldn't very well have burned his notes and stuff if he was already dead, could he?"

Kit said, "It doesn't make any sense to me, Chase. Do you understand what she is getting at?"

He looked at the recorder, ran the series through his mind for a moment, orienting the chronology of the sounds before responding. "Sure. Sammy is saying that someone came in here, killed your father, then burned the papers."

Defoe walked to the far end of the room, tried the glass door to the gun cabinet. It was unlocked. He remembered it from his youth, always locked then, with a child in the house. He recognized most of the firearms inside. A sporterized 30.06, with a scope. A .22 Remington pump gun, a gun he and Kit had fired countless hundreds of rounds through as the General instructed them in the fine art of bottle busting at the bluff behind the carriage house. The Browning automatic shotgun, fitted with a Polychoke, a Remington 12 gauge, and the little Purdey double; short and light, an upland game piece. "Put a side by side in his mouth and pulled the trigger," Defoe's father had said. The other weapons had a faint haze on their steel-and-walnut surfaces, a matte look. An unused look, a film of dust. The Purdey glistened, its barrels and receiver shining with a fresh coat of oil. He took it out of its place in the cabinet, sighted along the barrels, opened the action, and looked down the bore. Gleaming, polished steel. He closed it with a click, tilted the gun so that the morning sunlight angled off the steel. Smooth, clean, polished. No trace of dust or fingerprints. He'd bet a small fortune the other guns were covered with the General's loops and whorls. He sniffed the receiver. The familiar scent of Hoppe's powder solvent, but no trace of its recent discharge. Someone had cleaned it very, very carefully.

He replaced the gun and looked at Samantha. "That loud sound *could* be the shotgun; it's too short, too distorted, to identify. Any good police lab could take it apart, digitally, and identify it, though." He closed the door to the gun cabinet and walked back to the desk, noticed the way his leather heels sounded on the hard floor. "But that's not the problem, Sammy. I agree with you, this is certainly very suspicious. Only you're forgetting that this isn't a continuous recording. If this machine is anything like mine, when it's in the voice-activated mode it automatically shuts down after a few seconds of silence. So we really have no idea of how much time elapsed between the bits and pieces on the tape. But you're right, Sammy—if that sound was the gun firing. Even if the General did shoot himself, someone burned the papers afterward. The tape certainly proves that." He looked around the General's den. It was clean and orderly to the point of appearing sterile. "There certainly isn't any evidence here of what happened. Not even any ashes in the fireplace."

"Oh, that was your father's doing, Chase," Kit said. "I guess you know that Sammy found Dad, and called me. I didn't know what to do, so I called Uncle George. He hustled right over, got here before I did. Made one of his phone calls, and the next thing we knew there was a team of men in a blue van here, cleaning the room with all sorts of exotic equipment and chemicals." She shuddered at the memory of her father, the back of his head spattered across a large part of his den. "Anyway, I asked him how he was able to get someone so quickly, and he tapped his nose and said, 'Langley isn't that far away.' Then he hustled us out of here while the men cleaned up. They must have taken the ashes with them. I must say, they were very thorough. When they left, it was as though it hadn't really happened." Her eyes glistened, and she blew her nose on a tissue. "He was a godsend, Chase. Took care of everything, even dealt with the police. They didn't ask to interview us or anything. I mean, I know that even an accidental death has to get some sort of police investigation, but your dad took care of that, too. We're very grateful to him."

Yes, very thorough job, Dad. I wonder why, Defoe thought. Aloud he asked, "Sammy, what could have been in those papers that would make someone want them destroyed? Assuming for the moment that the General didn't burn them himself."

"I don't know. I can't think of any big revelation or secret. I mean there wasn't anything in them that would be a bombshell when it came out, like the thing about Ike screwing his English driver or Kennedy and the Mafia tootsie. But don't you see? If Grampy wanted to destroy the papers, if he burned them all up, then shot himself, what about the carbons? At my apartment. He knew I had a set there. Why would he burn the ones here, knowing I still had the carbons?" She shook her head. "No, somebody else did it."

Defoe looked at Kit. "What she says, Kit, makes sense. Unless your father's Alzheimer's was so advanced that he forgot about the copies. I know in its later stages it can cause some pretty queer behavior."

"Oh, bullshit!" Samantha smacked the surface of the desk with her hand. "Grampy wasn't anything like that. Sure, he'd call me Kit, or even Grammy Alice occasionally, and sometimes he'd forget things. But no way was he as bad as you're making out."

"Okay, calm down, Sammy," Defoe said. "I'm just playing devil's advocate, double checking every angle of this. Kit, you mentioned something about your father's will, at the cemetery? I gather that your husband wrote it?"

"Yes, about, oh seven or eight years ago, I guess. Jack had

to keep after him for months to do it. His old will must have been twenty-five years old."

"Do you remember, offhand, the terms of it? The new will, I mean."

"Oh, gee. Sure. It was pretty simple. He left most everything to me. What he had, I mean. The house here. Some securities. Stocks. I think Jack said they were worth about a hundred thousand dollars. I guess it's more than that now. I know he left fifty thousand dollars to Sammy, for her education. That was when she was still in high school. Why do you want to know about the will?"

"Well, Kit, without being too blunt about it, money's probably the number-one reason that people kill each other. Money and passion are really the only motives."

"Passion? What do you mean," Samantha asked.

"Love. Hate. Jealousy, fear. All, I'm afraid, reasons to kill."

"Well," Kit said, "*we* didn't do it, so I guess you'll have to look elsewhere. Assuming that someone *did* kill Dad."

"I'm far from convinced, too, Kit," Defoe said, then looked at Samantha. "How about letting me look at these carbons you have, see if I can uncover anything that might give someone a motive for wanting your grandfather dead?"

"Deal. They're at my apartment. Mom, shall we drive over there and get the copies?"

"Oh, I don't know if I'm up to it right now, dear. I'm pretty exhausted from the funeral, and now this. Can't it wait? Besides, Jack has his trip to get ready for, and I really should get home to help him pack."

Samantha rolled her eyes and looked at Defoe. "No, it *can't* wait. I have to work this afternoon, remember, Mother? How about you and me then, Chase? Run us over to my place and we can check out Grampy's memoirs over a glass of wine?"

Defoe reviewed his options; a few hours with a pretty girl against lunch with his mother and father and the latent war that seethed between them. "Sure," he said. "Why not? I'll go back and get my car."

Samantha zipped open her camera bag and dropped the recorder inside. "We'll both go. I've never been to your parents' house, but I've heard enough about it." She turned to her mother. "Go get Daddy ready for his trip, Ma, and we'll see you later, when I pick up my wheels."

Chase Defoe and Samantha Quinn stepped off the brick patio and headed across the smooth lawn for the rougher fields as Katherine Brill turned her Volvo toward Georgetown and her husband. Jack Brill was going to New York for one of his frequent client meetings, and he preferred, he told his wife, to ride Amtrak up the night before, have a leisurely dinner in his hotel, and get a good night's sleep over taking an early flight and dealing with rush-hour traffic to make a nine A.M. appointment.

Samantha linked her arm through Defoe's and matched him stride for stride as they crossed the sere turf. They passed the carriage house, the panes of glass in its single upper window staring blankly down at them, and she turned to Defoe, flashed a knowing smile as she squeezed his arm tighter. "I feel like I'm following one of those Trails of History they publish in all the guidebooks, Chase," she said with a laugh.

He looked at her, puzzled. "Want to let me in on the joke?"

"Oh, you know all about it, lover. Except I guess maybe you don't know *every*thing, after all." She stopped, looked into his eyes. Her wide pink tongue darted across her teeth as she smiled. "You didn't know, did you, that Mom kept a diary? Filled with absolutely *pages* of the most graphic descriptions." She made a double clicking sound in her cheek, and winked, said, "Hot stuff, Defoe. Tell me, is it really true? You guys once did it *four* times in less than an hour?" She laughed again as he blushed.

"Diary, huh? Does your mother know you're reading her darkest secrets?" He glanced over his shoulder at the carriage house as they entered the wooded area. The trunks of the beeches were like massive silver snakes, sinuous in the morning sun, the smooth surface inviting a casual caress as the hikers picked their way between them.

"Are you kidding? She'd absolutely *kill* me if she found out I'd seen it. She probably doesn't even remember that it's still around. I came across it accidentally last year, rooting through her papers, looking for some letters I'd written home from college." Samantha shook her head as they left the coppice and continued across the landscape. "Six weeks of concentrated loving. Must have been a memorable summer, right? I wonder what happened, to turn her into the dull and boring person she is now. I mean, it's like two different people, the one writing the diary and the other here today."

"You have to realize that the diary-writer was sixteen, Sammy. I think what happened is that she grew up. People tend to do that."

"Nah, not the way she did. She's *old,* Chase. Scared of life, folded up."

"Maybe losing your father played a part in that." He hesitated for an instant, added, "It can do that to a person, having a loved one die."

Samantha laughed, but there was no humor in the sound this time. "That's hardly apropos in her case. She's the one who killed my father."

"I thought he died in a traffic accident."

"Yes, but she was driving the car. The three of us, coming home from a weekend ski trip to Vermont. It was slippery and late and Mom had slurped up one too many mugs of mulled wine. I was just a little kid, asleep in the backseat. The car went off the road and rolled over. Broke Daddy's neck and my collarbone. She crawled out of the car without a scratch." She looked at Defoe, her eyes glistening. "I loved my daddy, more than you can know. And she killed him. The stupid witch, I wish it had been her that died."

Defoe stopped, turned to her, brushed the tears from the corners of her eyes with his thumb. "Don't say that, Sammy. I know it hurt, losing your father. But how do you think she feels? I knew your dad, he was a friend of mine. I was the one who introduced him to your mother, did you know that? And I know how much they loved each other. Don't you realize that she hurts as much as you do?"

"No way, man. Nobody can hurt the way I do. Not the way I hurt for my daddy." She walked a few paces in silence, then said, "But I'm not letting that interfere with my life, the rest of it, the living part." She looked at him and grinned. "Hey, you know something? You could have been my daddy, if the two of you hadn't been so careful, way back when. Daddy Chase," she said. "Daddy Chase, Daddy Chase." She nudged him in the ribs as they crossed the lawn to the front of his childhood home. "Something to think about, eh?"

It was eleven when Defoe rang the front doorbell and said to Samantha, "I really ought to see if there's a spare key I can borrow. I feel a little silly standing in front of the house I grew up in, waiting for the maid to answer the door."

"I know. Grampy gave me a key to his place, after we started working on the book." She threw her head back, looked up at the fluted columns of the porte cochere that soared to support the second-floor balcony. "So, what's it like, growing up in a mansion?"

Defoe admired her throat, the smooth muscles of her neck thrown into definition by the tilt of her head. "Mansion? Well, I'd hardly compare it to Monticello, but, yes, I guess it is a bit grander than most houses. To tell the truth, I never thought much about it. Guess it's the old saw about familiarity breeding contempt. It was just 'my house.' Why? Does your mother paint it as being a palace?"

"No, not really, but you have to admit that it's a heck of a lot more imposing than Grampy's place."

"True. But if you want to know a secret, it always seemed warmer over there, more casual. Your grandmother, Sammy, was the opposite of the General. Where he was, well, I'll have to say it, a bit of a martinet, she was a . . . a kind of a Mother Goose person, if that makes any sense to you. Rosy cheeks and a warm smile, flour in her hair and milk and cookies ready any time of day. And over there you didn't have servants lurking in the background. Sometimes this place felt more like a four-star hotel than a home. There we go. Hello, Anna, sorry to bother you. Is there a key handy that I can borrow? You have enough to do, without pulling door duty. How come it's locked, anyway? Oh, this is Samantha Quinn, Kit's daughter."

"How do you do, miss," Anna said, standing aside as they came through the door. "Your father said to keep it locked, since last year, when there was those break-ins. There's spare keys in your father's desk, in the library."

"Ah, good," Defoe said, putting the walking stick back in the umbrella stand. "I'll purloin one. Where is my father?"

"He's in there, sir, with the morning papers."

"Good." Defoe led Samantha into the library, said, "Dad. Mother around? I want to tell you both what's going on. Oh, and how about letting me have a key to the front door."

George Defoe looked up from his desk, stood up when he saw Samantha. "Hello there." He opened a drawer and handed his son a key. "What's all the running back and forth about? Your mother is fiddling with her plants, least she *was.*"

Defoe put his hand on the small of Samantha's back and steered her to the morning room. Mary Defoe got up from the floor where she had been root-pruning a large philodendron. She brushed her hands across the knees of her slacks and said, "Hello, you two. What's going on?"

"Sammy and Kit discovered a recording over at the General's. Without going into the details, I'll just tell you that he had a dictating recorder, and it was apparently running at the time of his death. It also seems likely that someone came into the room after he died and burned the notes and papers pertinent to his memoirs. Sammy and I are going to run over to her apartment, pick up the carbons for a look-see. Maybe we can find a clue that will shed some light on the mystery."

"Oh, dear," Mary Defoe said, looking at her husband. "It sounds all very confusing. Why would someone want to destroy Harmon's papers?"

Defoe shook his head, poked his toe at the tangled mass of the root ball on the floor. "Worse than that, I'm afraid. Sammy thinks that someone destroyed her grandfather."

"What!" Mary Defoe said.

"Oh, for God's sake, don't be ridiculous!" George Defoe added. "The old fool shot himself. Sorry, Samantha, but it's as plain as day that's what happened. Don't go stirring things up, Chase. I went to quite a bit of trouble getting this whole thing squared away. Had to throw my weight around with the local police; now don't go knocking the ducks out of line with a bunch of wild ideas."

Defoe looked at his father, wondered why he was so adamant about keeping the whole affair quiet. "Don't worry, Dad, we're just going to look over the General's notes, see if there's anything that might indicate a motive for—what do they call it in the Agatha Christies? Foul play."

"Huh! Well, do what you must. Please, I ask you, though. Clear anything you come up with with me before you go off half cocked. Damned embarrassing, for me, if you uncover something the local police want to follow up on, after I pulled out all the stops to cut them out of the loop."

Defoe backed the Jaguar out of the garage and leaned across, opened the door for Samantha. "Sorry about Dad. He can be a bit overbearing at times. At *most* of the times."

"He did seem sort of testy. Mom said that Aunt Mary told her you and he haven't been getting along too well since you came back from California. Something happened out there that started the whole thing, she said."

Defoe stared out over the steering wheel through the windshield. "I guess you could say that," he finally said. "My son was killed." He turned and met her eyes.

"Oh, I'm sorry, I didn't know." She reached out and lightly put her hand on his, where it rested on the gearshift.

"It's okay, I can talk about it. Now. I was in pretty bad shape when it happened. See, I was on the other side of the world, on an island in the middle of the Indian Ocean, when he died. Hit by a drunk while he was riding his bicycle. He shouldn't have been out, it was late, after dark. She, his mother, she was at a cocktail party at a neighbor's, few blocks away." Defoe paused, examining again, as he had countless times before, the facts of the event. Still hoping some new evidence would leap into focus, give a different slant to it. Finally he went on. "Andy was really the only thing we had in common. When he died I think we both realized that. She filed for divorce, I resigned from the Navy, drove east. Holed up at a friend's place in Pennsylvania, vacant while he was in Europe, tried to repair the damage to my psyche. Came down here a couple of times, looking for tea and sympathy. Dad wasn't much help. Didn't think Andy's death was reason enough to jump ship in midcareer. I tried to explain that it was a lot more than just my son's death, but he wouldn't hear it. I think I embarrassed him, made him look bad in front of his friends."

"Yes, he reminds me of Grampy, that way. 'My mind's made up, don't confuse me with the facts.' But men like that are so used to being right that I think the idea of maybe making a mistake is completely alien to them. Grampy and I got into a couple of doozies, arguing the Grenada invasion. Hey, this is a neat car! What is it?"

"Jag. A Mark Two, early sixties." He disengaged the clutch and blipped the accelerator a couple of times as they rolled down the driveway, sending the revs up the tach and listening to the rich rumble of the exhaust. "Zoom zoom! Defoe's folly. Where's your apartment?"

"Tyson's Corner. Hit Chain Bridge and take it to the mall. I'm in one of the new buildings. Super swank; I can see Bloomie's from my bathroom window."

Defoe chuckled. "Who could ask for anything more?"

"Yeah. Beats the view from the living room. That's of the apartment building next door, all of fifty feet away. It's kind of expensive, but convenient to Grampy's, and I had to get out of the Georgetown place. Mother was driving me nuts."

"Oh? How so?"

"Well, you saw her. Wimpy, I guess is as good a word as any. Tentative, unsure of herself. Not in control. I'm not that great with words, I guess that's why I'm a photojournalist, hey? Picture's worth a thousand words. A thousand of mine, anyhow. I'll show you my work, at the apartment." She looked over at him, sucked her lower lip. "Sounds like a line, doesn't it? Come up and see my etchings. Only in my case it's my prints. Black and white. I have a darkroom set up in what is supposed to be the bedroom; I sleep out on the sofa. Management would probably kill me if they knew what I've done to the place. Snuck a plumber up there, had him put in a big sink for me, then got a guy I know that's a whiz with a hammer and saw. Sealed up the door and windows so they're light tight, built me shelves and countertops for my printing gear. Hang a left. Park any place you can, up there."

Defoe eased his car between two smaller, newer ones and looked around. From the slight elevation they gazed across several hundred acres of brick- and stone-veneered buildings and the macadam parking lots that served them. One each of every department store Defoe had ever heard of competed with a thousand specialty shops on both sides of the highway for the dollars of the area's wealthy residents. "None of this was here when your mother and I were kids," he said. "It was just open fields." He shook his head and followed her into her building. At least back in Pennsylvania the two hundred-year-old stone farmhouses still stood, even if they were now surrounded with ever-expanding suburbia.

The elevator stopped and the doors slid silently apart on the fifteenth floor. *"Mi casa es su casa,"* Samantha said, keying the door and standing aside, letting Defoe enter ahead of her.

An entrance hall, not much more than an alcove, just large enough for a table and mirror across from a tiny closet, opened into the living room, light and airy with its nine-foot ceiling and pale broadloom carpeting. On the right side a gently arched doorway led to the kitchen and on the opposite wall a closed door hid the bedroom that was now Samantha's photo lab. An eight-foot sofa, upholstered in deep chocolate leather, was positioned in front of sliding glass doors that led to a small balcony and gave a view, diffused through gauze curtains, of the building's twin. A sheet of glass, supported on beige ceramic pyramids at each corner, served as a cocktail table, and a swooping cantilever of chrome steel ending in a bulbous lampshade overlooked the arrangement. The furnishings had an expensive and vaguely foreign look that Defoe couldn't quite place. Italian probably; they were the hot designers at the moment. Samantha had paneled one wall with homosote and completely covered it with black-and-white photographic prints, each held in place with four aluminum drafting pins. Defoe walked over to it and started in the upper left-hand corner.

"My rogue's gallery. What I've been up to the last couple of years. Glass of white wine?"

Defoe glanced at his watch and thought it a bit early, but what the hell. "Sure, why not?"

"Great, then I'll whip up something for us to eat while you're going over Grampy's ramblings." She went into the kitchen and Defoe turned back to the wall.

Carol and Arthur Ochs Sulzberger smiled and held wineglasses of the sort handed out at catered charity functions, Gloria and Jimmy Stewart did the same, and Oscar de la Renta showed his perfect teeth. Defoe recognized Malcolm

Forbes but not Mary McFadden sharing the print, identified Jeane Kirkpatrick, Al Haig, and John Sununu, but drew a blank at Honey Skinner, Nancy Sununu, and Georgette Mosbacher. "I'm afraid," he said, accepting a glass of chilled Chablis, "that the distaff side of the power elite is not my strong suit. Who's that?"

"Salut," Samantha said, touching the lip of her glass to his before tasting her wine. "Georgette Mosbacher. Husband's Robert? And that's Teresa Heinz and Helene Safire and down here, this is Lynne and Richard Cheney."

"Yes, Dick I recognize. He was a classmate of your father's, did you know that? You took all these pictures?" Defoe stepped back from the wall, rolled a swallow of Chablis over his tongue. "There must be hundreds."

"Hah. This is just some of the better ones. I have three file drawers full in the darkroom, and about ten thousand negatives that I never bothered to print. Sometimes I hit two or three of these things a day. Have a big one tonight at the Kennedy Center." She went to the darkroom door and disappeared through it, her voice echoing. "The Eagles—that's what the big money Republicans call themselves—are having a bash for the President. Supposed to be seven or eight hundred of the movers and shakers there. I'll shoot most of them, there or at one of the smaller parties afterward." She laughed, coming back into the room with a sweater and jeans over her arm and a pair of jogging shoes in her free hand. "Taking the pictures is the easy part; it's keeping track of who's who that drives you nuts. You can never count on the photo editors identifying the people, so you have to do that for them if you want to see your work in print."

"I guess. Him, I recognize. Bill Buckley."

"Yeah, and that's his wife, Pat. Better known than her husband, if you can believe it, to our *WWD* readers." She reached out to the wall and touched an eight-by-ten of a white-haired man in a dinner jacket. "You must know him."

"Paul Laxalt. He and Carol live just down the road, in McLean. You're a lucky girl, Sammy, to be rubbing elbows with this crowd, and getting paid for it." He looked around the apartment, added, "Pays pretty well I'd guess."

"Not as well as you think. Turn around," she said, putting

her wineglass on the cocktail table and kicking off her shoes. "I want to get out of these funereal drabs."

Defoe faced the windows and the neighboring building beyond, saw that, with the sun on the other side of the building, the glass was a remarkably effective mirror. Sammy peeled off her sweater and unhooked the short skirt, let it drop to the floor. She looked up and met Defoe's reflection in the blackness of the sliding doors as she rolled the black panty hose down her thighs. "Grampy's publisher gave him a fifty-thousand-dollar advance on his book, and he gave me half of it. I bought a car and put the rest in a money market fund, earmarked it to pay the rent on this place for a year." She wriggled into the jeans, worked them up over her rump and zipped, then pulled the sweater over her head and shook her blond hair free. "Grampy and I were going to split the royalties on his book, but now I don't know what's going to happen. If I don't increase my income by half again what I'm getting as a free-lancer I'll either have to find a cheaper place or—curses, curses—move back to Georgetown with Ding-Dong, the Wicked Witch. 'Kay, you can turn around now." She smiled and reached under her sweater, unhooked her bra and pulled it out, tossed it on the floor with her other clothes, then picked up her glass and looked at Defoe across the rim.

"Hmm." Defoe smiled back. *Slow down, girl,* he thought. *Old men don't like to be rushed; not when we've finally learned that getting there is half the fun.* "Well then, let's have a look at your grandfather's notes, see if we can come up with a crime scoop that you can sell to the *Washington Post* for a bundle."

"Hey, that's an idea." Samantha walked across to the other side of the room, put her wineglass on her desk, a black lacquered slab supported by a latticework of glossy red industrial steel shelving components. An IBM Selectric was centered on its surface, a cassette player with earphones and a foot switch was to its left, and a box of paper on the other side balanced the still life. The swivel chair was black leather and shiny chrome and had so many knobs and levers to control pitch, height, and yaw that it might have come from the cockpit of a fighter plane.

"What the—That's odd, I know I—" Samantha looked at the desk, puzzled.

"What's the matter?" Defoe walked across the room, stood beside her, and looked at her transcription equipment.

"They're gone."

"The copies? Maybe you put them someplace else."

"No. See, this is a box of two-part NCR paper. I finish transcribing a page, tear them apart, put the original facedown beside the box here to go to Grampy, and put the copy in the lid of the box, right there, behind the typewriter. Only it isn't there." She turned and looked at Defoe. "Except it's *got* to be. I mean, that's where it's been since we started this project. For six months, that damn lid was right *there,* behind the typewriter. Gradually filling up with paper. About two hundred pages by now. I don't understand it."

"Does anyone else have a key? Maid service? A, uh, boyfriend?"

"No, nuh-uh. I mean, building management can probably get in, but why would they take the notes?"

Defoe put his wineglass beside Samantha's and turned her toward him with a firm grip on her arm. "Sammy, are you absolutely sure about this? That the copies were right here, on the desk? No chance that you moved them, stuck them in a file drawer or something like that?"

"No! Absolutely not! They've been right the fuck *here,* for, like I said, about six months."

Defoe let go of her arm. "Then the only possibility is that someone got in here and took them. When was the last time you saw the copies?"

"Well, I guess they were here this morning, when I left for the funeral. But I didn't check; the last time I know for *sure* would be, uh, Monday. I transcribed a cassette Sunday night, and Monday morning I stuck the originals and the cassette in an envelope, dropped them off at his house. He wasn't home, so I left them in the basket. And then I went back, around five or so, 'cause I wanted to talk to him. That's when I found him . . ."

Defoe didn't comment, went instead to the apartment door and opened it, squatted to examine the lock. "Hmm," he said, surprised. More quality than he'd expected. Most rental unit locks can be opened in a couple of minutes with only rudimentary burglar tools, but this was a top of the line Yale deadbolt and the jamb was steel. No scratches around the keyhole; whoever opened it knew what they were doing. A professional. "You're absolutely sure that nobody else has a key? Didn't give one to your mother or stepfather, didn't stash a spare someplace. First place burglars look, after checking under the doormat, is the ledge over the door. An awful lot of people stick a key up there, figuring if you can't see it nobody would know it was there."

"No, nuh-uh. I told you, I just have the one key. They charge you five bucks for a duplicate, and I didn't see any reason to get another one."

Defoe looked around the room. "Sammy, I'm afraid it looks as though you're right. If someone broke in here and stole the copies, it certainly reinforces your supposition that your grandfather was murdered. Can you remember anything from his notes while you were transcribing them that would be a motive for murder?"

"Nuh-uh. I mean, I have no idea what was on the tapes. See, when you're typing from dictation, you don't really listen to the content, just the words. You concentrate on the typing, not what's being said." She shrugged. "He could have named his killer and I wouldn't have known."

"Yes, I've heard that. Well, I think it's time to bring the police into this. The recording you have of that mysterious visitor at the General's is the only solid lead we have. A voiceprint of it would give the authorities a starting point."

"What about your dad? Remember what he said about the local police."

"Yes. Well, I wasn't planning on dealing with the Fairfax County people. One of my college roommates is in the Justice Department. I was going to drop in on him anyway, while I was down here. I'll see what he can do with the information. Is there a Radio Shack in the mall?"

"What? Sure, I guess so. I mean isn't there always? Why?"

"I want to pick up an empty cassette, make a dupe of the one you have. Murphy's Law, subchapter number one. 'Never let the only copy of anything out of your sight.' I want a backup copy for insurance."

Samantha paled and put her hand on her chest. "Oh, my God, Chase, I never even thought about the cassettes. We'd better buy three blank tapes. Because there's the one I transcribed on Sunday; like I said, I dropped it off Monday morning with the typewritten pages. And the new one I picked up at the same time. Grampy has a basket in the kitchen, where he puts his mail. He's always getting packages from the National Archives, from that place up in Pennsylvania where I took him, and Suitland, over in Maryland, sends records to him, too. Not just by mail; UPS and Federal Express sometimes drop stuff off. I always leave my transcriptions there, and if there's a cassette for me to do, that's where he puts it. Because half the time he's not at home when I stop by." She waved her hand, dismissing her chatter. "Anyway, what I'm saying is that maybe the cassette and the transcription are still sitting there, in that pile of mail. And the one I picked up is in my car, in the glove box. See, I had put it in my windbreaker that morning, in the pocket, and it was still there that afternoon, when I went back to Grampy's. God, it was awful, Chase. I can close my eyes and see him . . . I guess I always will. Anyway, I bent down, over him, and got blood on my sleeve. And later, after all the people had come and gone and everything, when I left, I took my windbreaker off, in the car, because I was going to drop it to the cleaners. And I took the cassette out of the pocket and tossed it in the glove box. Forgot about it completely, until this moment. So, anyway. We've got three cassettes. Think there's anything on them that might be important?"

"I think, Sammy, we'd better get those cassettes and find out."

FIVE

Defoe tossed the three newly purchased cassettes in the Jag's glove compartment and at the same time extracted his own cassette recorder and put it in the breast pocket of his suit coat, then followed Sam's directions to the Brill house.

The exterior of the four-story brick dwelling was eighteenth-century Georgetown, but the interior foreshadowed the approaching millennium. Brill's designer had lacquered the walls pale peach, apple green, and citron yellow, then carpeted the entire first floor in an electric blue that flowed from room to room, mirroring the Atlantic somewhere south of Miami. The furnishings were an echo of those in Sam's apartment—very modern and very expensive.

Defoe glanced into the dining room as he and Sammy headed along the hallway toward the rear of the house, puzzled momentarily by the trompe l'oeil columns capped with pediments and an Egyptian frieze that gave way to a Nile-blue sky, complete with a pair of soaring birds. *A bit disconcerting,* Defoe thought, *having buzzards overhead during dinner*.

The living room opposite was one of the endless variations of postmodern; all the flutes, capitals, and dentils on the entablatures reminded Defoe of the façade of some nineteenth-century small town bank, trying very hard to impress its customers with its solidity and grandure but looking rather ostentatiously ridiculous instead, squeezed as it was between its board-and-batten neighbors.

Jack's den, where Defoe and Sammy found both Kit and Brill, looked out at the brick-walled garden that ran a hundred feet beyond the rear of the house. Brill had his briefcase open on his desk, a freeform slab of some exotic wood resting on a contrasting trestle formed from six-inch beams joined by intricately hand-cut Japanese joints, and was filling it with the manila folders he was taking from a tambour-doored oak cabinet beside the desk. He looked up as they came into the room. He wore cavalry twill trousers and a white cotton tab collar shirt with a deep maroon-and-blue regimental stripe tie that made his tan look darker than it really was. His navy-blue blazer hung over the back of a chair behind the desk, its gold buttons winking bright against the dark wool.

"Hey, guys," he said. "Didn't expect to see you here. Kit says you found a tape at the General's that indicated he might have met with foul play." He turned to his wife. "I thought you said they were going over to Sammy's, to read transcriptions."

Kit looked at Defoe and her daughter, blank bewilderment in her eyes. She'd changed from her black Chanel suit into a matching navy sweater and skirt, looked pale against the dark wool. "Yes. What did you do, dear, bring them back here with you? I didn't expect to see you for a couple of hours."

"They're gone, Mother. Daddy, someone broke into the apartment and stole them. Six months' work, gone."

"Huh!" Brill said. "You sure? Oh, hell, Jack, of *course* she's sure. This is Sammy you're talking to, not some damned nitwit." He came around the desk and wrapped his arm around her shoulder, led her toward the bookshelves filled with law journals. "Damned shame, sweetheart, losing all that work. I know how much it meant to you, the book. Especially after . . . after what happened. Had your heart set on finishing it up for him." Brill looked at Defoe. "She could have done it, too, fella. This is one hell of a talented little girl I have here. But I guess that's water under the bridge, over the dam, now, right?"

"I don't know about the book, Mr. Brill, but we still have three cassettes, according to Sammy. There may be something on them that will indicate why he was killed."

"Hey, Chase, my friend. Call me Jack, will you? After all," he added, glancing at Kit, "you're practically a member of the family. How 'bout a drink, short one before lunch? I bet Sammy could use one. How 'bout it, little girl? Down in the dumps, right? Let Daddy Jack fix you a little something, perk you right up." He went to a bar that occupied a section of bookcase and took an ice cube tray from the refrigerator concealed behind fumed oak, shucked it into a Waterford bucket, the cubes clattering against the crystal. "Specialty of the house, Chase," he said, smiling, pouring six ounces of Swedish vodka over the ice. " 'Brut Absolut.' The driest martini in DC." He stirred it with a rod, clapped a sterling strainer over the lip of the ice bucket, and decanted the chilled vodka into four stemmed glasses, dumped the dregs into the stainless-steel sink, and rinsed the ice bucket in one smooth move.

"Chin chin," he said, lifting his glass in salute. Took a mouthful of vodka, grinned at Defoe over the top of his glass, sucked air through his bared teeth. Swallowed, said, "Ah. Put starch in your shorts." Looked at Sammy. "Listen. How 'bout it, guys? Little lunch? Long as you're here. Mom and I were just going to zap a quiche and share a bottle of Meursault, before I hit the trail." He looked back at Defoe. "Kit's got a deft touch with the freezer; I always say that if I step in front of a bus she can go into the frozen food business. Seriously, she makes the best damned quiche, and then freezes them by the carload. Only way to go, with a lawyer who turns up for dinner at the oddest hours. How 'bout it, babe? Go get a couple out for us, put them in the magic box."

When Kit had left the room Brill put his arm around his stepdaughter once again and turned to Defoe. "Her secret—God, don't tell her I told you—after she microwaves the little devils she pops them under the broiler for a couple of minutes." He finished his drink. "Keeps the pastry crisp and gives the cheese just the barest soupçon of crunch, know what I mean?" He gestured with his empty glass at Defoe's. "Hey, how 'bout a refill?" Turned to Sammy. "Li'l darlin'?"

"Not for me, thanks," Defoe said, disguising his barely touched drink behind his fingers. Privately he thought, *this makes a great anesthetic, but I like to* taste *my booze.* Aloud, to Brill, he asked, "What's the Meursault? It's not a cru I'm very well versed in."

Brill said, "Hey, you a wino, Chase?" He let his hand fall to

Sam's bottom and smacked it twice, a love pat. "Go help your mom, set the table for her. I want to show Chase my cellar."

Sammy went left, toward the kitchen, and Brill steered Defoe along the hall, back toward the front of the house. Halfway there he opened a door and flicked on a light. "Watch the steps; they're steep. Our ancestors were pretty niggardly when they built these old houses. Didn't waste much space on closets and stairs." His voice boomed in the stairwell as they went down, his cane clunking against the wooden treads. "On the second floor I turned a whole extra bedroom into a walk-in closet and dressing area for the master suite."

The basement was whitewashed brick walls and a ceiling that was a few inches shy of seven feet above the slate floor. Defoe had a momentary glimpse in his mind's eye of the underground railroad that ran up through the area, up into Pennsylvania.

"I thought at one time of digging down a couple of feet, get a little more headroom." Brill pointed Defoe toward the back of the cellar. "But I figured, what the hell, spoil the ambiance of the old place." Unglazed flue tiles, eighteen inches across, were stacked on their sides against the wall, covering it from floor to ceiling. Each held a dozen bottles, a case, of wine. "Stays in the midfifties down here, year round. 'Course I help it a little, in the summer. Get's so damned hot and humid. But then you know that, right? Grew up in the area, didn't you?"

"Yes, more or less. Until I was twelve or thirteen, anyway, and got shuttled off to boarding school."

"Yes. Lucky fella; I grew up in Cincinnati, went to public school. Ohio State, then Georgetown, for my law degree. Played a little football, for Woody. You don't look big enough to have played the game. But I bet you were a jock, right? Got that look about you."

Defoe laughed. "Sure, I guess. I try to stay in shape, anyway." He looked at his host's larger, taller frame. "You must still play a sport."

Brill ducked his head to one side, ran his hand over it, smoothing his razor cut in a self-deprecating gesture. "Aw, yeah, I still work out a little. Keep the old gut firm. Some tennis. Weight routine, at the club." He looked at Defoe with a sly glance. "Got to, want to keep the ladies on line, right, my friend?" He lightly punched Defoe on the left biceps. "But I don't have to tell a super stud like you about performance, do I? Hey, you a shooter?"

"What, guns? Some smoothbore, now and then. I don't get out in the field much anymore."

"No, no, I'm talking pistolas." Brill glanced at his watch, a gold Rolex. "We got a couple minutes, let's pop a few rounds."

He led Defoe to the other end of the cellar, where a bullet trap, welded from sheets of half-inch steel, dominated the wall. Ten meters in front of it a two-by-twelve plank across a pair of saw horses served as a firing line. Brill opened a steel cabinet and pointed with pride to its contents. "Couple of Gold Cup .45's; the top one modified by Bill Wilson. The Accu-Comp; most of the guys that take the top honors at the IPSC World Championships use his guns. Then the .22 match pistol, just use it to keep my eye in." He pointed to the last gun in the cabinet. "Just got this one; Beretta nine, the new Army sidearm. Shoots nice, but no punch, not when you compare it to the old four-five. Step backward, if you ask me. What the hell good is an extra half dozen rounds, if they won't put your opponent down?"

"Afraid I'm not really up on the latest in sidearms, Jack. That little .22 is more my speed. May I?" He reached into the cabinet and took out the single shot, bolt-action match pistol, cradled it into his right fist. The familiar feel of its weight was comforting, and he slowly lowered it onto the bullet trap, sighted over the heavy barrel.

"I thought you were in Naval intelligence. I think that's what Kit told me; or maybe it was Harmon. Wasn't handgun proficiency part of the training? That, along with unarmed combat, escape, and evasion, all that good stuff."

Defoe put the .22 down. "Not for me it wasn't. To tell you the truth, I was more involved in keeping government contractors honest than in catching Russian spies. I knew a lot of those guys, though, ran a few as a case officer."

Brill took a plastic sleeve of .22 ammo, fifty rounds, out of the cabinet, put it on the plank. "Me, too." He looked at

Defoe and smiled. "Knew a bunch of the spooks, I mean. I spent about ten years as assistant counsel over at the NSA. Whenever one of them would screw up, run afoul of the judicial system, I was responsible for defending them." He shook his head. "Had some pretty whacky dudes there." Brill pushed the ammunition toward Defoe. "Okay, my friend, let's shoot us a few." He clipped a pair of paper targets, five bull's-eyes on each sheet, to the overhead wires, ran them out to the bullet trap. "Ten rounds, loser cleans the weapon. Guest draws first shot."

Defoe took a .22 long rifle cartridge, an inch long and slimmer than a pencil, and dropped it in the chamber, locked the bolt. Cold barrel, adjustable rear peep, he'd have to figure that Brill had it sighted in for the distance. Touch the first round off very carefully, see where it went. He extended his arm, raised the pistol over his head, and slowly, slowly, lowered it on to the top of the ten ring. Breathe in, exhale as the muzzle approached the stopping point, the X ring, dead center. A black spot, not much larger than the diameter of the little .22 bullet, and thirty odd feet away. He could feel his heart, his pulse. Bad; you were supposed to be past all that. But it had been years.

Defoe was a two-eye shooter, learned the then-new technique at the École Militaire, in Antibes. Don't squint and shoot, keep your binocular vision intact. The combat theory. The école's full name was the School of Fencing and Military Sport. Defoe had spent six weeks there, training for the pentathlon, the modern one, the military event. Ride and shoot; run, swim, and fence. He'd not made the cut for the U.S. team, but the training had stayed with him, and proved useful in his career with the Navy; four years later, at the time of the next Olympic Trials, he'd been busy using those skills to stay alive. He centered, held on target, touched the trigger.

The .22 fired with a small report and no measurable recoil from the heavy gun. Defoe admired the crisp release of the trigger and focused on the target, fifty feet away. Virgin paper stared back at him; either he'd aced the center ring or missed the whole damned eight-by-twelve sheet of paper. *I'm not* that *rusty,* he thought. Sights appeared to be dead-on. He ejected the empty cartridge and loaded another round, raised the pistol, and dropped it once again onto a fresh target. Take up the trigger, creep, concentrate, squeeze. Snap. A ragged hole in the nine ring of the target, a few degrees up and to the left stared back at him. Maybe drift just a hair right of dead center with the third shot, to compensate for the warming barrel. Under match conditions there is time between shots for the barrel to cool, for metal to realign itself. Need to use all the angles; this guy talks like a player.

Repeat the exercise three more times on the remaining targets. An X and a ten, three nines, running high and to the left. He looked at the paper that Brill had scooted back on the overhead trolley. "Not bad," his host said, looking at the gray, puckered holes in the paper.

Damned fine, Defoe thought, *considering that I haven't done this in about twenty years.* "Yeah," he said aloud. "It's a skill that never really leaves you. Kind of like riding a bike, I guess."

Brill loaded a round in the single shot pistol. "This, this business, with the General's tapes," he said, dropping on the target. "You really think there's something there?" Snap. The bullet punctured the top target in the center of the X ring. "Hey, I think I got lucky. Aced that one."

"That you did. She seemed to be pulling a little bit to me, once she was warmed up." Give him something to think about, sow a seed of doubt. "Guess I was wrong. Hard to say. About the tape, I mean. Sammy's got it, upstairs. We'll play it for you, see what you think. Sounds to me like the General had a caller before he died, and the caller, or someone else, was there, after. Tell you one thing. The sounds pretty well prove that he didn't burn the papers."

"Uh hum." Brill ejected, reloaded, lowered on target. "Of course, as a lawyer, I would have to tell you that a tape like that would never be admissible as evidence." Snap. "Shit. High and to the left. That's where your second shot went; I think these sights *are* off." He went to the cabinet and got out a small gunsmith's screwdriver.

"I realize that, Jack. But I'm not offering the tape as evidence, not to you. Just as a corroboration of Sammy's feeling that the General wouldn't kill himself. Or that he didn't burn the papers."

Brill exhaled and fired his third shot, rushed it. "Nine ring, nine o'clock," Defoe said, looked at the gun, then the lawyer. "Did you turn the windage adjustment clockwise or counter-clockwise?" He could see Brill looking at a clockface in his mind, figuring which was which.

"Dammit! I think I turned the sight a click the wrong way, went left instead of right." He picked up the screwdriver again and bent over the pistol.

"What about the papers stolen from Sammy's apartment? That must indicate something." Defoe pressed the red record button and slipped the machine back in his breast pocket.

Brill got the sights the way he wanted them and reloaded. "Hearsay. Again, inadmissible as evidence. We don't even know that these so-called copies ever existed." The muzzle slowly dropped on target, Brill exhaled, held, held, too long. Exhale, drop the pistol to his side, breathe. Raise it once again above his head, lower it. Hold, squeeze, fire. Eight ring, nine o'clock. "Shit!" He looked at Defoe, puzzled, wondered if he'd been conned. "I had it right the first time." He bent over the gun with the screwdriver. "I'm not saying that your evidence doesn't exist, Defoe, Chase," he said, ejecting the brass shell and reloading a fresh bullet. "Just that it is pretty weak, if we had to take it to court. Maybe someone burned the papers. Maybe someone stole the papers. Maybe someone killed Harmon." He raised the gun above his head for his fourth shot, started down. "Need something more substantial to take to the police, get them to open an investigation." He paused for a split second, then fired. "Yes! *That's* the way it's done! Knew that bastard was an X ring before I let it go." He turned to Defoe. "See what I'm saying?"

"Sure. But let's look at it logically, never mind from a legal standpoint just now." Defoe paused, turned, walked a few steps away, pressed the stop button. As he turned back he saw Brill pointing the pistol at his stomach. There was a split second where each man measured the other, then Brill dropped the gun to his side.

"Sorry," he said. "Didn't expect you to walk off like that." He put the pistol on the bench.

"No, it's my fault. My point, the point I was going to make, is that never mind what I've been telling you. Listen to the tape, make up your own mind. I . . . we—Sammy and I, and I guess Kit also—don't have to convince you, or anybody else. Not right now. What we need is for you to listen to the tape and make your own judgment. Interpret it for yourself." Defoe shrugged. "That, after all, is what the three of us did."

The sound of the door at the top of the stairs reached them. "Jack? You two still down there? Lunch."

"Okay." Brill raised the pistol, turned, dropped it on the target, and fired, all in one smooth move. "Shit. Looks like a flier. I'm going to take that one over, with your permission." He opened the breech and laid the gun on the plank. "I have to tell you though, I'm going to look at it as an interested party. As counselor to the decedent's only heir, I don't want to make any waves. Because waves, the kind you're talking about, could push probate back six months." He turned to Defoe as he closed the bolt on the final round. "And that, my friend, means dollars right out of our dear little Katherine's pocket." He turned and fired, casually. "Keep it in mind."

Defoe thought that the quiche was good, but was probably better before it had been frozen. The Meursault was a disappointment; flinty and in need of more aeration. He and his host were shooting in the cellar when they should have been pulling the cork on the wine. Why the veiled threat about probate? He looked around. No penury here. Cut flowers in the crystal bowl centered on the flawless four-yard stretch of mahogany. The cellar had been full, they were now sampling an investment from the past, but this year's vintages had already been laid down. Still, with money matters you never knew. A man's mortgage might be six months in arrears, but he's still playing the ponies and drinking champagne from ladies' slippers. If money *was* a problem, the General's little piece of northern Virginia had to be worth . . . millions.

Brill stood and refilled their glasses with the last of the wine. "Chase was telling me," he said to the two women, "about the General's tape."

"Tapes, Daddy," Samantha said. "There's three of them, what with the one in my car and the one I dropped off at Grampy's the day he died."

Brill looked surprised. "Interesting; we'll have to see

what's on all of them. Of course the important one, from the way you three talk, is the one recorded at the time of his suicide. But I want to listen to it myself, form my own opinion. Only it will have to wait until I get back from New York." He looked at his watch. "I'm behind schedule now; I have to stop at the office for a couple of hours and tidy up a few things, make some calls before I catch the train." He tossed off the last of his wine and offered his hand to Defoe. "Nice meeting you, Chase. Hope to see you again, when I get back from the Big Apple; give me a chance to play catch-up in the second half of our pistol match." He turned to his wife. "Run upstairs and get my bag, will you, hon, while I'll fetch my jacket and briefcase from the den." He leaned over his stepdaughter and kissed the top of her head. "Take care, li'l darlin'; see you in a couple of days," he said as he left the room.

Samantha got up, said, "Hey, I've got to get out of here, too. I want to stop at the Kennedy Center, pick up a copy of the table settings, see who's where. Then I have to buy some fresh darkroom chemicals, get my dress from the cleaners, and wash my hair. Gotta scoot."

Defoe stood, put his napkin on the table. "What about the other tape? The one in your car. Why don't you give it to me, maybe your mom and I can go out to your grandfather's place and pick up the third one, see if there's anything that might be a lead, a clue."

"Good idea."

"What's a good idea?" Kit asked, coming into the room with a large pigskin suitcase at her side.

Samantha turned to her mother, said, "Chase suggested that you two run out to Grampy's, give all three tapes a listen. And I said it was a good idea, good because I'll be tied up all night with this do at the Kennedy, the Watergate parties that'll follow. After which I have to develop and print, write some copy, then send the happy little rascals on their way to New York. At which time I will collapse into bed and sleep until noon." She turned to Defoe. "When you will call me with the earth-shattering news you guys have discovered on the tapes, right? Then we can . . . what did your father say? Line our ducks up in a row? For Daddy, when he gets back from his trip. And, brilliant lawyer that he is, he'll take our evidence to the cops and they'll grab the bad guy, right?"

Defoe laughed. "You have the whole scenario laid out, don't you? Okay; if you're game, Kit, let's run out to the country and check out these tapes. Maybe Sammy's right. Maybe we'll catch a killer."

SIX

Defoe looked in his rearview mirror at Kit behind him in the Volvo. "I'll follow you to Dad's," she'd said. "No sense in you having to run me all the way back to town when you're two skips and a hop from your own place out there."

No sense at all. Besides, it avoids the embarrassment, the temptation, the, the—what? *Inevitability? Of us winding up, back at your Georgetown house, alone.* He recalled her husband's sly reference to Defoe's amatory abilities, wondered how much of their childhood she had shared with her second husband. Best, yes, to take both cars. He touched the turn signal and swept off 66 at the Fairfax County line.

"I want to stop for a moment at my parents'," Defoe had said as they left the Georgetown house. "To pick up my briefcase, or at least the bible in it."

"Bible? We're going to be needing divine help with this?"

"No, at least I hope not. My bible is my address book. More than that, really. It's the vital statistics on most everybody I know or have ever met. Useful when you want an answer to a specific and very arcane question. As the old saying goes, 'It's not what you know, but who you know.' Especially if the Who knows the What."

Defoe unlocked the front door and left Kit in the hallway beneath the watchful eyes of dead Defoes as he ran lightly up the wide staircase to his bedroom. When he came down, his father and Kit were standing under the big Whistler of his great-grandmother and her two daughters. They'd sat for it in Paris, the year of their Grand Tour; it reminded him of the Beardsley drawing of Salome holding the head of John the Baptist. He couldn't decide if it was the expatriate artist's style or the subjects who sat for him, but Whistler's paintings always seemed slightly decadent to Defoe.

". . . over to Dad's, to listen to the other tapes," she said.

"What? There's more than one?" George Defoe was uncharacteristically casual, wearing a beige cashmere cardigan over his white shirt and tie instead of his ubiquitous suitcoat.

"Sammy came up with two more," Defoe said. "The immediate predecessors to the one that was on the General's body. I gather that they are the end result of his final week's work. May very well contain some interesting tidbit."

"Pssh!" George Defoe made a noise like the doors of a municipal bus. "Don't see why you have to go poking into things. Won't bring him back. Let the man rest in peace." He turned to the General's daughter. "Are you part of this nonsense, Kit? Thought you had more sense. Won't do your husband any good, the gossip this will stir up."

Kit looked pained. "I know, Uncle George. Jack more or less said the same thing, when I told him about the tape this morning. But I can't just toss them out, not without at least listening to them. Besides, Sammy is convinced that Dad was murdered, so whatever I think or do is really beside the point."

"Ahh; it's all a batch of blather, if you ask me." George Defoe shook his head. "The ramblings of a senile old man." He made dismissive wavings with both his hands. "Go on, then, the two of you, listen to your tapes." He turned to his son and grasped his forearm with a surprisingly strong grip. "All I ask, Chase, is that you come to me before you do anything foolish."

I hardly intend to do anything foolish, Defoe thought, *but then who does?* He smiled, patted his father's hand. "Sure, Dad." His father would sooner be shot than patronized. The former meant you were dangerous, the latter that you weren't. After thirty years of combat, they knew all the moves.

"I think it might help to orient us if we put the cassette player on his desk," Defoe said as they walked into the kitchen of the General's farmhouse. "According to Sammy that's where he did all of his dictation. Not," he added quickly, "that I think we're going to hear another visitor come in through the French doors, or anything like that." He looked around the kitchen. "Sammy said there's a basket that your dad put his mail in. That's where the third tape and transcript are supposed to be."

"Yes, on the end of the counter there, under the wall phone." Kit went to the refrigerator and opened it. "Want something to drink? I'm going to have to clean this thing out; there must be vegetables in here from the year one." She held up a carrot that drooped. "Dad was never much of a cook; I don't know how he survived between Mom's death and the invention of the microwave." She took out a half-empty bottle of Graves and wiggled the cork out. "Chase?" She held the bottle in his direction.

"Not for me, thanks. God knows when he opened it."

Kit took a glass from a cabinet and poured a dollop of wine in it, tasted. "Seems okay to me. There's some diet soda in there."

"No thanks. Maybe I'll boil some water if you can find a tea bag. I don't see the envelope that Sammy mentioned, the one with the transcript she dropped off." Defoe rooted through a stack of sales fliers and bulk-rate direct-mail offerings. "Here's a cassette, though." He picked up the tiny recording, smaller than a matchbox. "Maybe this is it."

Kit poured her glass full of the chilled white wine, put the bottle on the table in the center of the room. "Here's where he keeps the instant coffee and tea bags." She peeked into a large, lidless square tin that had once held imported English tea biscuits. "Orange Pekoe bags, a box of Red Zinger—that must be Sam's—and some with Chinese writing on them. Left over from a take-out dinner, I suppose. Sammy brings them to him, every so often, when they're working at night." She turned to Defoe with tears in her eyes. "God, Chase, I'm talking about him in the present, as though he were still alive."

He came across the room and pulled her into his chest, put one arm across her shoulders and held the back of her head with the other. She buried her face in the lapel of his jacket and sobbed silently.

"It's such a shock," she finally said. "Coming so fast, the way it did." She looked up at him. "The violence of it all."

She pulled away, got a tissue from her purse, and blew her nose. Took a sip of wine. "When Mom died, at least there was a little warning, some time to let the subconscious prepare. Not much; she had the heart attack, and we rushed her to the hospital. But even that half hour, somehow . . . with Dad, it was Sammy on the phone, saying that he was dead. Boom, just like that."

Defoe found a pot and put it on a burner, found a cup and put a tea bag in it. "I know. God, do I know. My—Andy, my son, he'd been dead for three days by the time I found out. Yesterday's news." He touched the handle of the pot, centering it on the burner. "By the time I got to San Diego from halfway around the world the funeral was over." Defoe looked up, out the window over the sink, at the first tentative buds beginning to swell on the apple tree between the house and garage. "It made the whole thing very abstract, Kit, hard to believe, to accept."

He poured boiling water over the tea bag and began to dunk it up and down. "I always thought that viewings were a primitive, ghoulish rite, but I can understand their function. Seeing the dead body, lying there in front of you, it gives the mind something tangible to grasp as the psyche adjusts to the reality that the person is gone." He took the bag out and put it beside the sink. "Without any of the ceremony, the religious trappings, I had a hard time dealing with Andy's loss. Intellectually I knew he was dead, but down deep in my gut I just couldn't believe it." He sipped the hot liquid, looked at Kit through the steam that rose from the cup. "There are moments still when I think of him in the here and now, after all these years."

Kit put down her glass of wine and took two steps across the room to him, put her hand lightly on his cheek. "I can't even begin to imagine how awful it must have been for you. The death of a child." She shook her head. "When Dee, the accident, I—he was dead, Chase, I knew it right away, I mean. There just wasn't any doubt in my mind, when I saw him there in the car beside me. Bang. Flash; he was dead, I just *knew.* I don't know how. But the thing is, the tiniest fraction of a second after I looked at him, before even, before, I guess, that I even *realized* he was dead, I was thinking about

Sammy, in the backseat. My child. I just abandoned him, threw him out of my mind, and concentrated on her." Kit swallowed the last of her wine, then refilled the glass. "She was crying, she'd been thrown off the seat and was on the floor, more scared than anything, I realized, after I got her out of the car. I mean, she was fast asleep, and the next thing I knew she was upside down in a ditch, with a broken collarbone. I was so relieved that she was all right, the knowledge of Dee's death just wasn't *there.* Not right then, not at the moment. It's as though her survival canceled his death." Kit ran her finger around the rim of her glass, studied it. "Sammy immediately, though, wanted to know about Dee, wanted her daddy." She looked up at Defoe. "They were very close, Chase. Made me a little jealous at times, to tell the truth." She hesitated for a moment before saying, "Sammy blames me for his death."

Defoe sipped his bitter tea. "I know. She told me as much, this morning. Told me how much she loved him, too. Maybe, Kit, she doesn't really blame you for his death, not deep down inside. Maybe she just needs to hold on to him, his memory, all for herself. Doesn't want to share it. Remember, she was just a kid when it happened. By blaming you for his death she's able to cut you out of the picture, negate the love you and Quinn felt for each other. That way the Quinn that's still alive in her memory can concentrate his affections on her alone." He reached out and squeezed her hand, his grip warm from holding the teacup.

"Thanks," she smiled. "I guess that makes sense. But her hate still hurts. And she's right, in a way, you know. If I hadn't been driving, it would have never happened."

"Hey, don't play that game. 'What if.' There's no looking back in life, no second shots. What's done is done. Accept the past and get on with the future, Kit."

"I suppose. Yes, you're right." She picked up the bottle of wine and her glass. "Then let's do it. Listen to the tapes, I mean. Deal with the past and get on with life." She carried the wine to the back of the house, put the bottle and glass on the low table in front of the sofa as Defoe set up the General's cassette recorder, connected it to his own with the patch cord he'd bought along with the blank cassettes, and punched the play button on the former and the record button on the latter.

. . . thirty days to go a hundred and twenty-five miles from the crossing at Remagen to Ohrdruf, a village south of Gotha, in the Thuringerwald Mountains. Four miles a day, and we fought every inch of them. My battalion took heavy casualties; Patton's Third Army, of which the Ninth Armored Division was a part, lost 29,000 men since taking Metz, fighting our way through the Siegfried Line, and plunging into the Saar. The 37,000 prisoners we captured served to slow us up, too. As I said, a large number of my troops were green, having arrived less than six weeks earlier from the States. I had lost many men, many friends, during the Battle of the Bulge the previous December, and my front line units were both under strength and largely commanded by junior officers that had experienced almost no combat. It was difficult for me to conduct any sort of effective military action with men whose talents I didn't know, and I found myself frequently giving crucial battle assignments to men I had only met hours before.

So it was with this sort of organizational chaos that we rolled into Ohrdruf. I deployed my armor and left Captain Jenks in charge while I took my jeep and driver north to Gotha, to report in at XX Corps headquarters.

Upon my return, later that afternoon, Jenks told a curious tale. The local bank had been pretty well demolished during house-to-house fighting when we took the town a few days earlier; German troops had made a last stand in the big stone-and-concrete building, set up a light machine gun on the roof and managed to wrestle an antitank cannon into the lobby. Took out one of our tanks with it, before we brought the whole damned thing down around their ears. Nothing left but the vault, standing like a big steel cube in the midst of the rubble.

The president of the bank showed up at HQ, identified himself, told Captain Jenks that he wanted to cooperate with us, told him that there was a cache of Nazi art works locked in the vault. Guess he figured sooner or later we'd get around to opening it up, and he wanted to be assured that he was standing on the right side of the line when we did. We had all heard the stories about the enormous hoard of stolen treasure that had just been found in the mountains of southern Germany. By uncovering it the Allies were able to nip the Elsa in the bud, and destroy the Werewolf plans before they ever got going. Make a note to me, Samantha, to ask George about the role he played in uncovering the Elsa people.

Anyway, Jenks, the CO of the MP company, and this little banker clambered over the rubble, cleared the door to the vault, and opened it up. Jenks had an inventory, showed a copy to me later that night. I remember there were a couple of paintings by Rubens, because Jenks, an OCS man with, as I recall, just a high school diploma, said they were "big pictures of some fat, naked broads." And one or two Dürer prints, plus a truckload of less well-known but no less significant paintings. Mostly Italian. Caravaggio, Correggio, something like that. Unfortunately, the list is gone, so I can't be sure. But that's only part of the story. Jenks and the banker went into the vault, where the banker showed him the loot and told him that the camp commandant had delivered the artworks to the bank a few days earlier, for temporary safekeeping. The banker swore that he protested, but probably not terribly forcefully. Anyway, Jenks took one look at what was in the vault, remembered the story making the rounds about the big find at Merkers, and called Corps HQ, screaming for someone from the Roberts Commission. We'd had one of their fellows with us, back when we took Metz, to ID the artworks there and supervise their removal to safekeeping, so when Jenks saw the contents of the vault, he knew what to do.

Corps sent a historian down, along with a Signal Corps photographer, and they set about clearing the paintings out of the vault, documenting them with photographs, and getting them loaded on a couple of trucks, with the idea of moving them back to Corps HQ for storage with the main part of the treasures. A damaged vault in the middle of a ruined building wasn't too secure. Along with the paintings, as I said, several truckloads, there were two wooden artillery-shell boxes, about a foot square and four feet long. Jenks and this Roberts historian opened them up.

Both boxes were filled to the brim with gold ingots. They estimated the boxes at two hundred pounds apiece; it was all the MP's could do to drag them out of the rubble and load them on the historian's jeep.

Well, this was our baliwick, and Jenks had enough smarts not to let this fellow take off with the treasure, so he turned command over to my number three and took charge of the convoy, climbed into the lead vehicle, and headed for Gotha, figured to sign the whole lot over to Corps and let them handle it.

The General makes a coughing sound that turns into a chuckle, and Defoe turns to Kit and smiles, feeling for just a moment that the General is there, in the room with them.

Jenks told me he figured it out on a scrap of paper, while they were driving to Gotha. Four hundred pounds of gold, at the then fixed price, in America, of thirty-two dollars an ounce, was about two hundred thousand bucks. Damned fool didn't realize that the artwork was probably worth ten times that, even then. Anyway, the three vehicles, two trucks, and a jeep bringing up the rear, were high tailing it north to Corps HQ, ten miles away, on a sunny afternoon in early April. And the next thing Jenks knew, a Messerschmidt was dropping down between two hills in front of them, its machine guns raising geysers of dust in the middle of the road. The trucks swerved right and left and the MP sergeant next to Jenks took a bullet in the chest. The driver kept control of the truck and headed for HQ. Jenks leaned out the window, saw the second truck right behind them, and the historian's jeep bouncing down a donkey track toward the stream that ran alongside the road.

By the time they got to Gotha it was dark. Jenks signed off what was left of his convoy and went back with the patrol to look for the missing jeep. Of course they came up empty; they searched the area with flashlights, but it was a waste of time. By the time he got back to our own HQ it was midnight, but I was still awake. We broke out a bottle of prewar French brandy that we had liberated from the

Germans who had done the same from the French and he filled me in on the details.

"He was a queer duck," Jenks said, describing the Roberts man. "No soldier, I can tell you that. Had the uniform and all, wore first lieutenant's bars, but no unit markings or insignia. But then the other one was like that, too. Remember the guy back in Metz? Wanted us to climb up, in that cathedral there, and take down those . . . what, icons? Afraid, after all that building had been through, they were going to get damaged now!"

"Right, yes, I said. "Tell me about what happened, on the road. You didn't see any sign of the jeep? It didn't get hit by the strafing?"

"No, not that I could see. The plane missed him the first pass, because he was heading down through the trees toward the water and the Jerry was disappearing up in the clouds. The pilot couldn't have come around for a second run or we would have seen him. What I figured was that the driver turned around and headed back here. I don't know where he is, Colonel."

"Damn it, man, how could a jeep and two men just disappear?" I tossed off the glass of brandy I'd been toying with while he told his tale, and poured another. I saw the hurt in his eyes and got up, put my hand on his shoulder. Jenks was a good trooper; certainly no horse soldier, but a fine administrative hand, and I needed him as my Number Two. "Don't take it personally, Carl," I said. "When it comes right down to it, you didn't even need to escort the convoy to Corps HQ. But since you did, damn it, I want you out there at first light, with every man in the battalion if need be, to find that jeep!" I filled his glass and added, "Between now and then, go get some sleep. I got word from General Patton today that we're pulling up stakes in forty-eight hours, heading for Berlin."

Jenks stood up and grinned, lifted his glass in a toast. "Berlin!" he said. "By God, Colonel, but that sound's final. Maybe the war's over at last, and we'll all be going home."

Captain Carl Jenks, US Army. Twenty-seven years old, hometown: Stockton, California. Married, no children.

And never would have any. For, at that moment, the ceiling came down.

The ceiling came down just a half second after the four walls went out, in four different directions.

When the German SS Grupe abandoned the town of Ohrdruf they left behind an artillery shell in the basement of the town hall, wired to a seven-day time delay fuse, the same type of device used on the V-2 rockets they launched on London. V-2's were, after all, assembled in the nearby Hartz Mountains.

The roof came down; big, two-hundred-year-old oak beams, and several tons of plaster. It killed Captain Jenks instantly, shattered my leg, and buried both of us under six feet of rubble. Luckily the explosion occurred in the dead of night and our radio operator, a technical sergeant from New Jersey, was the only other man supposed to be in the building. Lucky for both of us he had just gone outside to answer nature's call, and he was able to dig through the rubble and point the rescuers to me.

My leg was broken in two places, I had a couple of cracked ribs and a nasty cut on my head. They evacuated me back to a field hospital somewhere in France and set my leg, then flew me to Cherbourg, where I sailed for home. I thought my war was over.

The tape ran for several seconds and stopped. Defoe got up and went over to the desk, looked down at the cassette player, said, "Side one." He shook his head. "Sammy was going to have her work cut out for her making this into a book if all the tapes were this disjointed." He reached inside his jacket and took out his Mont Blanc pen, jotted a couple of notes on a three-by-five card. "I never knew that your dad was wounded."

Kit got up from the sofa and stretched, picked up the empty wine bottle. "Yes; he had this awful scar on his leg. I think he was sensitive about it, he never wore shorts unless Mother absolutely forced him into it. You want something to drink? I'm going to the kitchen, see what I can scare up."

"What?" Defoe looked up. "No, thanks." He ejected the tiny cassette, turned it over, and snapped it back into the player. More unanswered questions, he thought, and walked down the hall to the kitchen. The sound of a toilet flushing told him that

Kit was in the powder room, a few steps farther along the hall, toward the front of the house. He rinsed his teacup in the sink, filled it with cool water and drank. Kit came back into the room.

"Wasn't that awful, about the booby trap? He never talked about it."

"I can see why. Generally speaking, the less action one sees the more one likes to tell war stories. It's the guys who spend their military service in a supply room in Kansas that have the bloodiest tales to tell."

"I know. Dee never liked to talk about Vietnam, what he did over there. It's not that he wouldn't talk about it, just that he *didn't.*" Kit opened a cabinet beside the refrigerator and rummaged in the liquor supply. She took out a bottle and waggled it at Defoe, sloshing its contents from side to side. "Scotch? A wee dram?" She smiled.

"Oh, okay; just a wee, wee dram. Speaking of which, I think I'd better *go* wee wee, make room for it." He went along the hall, thinking about General Kilgallen and his daughter, opened the powder-room door and stepped inside, feeling for the light switch, and almost fell down the cellar stairs. He caught the doorframe as his foot descended into blackness. His heart gave a stutter and thud and his skin broke out in a cold sweat with the realization that he had nearly gone head over heels down to the basement. *Damn,* he said to himself, *I'd forgotten that this place even had a cellar.*

The powder room was not what he remembered from twenty-five years earlier, either. Now it had a blue toilet and sink, matching shag carpeting, an exhaust fan that automatically went on with the lights, and a big print over the john that Defoe tentatively identified as the Charge of the Light Brigade.

Kit was back in her father's den; ice, glasses, and Scotch on the table in front of the sofa. She bent over, lifted several ice cubes out of the silver bucket, and dropped them into a glass, then repeated the process. "Say when," she said, pouring Scotch.

"Whoa! Hey, enough, when," Defoe said.

Kit looked up, then poured half as much into the other glass. "Here, then, I'll take the big one," and she handed him the second drink. "Here's mud in your eye, sailor." She raised her glass in salute. "Ready for side two of the General's Greatest Hits?"

Defoe pressed the play button and sat beside Kit on the sofa. She crossed her legs and tugged her skirt over her knee, leaned back against the leather cushion and closed her eyes. Her throat, Defoe noticed, watching her swallow, had the slender, delicate look of some African gazelle. She still had the firm skin and slim body he had known so long ago. Only when he looked closely at her eyes, around her mouth, could he make out the telltale lines and puckers of age. *Ah, well,* he thought, *better the honest marks of time, earned in life's combat, than the hidden nips and tucks of vanity's surgeon.*

My war with the Germans was over, but the war with my own body had just begun. They'd botched the job in France, and by the time I got back to the States, my leg had healed enough so that correcting it was not going to be an easy task. We landed in New York, and along with most of the other passengers who limped, hobbled, or were carried off the ship, I made my way back onto American soil for the first time in nearly three years. A Red Cross gal got me into a wheelchair, one of those old wooden-and-cane things that you only see in museums nowadays, and got me and my scant baggage through all the paperwork entailed in entering the United States. The one dress uniform I had was six years old, and after three years of combat was two sizes too large. But it was that or wear combat fatigues, so I came home, looking a bit less than Hollywood's idea of a war hero.

The Red Cross lady got me into a cab at the pier and the cabby got me onto a Washington-bound train at Pennsylvania Station, where he looked down at my crutches resting on the seat beside me in the Pullman car. "I tried to join up, in '41. Only I got bad eyes and flat feet, and now I'm too old and got the hemorrhoids besides. So I'm stuck, doin' my part back here. Tryin', anyhow. But it ain't nothin', don't think I don't know that, to what you guys been goin' through over there. Makin' it possible for guys like me to live here, peaceable, in this country, to do what we do, live the way we want to. God bless you, General," he said, standing and backing toward the door to the railway car. "And welcome home, sir." He raised his hand in a salute and left the train. I leaned against the grimy glass and thought about him, and the millions of other Americans back here, as the train slowly pulled out of the station, then began to pick up speed before plunging under the river and heading south to our nation's capital. I'd been a soldier for so long, fought because that was my job, that I'd forgotten what our purpose really was, and I thanked that nameless taxi driver for reminding me.

Union Station was a madhouse, bedlam, compared to when I had last visited Washington. We had heard, of course, from officers who had recently returned to the front from the capital what it was like in the District of Columbia, but you really had to experience it for yourself to believe it. Wartime Washington was a crazy turmoil of people in constant movement. Too little of everything—transportation, housing, parking spaces, gasoline, food, and people to do the work. When I had left for Europe in the spring of '42 it had been a sleepy little southern town with broad streets and only the beginnings of wartime bureaucracy touching it. Now, just a few short years later, it had changed so that I hardly recognized it. "Tempos" the cab driver called them as we drove down Constitution Avenue toward the Lincoln Memorial. Great, ugly, shoebox buildings cheek by jowl in what had been open, grassy park. They stretched forever, on either side of the reflecting pool, and housed countless thousands of government workers, vital to the war effort. People, he told me, were sleeping three to a bed, in shifts.

We turned north at the river, toward Rock Creek Park and Walter Reed Army Medical Center, and he told me a joke that was making the rounds of Washington. A man was crossing the Fourteenth Street Bridge and saw a man drowning in the Potomac. "Where do you live," he yelled at the man, then ran off to the address and told the landlord he wanted to rent the room. Too late, he was told, the room's already rented to another fellow. "Impossible!" the man shouted, "I just left him, drowning in the river!" The landlord laughed and replied, "I know, I rented the room to the man who pushed him in."

Walter Reed, at least, was an island of green in the sea of humanity. And those of us there were far from able to hustle and bustle; I checked in, feeling a bit sorry for myself, knowing that I faced surgery on my leg to correct the damage done in France. But when I saw some of the other patients I mentally kicked myself in the rear end. Blinded, missing arms and legs and both; I took another look at myself and realized how lucky I was.

All that was before they operated. Afterward, after they had cut me open and put the pin in my leg and had me wrapped in plaster from toe to hip, suspended in traction with my leg angled skyward like a field howitzer, I got myself right back down in the dumps. Alice was back in Omaha, living with my folks, and had so far been unable to get a train east, and all I had to look forward to was the long and painful process of learning to walk again.

My leg was suspended on a series of weights and pulleys over the bed like a log on the way to the sawmill, and I was damned uncomfortable, so I am afraid I was rather rude to the handsome young woman who came into the ward with her pushcart of books, magazines, cigarettes, and candy.

"Well," she said in a too bright and too cheery voice, looking at the chart at the foot of my bed, "You're a new one. Colonel Kilgallen, is it? An Irishman, would you be now?" she asked, affecting an accent. She had auburn highlights in her hair and for a moment I was reminded of the young actress Maureen O'hara. But then she dropped the accent and smiled, straightened my covers and pulled up the visitor's chair beside the bed. "My name's X," she said, and sat down. "I hope you don't smoke."

"No." I laughed, in spite of myself. "It's too darned difficult to do outdoors, with other fellows shooting at you, and I never picked up the habit."

"Good; then, Colonel, we've got that out of the way. I can offer you candy bars, but you probably won't want them, either, not if you want to stay as slim as you are. Because I can see, with that leg, you won't be getting much exercise for a good while yet. All that leaves is my books. I have westerns and detective thrillers, but quite frankly, I'd suppose that you've seen quite enough action in real life. I don't think the books would hold much amusement for you. That leaves the romances." She glanced at her cart. "And nobody wants to read them!"

We both laughed, and I asked her if she was as forthright with all her clients.

"Oh, I try," she said. "My real job is to make things a little happier for you, do whatever I can to make life easier. Now you're a Colonel, Regular Army, so you're different. I mean, most of the boys are just temporary soldiers; as soon as they get out of here, they are free, heading back home, to their civilian lives. But you, when they get you back on your feet, I bet you are going right back to the war, wherever it is, aren't you?"

I thought about that for a moment. Curious. First, a taxi driver in New York, and now this pretty young woman in Washington, making me question, for the first time in my life, what I was doing. "Yes," I said, "I suppose I will. It's my job, it's what I do."

"You went to West Point, didn't you? I can tell. I had a friend, he went to West Point." She looked out the window, sad. "He died." She turned back to me, reached out and took my hand. "Don't die, Colonel Kilgallen, please. Promise me? I can't take much more death, not now."

I guessed her age at twenty-one, or -two, perhaps, a good fifteen years younger than I was, so young to be so desperate. She must have seen so much death in her time. "No, X," I said, "I won't die." I smiled at her as the sun came back into her eyes. "But only if you call me Harmon. Colonel Kilgallen sounds like such an old man!"

We both laughed, and she promised to come back and see me the following day, see if she couldn't find a history book or two in the hospital library.

Each day she would stop, sit with me and talk for a few minutes, ask about my wife, the history book she'd brought me, but never about the war. She was married, she told me, to an older man, one with some vague government position, a job that often took him away from home for weeks at a time. Home was a farm across the river in Virginia. I gathered that her husband was well-to-do and the job at the hospital was a voluntary one, a way for her to pass the time and feel that she was doing something for the war effort.

They cut the cast off my leg and started me on physical

therapy, an agonizing process, but the strength returned gradually to my muscles and it wasn't long before I could hobble up and down the long corridors with a cane instead of the crutches.

Alice finally arrived in Washington and we were reunited at the hospital. It had been three long years since we'd seen each other, and had a great deal to catch up on. Unfortunately all of the hotels in town had a three-day maximum that they would allow a guest to stay, and we were unable to find more permanent lodging for Alice, so she returned to my parents' home in Nebraska, to await a more final reunion, after I was mended and released from the hospital. It was becoming more and more obvious that the war in the Pacific would be over by the time I was fit enough to return to active duty, and I began to think about my place in the peacetime army that was fast approaching.

My cheerful companion with the cart of books and sweets had an automobile and a B card, so she was able to drive most anywhere she pleased. She began taking me out on the town, finding different diversions that would not tax my leg too much.

Our first trip out in public was to Lewis and Thomas Saltz's men's store on G Street, to have some decent uniforms made for me. She ferried me back and forth over the next few days for fittings and I told her how much I appreciated the attention and time she was devoting to me, what a lucky fellow I was.

"Are you kidding?" she asked. "I'm the lucky girl, having a tall and handsome wounded colonel all to myself. You're a very sought-after commodity just now, and I plan to keep you all to myself for as long as possible!"

She loved, she said, to ride, and being a cavalry officer of the old school, I prided myself that I could sit a horse with the best of them, so one day we rented a pair of plugs from a riding stable in Rock Creek Park and spent an afternoon exploring the trails through the wooded park.

Another time we rented a canoe at Fletcher's Boathouse in Georgetown and paddled down to the Watergate with a picnic luncheon she'd prepared for us.

She took me to a party at the home of one of those

mysterious Dollar a Year Men who had descended on the town with the onset of war, businessmen who gave up high-paying positions to run obscure government offices like the WPA and the OPC. I met Alben Barkley there, the senator from Kentucky. I'd spent a tour of duty at Fort Knox, and we discussed armor and horses for a few minutes, then he told a story, one that I later discovered he trotted out on most public occasions. He'd asked an old Kentuckian for his vote in the coming election, reminding him that the senator had gotten his brother a job with the post office, arranged a loan to save his farm, and gotten the man's son out of jail. "Yes," the voter answered, delivering the punch line that has become a part of the language, "but what have you done for me lately?"

I discovered that a well-tailored colonel with a cane and a slight limp was indeed a sought-after commodity, particularly when he had a lovely young woman on his arm. We went to different parties almost every night, and I began to meet the men who would be shaping our country's future when the war finally came to an end. It was during this period that I learned that if I planned to stay in the Army I would have to base myself in Washington. With X's help I began to look for a house for myself and Alice.

Across the river, just a half hour's drive from the chaos that was the District of Columbia, she showed me rolling fields just turning green in the first week of April, wide-open spaces little changed since the days when Sheridan chased Lee across them to Appomattox. We found a modest tenant farmhouse with a few acres and I put down money on it on April the eighth, the day Germany surrendered. That night I took X to dinner at the Willard Hotel, and afterward we walked through the crowds on the mall, listened to President Truman's announcement of the signing of the surrender documents on a radio that someone had placed in the window of one of the temporary buildings. A few moments later, at eight-thirty, the lights of the Capitol were lit, for the first time, someone in the crowd said, since December 9th, 1941. The great white dome blazed in the sky, a splendid sight. I turned to X and we kissed, there on the mall at the end of the war.

She took my hand and led me to her car, drove us back

across the bridge to Virginia, and took me to her house. That night I fell in love with Fairfax County, and a little bit, too, with X, the angel with her trolley of books and sweets and ready smile.

I was released from Walter Reed at the end of April and took the train to Nebras—

The cassette stopped with a click and Defoe looked over at Kit, holding her empty glass in both hands, tears running down her cheeks. "So sad and so beautiful," she said, and smiled. "I'm a mess." She put her glass on the table and stood up. "I've got to go and fix my face. Don't start the other tape until I get back."

Defoe sat and stared into the middle distance, puzzled by what he'd heard. Why the "Madam X" bit, and what had happened to the transcript of the recording that Sammy had typed? If the person who had burned the other papers had found the transcript in the basket in the kitchen, he certainly would have destroyed the cassette as well. He went to the French doors and looked across the lawn at the old carriage house. The grass was beginning to make the transition from dormancy to growth. It was just about this time of year, nearly half a century ago, Defoe thought, that Colonel Kilgallen first laid eyes on this scene, he and his mysterious young woman. The telephone rang.

Kit picked it up in the kitchen; he heard the low whisper of her voice but not the words. She came into the den. "For you, Chase. Senator Kinship."

He raised his eyebrows and picked up the phone on the desk. "Hello, Senator."

"Chase, my boy. Glad I was able to track you down. Listen, son, your father called me a little while ago, told me you and the Kilgallen girls have come up with a tape of the General's. Says you think there's something on it that might indicate that Harmon was killed?"

"Yes, sir, it does seem that way. Pretty obvious, anyway, that his papers were burned after his death. There are three tapes, by the way. Kit and I are just listening to them now, trying to get a handle on this."

"Good, good. Listen, son, I know you know your way around this sort of business, and I won't interfere. The thing is . . . dammit, I don't know how to put this. What it is, Chase, well, your father wanted me to convince you to let this thing lay, not stir up any publicity. Felt pretty strongly that it wouldn't do Harmon's memory any service to go airing dirty laundry."

"I'd hardly call murder 'airing dirty laundry,' Senator Kinship."

"Oh, I agree, I agree. Don't tell George that I said so, but I'm with you on this thing. If he *was* murdered, I want it to come out. We can't have the memory of a fine soldier tarnished by suicide if it isn't true."

"Yes, sir."

"If there's anything I can do to help, let me know. Keep me up to speed on this, son."

"Yes, sir. You may, as a matter of fact, be able to do something. The records that he was working from were all burned, but if we get an indication of what they were from the tapes, perhaps you can get us duplicates. I know it wasn't just his own diaries he was working from. Samantha said that he had gotten material from the National Archives and the library up at Carlisle Barracks. If he mentions some specific document, maybe you can use your influence to get us the material a bit quicker than we could."

"Consider it done. And, Chase . . . ? Keep me posted on this. Harmon and I went back a long way. Hate to have this swept under the rug as a suicide, if it wasn't."

"Will do, Senator. We're about to listen to the second tape; I'll give you a call as soon as we have anything concrete."

"Good, good. So long, then, son. Keep in touch."

"Did you hear all of that?" Defoe asked Kit as she came back into the den.

"Uh huh, I listened in. Your dad certainly is stubborn. I wouldn't think he'd put so much stock in propriety, over truth."

"No," Defoe said, and put the second cassette in the player. "Neither would I."

> Samantha, I don't know how to deal with the following information, how we are going to work it into the book. I only just uncovered what I'm about to tell you in the last few days, but it is part of the story that began forty-five years ago. The fellow from the Roberts Commission and the missing boxes of gold.
>
> I guess the best way to do this is, I will just tell what I've

found, and after you've heard it, typed it up, we can decide how to work it into the manuscript. You know more about these things than I do—narrative thread, flashbacks, all that author business.

Well, a couple of days ago I got to thinking about the missing gold, wondered if anyone else had investigated its disappearance after Captain Jenks's death, so I drove over to Suitland, in Maryland. That's where the National Archives have stored the records of individual units. I went through our own, as well as the MP company and the records of XX Corps Headquarters, trying to track down anyone involved with that convoy. I came up with several leads out there. The commanding officer of the MP outfit that had transported the artworks from Ohrdruf to Merkers had filed a report, both on the incident with the German aircraft that strafed the convoy, and the subsequent search for the missing jeep. It pretty well matched up with what I remember Jenks telling me that night, just before the building came down on us. Only the military police personnel were named, not Jenks or the Roberts Commission man. The driver, Pvt. Allen Czynski, was listed as missing in action against the enemy. This made me perk up my ears, as you can imagine, and I pursued the matter further. Unfortunately, what had seemed a promising lead came up a dead end when I ran Pvt. Czynski through the master records section. There he was listed as dead, killed in action. No date was given, but that wasn't all that unusual at that time. We often found the remains of soldiers, originally listed as missing, months after a battle had taken place. I then turned my attention to the other members of the convoy.

XX Corps HQ had supplied the Signal Corps photographer that documented the stolen artworks. I remembered Captain Jenks telling me that a tech sergeant had taken photos of everything that was in the vault, so I had one of the research assistants out there at Suitland see if he couldn't track down the photographs. Apparently Signal Corps photos are at the DAVA, in Washington. The Defense Audio-Visual Agency. Only he drew a blank there. I was ready to give it up, but this young fellow knows his way around the world of research scholarship, and he dug a little deeper, made some calls to people in other agencies. To make a long story short, he called me back in a couple of days, said he'd talked to a friend up at the Army Military History Institute and found out that the Office of War Information released a lot of Signal Corps photos for general media use during the war. All that material is now at the National Archives, in the still-picture collection. We had the sergeant's name, his unit, and the date the photos were taken, so I called the director of the Archives, who put me in touch with the proper person, and I ordered a set of prints, everything the photographer shot that day. He assured me that I'd get the photographs in a day or two, so I am expecting them tomorrow or the next day. I look forward to seeing them; from the way Jenks described the scene there should be some rather dramatic pictures of the large Rubens canvases, standing atop the rubble of the destroyed bank.

While this young research assistant was busy tracking down the photos I turned my attention to uncovering the identity of the mysterious officer from the Roberts Commission. The official name was the American Commission for the Protection and Salvage of Artistic and Historic Monuments in War Areas. They were largely responsible for finding and recovering many of the art treasures stolen by high-ranking Nazi leaders. Not only Hitler, you know, Samantha, but Himmler and Goering; both also had acquired substantial collections during their rape of Europe.

Because many of these treasures were necessarily located in what had become combat zones, it fell to the OSS to get these men from the commission up to the front lines as quickly as possible. I remember that the Roberts man in Metz was busy documenting the artwork in the cathedral while small-arms fire was still ricocheting off the walls outside. Anyway, I went through the commission records and came up empty, drew a blank. Apparently he wasn't one of their boys after all. So I tried the CIA; they have all the old OSS records. Of course getting anything out of that bunch is like pulling teeth, even with the Freedom of Information Act. I wound up contacting some of my friends in the intelligence community, never mind who they are, Sammy. Hah. I sound like another one of them, don't I? Anyway, the historian over at Langley sent me a Xerox of the personnel file of the agent responsible for cataloging the artwork in Ohrdruf. I have it here . . .

The sound of papers moving on the General's desk are followed by the rumble of his chair rolling across the floor.

Here it is. Pierson, Calvin R. Pierson. Vice President of Acme Machine Tool and Die Co, Akron, Ohio; a lieutenant in the Army Reserve and called up in 1941, right after Pearl Harbor. Recruited into the OSS in '42 and assigned to the Research and Analysis division in Washington, then sent to Europe in late '44. There is a list of recovery projects he directed, including the one in Ohrdruf. Hmph. Two more after that, so we know he survived the event. And then, about six months later, in the fall of 1945, he was killed in Greece, during the civil war. Don't know how an art historian got involved with that mess. Funny. For that matter, how's a VP of a manufacturing company get into the art-recovery business? War made some strange bedfellows . . . I suppose there is a report, buried over in the OSS records, of his version of what happened to the jeep and the gold, but ferreting it out would be a task, and what's the use, with him and the driver both dead? So, Samantha, whatever happened to the jeepload of gold, neither the driver nor Mr. Pierson will ever be able to tell us, and I guess the saga comes to an end. It will make a nice little sidebar to the story of the part I played in World War II, Sammy, and one of the photographs will be interesting to include.

So, back to the postwar period, a short one for me. Japan surrendered in September of '45 and North Korea invaded the South less than five years later, in June of 1950. But they were five busy years, for after three weeks leave in Omaha with Alice and my parents, she and I headed back to Washington, back to my new assignment at the Pentagon and our new house in Virginia.

There is a pause and then static sounds from the cassette. Evidently the General has removed the recorder from his pocket, as his voice is both louder and clearer.

I see that the tape has almost run out; it's late and we seem to be at a breaking point. I'll put this one out in the basket for you, Sammy, and begin tomorrow with a fresh tape.

The tape continued to run, silently, for several minutes, then stopped with a click and Defoe looked up from the three-by-five card on which he was writing yet another note to himself. He frowned, went to the machine and ejected the tape, turned it over and punched the play button. Nothing but the hiss of blank tape. He cued the fast forward button a few times, scanned the tape, and found it unused. "Well, that's it. I guess he didn't realize that he hadn't used the second side." He put the two copies he had made in the right-hand desk drawer, dropped the originals in his pocket. "I don't think we have much to go on here," he said to Kit, and stood up. "I'll copy the last tape and see if we can get a voiceprint of the General's mysterious visitor. I'm afraid that it's still the only solid lead we have." He inserted the last cassette, put a fresh one in his own recorder, and activated both machines.

The Second World War, a war that started with a Polish cavalry charge into the teeth of German machine guns and ended with an atomic blast, introduced new weapons and new techniques of warfare. Rommel had revolutionized armored tactics and my assignment was to help our post-war army rewrite the book on mechanized warfare, incorporating everything we had learned in the past five years. General Burd—

Defoe hits the stop button and looks at the machine, then at Kit. "This is the first side of the last tape, the one that was in the machine when he died. We never thought to play it. It's the second side that has the unknown visitor and the sounds of the papers burning." Defoe rewinds a few inches and hits the play button again, saying, "Maybe this will clear up the mystery."

—ive years. General Burden was the CO of the group, an armchair commander who'd not seen combat since the First World War and didn't understand armor, so we—damn! There goes the doorbell.

The sound of the General's chair wheeling back from his desk is overwhelmed by the scrape of his tweed jacket against the built-in microphone of the cassette recorder. His footsteps sound on the floor, echoing, then fade to a duller, measured beat as he walks along the carpeted hallway toward the front of the house. He coughs, opens the door.

Yes? Oh, ah. Hello, young man.
Federal Express, sir. General Kilgallen?
Yes.
Sign this; no, there, sir. Thank you.
Yes, certainly. Let's see, what . . .

The sound of the door closing is followed once more by the muffled footsteps of the General as he returns to the rear of the house.

Ah; the photographs.

A door opens and there is the sound of water, then the flushing of a toilet. Footsteps as the General crosses from the powder room to the kitchen. Once again the sound of running water, the clatter of a metal pot being removed from the drawer beneath the stove, the water running into the pot. The General's footsteps move across the linoleum tiles, there is the rattle of china as he evidently prepares coffee or tea. The refrigerator door opens, then closes with a dull thump. The General coughs, whistles tunelessly between his teeth, turns on the radio.

—igh of fifty-five, with some sunshine. Gonna get chilly tonight, folks, overnight low of thirty-five in the city and a chance of scattered showers after midnight, which might appear as flurries in the outlying areas. Old man winter hasn't left us yet, Jennifer.

Right you are, Ray. Checking traffic, the outbound arteries are running normal and the Beltway is experiencing its usual ten-minute delay at the construction area. A minor fender bender reported on the Georgetown Pike at exit thirteen; otherwise it looks like clear sailing out of the city. Now something from the Miami Sound Machine to ease your traffic tensions on your way home at twenty-seven minutes before the hour.

The music mingles with the sounds of the General drinking his coffee or tea, followed by a slight belch, and the radio fades as he moves from the kitchen to his den at the rear of the house. The transition from carpeted hallway to the bare floor is evident, as is the rasp of the chair's casters as the General sits behind the desk.

Now then . . .

There is a tearing sound as the General rips the tab at the side of the padded shipping envelope and spills the photographs onto the desk.

Hmph, quite a stack. Let's see . . . Yes, there's Jenks. Shock, seeing his face, after all these years. God, how young we were. Good man. No horse soldier, that's for damned sure, but a fine administrative officer. Ran the outfit the way I wanted it run.

The crisp sound of glossy photos against one another underlie the General's ruminations.

Must be the Rubens. Bunch of naked broads, eh? Heh heh, yes, and the men, too. And horses and angels besides. Ah, well. Big damned thing. I wonder where it is now. Well. Let's see. There's Jenks, and that has to be the banker. Looks well enough fed, but . . . This must be the lieutenant in command of the MP detachment; he's got an armband. Big enough youngster, too. Well, they should be identified, on the back of the prints. Standard procedure. Yes. Capt. Carl Jenks, 4Bn, Armor, XX Corps. Lt. Bruce Hommanger, MP det. XX Corps, Sgt. David Sprague, MP det. XX Corps. Another Rubens. Ah, here's the Italian paintings. Bit smaller than the others. One man can hold them up. Good clear photos. But I think the first one, the one with the horses, and Jenks, of course, is the one we'll use. Ah. This must be the Roberts man. What was his name? Pierson. Yes, Pierson . . . OSS, I mean, not the

> Roberts Commission. Hmn . . . No ID on the back. Just First Lt, XX Hq. Of course the photographer wouldn't necessarily know who he was. People coming and going in those days, confusion at the end of the war. We had new faces showing up almost daily. Wait a minute. Here he is, better focus, a smaller painting. Damn. Forty, forty-five years ago. But that looks like . . .

There is the sound of photographic prints rapidly shuffled against one another, and the General says once again

> Damn! It has to be . . . What's he doing . . . never told me he was . . . Son of a bitch!

There is the sound of a desk drawer opening, the ruffle of pages spilling from beneath the General's thumb, then the crisper sound of individual pages turning.

> Call, see what he has to say about this. Queer. I wonder why he never said that he—Hello? Hello! Harmon here; lis—

The tape stopped with a click that seemed louder than the others and jolted Defoe and Kit from their concentration. "Hell," Defoe said. "What a time for the tape to run out."

"Why? What do you mean?" Kit sat up straighter and looked at Defoe.

"I think your father recognized the OSS man, this Pierson." Defoe hit the rewind button and the General's voice squealed at high speed for several seconds.

> —fusion at the end of the war. We had new faces showing up almost daily. Wait a minute. Here he is, better focus, a smaller painting. Damn. Forty, forty-five years ago. But that looks like—

There is the sound of photographic prints rapidly shuffled against one another, and the general says once again

> Damn! It has to be . . . What's he doing . . . never told me he was . . . Son of a bitch!

There is the sound of a desk drawer opening, the ruffle of pages spilling from beneath the General's thumb, then the crisper sound of individual pages turning.

> Call, see what he has to say about this. Queer. I wonder why he never said that he—Hello? Hello! Harmon here; lis—

The tape stopped with a click and Defoe said, "See? He recognized Pierson. And he called someone about it. Don't know who, or why." He looked at the telephone on the desk. "Too bad it's a push button; if it was one of the old rotary phones we'd have picked up the clicks and could figure out the number." He turned to Kit. "Do you have any idea?"

Kit looked over at him. "No, nothing. I don't understand what this is all about."

"Neither do I. Well; when his telephone bill arrives at the end of the month the number he called will be on it." Defoe pursed his lips and looked through the French doors at the world outside. "But I think identifying the mysterious voice at the French doors is the key to the whole thing." Defoe went to the kitchen and got his "bible" from where he had left it on the table when they'd first entered the General's house several hours earlier. "Did you ever meet Doug Winston? He was one of my roommates."

"No, not that I remember, anyway."

"He's in the Justice Department, an Assistant AG, one of the top guns. Head of Criminal Division. He should be able to hook me up with the right person across the street, get a voiceprint of this tape."

"Across the street?"

"Hoover Building. FBI." Defoe flipped through his loose-leaf book, picked up the phone. "Most of the FBI people I know are on the West Coast. Besides, coming in from the top, with Doug, we'll get quicker results." He winked at Kit as he put the receiver to his ear. "Clout," he said. "Politicians ain't the only one's who find it useful. Hello, Chase Defoe. I'd like to speak to Doug Winston. Yes, Defoe. Thank you." He flipped his notebook closed and leaned against the desk, met Kit's gaze. "Doug! How's the boy? Fine, thanks. No, I'm in town, well, across the river. Yes. Next door, actually. General Kilgallen's; I suppose you heard about his death; I'm down for the funeral. His daughter and I are old friends." Defoe looked at Kit, returned her smile. "Listen, Doug, I wanted to get together with you while I was down here. Maybe take you and Joan out to dinner, if you guys can fit me in. Only something's developed here, got a small project going, and I wondered if I could drop by for about fifteen minutes this afternoon, twist your arm a little. No, no, nothing like that. Yes, I remember. But don't forget that you owe me one, also, for the Peacoat Caper that I did all the work on and then dumped in your lap, gave you all the glory. Yeah, same to you, sport." Defoe looked at his watch. "Give me about an hour, maybe an hour and a half. Let's make it, say, four-thirty? Good. No, honest, fifteen minutes, that's all. Room 2107? Got it. Yes, do that, please; I don't have ID that would get me into your building, let alone up to your office. See you then, Doug."

Defoe hung up the phone, ejected the original tape from the General's recorder and the copy from his own, and unhooked the patch cord connecting the two machines. "It's all set. I'll run this down to Justice and see where it leads." He looked at his watch. "I should be finished there by five-thirty, six. Can I take you out to dinner? I assume, with both Jack and Sammy away, that you're free."

"Yes; I mean, I haven't made any plans, even *thought* about dinner. To tell you the truth, though, Chase, I don't really feel up to going out. Not after today. How about if I make dinner for us? Here, I mean," she added quickly. "I could run into McLean and pick something up at the market. I want to get some boxes anyway, and start sorting through Dad's stuff. It has to be done sometime, and I've got to keep busy." She picked a piece of lint off her sweater and rolled it between her thumb and forefinger, swirling it into a ball. "I can't face going home right now, to an empty house, spending the rest of the evening thinking about today." She looked around the den, still filled with the paraphernalia of her father's life. "Jack wants to put the house on the market right away, so that by the time the will is through probate we'll have a buyer ready to make settlement."

Defoe put the third original cassette in his pocket with the other two, and dropped his three copies into the desk drawer on top of the telephone book. "You're not going to keep the place, then?"

"No. We talked it over, and Jack doesn't want to live out here, says commuting is too much of a hassle. Besides, he's not a country person." She smiled, then chuckled. "Jack's such a dandy. He was dressed conservatively today. Usually he can give Tom Wolfe a run for his money. Strictly the dude from the city. He's already had the place appraised, already has ideas of how to invest the money. How does steak sound? Baked potato, a salad?"

"Sure."

"Okay, great. We can get Dad's gas grill out and do the steaks out on the patio." She looked around the room again, picked up her purse. "Well, I guess that's it, then. Let's go, I'll drop you off at your car."

"No, don't bother; it's in the opposite direction if you're going into McLean, and I want to go over the tapes again in my mind. The walk across the field will help me to sort it all out."

He went out through the French doors and Kit locked them behind him, then left by the front of the house and got into her car.

SEVEN

Defoe let himself in the front door and stood in the hallway, listening to the sounds of the old building. His grandfather had bought it during Wilson's second term, renovated both the house and grounds, used it as a way station between Palm Beach and Newport, then willed it to his eldest son upon his death in 1937. It stood vacant for five years, until Defoe's father moved from New York with his new bride, to wartime Washington.

Cool and dark, with polished marble underfoot, and walls that soared eleven feet to the Georgian moldings delineating the junction of wall and ceiling, the entry hall had always been for Defoe a place to pause and exchange the bustle of the external world for the quiet serenity that waited in the rooms beyond. Even after relations with his father had deteriorated, decorum and propriety took precedence over the heated retort. For twenty years the subversive skirmishes had been conducted sotto voce. Defoe went into the library.

His father was at his desk; the afternoon sun filtered through the draperies behind him, illuminating the wood and leather and fabrics in the room, the cool light casting sharp shadows across the surfaces. Shades of umber and sienna, oxblood and beige, it reminded the younger Defoe of some quattrocento canvas by Da Vinci, the haze and light of his spectacular *sfumato* overwhelming the subject itself. "Dad," Defoe said carefully, "what was Elsa?"

The elder Defoe looked up from his labors with pocket calculator and the financial pages of the *Times* and studied his son over half-moon reading glasses, their gold frames catching the light. He held his Cross pen in the center of its slim barrel and beat a paradiddle on the yellow legal pad beneath it. "Not 'who,' but 'what,' eh?" He shoved back slightly from his desk and sat erect. "Elsa was a lioness, wasn't she? A rather anthropomorphized beast in a rather saccharine tale out of Africa. *Born Free,* I think it was. Nineteen sixty something. Book first, then a film." He waited for his son's response with eyebrows forming twin circumflexes above his pale, unblinking gaze.

"I think not. Something out of Nazi Germany, not Africa." Defoe walked over to the sofa and rested his thighs and buttocks on the upholstered arm, faced his father. "Harmon Kilgallen left a rather cryptic sentence on one of his tapes. 'Talk to George about his role in uncovering the Elsa people.' I admit George is not an uncommon name, but somehow you were the one who sprang to mind."

"Yes. Elsa, eh?" George Defoe worked his lips for a moment, buying a little time. He put the pen on the pad, centered it on his desk. "Well, I guess there's no harm in discussing it. The whole thing's pretty much available —here, there, and everywhere. Carlisle. The National Archives. Old fools like Kilgallen have been setting their version down in print for the last forty years. Even the stuff that was classified I imagine has come out in the open by now, what with the damned Freedom of Information nonsense." He scratched his chin and contemplated the near distance. "Things were different when Dick Helms was running the show. Hell, you must remember him. DCI when you were active; late sixties till about '73.

"Of course, I knew Helms when he was in London, back in '45, when he and Bill Casey were there. Couple of rah-rah boys. Parachute drops behind enemy lines, forming Jedburgh teams; *your* sort of thing. Anyway, after the war Richard joined the newly chartered CIA in 1947, went on to become director twenty years later. Got shafted when he refused to testify before the Senate about Agency operations in Chile. Of course it was a Nixon vendetta; damned Democrats couldn't nail Richard the First, so they went after Dick. Best they could come up with was a suspended sentence and a two-thousand-dollar fine, which was paid off; at a testimonial dinner out at the Kenwood Country Club in Bethesda, four hundred retired intelligence officers passed a couple of wastebaskets around the room and stuffed them full of cash."

"Interesting, Dad. Did you go to the dinner? Toss a few bucks in the kitty for old Dickie Helms?"

His father cleared his throat and blew his nose on a handkerchief he pulled from his hip pocket. "Never mind. The point I wanted to make was that Helms goes back to the early days of the OSS. Was in on the whole thing from the word go. And he always said, 'We are the silent service, and silence begins here.' Got that from the Brits. Where American Intelligence was spawned, y'know. From British Intelligence. And I've always gone along with that regulation. Kept my mouth shut."

"Well, I'll bear that in mind, Dad. Bear it in mind as I listen to your answer to my question about Elsa."

His father said, "Yes, Elsa. Well, then, I suppose to begin at the beginning, get the players into the proper perspective, we have to start with Anastasia, the youngest daughter of Czar Nicholas II." He looked at his son and was gratified to see that the mention of the almost mythical princess had gotten his attention. "Bill Donovan is, of course, the thread that runs through this tale. You remember General Donovan, don't you? Knew almost as many people as I do."

"Wild Bill Donovan? Sure. A bit past his prime the few times I saw him. I guess I was still in prep school when he died."

"Brain atrophy, they said, the people at the Mayo Clinic. Ought to know. Anyway, the story starts with Donovan, it was Colonel Donovan then, back in the mid1930's. He was a hero in the First War, did you know that? Congressional Medal of Honor, DSC, Purple Heart. Bunch of others. Second generation shanty Irish, from Buffalo or some damn place. But a patriot, by God. Nobody loved this country more than Bill. And a fine lawyer. Had a firm in New York, started it up right before the Crash. Anyway, as I said, the story starts in the midthirties. Otto Kiep, he was the German consul general in New York, was instrumental in Donovan developing contacts in Berlin. And Dr. Paul Leverkühn, a lawyer from Berlin, was also in New York quite frequently. Donovan had met him in Washington when Leverkühn was with the German War Reparations Commission. But he was in New York representing the young woman who purported to be the Princess Anastasia. Surely you know that story."

"Sure. The czar was murdered, what, in 1918, as was his family. Only the girl supposedly escaped."

"Right. And there was rumored to be a substantial estate in this country. Millions. Of course she wanted the money. Hah. So did the Soviet government. Donovan was hired to help set up a US Corporation with Leverkühn, with the idea of getting control of the fortune for this girl. All that was parenthetical, though, just a cover for the real business they were doing together. Leverkühn was, you see, a high officer in the Abwehr."

"Abwehr. That was the German Secret Service, wasn't it?"

"Well, more or less. One of them, anyway. It was the intelligence and counterespionage service for the German General Staff."

"Which the Germans, under the Treaty of Versailles after the First World War, were forbidden to have. So the German Navy began to reform the Etappesdienst under commercial cover."

Defoe's father looked surprised at his son's knowledge. "You've done your homework."

"Not really. Paid attention during Charlie Garside's Modern European History lectures, though. Admiral Wilhelm Franz Canaris ran it, right?"

"Right. Except he was Lieutenant Commander Canaris back then. And, if you've studied the history, you know he was plotting to overthrow Hitler."

"Back then? I know he was, later, when the war was well under way. I think Hitler had him killed."

George Defoe waved his hand at his son. "You're getting ahead of the story. Remember, this is back in the mid, the late, thirties. When we were Fortress America, and that damned New Dealer was basically telling Great Britain to go piss up a rope. Only a few Americans knew what the hell was really going on over there, and Donovan was one of them. He saw where things were headed. So did Canaris." The elder Defoe stood and tugged his vest down. "He was, from what I've heard and read, a remarkable man. A true visionary. He foresaw a United States of Europe, led by the Brits, along with France, and, of course, Germany." He went to the butler's tray and poured himself a splash of whiskey, added a dollop of water, then pointed a bony finger at the tray and offered his son an unspoken invitation with his eyes.

Defoe shook his head. "No thanks."

"Well then." His father tucked the fingers of his right hand into a vest pocket, hooked the thumb under his watch chain, and took a swallow of his drink. "With what's going on in Europe today, the Eastern Bloc finally waking up to the reality of the moment and cleaning house, I think Canaris may have had greater vision than anyone in this century, Churchill included. Time will tell. You're lucky, Chase. You'll be around in the year two thousand to find out."

"Come off it, Dad. You'll be what? Eighty-eight? No reason to think you won't be there for the millennium."

"Think so, eh? *Hmph.*" He went back to his chair behind the desk. "Well, anyway, in '33 Hitler repudiated the Versailles Treaty and started to rearm. You know all this. One of the things he did was appoint Canaris chief of the Abwehr, told him to model it after the British Secret Service.

"Only Canaris saw Hitler for what he was, a megalomaniacal thug, and, while doing what Der Führer told him to do, he also appointed many high-level contact men who dealt with foreign secret services." George Defoe leaned back and looked at the ceiling, checking his files. "Fabian von Schlabrendorff, a Frankfurt lawyer, made contact with the people in Britain's secret service. And in Bern, a Gestapo lawyer, Hans Bernd Gisevius, kept contact with Claude Dansey, also a Brit. Another lawyer, one from Munich, Dr. Josef Müller, made connection with the Vatican. You know what the Sicherheitsdienst was?"

"That was the Nazi's intelligence service, wasn't it?"

"Yes. Don't forget, the Nazis were a political party, one that didn't necessarily speak for the entire German populace. So they had their own secret service, to keep an eye on the opposition. And the Sicherheitsdienst uncovered this Vatican connection and the Canaris conspiracy. They gave it the code name Schwarze Kapelle. How's your German?"

"Schwarze is black. Something about music, right?"

"Orchestra. Black Orchestra. The man who made contact with Donovan, and therefore the United States, on behalf of the Black Orchestra, was Paul Leverkühn, the same Paul Leverkühn who had worked with Donovan on Princess Anastasia's behalf. So right from the start, *before* the start, really, we had penetration into the German intelligence service." Defoe Senior leaned back and put his hands behind his head. "Or Bill Donovan did. And Bill, as you know, went on to found the OSS, our own secret service. Didn't really get going, of course, until much later. It wasn't until after Pearl Harbor that FDR finally woke and saw the light. Didn't establish the COI until June of '41."

"COI?"

"Office of Coordinator of Information. Put Donovan at its head. Had a terrible time of it, fighting tooth and nail with the people over at the War Department. See, Naval Intelligence and the Army people, Roosevelt told them to share their information with this civilian and his newly chartered outfit. In a pig's eye." He looked at Defoe. "Thirty years later, how much did you share, when you were in Naval Intelligence, with the CIA? Hmm?"

"Point taken. What's this all leading to? You were going to tell me about Elsa."

"I'm getting there, but if you want to understand the facts rather than just know them you need background. Now when General Donovan was back in law school, at Columbia, he met Ellery Huntington. Yalie, by the way. An all-American quarterback. Anyway, between the First and Second World Wars, Huntington joined the Equity Corporation, in New York. There he had some business dealings with a fellow named von Gaevernitz. Who, in turn, became friendly there, at Equity, with another German, Edward von Waetjen. All those von's! Minor royalty, I guess. Today we call 'em Eurotrash. Von Waetjen's sister was married to Godfrey Rockefeller. Not a crowd I traveled much with, you want to know the truth. Never much into that heel-clicking and hand-kissing business. Of course Donovan, never mind his background, was a good twenty-five years older than I was. Whole generation's difference. Anyway, this Gaevernitz left Germany in '39, went to live in Switzerland. He and Huntington maintained their friendship, and when, in the first year of the war, Donovan recruited Huntington into the COI, Ellery in turn recommended Gaevernitz. Enter Allan Dulles. Donovan sent him to Bern as the OSS rep. By that time COI had become the Office of Strategic Services. Hah. 'Strategic.' Still hated to use the Ess word. Ess Pee Why. 'Gentlemen don't read other gentlemen's mail.' That was that pantywaist FDR's doing. Wonder we won the war. Wouldn't have, if it hadn't been for men like Bill Donovan. And men like Admiral Canaris on the other side. So, when Dulles showed up in Bern, not knowing bullocks from beans, he contacted, had a letter of introduction, and he contacted this Gaevernitz. They hit it off, and Allen asked him to come on board the OSS as his number-one assistant. Lucky for us, because he was in close contact with the fellow I mentioned earlier, von Waetjen, Canaris's rep in Switzerland, operating under German consular cover. And von Waetjen, in turn, had access to the whole damned German, Finnish, Hungarian, Rumanian, Bulgarian, Croatian, and Japanese intelligence and diplomatic community. Did I mention that this Edward von Waetjen was also a member of the Black Orchestra? As was a third man, the Gestapo lawyer, Gisevius. He was politically aligned with Canaris and was sent to Bern with the sole purpose of maintaining contact between the admiral and Donovan, through Allan Dulles. All this was in '39, right at the start of hostilities. Well before we got into it.

"Jumping ahead now, to the last days of the Reich, middle of 1944, the German General Staff, soldiers, remember, not Nazis, they saw the handwriting on the wall. Sent their man, Baron von Weizsäcker, he was the ambassador at the Holy See, to arrange, through Pius XII, talks with Donovan. What they wanted, both General Guderian, and Field Marshal von Rundstedt, was a conditional surrender, one that would permit the Wehrmacht to keep fighting the Soviets on the eastern front. This was after, you realize, the July 20 bombing attempt on Hitler. Canaris had been arrested by then and was in an SS concentration camp. He'd played his part, set up the channel between the German General Staff and the OSS. But it all came to naught. Eisenhower said he'd accept nothing less than unconditional surrender. Fool. Of course he was taking his cue from the decision just made at Yalta. Joe Stalin got his back up, said that he knew the Germans were negotiating separately with both us and the Brits. Which they were. FDR and Churchill gave in to him; well, you know about the Yalta Conference. Winnie was senile and FDR was a dead man. Actually got around to doing it a few weeks later, down there in Warm Springs, with his lady friend. So the war went on, with the United States and Great Britain pushing into Germany from the west and Russia moving from the east.

"Then something strange happened. The German General Staff somehow failed to destroy the Ludendorff Bridge."

"The bridge at Remagen. The one the US First Army used to cross the Rhine and sweep up into the belly of Germany, ahead of the Soviets."

"Exactly. Without that bridge the Russians would have taken most of Germany for themselves. They, the Germans, tried to blow the bridge, but the wires had been cut. Some evidence points to a group of Polish engineers doing the job, perhaps at the instigation of the OSS. Another theory says that shrapnel from exploding shells cut the wires. Hitler certainly thought differently; when the bridge fell he relieved von Rundstedt of command and executed anyone involved that his Gestapo could get their hands on. He'd already, by then, murdered the man ultimately responsible for the bridge falling into our hands. Admiral Canaris. Because it was Canaris who had, six years earlier, first set up the link between himself, and therefore the General Staff, and Bill Donovan. So Donovan had a very real, very personal interest in finding Canaris. And his wife and two daughters.

"Donovan put Otto Nordon, a New York lawyer, on the trail sometime in March 1945. It wasn't until the end of April that Nordon discovered that Canaris had been hung in the Flossenburg concentration camp on April ninth. Reenter Dr. Josef Müller, the lawyer from Munich and the man who had been the member of Black Orchestra in contact with the Vatican. He was a guest in the same concentration camp and was able to give Nordon a first hand account of the admiral's execution. So they teamed up and continued to search for Frau Canaris, finally found her and her children about six months later. And while they were looking for her, they uncovered evidence of the Werewolf. Nordon, see, discovered that the SS had hidden gold somewhere in south-central Germany. The OSS detachment with Patton's Third Army took Nordon's information and found a huge cache of bullion, art treasures, jewels. Apparently it was destined to be used by the Nazi underground to finance a reawakening of the Reich."

"Yes," Defoe said. "Kit and I just heard General Kilgallen's version of it. Apparently he played a minor role in the story."

The elder Defoe gave his son a dubious look over the tops of his glasses. "If he said so. Well, the OSS people captured a young SS man, and under interrogation he told them about Werewolf, and Elsa. Elsa was the parent group, groups, really. There were counterparts in each of the forty-two administrative districts in Germany. The Elsas would spawn Werewolf groups, small bands of former members of the Gestapo and the Sicherheitsdienst, along with some of the more fanatical kiddies from the Hitler Jugend and the Hitler Mädchen. These Werewolves would terrorize the German population and murder anyone who collaborated with the Allied Military Government.

"One of Donovan's OSS boys, a German-born New York Jew, penetrated the Munich Elsa, and, in turn, the Munich Werewolf. Only a matter of time before the OSS broke the whole thing wide open, rounded up about a thousand or so Nazis. This was in April of '46, and was the final spike in the coffin of the Third Reich. So now you know." He picked up his glass and finished the swallow in it.

"So now I know." Defoe got up from his perch on the end of the sofa and looked absently at the wall of books beside his father's desk. "Everything but why Harmon Kilgallen would leave a note to himself to ask what part you had played in this." He turned to his father. "So far, Dad, what you've told me is popular history. Probably been published a dozen different times, both, as you said, by people writing their memoirs and by some of the more serious historians. What did General Kilgallen think you could tell him that he couldn't get from published sources? He said, and I quote him, 'Ask George about the part he played in uncovering the Elsa people.' From that remark one might assume that you played a clandestine role in the affair."

"Oh, fiddle faddle! Clandestine, my foot." He got up and fixed himself another drink, a more solidly constructed and rather larger one than the first. "I suppose you know that I was in the OSS back then?"

"I'd rather figured that out, yes. You and General Donovan, closeted in here, while Mother and I were hustled off to some small-boy amusement, with Butterfield in charge."

"That? Oh, hell, that was well after the war. The period between the breakup of the OSS and the charter of the CIA. What he and I were working on, incidentally. That fool Truman didn't want to have anything to do with an American intelligence organization during peacetime; the ink was hardly dry on the Japanese surrender documents when he abolished the OSS. September of '45. But that's got nothing to do with what you're asking about. The war. I was in the OSS early on. Recruited by Archibald MacLeish. He was Librarian of Congress at the time, and drafting every Old Blue he could get his hands on. He was Class of '15, y'know, as was Dean Acheson. Skull and Bones, the bunch of 'em. Stimson, Averell Harriman, Henry Luce. Thick as ticks. Most of us were in R&A, Research and Analysis. 'Weak eyes Brigade,' they called us. Brains of the whole thing, you understand." He looked at his son once again over the tops of his glasses. "Not like the rah-rah boys in Special Op, X-2. Counter Intelligence. More to your liking, the field side of the business, eh? Judo, disappearing ink, and that sort of malarkey. We, the men in R&A, were responsible for coming up with the information that those men in the field used. I was only in the outfit officially for a year or two. Analyzing the information coming in from the field. Take all the bits and pieces, and make some sense out of it. Spot bottlenecks in German war production. We discovered, for example, that there was a ball-bearing plant that was vital to the arms industry, and were responsible for it being bombed by the RAF. Not very exciting work. Translating train schedules from eastern Europe, for example, poring over shipping and billing manifests from Hungary, from the Ploesti oil fields in Rumania. See, before the war, petroleum received preferential rates, so by identifying shipments from the billing manifests, we were able to target specific trains for our bombers. Then I got involved with the Roberts Commission, drawing up lists of art treasures, what they were and where they were. Probably never heard of it, right?"

"As a matter of fact, I hadn't, not until a few hours ago. But I thought it was involved in recovering stolen artwork, Himmler's famous paintings, that sort of thing."

"No, no, that was just a small part of it. We had that report pretty well finalized by 1944. No, mostly what we did was make maps, very detailed ones. Again, for Allied bomber pilots. Only these maps pinpointed places *not* to bomb. Cathedrals, historic structures, museums. My job was coordinating the production of these lists and maps. Spent a good part of my time rushing around the countryside. About twenty percent of the people involved in it were from Yale, y'know. Both the galleries, and the art and history departments. Classmate of mine, Sumner McKnight Crosby, ran the show up there. I was back and forth, between here and New Haven; got across the pond a couple of times toward the end of the war. Your mother was pretty well abandoned for a while there. She had her volunteer work to keep her busy, though." George Defoe looked into his glass. "Too busy. Well, anyway, last time I went over to Europe, was in the spring of '45, toward the end, a few weeks before VE Day. Running interference for the government on a little project. It was decided that some of the art objects should be brought back here, for storage—safekeeping, you see. Just temporarily. Germany was a shambles, couldn't leave them there." George Defoe chuckled and sipped his whiskey. "Crosby got his dander up about that. Thought it was a thinly disguised way for us to appropriate the treasures that his people had just rescued from the Nazis for American galleries. Of course he was right. Naive, but right. Resigned, went back to Yale in a huff. Lost a lot of damned fine art for the university, too. Ah, well. Difference of opinion; what makes for horse races, right?" He put his glass on the desk and raised his hand in advance of his son's interruption. "Yes; yes, I know, what's all this got to do with Elsa? Well, when I was over there I worked pretty closely with the boys in the field, the OSS lads on SO,

Special Ops, tracking down these Elsa groups. Because the Elsas were funded by these hidden caches of gold and currency, don't you see, it stood to reason that if we could find their booty, then the underground Nazis wouldn't be far away. And I was coordinating what the people in R&A, back here, were coming up with, and directing the people in the field, over there. Not much more than a glorified telephone operator, you want the truth. Passing messages back and forth. My part in the whole thing only lasted a few weeks, while I was there. Satisfied? Not quite the clandestine activities you were picturing, eh?"

"I wasn't really picturing anything at all, Dad. Hard to imagine things when you have no base to start from. You know, you've never talked about your role in the war, and Mother never said anything about it, so I assumed it was something you didn't want to bring up. Painful memories, I supposed. I remember asking General Kilgallen about the war, when I was ten and bloodthirsty, but he'd never talk about it, either. When I was little it was all too abstract to comprehend, and then, when I was old enough to understand I—we—had this block that prevented an open dialogue." *Had?* he thought. Still have, guess we always will.

"Hah. Sorry to disappoint you. Boring memories, more the reason. No bloody tales of hand-to-hand combat, knife between my teeth, best friends leaping on grenades to save their buddies. Most war stories are best left untold. High point of my life was always what I was doing at the moment, what I was going to do, not what I'd done. History is for people who have quit, hung up their shield. Most histories are shaded, anyway, by the teller of the tale." He gazed across the expanse of his desk. "Believe half of what you read, and even less of what you hear."

Yes, Defoe thought, *I'll keep that in mind. Even when I examine this history you've just related, Dad.* Aloud he said, "I suppose I should feel honored that you finally filled in a gap in your past for me. I only wish you had volunteered it before the death of Harmon Kilgallen forced it from you."

His father looked at him for a long moment before picking up his pen and returning to his calculations. "Some people, Chase," he said, not looking up, "put too much stock in what they've accomplished." He paused, then added, still not looking up, "Harmon was one of them."

Defoe watched his father compute his worth for several minutes, then left the library. *An interesting tale,* he thought. *If only I could be sure it was true.* He found his mother in the kitchen, performing some arcane culinary feat with the food processor and a smoking skillet of pork fat.

"Chase, darling! How opportune. Turn down that burner, will you? And hand me the flour. Anna! Come and take charge of this roux, I've done all the hard parts. You can stand and stir while my son and I have a cup of tea." Mary Defoe whipped the dish towel from the waistband of her skirt and tossed it on the counter, confided in her son that "Anna's afraid to grasp the thistle, even after all these years." She leaned toward him and whispered, "Your father still intimidates her; she can't so much as boil water if he's in the room." She straightened and pointed to the stove. "Turn up the burner under the kettle, dear, and I'll brew us a pot. I've got some Ceylon black tea that will knock your socks off. Standing rib roast tonight. You'll be here for dinner, won't you?"

Defoe hesitated, said, "Afraid not, Mother. Kit and I are having dinner together tonight. I'll be here tomorrow, though. Promise."

Mary Defoe said, "Well, I hope so!" and busied herself with rinsing a small ceramic pot with hot water, filling an infuser with a very black gunpowder tea, and slicing a fresh lemon while her son fetched a pair of Belleek cups and saucers from the china cabinet in the dining room. He looked at her raised eyebrows as he put the translucent Irish porcelain on the tray she was preparing.

"I know, I know," he said, "Oriental teas in fat and rustic hand-thrown Japanese thimbles; use the Belleek and Wedgwood for teas that take milk and sugar." He smiled, and added, "But after all, Mother, rules were meant to be broken. And somehow that dark and tannic tea you are brewing seems to call for the crisp edge of high-fired porcelain."

"Well, darling, whatever you propose. I'm game. Sugar or honey?"

"Neither for me. Lately I've developed a taste for the bite

of the tea itself. A slice of lemon will probably be lovely with the Ceylon, though."

"Oh, you! That gourmet pallet of yours, always striving for the ultimate in—what is it . . . the Zen of food?" His mother laughed and picked up the tray holding the teapot, china, and ancillary paraphernalia, headed for her sanctum that was the morning room. "Next thing we know," she said over her shoulder, "you'll be importing air in canisters from the Kalihari, breathing it through those silly little masks the football players all clap on their faces during the warmer months." She put the tray on the glass-topped table his parents and Senator Kinship had surrounded that morning. "Your father has discovered professional football in his dotage," she explained. "He and Jack Brill were a regular item every Monday night last fall. Ever since Dad and Harmon took Jack duck-hunting a couple of years ago, and Jack absolutely corrupted the both of them." She smiled and poured the tea. "You didn't even notice, did you? The big television in the library. Swore, thirty years ago, he'd never have one in the house, then finally broke down when you were in high school and got the little RCA. Now he has a Japanese set a yard across, hooked us into the local cable system." She laughed a high trill, leaned forward as she squeezed a translucent slice of lemon over her cup. "Has it hidden behind the Chinese screen, in the corner. Just the football games, at first. Now he watches 'MacNeil, Lehrer.' And 'Wall Street Week,' on Sundays, before his games." She dropped her voice. "They *gamble.* Dad has a—what do you call it? A man he telephones on Friday. Bookie, that's it! All very complicated; point spreads seem to play a large part in their conversation. Dad plays twenty or thirty dollars a week, mostly on the Washington team, although sometimes he bets on the others, too. Jack, I think, is a bit more serious about it." Mary Defoe, unlike her son, dropped a lump of sugar into her tea, stirred it with a small sterling spoon. "He, Jack, bets on the college games on Saturday as well. Dad just plays the professional teams. Says it's not unlike the stock market, if you look at it the right way. He tried to explain it to me once, but I really don't have the interest." She laughed again and leaned toward her child. "Don't breathe a word of this to him, dear, but I *do* enjoy watching the games with him. Those absolutely marvelous young men, leaping through the air, crashing into one another. And the skintight trousers they wear." She sipped her tea and paused in her paean to professional football. "The *definition* is positively amazing." She looked at her son. "Am I shocking you, darling? A graying old lady ogling the buns of a twenty-two-year-old black man?"

Defoe laughed out loud, put his cup down on the table. "No, Mother, not in the least. I find your openness refreshing, especially after talking to Dad about the part he played in the war." Defoe picked up his cup, looked at the dregs of the tea in its bottom, then put it back on the table beside the tray. "I hope you will be equally honest, Mother, in telling me about what you did during the war." He put his palms together, forming the beginning of "here is the church, here is the steeple," but instead of interlocking his fingers for "open the doors, here are the people," he put his forefingers on either side of his nose, his thumbs under his chin, and looked at his mother. "Does," he asked, "the name 'Madam X' mean anything to you?"

Mary Defoe put her cup, nearly empty, on the tray, and snatched a linen napkin, its corner showing the letter D in point coupé, from her lap. She used it to cover the color that came to her cheeks and buy a moment to gather herself. "You have evidently been listening to Harmon's reminiscences," she said, putting the napkin carefully on the tray, concentrating on the small task. "I'd resigned myself this morning to the fact that you would hear it, sooner or later, when you and Kit said that you had discovered tapes at his house." She finally looked at her son. "Yes, Chase. I was his mysterious 'Madam X.' Took him under my wing, the poor, wounded colonel. You would never know that he was a dozen years older than I was. Such a bumpkin! I don't mean that in a derogatory way, dear, but Harmon *was* rather provincial. Anyway, what he said, at least what I read in the transcript he brought me, was true enough. We did all the things he set down." She looked down at her lap, added, "Including coming here, the night the Germans surrendered." She raised her eyes to her offspring. "Your father was off on one of his Oh-So-Secret trips to God knows where; he had been gone for weeks, before I'd even met Harmon. I'm not offering it as an excuse. It's just one of those things that happened. The one time, that was it. An evening, and he was gone, back to Alice out in the Midwest." She smiled, a distant, abstract gesture. "You know, she and I became quite good friends, after they moved into the old farmhouse. You were born, and then Katherine, a year later, and both our husbands off pursuing their careers." Mary Defoe jerked herself back to the present and sat straighter. "Well. Harmon brought the transcript over to me, sometime last week. The morning of the day he died, as a matter of fact. Asked me to read it, gallantly requested my permission to include it in his book. I didn't know what to say. It was, I suppose, a legitimate part of his story. He was, after all, rather badly wounded toward the end of the war. And I guess I did play some part in getting him back on his feet. Anyway, the whole thing was taken out of my hands when your father found the pages that Harmon had given me to read.

"An absolute tirade! You'd think that Harmon and I had been surprised, flagrante delecto, that morning. Never mind that the whole thing took place nearly fifty years ago. Your father wanted to go over there and *confront* Harmon! *Really.* Talk about overreacting. Grabbed his hat and a stick from the hall, stormed out of the house. Said he was going for a walk. Well, he went off by himself for a few hours, came back in worse shape than he'd been in when he left, and we've been at each other ever since. I suppose you picked up on it the moment you walked in the door."

"Yes, I did, Mother. Pretty obvious that something was wrong."

"Certainly. Well, now you know." Mary Defoe poured the rest of the tea into her cup. It was cold, and very strong. "Never mind that your father has enjoyed his little peccadillos these past, what is it, nearly five decades, now? Once, just once, I had a momentary lapse, and he reacts this way." Mary Defoe buried her face in her napkin and began to cry. "It's not fair, dammit! It's not fair."

Defoe got up and crossed to his mother; bent, feeling awkward, put his hand on her shoulder. "I know, Mom. It never is." He shook his head as she continued to sob into the crisp linen. He didn't know what to say, what he *could* say, so he said nothing. Stroked her hair, once, sighed, and left the room. Left the house, started his car, and drove to Washington.

EIGHT

Steak and a baked potato, she'd told him; and a salad. Kit wheeled the shopping cart through the automatic doors of the supermarket and decided that it was best to assume that there was nothing but cooking and eating utensils at her father's house. She put a five-pound bag of potatoes in the cart and began a careful selection of salad vegetables. The quality and variety of food in a market is directly related to the level of income of the customers it serves, and the residents of northern Virginia can compete with those of southern Connecticut, Marin County, and Central Park South.

Kit put a head of Chinese cabbage in her cart; its crisp leaves, a pale, pale yellow with just a tinge of green at the tips, would be a good foil, both in color and texture, to the spiky leaves of the winter spinach and the deep-green peppery-tasting watercress she had already tucked into plastic bags and dropped into the cart.

She looked at the Belgian endive and saw that it was more green than white. Likely to be too bitter, she thought, and opted instead for the Boston lettuce. The warm, yellowish green of the soft, rounded leaves would add yet another subtle shade to the salad she had decided would be a single color. With that scheme to build on she bought chicory, both for its slightly bitter taste that would be a nice counterpoint to the blander Boston, and its curly, rather tough leaf that would serve the same contrast in texture. There were some young chives in the herb section, as well as chervil to add a fresh and spicy bite to her dressing. And a few French tarragon leaves; she crushed one, rolled it between her fingers, and inhaled the glorious aroma. The damned salad was going to cost more than the steaks!

After the produce section she was able to move more quickly through the store. A small bottle of Italian *aceto balsamico* from Modena, an even smaller bottle of cold-pressed French walnut oil, and a larger one containing extra virgin olive oil would form the basis for her vinaigrette. A bottle of dry Dijon mustard and a bottle of white peppercorns, along with the chopped chervil and tarragon, would provide the piquancy of the dressing. She went back to the produce section and bought a big lemon to balance the strong Italian vinegar, then sailed her cart down the aisle of wines and selected a bottle of Chablis; a tablespoon for the salad dressing, and something for the chef while preparing it. Also a bottle of red, to drink with dinner. Wine selection was Jack's department, but Pommard was always safe, and she bought blindly, by price, knowing that anything that was over twenty dollars a bottle would please. A pair of steaks and a pint of sour cream completed Kit's marketing. She asked the bagger to put her groceries in boxes; she'd use them to pack some of the mementos back at the farmhouse. As she stood, waiting at the checkout counter while a bored, gum-chewing fat woman in a maroon-and-white polyester tunic swept her selections across the laser scanner, she caught sight of her reflection in the plate-glass windows, a translucent image overlaid on the more substantial one of two younger women just entering the store, girls dressed in bright print dresses, short and vibrant, like the ones that Sammy wore. The plain navy sweater and skirt suddenly made her feel her middle age and she decided to drive over to Tyson's Corner and do something about it. Chase wasn't due back at the farmhouse for a couple of hours.

NINE

"Federal Supply Company."

"Good afternoon, Eumenides."

"Odin! Years of silence, followed by contact twice in the same day. By the way, we can dispense with the code names, this line is secure. I must sweep it half a dozen times a day, demonstrating different pieces of equipment to customers."

"Don't be a fool. No line is ever secure; you, of all people, should know that. Have you destroyed the papers I sent you for?"

"From the girl's apartment? Of course. You told me to."

"I know. Unfortunate that you are so efficient. I now find that they were transcribed not from his notes, but from tape recordings. Which are still in existence. At General Kilgallen's house, west of MacLean. I'll give you directions and a number where I can be reached. Go there and secure them. Call me when you have the tapes and I'll arrange for us to meet. I will need to hear what the General said."

"Now? Hey, I'm trying to run a business here."

"Yes, now. Must I remind you of the part I have played in keeping your business the success that it is?"

"Yes, I hear you. It's just that, ducking out here, twice in the same day, is hurting me. I mean, I have to close up. This isn't the kind of place where I can get some geek in here on a moment's notice to fill in for me."

"Don't worry, my friend, you are being amply compensated for any lost revenue."

"Okay, okay. What do I need to know about this operation?"

"I understand that there are three tapes. The General

worked in his den, at the rear of the house. That would be the most obvious place to start. French doors open onto a patio; it's shielded from the road and the lock will be much less of a challenge for you than the one at the front of the house."

"Good. Any personnel involved?"

"Unfortunately, yes. The General's daughter, Katherine. Slim, dark hair, midforties, and a man, Chase Defoe; about five seven. Also middle forties, but fit. Ex Navy Intelligence, so you will have to respect his abilities; don't take any short-cuts. The two of them are listening to the tapes, trying to find a motive for the General's suicide. You will have to get the tapes without contact; I can't afford to have this escalate. One death is enough."

"I'm beginning to think that this General didn't shoot himself, after all."

"Don't think. That's not part of your job. Just carry out your instructions."

"Hey, don't start sounding like a case officer, handling one of his agents. Those days are way behind both of us."

"Don't remind me. And don't forget that this work is much more lucrative, much, much more lucrative." There was a pause. "Besides, Eumenides, one never really retires from The Company, you know that."

The owner of Federal Supply Company was called Eumenides by a single man. To everyone else he was Randolph Kronenberger, a fifty-eight-year-old retired Central Intelligence Agency officer and operator of a small business not far from "The Campus," a business that dealt in weapons, surveillance equipment, and ancillary goods. His still-dark hair was clipped as short as his mustache and he carried two hundred pounds on his six-foot frame with the easy grace of an athlete. His sport was, in fact, tae kwon do, a skill he had acquired in Korea during the "police action." It was also there that he had been noticed by The Company, and recruited. Later, as a case officer, he had run a string of agents in southeast Asia and come under the control, in turn, of the man he still called Odin.

The man he still called Odin had moved on to other, larger, playing fields, and Kronenberger himself had retired when he realized that, without the requisite Ivy League background and access to circles such a background offered, he had reached the highest level that he would achieve within the agency. Dealing arms in the shadowy realm that existed between the two worlds those in the business termed "legitimate" and "notational" proved to be far more profitable than service to country had ever been.

His company was located in an anonymous, windowless structure, clad with buff-colored aluminum siding, on a dead-end street behind one of the industrial parks that encircled Washington like the Capital Beltway that carries their customers to them.

The building was largely a warehouse; Kronenberger advertised the bulk of his product line in male adventure and soldier of fortune magazines, selling surplus flak jackets, parabolic eavesdropping devices, and electronic gear alleged to detect wiretaps and freestanding bugs. A disclaimer in his ads said:

> WARNING: not to be used for surreptitious interception of communications. All electronic equipment is subject to Public Law 90-351, Title III, 18 U.S.D., Section 2511A

and served to increase sales of these items by approximately twenty-five percent.

A smaller portion of his wares, those banned from interstate mail order commerce, were displayed in the showroom area just off the six-car parking lot at the front of the building. There he sold domestic and imported handguns and semiautomatic assault rifles of the type favored by survivalists and closet Rambos. Citizens with the proper identification; that is, anyone able to prove that they were twenty-one, sober, and not currently a resident of a federal penitentiary, could walk in and buy one.

In an even smaller area, at the rear of the building, behind a steel fire door, where he had an office furnished with a large sofa, a small refrigerator, and a government surplus desk and chair, there was an even smaller range of products available to more uniquely qualified buyers. The fully automatic Uzi, with a 900-round-per-minute cyclic rate and the thirty-two shot magazine so popular with the Secret Service, as well as the more prosaic Mac 10 and assorted Heckler & Koch assault weapons, were aligned in neat array on sturdy steel shelving. As was exotic ammunition, silencers, and other devices designed to break a number of federal and state laws. Members of the clandestine community, Special Agents of the FBI, and active-duty police officers, could, by producing proper documentation and purchase orders, buy these weapons and devices. By substituting a large amount of cash for the proper documentation, less officially qualified individuals had been rumored to have made purchases in Randolph Kronenberger's back room. This was a fact suspected but not confirmed by several law-enforcement agencies, especially the people at BATF charged with regulating the laws concerning alcohol, tobacco, and firearms. Friends in high places negated any undue interest field investigators from the Bureau showed from time to time in Kronenberger's business.

He sold a vacationing police officer from Canton, Ohio, a pair of nickel-plated handcuffs and a speedloader and pouch for his .38 service revolver, ran the policeman's Visa card through the electronic scanner, then locked the front door behind his last customer of the day, and flipped the OPEN sign over to CLOSED.

In his office in the back of the building, he opened a cold bottle of Beck's, tossed the cap and bits of foil in a steel wastebasket, and considered his needs for the Kilgallen Operation. While he drank the beer he put an assortment of items in a black nylon carryall, fastened the Velcro straps of an ankle holster under his right trouser leg, loaded it with an Airweight Chief's Special in .32 caliber, put a six-inch slide knife in the breast pocket of his gray tweed hacking jacket, and finished the beer. He then left the building by its rear door, after setting several sophisticated intruder alarms.

He put the carryall on the passenger's seat of a black Bronco with smoked glass all around and drove out of the industrial park, heading southwest toward Leesburg Pike and General Kilgallen's farmhouse. Avoid contact, Odin had said. Easier said than done, my friend.

TEN

7′ 5″ CLEARANCE it said on the four-inch steel bar that spanned the entrance to the parking lot of the Galleria at Tysons II. If your vehicle stood taller than the bar, you weren't the sort of person they wanted in their lot, much less inside the tri-level mall that looked more like a sanitized section of the Amazon rain forest than the most exclusive shopping center in North America. The Hanging Gardens of Babylon, with climate control. No Mercedes stands taller than four feet six, and the roof of the lowly Isuzu Trooper is barely six feet above the roadway.

Kit ignored the valet parking service with its blotchy faced boys lurking in its kiosk and eased her Volvo sedan into a slot just vacated by a young blonde in an old Lancia a hundred yards away from the impressive arch of the brick-and stone-façade that soared twenty feet above the mirrored glass entrance. The March winds tore at her skirt and tormented her short hair and she leaned into it, almost tacking, as she sailed toward the heavy, brass-handled plate-glass doors.

Inside, she paused and caught her breath, tried to do something with her hair. Mirrors, mirrors, everywhere, she thought, looking at herself in a storefront. This place is a Sybarite's paradise. Her cheeks were flushed from the wind and her heart pulsed at her breast after the brisk walk across the parking lot.

She didn't have time to shop the mall; best to hit Nieman Marcus and see what their large selection had to offer. She hadn't bought a new dress since Christmas, when she and Jack had done the usual round of holiday parties.

The salesgirl was her daughter's age and wore too much

makeup and Kit saw her surreptitiously stick a lump of gum behind a potted palm on the scarf counter as she asked with a nasal whine if she could help her. And then misread Kit completely when she told the girl that she wanted to see something young and fresh; brought her a Christian Lacroix print as soft as water lilies, short as Reagan's memory, and twenty-seven hundred dollars. She barely glanced at herself in the changing-room mirrors before whipping it back over her head and tossing it to the clerk, saying, "Not *that* young, dear! I meant fresh as in *new.* Besides, I'd like to be able to sit down in it."

The Ungaro Parallèle, a floral print in silk, was marginally better, but showed too much cleavage and the colors really needed a tan that she didn't have. Should have gone to the islands with Jack and Sammy, but he'd been such a grouch, with his broken knee, that she'd stayed home alone. It seemed that they had been at each other the whole week before the trip, almost as though he was looking for excuses to start a fight. He'd been that way since his fall, irritable. Jack wasn't used to being held back by anything, and she guessed that the knee bothered him more than he let on.

The girl gave her a poisonous look when Kit told her she didn't like any of the dresses and to show her something else. But the next batch was better, and the Arnold Scaasi black-and-white print was not only perfect—a sexy, clinging silk that hinted rather than displayed—it was also marked down from fourteen ninety-five to eight hundred dollars. She bought a pair of shoes and some of the new Lancôme makeup, then stopped at Victoria's Secret for a half slip, stockings, and lace bikini panties, all in black to match the dress. Once again she checked herself in the mirror and decided that her breasts were small enough and firm enough to obviate the need for a bra. Besides, the Scaasi dress cried out for a bare torso beneath it. She smiled as she handed the saleslady her credit card, a heavy-breasted woman who couldn't have been a day over forty and who said she wished she was young enough to wear "those styles." Kit was feeling better about herself by the minute.

ELEVEN

Defoe was looking forward to seeing his roommate after a hiatus of nearly five years. Even the frustrations of trying to find a parking spot less than taxicab distance from the Justice Department building at Ninth and Constitution did little to dampen his enthusiasm.

Douglas Winston, Assistant Attorney General, Criminal Division, had a secretary with perfect calves and an excellent bottom above them, and Defoe had a difficult time tearing his attention away as they waited for the elevators in the 1700 corridor off the Pennsylvania Avenue entrance. But he managed to give the building's directory board a brief glance before the elevator doors opened, and saw that the place contained the offices of not only dozens of assistant attorneys general, but also myriads of deputy assistant attorneys general, as well as special assistants, special counsels, senior counsels, and, down the hall from his old friend and roommate, the office of someone who was the deputy special assistant to the assistant deputy attorney general. He made a mental note to ask Doug if he knew how many lawyers it took to change a light bulb.

"Why certainly; as many as you can afford," Doug answered, and gave Defoe a sly smile as he released the shorter man's hand. Winston was an inch over six feet, developing a middle-aged spread and male-pattern baldness, but gave off the aura of power inherent to the top echelons of Washington. "And, as long as we are trading barbs, I suppose you know the joke about the consultant who leaped from a sinking boat into shark-infested waters and swam safely to shore, don't you?"

"Something to do with professional courtesy, isn't it?" Defoe smiled and looked out his roommate's window at the tourist traffic stuttering down Pennsylvania Avenue toward the Capitol. "I wasn't schmoozing you earlier when I said I wanted to take you and Joan out to dinner some night during my stay in town, Doug, and I also remember that I promised to make this a brief visit today." He turned and slid into the visitor's chair. "I have a tape here," he said, carefully placing the tiny cassette on the desk, "of the last few minutes in the life of Lieutenant General Harmon Kilgallen. I suppose that you are more or less familiar with the events of the past week, with regards to the recently departed General?"

Winston smiled and shook his head. "You still have the knack, don't you? Of sounding like a pompous asshole, I mean. Yeah, Chase, I have a radio. Two of them, as a matter of fact. One in the car, and Joanie bought one of them newfangled things also, has it in our bedroom. Goes off every morning, wakes me up. Why, I even take a couple of newspapers. Believe it or not, reports of the General's suicide made not only the *Washington Post,* but the *Times* as well. And I don't doubt that the *National Enquirer* will soon be reporting that he's really alive and well and playing in a garage band with Elvis and Liberace in the Baltimore Combat Zone." He picked up the tape, examined it. "What are you into? More to the point, what are you getting *me* into?"

Defoe grinned and leaned forward. "Got you hooked, don't I? That tape, as I said, records the last moments of his life. He had a pocket recorder, and was using it to dictate his memoirs. His granddaughter was transcribing them, the two of them were writing a book. As I told you on the phone, General Kilgallen lived next door to my parents, was an old friend of the family. His daughter and I grew up together. Hell, you met her. Kit, Katherine? I had her up there, prom weekend. You remember Quinn, Delaney Quinn. He married her, right after we graduated. Anyway, it sounds like the General didn't kill himself, at least not when you listen to this tape. Which is where you come in, old pal. I want an entrée over there, across the street; connect me with someone who can do a voiceprint, analyze this tape, tear it apart, computer-enhance the thing, and put it back together the way the record companies are doing with the old rock 'n' roll master tapes. Because I think that the man was murdered. Especially after I found out, a few hours ago, that someone broke into the granddaughter's apartment and stole the carbon copies of the notes she'd transcribed. Copies of the originals that General Kilgallen supposedly burned, right before he put a shotgun in his mouth and touched it off."

Winston leaned back in his chair and contemplated his roommate. Chase was a difficult man to pin down. Just when you had him pegged as a total gadfly he'd come through with something, out of left field and of no use to himself at all, but something that would advance your career in a way that you could never have done on your own. Like the recording of the Buffalino meeting in Scranton he brought me, ten years ago, when I was an assistant U.S. attorney. A tape that helped put me in the chair I'm sitting in at the moment.

"I don't really deal with the technical people, but I guess I can take you across the street and introduce you to the chief honcho of ID. Lately he and I have been seeing more of each other than our wives have. Ultimately I guess that's what you want, anyway. After you get your voiceprint. Identification of the man behind the voice. It is a man, isn't it?"

"Yes. Pretty bad quality, though. You can't tell what he is saying."

"Yes, well, they can work miracles in the basement over there." Winston looked at his watch. "Come on, I'll run you over and connect you with the assistant director who heads up the ID division. Then I have to get back; I'm due down in the Andretta conference room in half an hour, to meet with a group of US attorneys."

They used the tunnel under Pennsylvania Avenue that connected the Justice Department and the J. Edgar Hoover Building, and Defoe swapped his Justice Department visitor's badge for an FBI one. Winston took him up to Room 11255 and introduced him to Carlton Jarinko.

"I don't know why I'm doing this, Carl," he said. "But give this guy whatever assistance he needs. It was my bad luck to draw him as a freshman roommate thirty years ago, and I've been saddled with the Defoe Curse ever since."

The three men exchanged the requisite smiles, chuckles,

and handshakes, Defoe and the FBI man swapped business cards, and then Doug Winston left for his meeting with his federal prosecutors and Chase Defoe began to work Carlton Jarinko.

"Doug's just jealous, because I cruised through college with a philosophy major, a subject that required more bullshit than facts for a passing grade, while he was sweating bullets, going for degrees in both history and computer science at the same time."

"So," the FBI man said, "you've known Winston since college. I guess that takes precedence even over me. Doug and I met at Columbia, when he was studying for his law degree and I was on temporary leave from the FBI, getting my master's in computer science."

Defoe guessed that Jarinko was a few years older than he and Doug and the mandatory FBI retirement age of fifty-five was looming on the horizon.

"Computer science." He figured that the gray-haired man with the soft look of too many years behind a desk was about the right age to have been involved in the development of MAGLOCLEN and said so.

Jarinko showed his surprise and Defoe added, "Middle Atlantic–Great Lakes Organized Crime Law Enforcement Network." He smiled as he said, "A centralized storehouse of intelligence information, like your own AIDS setup, only the Pennsylvania Crime Commission is the host agency. That's how I know about it; I live up there and have a couple of contacts in the state police."

"You do, eh? What line of work are you in? And how do you know about AIDS?"

Defoe pressed, showing off, needing the advantage. "Automatic Identification Division System. Your in-house setup for fingerprint searching, computerized name search of criminal indices, computer storage and retrieval of arrest data. Shared, grudgingly, with other law-enforcement agencies. I'm betting, with your computer background dating back to the stone age of data processing, that you were in on the development of both systems. I know about them because I spent nearly twenty years in Naval Intelligence and dealt with more than a few of your four hundred and sixteen resident agents around the country during that time."

"Naval Intelligence," the FBI assistant director said, and looked up at the low ceiling of his anonymous office in the dirty yellow concrete blockhouse that was the headquarters of the world's most famous crime fighting organization. "Wait a minute, Chase Defoe." He brought his eyes down ninety degrees and focused an unblinking stare at the man seated on the other side of his desk. "Nineteen, nineteen seventy . . . eight. The Soviet delegation's new quarters at the UN. Plaster wasn't even dry on the walls, guy walks in, with piss-poor documentation, so obviously forged that the Residentura actually called the New York *cops,* and . . . that was *you?* Yeah, it was, wasn't it?"

"Afraid so. My younger days. Heavily influenced by Newman and Redford. Remember *The Sting?*"

"Yeah; and we were still picking up transmissions, ten years—Hey, you're a fucking *legend,* you know that?"

"Oh, bullshit. I got lucky; they fell for the decoy and didn't even look at the . . . Anyway, what I'd like some help with, right now, today, is with this little audio tidbit." Defoe fished the tiny plastic cassette out of his pocket and put it on the desk. "I have two others, all three recorded by General Killgallen shortly before his death. But this one seems to be the key. I don't want to say anymore, not until you've heard it. I know enough about this sort of thing to realize that you have to bring an unbiased mind to it. Let's just say, after nearly twenty years in Naval Intelligence, and about ten more in the private sector, I find the tape . . . interesting."

"Okay, sure." Jarinko stood up and scooped the cassette off the desk. "Let's go down to the subterranean realm and see what we can find out about your tape."

The basement levels of the FBI Building were occupied by the labs, and Defoe noticed that the personnel they encountered as they made their way down seemingly endless corridors seemed to stand a little straighter and walk with a bit more purpose as they passed Jarinko and his guest. The audio lab was a techno-freak's paradise.

"Joe," Jarinko said to a slender man in his late twenties, "we have a micro for analysis." Joe looked up from a Nagra body recorder he had dissected and spread across the benchtop, reached up to the transistor radio on the shelf above his magnetic tool rack and dropped the volume on Washington's number-one hard rock station to a barely audible level.

The flesh-colored plastic frames of his glasses held lenses thick enough to give his eyes a watery, Woody Allen look, and his hair had to have been cut by his mother, with the aid of a Tupperware bowl. He scratched at a reddish eruption on the side of his neck as he took the cassette from his boss. "IPS?" he asked.

Jarinko looked at Defoe, who looked at Joe. "Oh," he finally said, pulling his recorder from his pocket. "Two point four," he answered, looking down at the speed switch on his own machine.

"Thank God for small favors," Joe said. "Inch and a half and you might as well forget any meaningful interpretation. Guys want a soda?"

No, they both said as the technician slid off his stool and drifted across the room to a grungy Playmate cooler. The guys in forensic had unlimited refrigerator space, if you didn't mind sharing it with unmentionable organic things shipped in from the RA's across the country, and the photo lab people had a big unit also, but here, at the other side of the building, nobody had yet been able to come up with a reason for one in the audio department. He cracked the tab on a Mountain Dew and slipped the little cassette into a state-of-the-art machine on his bench, inserted a blank cassette beside it, then drank deeply from the can as he played the keyboard with his left hand and watched an oscilloscope above it.

General Kilgallen's slender, slightly arthritic fingers sort and resort the dozen photographs, as though by the mere act of noisily shuffling the glossy black-and-white prints, the images can be modified to meet the preconception the General brought to the task of studying the pictures.

He is therefore not pleased when he hears a sound at the French doors that open onto the brick terrace overlooking his rolling fields, and looks up to see what the interruption is.

Patience, tolerance, compromise, and understanding are

all laudable traits, and the man possessing them is to be admired and commended. They do not, however, serve the soldier well in battle, and Harmon Kilgallen is a soldier.

But appeasement and compromise are safer avenues to pursue now that armaments are measured in megatons, and men like Harmon Kilgallen find that fourth star elusive and retirement a welcome alternative to a meaningless command and the patronizing smiles and winks from the young lions of the post-Glasnost army.

The right-hand French door, the one with the exterior handle, opens and the General's visitor enters, the muffled click of the latch signaling the closing of the door behind him as he repeatedly taps the floor, playing a nervous tattoo.

"A cane?" Director Jarinko asks.

"Or a walking stick," Defoe replies.

Joe touches the pause button, says, "Or an umbrella, one of the ones with a plastic, not metal, ferrule" as he restarts the tape.

"What?" the General says, no doubt shading his eyes with his hand, *"Ah, it's you, is it?"* The tone of the General's voice can be categorized as irascible, even angry. He is not happy to see the visitor, but his appearance is not altogether unexpected. This from a single word; not even a word, really, just a sound. "Oh, it's you" would denote a slight element of surprise, whereas "Ah, it's you" indicates a certain expectancy. Nevertheless, the overall tone of the General's voice definitely carries a hint of annoyance above his usual irritability.

"Pissed," Joe says, eyes on the big speaker above his bench. He adjusts a few controls and the sound seems crisper to Defoe.

Harmon Kilgallen always had that impatient quickness in his speech, and a listener had to hear just a few words before he knew he was in the presence of a man who did not suffer fools gladly. But lately, over the past six months or so, the irritability and impatience has taken on another subtle nuance that is most noticeable late in the day, when he is tired. A hint of hurried desperation creeps into his voice. The General has read a book on the subject and is convinced that he is afflicted by Alzheimer's disease. His disorientation and memory loss are still largely confined to the present so that he frequently finds himself calling his granddaughter Samantha by her mother's name, or by the name of his late wife.

The General's caller says something in response from across the room, but the voice is far away and the words are indistinguishable. It is a mature male voice with a sureness that transcends its incomprehensibility.

"There!" Defoe says, "that's what we want to concentrate on." The other two men look at him and he quickly adds, waving his hand in dismissal, "Just tuck it away, for later."

There are several Oriental rugs in the General's den between the dark leather sofa and the fireplace and a longer, narrower runner leading into the hallway and the interior of the house, but the path from the doors to the desk is bare and highly polished oak and the visitor's footsteps click on the floor with the hard sound of leather soles and heels as he crosses the room. It is an infrequently heard sound in this day of the Adidas and the Nike and the rubber-heeled street shoe. The General's chair squeaks and its casters rumble on the floor as he shoves it back and rises. *"What the devil d'you—"* he says.

"Sounds like leather heels," Joe says, stopping the tape. "Rich man's shoes. I'll try to measure the stride, but at two point four inches per second it's going to be tough to size the guy closer than about six inches either way. May be able to use it to reinforce other data, though. Do you know where this was recorded?"

"Yes," Defoe answers. "I guess what you're asking is about the floor. Hardwood; oak, yellow pine, a residential dwelling. The man recording this is sitting at his desk, the machine is supposedly inside his jacket and set for voice activation."

"I know that," Joe replies, pointing at the oscilloscope. "The breaks are obvious." He rewinds the tape a few inches.

The General's chair squeaks and its casters rumble on the floor as he shoves it back and rises. *"What the devil d'you—"* he says.

There is a sharp, puzzling sound, then an *"uhhh,"* and the General noisily falls to the floor, bringing the chair with him, then books and papers from the desk. Perhaps he has caught his foot in the chair as he stands and has lost his balance. The leather heels click again, fade; there are sounds from the far end of the room; the footsteps return. A rich, mechanical sound, precision machined metallic parts against each other as though the tumblers of an expensive lock are being worked, is followed by a sudden, deafening noise, so short and yet so overwhelming that it is unintelligible.

Joe springs into action and touches buttons on his console with a flurry that requires two hands. He puts the can of Mountain Dew on his bench as he watches the oscilloscope, playing the few seconds over and over.

"Gunshot," he finally says, swiveling to face Jarinko and Defoe. "Shotgun, I think, see this part of the sine wave? Handguns don't go down there, and a rifle . . . Damned voice-activated recorders lop off half the signal before they start up. Never get it introduced as evidence, boss, but it's a shotgun. Stuff before it I can't tell you much about. My guess, and that's all it is, is that the one guy hit the other with something, the stick, umbrella, whatever, then walked off and came back with a gun to finish him off. But the 'scope shows a couple of stops in the action, so who knows what happened."

"Yes," Defoe says. "Very good. There is a gun cabinet at the far side of the room. That's where the General kept the shotgun that he allegedly killed himself with. Nice work, Joe."

The technician smiles at his superior and says, "How about putting me in for a jump in grade, boss" as he once again rewinds a few inches and restarts the tape.

The deep, ball-bearing rumble of a steel filing cabinet drawer being opened, then closed, is repeated, followed by the sounds of the surface of the desk being quickly cleared. The noise of these activities is followed in turn by the crackle of flames. Ten minutes later the French doors are opened and quietly closed again. The sound of the fire continues for another seventeen minutes. Long before then Defoe has told them that there is nothing else of interest on the tape.

Joe tossed his empty can into a wastebasket and rewound the tape. "Someone burned something. Paper, lots of it." He went to his cooler for another soda. "Sure you don't want one?"

"Can you do anything with that voice, back toward the

beginning?" Defoe eased his rear onto the workbench next to Joe's stool and looked at the technician.

"The mystery man. One who came in through the doors." Joe shook his head slowly, not so much in negation as in frustration. "Awful bad quality, and at two point four, there isn't much for me to enhance. Of course I'll do what I can. But you heard the recording. The man was pretty far away, and if what you said is true, that the recorder was in the victim's pocket, then we aren't going to get much enhancement; all the highs were filtered out, deadened by his clothing, before they ever got to the mike."

"Hmm." Defoe slid off the bench, stood up as he took his own recorder out of his jacket once again. "I recorded someone earlier today. It's a long shot, and I hesitate to even give it to you. But he stands to gain, indirectly, from the General's death, and I guess he could have a motive, although I don't know what it might be."

Both Joe and Carlton Jarinko looked at him with questioning stares. "He's the son-in-law of General Kilgallen. His wife will inherit a couple of million dollars worth of real estate." Defoe put his hands up, defending his suggestion. "I know, it ain't much. But it's all I have." He turned to the technician. "And, Joe, you've at least seconded my suspicion that the General was murdered."

Joe looked at his boss, ejected the original tape from his player and handed it to Defoe, then put the duplicate into a plastic evidence sleeve, made a note on it with a felt marker. "He's right there, Mr. Jarinko. Worth running a match, anyway." He turned back to Defoe. "Don't get your hopes up, though, sir. You know about voice prints?"

"No, not really. Just that you print them out on paper, compare the spikes."

"Yeah. What we do is measure resonance, pitch, and volume of a voice. That gives us an acoustic spectrogram. What you call a voiceprint. Only it's made from the articulation of common words, like 'you,' 'me.' And we don't have a recognizable word on this tape. See, your voice, produced by the unique conformation of your vocal chords, structure of your mouth and throat, is just like your fingerprints. You can't modify it, disguise it, not after I break it down. Unfortunately, the courts don't agree with me, at least not yet. Be a while before I can put on a tie and go into court, testify alongside the loops and whorls department." He brightened. "That day is coming, though. Look at the breakthrough we just made with DNA identification." He looked back at his audio equipment. "I don't hold out too much hope for this one, though. The recording of the voice on the tape is too tentative to get a decent print from."

Jarinko stepped forward and slapped Joe on the arm as he addressed Defoe. "If anyone can do it, this guy can. Give him your suspect and we'll see what we can do." He smiled and added, "You realize that murder isn't a federal offense, though. The FBI really shouldn't be getting involved. I'm only doing this as a favor to Doug Winston."

"Maybe, if you can match these two up, Doug can come up with something to charge him with."

"Sure," Jarinko replied. "There's always violating the victim's civil rights."

All three chuckled and Joe took the recording from Defoe, dropped it into a second evidence pouch. "Who's this? To ID the cassette, I mean." He picked up his felt pen.

"Oh, right. General Kilgallen's son-in-law. Brill; John Brill."

Joe looked at his boss for a split second before dropping his eyes to the bag and jotting the name on the plastic.

His boss looked at Defoe for a split second, then turned to the technician. "Run it, Joe, see what you come up with. Send the results up to my office when you have them." He turned to Defoe, jerked his head toward the door, said, "Defoe, let's go back to my office. We have to talk."

The assistant director, identification division, of the Federal Bureau of Investigation sat once again behind his desk in Room 11255 of the JEH Building. He punched up a number on his phone and waited for an answer as he and Defoe drank coffee from foam cups.

"Still down with his prosecutors," Jarinko said, looking at Defoe over the top of his cup. "Winston did say to give you every cooperation. And, if you were Naval Intelligence, you probably had higher clearance than I do." He drummed the fingers of his free hand on his desk as he examined the contents of his cup. Finally he came to a decision, stood up, and walked to the steel bookshelves that took up a large part of his office. "The tapes are down in the lab," he said, pulling a partition folder, one of several thousand, off the second shelf. It had a tan cover and a double gusset, reinforced with darker brown Tyvek. "Limited Official Use" was stamped on the cover and a lighter manila sheet, held in place by folded metal rabbit ears, displayed three stick-on letters, half an inch high and coded in different colors. BRI could be read from across the room and in smaller typescript beside it was BRILL, JOHN C. Reg. 01795-000. "This is the transcript of his file, current as of—" he flipped it open to the first sheet—"thirteen March. We'd written him off as a dead end and dropped direct interception." Jarinko eased back into his chair and put the binder on his desk. "Maybe we made a mistake, pulled our wires early."

"Wait a minute," Defoe said, putting his coffee cup on the desk. "What do you mean? You guys were running surveillance on Jack Brill? Why?"

"848, the Kingpin Statute. You familiar with CCE, RICO?"

"RICO, I've heard of; ah . . . Racketeer Influenced and Corrupt Organizations, right?"

"Right. The Organized Crime Control Act, title IX, US Code 1970. CCE is lesser known; that's Continuing Criminal Enterprise. Title XXI, Section 848. Both carry a ten-year-to-life sentence, with no chance of parole. And asset forfeiture. That's why all the field guys are driving 560 Mercedes and Lamborghinis. While I'm stuck with a three-year-old Plymouth with vinyl seats."

"Wait a minute. You're telling me that John Brill is involved with organized crime?"

"Some of the boys over at Justice seemed to think so, a few weeks ago." Carlton Jarinko pushed the binder toward Defoe. "Maybe you'd better read this, my friend." He turned his chair from his desk to the window. It offered a broad view of the Justice Department across the street, a narrower slice of the National Archives in the next block, and a tiny sliver of the Capitol dome six blocks away. Defoe dropped his eyes to the file and flipped the cover open.

SUPERIOR COURT
COUNTY OF MONTGOMERY
AT ROCKVILLE
MARCH 2nd 1991
BEFORE:
HON. WALTER WEINBERGER, JUDGE
PRESENT:
CALVIN HORNE, ESQ.,
DEPARTMENT OF JUSTICE
ROBERT SCOTT, SPECIAL AGENT FBI
CPL. DANIEL SMITH,
MARYLAND STATE POLICE

THE COURT: Make a statement, if you will.
MR. HORNE: This is an application under the authority of Osborne v U.S., 385 U.S. 323, for use of electronic surveillance on an individual identified by a previous wiretap authorized by this court.
THE COURT: Wait a minute. Is this more of your CCE investigation, Mr. Horne? The same case you were before me with back in December?
MR. HORNE: Yes, Your Honor. From that telephone intercept and surveillance authorization we have identified other individuals connected to Mr. Iezzi.
THE COURT: Sam the Slam.
MR. HORNE: Yes, sir. Samuel Anthony Iezzi.
THE COURT: Okay now. Who is this latest wiretap victim?
MR. HORNE: John C. Brill, your honor. A member of the Bar of the—
THE COURT: I know who Jack Brill is, Mr. Horne. I wonder if you do.
MR. HORNE: Yes sir. Your Honor, Special Agent Scott will testify as to a telephone conversation he recorded, on February the eighth

of this year, between Mr. Iezzi and Mr. Brill. Illegal wagers on a sporting event were discussed, and—

THE COURT: Oh for chrissake, Mr. Horne. Sam the Slam is a bookie, everybody knows that. And I personally happen to know that Jack Brill likes to get a few bucks down on sporting events, now and then. He plays the ponies, too. If you think I am going to authorize a fishing expedition for the Justice Department, just because—

MR. HORNE: Your Honor, it's more than just sports betting. I mean, the amounts discussed—

THE COURT: No. This, what you have here, in this request, is an invasion of privacy. Private telephone intercept, his home number. The mobile unit in his automobile. Two lines, in his office. All this because Mr. Brill called his bookie and—

MR. HORNE: Excuse me, Your Honor. Perhaps I didn't make myself clear. The telephone call that Agent Scott recorded was originated by Mr. Iezzi. He placed the call. The Pen Register we have on his line identified the number being called as that of Attorney John Brill's office in Georgetown. A private line, an unlisted line.

THE COURT: Who the hell authorized a Pen Register on Mr. Iezzi's telephone. I know it wasn't me.

MR. HORNE: Excuse me, Your Honor. We don't need authorization for the device. The Supreme Court has ruled that its use is not an invasion of privacy, and—

THE COURT: Okay, okay. I still think you're fishing, Mr. Horne. Tell you what I'll do. Put an intercept on this unlisted line of Jack Brill's, the one Sam the Slam called. None of the others. Not his home phone. Not the one in his car. And I want to see you in my courtroom, two weeks from now, with evidence from this intercept that convinces me to let you continue to run it. How's that sound?

MR. HORNE: I guess it'll have to do.

THE COURT: What did you say?

MR. HORNE: I said thank you, Your Honor.

THE COURT: That's what I thought you said. Now get out of here. Two weeks, Mr. Horne.

STATE OF MARYLAND:
COUNTY OF MONTGOMERY:
ROCKVILLE, MARCH 2nd, 1991

I hereby certify that the within and foregoing represents an accurate transcription of the testimony received in the hearing before Hon. WALTER WEINBERGER, a Judge of the Superior Court, at Rockville, Maryland, on March 2nd, 1991.

Naomi Strega
ASSISTANT REPORTER
SUPERIOR COURT

Defoe looked up from the last page of the wiretap request. "Don't you guys have a tame judge somewhere who hands out anything you ask for?"

Jarinko turned from contemplating the traffic jamming the streets outside. "Yes; unfortunately he was in Bethesda, getting his prostate attended to. Weinberger usually is more cooperative than that. But you know how lawyers are, stick together, no matter what. Off the record, I think he was right. I think Horne was on a fishing trip. The fact that we dropped Brill from the tap before the two weeks expired is evidence of that. He was into Iezzi for some pretty hefty change, but that was all it was. You know what kind of money these Washington lawyers can pull down, and we didn't think too much about it. Only now, with you bringing General Kilgallen's suicide in here as a possible homicide, and Jack Brill's wife in line to inherit a few million dollars . . ." He drummed his fingers on his desk and chewed his lip. "I don't know," he finally said. "Brill is hurting for cash. Read the rest of the report. You know the man, give me your opinion after you've seen what he's involved with."

I don't *know the man,* Defoe thought, but turned anyway to the report and began to read the transcripts of the wiretap on Jack Brill's unlisted line.

Federal Bureau of Investigation
Date of Transcription
3/13/91

The following information was derived from an investigation conducted by Special Agent Robert Scott of various telephone intercepts on the private telephone line of John C. Brill, Esq., an Attorney residing in the District of Columbia. This document contains neither recommendations nor conclusions of the FBI. It is the property of the FBI and is loaned to your agency; it and its contents are not to be distributed outside your agency.

CONFIDENTIAL

1645 HRS 3/4/91

BRILL: Hello?

FEMALE CALLER: Dandy Jack! How's it hanging?

BRILL: Hey, doll. I was just thinking about you. Want to spend a couple of days in New York with me?

FC: I can't, I have something I have to do. Will I see you before you go?
BRILL: Bet on it, kiddo.
FC: What about her?
BRILL: I told her I'm taking Amtrak up, like always. So we can spend the night at your place. If you'll make sure I get to the airport for the earlybird shuttle.
FC: I'll do my best. When are you coming over?
BRILL: About an hour. Damn, I'm horny. (LAUGHTER) Maybe I'll come over now.
FC: Do that. I'll wrap a lip lock on your root.
BRILL: Hey, such language.
FC: (LAUGHTER) You love it. Hurry up, Dandy, I'm all wet now.
BRILL: Okay, I'm coming, I'm coming.
FC: You better not, not until you get here.
BRILL: (LAUGHTER) G'bye darlin'.

Defoe looked away from the page. *Oh, Jesus, Kit. He struck me as that kind of guy, the way he talked while we were shooting down in the cellar.* Defoe shook his head and flipped the page. *Not really any of my business, I guess. And I don't see how I can tell her, anyway. Not without violating the confidentiality of this information.*

1742 HRS 3/7/91

BRILL: Hello?
IEZZI: Hello, fancy man.
BRILL: Sam; hey, ah, how's it going?

IEZZI: Depends on whether you got something for me or not.

BRILL: Yes, I, ah, Sam, this is not a good time for me right now. Can we—

IEZZI: Hey, Counselor, no time is a good time for you anymore. What, you don't have time for me, now that you owe me some scratch. You had plenty of time, when you wanted to play, wanted to put something down—

BRILL: No, it's not that, Sam. It's just that . . . look, I need a little time to get the money together.

IEZZI: Big shot like you, can't come up with two large? Come on, Counselor. Don't play games with me.

BRILL: Listen, Sam, maybe a guy like you has that much in cash lying around, but not me. Or anybody else I know. It's going to take a few weeks to get it together. You'll just have to wait.

IEZZI: Hey, who the fuck you think you're talking to, you—you were quick enough to put ten on the Hoyas, back there at Christmas, right? What, you think I'm carrying you. Listen, Counselor, the vig's at five a week, in case you lost track, and I ain't seen nothin' for . . . for it's been seven weeks now. So figure it out. We're talkin' two large, what with the love affair you had with the 'skins last fall.

BRILL: I know how much it is, Sam. You'll get your money, don't sweat it. I got something I'm working on.

IEZZI: I ain't sweating it, my fancy friend. But you better be. And you better be gettin' something together for me, 'cause I'm sending the fat guy over to see you, tomorrow. For this week's vig. So you better do something. Go get one of them equity loans on that place in G town. Sell that fuckin' car you got. I don't care what you do. But I tell you this, pal. You ain't playing until you start paying. Tomorrow.

BRILL: Don't threaten me (IEZZI BREAKS CONNECTION) shit!

0945 HRS 3/8/91

BRILL: Hello, this is Jack Brill, calling for Mr. Mandellio, please.

FEMALE VOICE: Just a moment, sir.

MANDELLIO: Hello?

BRILL: Tony! Hey, good morning. Jack Brill here. How are you?

MANDELLIO: Fine. What can I do for you, Jack?

BRILL: What—hey, remember what we discussed, last night? The, ah . . . loan? Twenty thousand?

MANDELLIO: Oh, yeah. Listen, I don't think that I can—

BRILL: Tony, it's me, Jack! You know I'm good for it. Short-term thing, six weeks, tops.

MANDELLIO: Yeah. The thing is, I hear you're into Sam the Slam for two hundred. Going back to last fall, and that Redskins habit you got. Know what I'm saying?

BRILL: Aw, Tony, Sam's a big mouth. No way am I into him that deep. How about it, my friend? Twenty, for four weeks. At your usual rate?

MANDELLIO: Sorry. No can do, not this time. Good-bye, Jack.

1013 HRS 3/8/91

BRILL: Hello?

IEZZI: You disappoint me, Jackie boy. The fat man came back here, said you ducked out on him. Saw you gettin' in that car of yours from the window. After your secretary told him you wasn't in. That wasn't nice, Jackie.

BRILL: Sam. Hey, I was going out to pick up the cash. I got it here, now. How about you meet me tomorrow night, wherever you say.

IEZZI: Don't fuck around with me, pal. The fat man is gonna be there in the morning, same time. And you better be there too. With the five. You got that?

BRILL: Got that. Listen, don't wor—hello? Hello? Shit.

1430 HRS 3/8/91

KIT: Hello?

BRILL: Hi, Kit, it's me. Listen, I need a favor. Jump in your car, and bring the key to the safety-deposit down here. I need to, ah, get some papers out. Oh, and get the Corum out of my dresser, bring it along.

KIT: Sure. What's up?

BRILL: Nothing. Just I'm nervous, having a piece of jewelry that valuable in the house. I never wear it, anyway; might as well stick it in the box, along with your jewels.

KIT: What do you mean, you never wear it? You wear it all the time, Jack.

BRILL: Hey, I didn't call you up for a fight, sweetheart. Just do what I ask, bring the key down, chop chop, okay?

1315 HRS 3/10/91

MS. COOKE: Good afternoon; Mr. Brill's office.
IEZZE: Hello. Who's this? Lemme talk to Jack.
COOKE: This is Mr. Brill's secretary. Mr. Brill is not in today. May I ask who is calling?
IEZZI: Yeah. Sammy Iezzi.
COOKE: Mr. Iezzi, Mr. Brill had an accident, he'll be out for a few days. Actually, he is still in the hospital. He slipped on the ice, day before yesterday and fractured his knee.
IEZZI: No shit. That's what happened, huh? Well, you call him up at the hospital, honey, and you give him a message from me. Tell him I deal in cash, I don't take no jewelry, TV sets, nothin' like that. And tell him the fat man's gonna stop by again, next week, with his ballpeen hammer. Tell him that, honey. The fat man, and his ballpeen hammer.

Defoe looked back at the top of the final transcript, noted the date. About a week before the General's death. He closed the file and put it back on the desk.

"Well?" Carlton Jarinko squared the file with the sides of his desk. "Think there's a motive there?"

"If I owed a bookie two hundred thousand dollars and he'd just tapped my patella with a machinist's hammer, I certainly might be driven to drastic measures to pay off the debt." Defoe stood up and went to the window, then turned and waved his hand at the folder. "But that can hardly be considered evidence that he killed his father-in-law, can it?"

"By itself, no. I'd have to check with Doug Winston, but I wouldn't suppose it would even be admissible, not on a murder. Justice was after Iezzi, not Brill, with the telephone intercepts, and for bookmaking and loansharking, not homicide. No, my friend, all these transcripts do is give us a motive. And I'm not even going to turn them over to the Virginia authorities in order to interest them in opening an investigation into the General's death. Not unless Joe can come up with something from the tapes you brought him." He picked up his phone and punched an internal number. "Joe. How are you coming on the Brill tape?" He listened for several minutes, then said, "Okay, put it in the file."

Jarinko broke the connection and turned to Defoe. "He got a poor set of spikes from the tape that General Kilgallen made. Not good enough to make a match with, but he says he has enough points to compare it with the one of Brill that you made. Inconclusive. Might be Brill, might not. Sorry. We can't place him in the room, not from the tape, anyway. Forensic might come up with something. Fibers, that kind of thing." He looked across the desk at Defoe, hopeful.

"Afraid not. The room was most thoroughly cleaned, shortly after the incident." Defoe stood up. "Well. That's that, I suppose. Looks as though we are at a dead end."

"Unless you have another suspect for Joe to run against the tape."

"Not at the moment." Defoe looked at his watch. "I'm having dinner with the General's daughter; maybe we can come up with a new angle on this."

"Okay. If you do, give me a call; you've got me intrigued with your mystery. You have my card; my home phone is on it also. Just don't go doing anything, ah *rash,* with that tape recorder of yours. Remember due process, Mr. Defoe. Don't ruin a possible case playing fast and loose."

Defoe held his hands up, palms out, declaring innocence. "Hey, I'm strictly on the sidelines. Anything I come up with goes right to the proper authorities."

He thanked Jarinko and left the building, headed for his car. The late-afternoon sun was turning the monumental federal buildings facing the mall a rich gold, and Washington's famous cherry trees were poised, awaiting the approaching conjunction of calendar and weather to burst into bloom.

The tranquility of the moment was lost on Defoe, who walked quickly, his head down, noticing nothing of the world surrounding him. He unlocked the Jag, got a fresh cassette out of the glove compartment, and snapped it into his recorder. Before this time tomorrow he knew he had to return to the FBI lab, delivering a tape recording of his father's voice.

TWELVE

Kit put the boxes of groceries on the kitchen table, stuck the wine and steaks in the refrigerator, then took her new dress upstairs and hung it in the closet of her old bedroom. She looked around at the small space she had not slept in for nearly thirty years. The antique four-poster bed with its frilly pink canopy and matching spread looked as lumpy as she remembered it, and after bouncing once or twice on its edge, then lying back across its surface, she didn't change her mind.

And musty-smelling; she peeled back the coverlet, saw the mattress was bare beneath it. Kit got off the bed and opened the window, letting the crisp March air swirl into the room. She leaned out, looked down at the easy slant of the gray shingled roof above her father's den, and smiled, remembering warm nights when Chase would ease over the sill and into her arms. And hours later slip back out onto the roof, then drop lightly to the grass below and fade into the darkness toward his own home across the fields. Ah, how long, long ago that was, she thought, and stripped off the coverlet, hung it out the window to air.

She then went to the linen closet beside the bathroom and made her bed with fresh sheets. *What are you* doing, *Katherine?* she asked herself, and blushed, catching sight of her reflection in the mirror above her old dresser as she tucked the sheets beneath the mattress. Then she laughed aloud and ran lightly down the stairs and into the kitchen.

She found a corkscrew, opened the white wine and poured herself a glass, sipped it while she searched for the other utensils she would need. No pepper mill, but a mortar and pestle that probably had last seen duty when her mother was alive did a good enough job on the handful of white peppercorns. She put salt and pepper into the Italian vinegar and gave the mixture a brief whisk, then beat in a little of the walnut oil to complement the olive.

She halved the lemon and squeezed it over a teacup, added a dollop of the Chablis and poured it into the vinegar and oil mixture, whisked it until it was creamy. Testing and tasting, she added and balanced ingredients until the power of the balsamic vinegar had been subdued but not defeated. Then she added dry mustard, minced the chervil and tarragon and a few of the chives, saving some for the baked potatoes. Pouring the dressing into a quart mason jar, she tossed in the fresh herbs and vigorously shook the mixture, then put it in the refrigerator to let the flavors blend. She refilled her wine glass and carried it, along with the empty cardboard boxes, out to the den.

Where to start? Jack wanted the personal effects, the small things, out before the real-estate people started showing the house. She guessed he was right, the temptation to pilfer souvenirs would be awfully strong. Still, there was so much here. She'd start with the knickknacks, bric-a-brac on the bookshelves, all the silver trays from units he'd commanded, an ashtray made out of an artillery shell, bits and pieces of captured armaments that no doubt had held strong memories for the General, but held little meaning for her.

Clear the desk, use its surface as a staging area. Wrap the more fragile things in newspaper. The cassette recorder was where they had left it earlier. She picked it up and put it in the right-hand drawer, with the three tapes that Chase had made. She noticed that her father's personal address book was there, under the telephone directory. She briefly considered packing it with the other stuff, but left it where it was.

There was a stack of newspapers by the fireplace and she began to wrap and pack the treasures that had been her father's life, sipping wine and humming as she drew memories from her mind and attached them to items she could identify.

* * *

Randolph Kronenberger eased the Bronco off the blacktop a few hundred yards past the General's driveway and shook a Camel from a soft pack, fired it with a battered Zippo, and absorbed the territory. Rural; the nearest neighbor was a new split-level with white vinyl clapboard above antique brick and raw clay where the lawn would be. Several hundred yards back, on the opposite side of the road. So new that it might not yet be occupied. Kronenberger scanned it for a few moments with a pair of 8×40 Nikons, then focused them on the Kilgallen place.

Blue-and-white frame farmhouse at the end of a short driveway. Tan Volvo by the front door. An outbuilding, a garage or small barn, a few hundred feet beyond the house, bordering a patch of woods. Good potential escape route. He swung the binoculars toward the other side of the property. Always have an alternate.

Above ground power and telephone wires entered the house at the left front corner. Be visible from the road if they had to be disconnected. Still, from the edge of the building you could see a couple of hundred yards up and down the line. Probably no need to take out the utilities, anyway. But it always paid to check. Kronenberger remembered men who hadn't bothered to touch all the bases. A memory was all they were.

He twirled the wing nuts that held his Virginia plates in place, replaced them with the set of Maryland tags he kept beneath the driver's seat for use in emergency operations such as this, then tied a white handkerchief to the door handle. He changed from his oxblood brogans into a pair of running shoes and slung the shoulder strap of the black nylon bag over his arm.

Kronenberger crossed the road and slipped into the second growth, moved away from the road, and found a secluded spot where he could study the rear of the house with his binoculars. He settled down and got comfortable, his back against a slender ash. Plenty of time. Patience was the key.

Kit put the last of the photographs, faded black-and-white pictures of unknown uniformed men in faraway, unidentified lands, in the second box and closed its flaps, then turned and surveyed the results of her work. Nothing left on the shelves but books; surely they could stay and make the room seem warmer to some prospective buyer; they'd be unlikely to steal the *books.* She'd checked the gun cabinet, packed her father's pistol that she had found in the drawer under the rifles and shotguns, packed all the bullets and cleaning gear, the other stuff that was with the gun. The big guns she could wrap in a blanket and put on the backseat of the car. Maybe Chase would help her with them, later. There had been nothing in the desk that couldn't stay, and she had filled the remaining space in the cardboard boxes with the Currier & Ives hunting prints that adorned the walls on either side of the fireplace. Kit carried the two cartons out to her car and locked them in the trunk, left the front door on the latch for Chase, then poured herself another glass of wine and went upstairs to take a shower and dress for dinner.

Must be the daughter, Kronenberger thought, focusing on Kit as she bent over the trunk of her car. *Nice. Very nice, for forty something. Down, boy. You know I never mix pleasure with business. I'll take care of you, later. No sign of the man. Defoe. The Naval Intelligence officer.* Kit went back into the house, reappeared with another box. *Must be alone; an officer and a gentleman would surely help her with those boxes; they looked heavy.* She reentered the house a second time, turned on the porch light. Dusk was half an hour away.

A minute later a light came on upstairs, and Kit appeared, briefly, as she passed the window. Then another light came on, next door; a warm yellow rectangle on which appeared the silhouette of a naked woman. Window shade; bathroom, had to be. *Move, Kronenberger! Seize the moment.*

He slipped from the cover of the underbrush and kept to the lengthening shadows as he approached the rear of the house. At the French doors he opened his bag and rolled a pair of rubber surgical gloves over his hands, then took a thin piece of steel from an inside pocket of his carryall and a few seconds later eased inside the house.

He stood, motionless, feeling the layout of the rooms, luxuriating in the power and control, stretching out that moment of entry into another person's world, reveling in the feeling of domination, of . . . violation. Kronenberger moved swiftly, lightly for a big man, along the hall, listened at the foot of the stairs to the faint sound of the shower. She must have left the door open. *Uhmm;* to slip up there, surprise! surprise! all wet and soapy . . . Purse on the kitchen table, a pile of lettuce and cabbage beside it. The den, Odin had said. Get to work. He automatically checked the doors as he moved along the hallway, back to the rear of the house. Powder room, cellar stairs. And, just inside the doorway to the den, a closet. Raincoats, rubbers, boots, an umbrella, a pile of duck decoys at the rear.

The desk was unlocked and seemed the most obvious place to start. The center drawer yielded nothing but ballpoint pens, paper clips, a few stamps. Brass letter opener, wooden ruler, pair of scissors. Top left, a box of envelopes and a box of writing paper, roll of stamps.

Second drawer. This year's income tax forms, unopened, still in the government envelopes, and underneath them a pile of receipts, Visa carbons, sheets of yellow legal paper filled with columns of numbers written in a wavery hand. Kronenberger smiled. *At least that's one thing you won't have to worry about, General.*

The telephone rang, its harsh bell breaking the silence of the room with such force that the instrument seemed to jump on the surface of the desk, like the ones in animated cartoons. He felt his heart skip and concentrated on regaining his composure. Getting *old,* Kronenberger. Out of practice.

Kit cocked her ear and pulled the shower curtain back. Damn! The phone. Let it ring; it was probably someone selling aluminum siding or one of the ghouls who crept out of the woodwork after a funeral and peddled memorabilia to the bereaved. But maybe it was Chase; she turned off the water and wiped shampoo from her eyes with the washcloth, then wrapped a towel around her torso and ran along the hall to her father's room.

"Hello?"

"Mom. Hey, I caught you! You guys are still there."

"No, just me. Chase is in town. I was taking a shower. What do you want?"

"Oops, sorry. Listen, I'm at the Kennedy Center. Just had a chat with a lawyer, she's in the publishing business. I was telling her about the book Grampy and I were working on, and what happened and all that. Absolutely floored me, said that we probably would have to give back the advance Grampy got from the publisher, unless we deliver a manuscript. Depends on what's in the contract. Anyway, what I need is the number of the editor who was dealing with Grampy. He had it in his address book. Obelus Press is the publisher, but I need the name of his editor. This lawyer said she'd call him up and talk to him for me. You have any idea where Grampy's address book is? God, I hope it didn't get burned up."

"No, it didn't get burned. I know exactly where it is, I saw it when I was packing some of your grandfather's things not twenty minutes ago. Hang on, I'll go down and get it."

The telephone stopped ringing. *Moving right along now, Kronenberger, never mind the phone, she picked it up upstairs. Bottom drawer, empty; go to top right. Bingo. Recorder, three cassettes beside it. So easy; drop the little darlings in your pocket. Better take the machine too; in for a penny, in for a pound. Don't rely on Odin having one that will play these microcassettes. That's the advantage of having me on the job, Odin. A man who can think as well as act. What had he said on the phone? "Don't think, Eumenides, just do as I tell you." Maybe I should leave the recorder—no; don't be an ass, don't play games. But I will mention it to him, when I hand him the machine. After all these years, I never asked him who the hell Eumeni—* Jesus Christ—*footsteps, on the stairs.*

He knew that he wouldn't make the French doors across the room in time and ducked into the closet as Kit came into the den, her bare feet leaving wet impressions of her toes on the smooth floor. She refolded the towel tighter around herself and picked up the phone as she pulled open the drawer.

Kronenberger eased the door open a half inch and looked at the back of the daughter as she bent over the desk, a dozen feet away. Nice, nice legs. *Shame the towel is so big. Damn, she keeps striking that pose, almost as though she's inviting . . . She's opening the drawer where the tapes were. If that's what she's looking for . . .* He touched the breast pocket of his jacket, felt the knife.

Kit pulled her father's address book out from beneath the telephone directory and flipped it open on the desk, saying, "Sammy, how am I going to find this editor's number, if I don't know the man's name?"

"Look under Obelus Press, Ma."

"Oh, of course. Yes, here's the number. 872-8110. And a name. McCreight, C.J. McCreight. Is that it?"

"Yes! That's it. Thanks a mil. G'bye."

"Good-bye, dear," Kit said, and hung up. She closed the address book and put it back in the drawer, on top of the telephone directory.

Something was wrong. Different. The sun was low on the horizon and here in the house it was all long shadows and dark pools around the furniture and along the walls. Kit reached out and clicked on the gooseneck desk lamp, and its forty-watt bulb splashed a cone of yellow light across her face, illuminating her as she stood beside the open drawer, a puddle of water slowly forming on the floor around her feet. She felt a sudden chill as the coolness of the room began to penetrate the warmth her skin had drawn from the steamy shower. The *tapes,* that was it. Chase had put them in the drawer, on top of the phone book, hadn't he? She was sure he had, because she remem—She stiffened, fear rather than the temperature of the room raising goosebumps on her exposed flesh. The *recorder.* It had been on the top of the desk when she had started to pack the boxes. She had put it in the drawer, with the tapes. Half an hour ago, it had been . . . right . . . *there.*

She knows it's missing, Kronenberger thought, reading the woman's body language as she bent over the desk. He reached, slowly, into the breast pocket of his jacket and took out the slide knife, pressed the release, and heard the razor-edged blade fall into place with a faint click. Three swift steps across the floor, never mind the slight sounds his rubber and canvas shoes might make on the polished boards; he'd be on her before she could turn.

Kit began to tremble; she could feel her body start to

shudder uncontrollably, like the washing machine when something heavy threw it out of balance. *Someone came in here while I was in the shower and took the tapes.*

She was suddenly aware of the multitude of sounds in the silent, empty house, starting with the intimacy of her own blood, a roaring surf that surged within her ears. She held her breath and her auditory world widened gradually, like a pebble in a pond; she heard a click as the refrigerator's compressor started, listened to the steady beat of the tall case clock beside the front door, so far away and yet so clear. Wind eddied at the eaves above her head, whispering, and the old house creaked and popped as beams and boards worked against each other with the changes in temperature and humidity. And far, far away, on the very fringe of her consciousness, she heard a plane overhead, making its final approach to Dulles. God, to be up there, in the safety of the sky, she thought, and slowly looked up, across the room, realized why it felt so cold. The French door was open, and the evening breeze was filling the room with chilly air. The hair rose on the back of her neck. *He's still in here,* she silently screamed and spun around, looking behind her.

Defoe stopped his car in front of the house, left the keys in the ignition. The fuel gauge was inaccurate at best and often didn't work at all. He took the little notebook out of the glove compartment and jotted the current odometer reading above the one he'd entered when last he'd filled the tank. Subtract, divide by the fifteen miles per gallon the car averaged . . . there was still six, maybe eight gallons in the tank. Time to start thinking about a fill-up. The high octane fuel the dual overhead camshaft engine thrived on was no longer an easy commodity to find. He put the notebook back in the glovebox, checked the cassette recorder in his breast pocket, and went inside. The cool and tranquil hallway suddenly struck him as cold and forbidding, permeated with a distant, uneasy silence mirrored by brooding portraits passing judgment on their progeny as he ran the gauntlet of their stares. Even Anna, preparing dinner in the kitchen, seemed more formal than usual. *What's happening to us all?* he thought and looked in the morning room for his mother. It was cool and dim there, too. Back in the kitchen Anna said that Mrs. Defoe had gone upstairs a little bit ago, to lie down before dinner. His father, as always, was in his library.

That room was as dark as the rest of the house, as though the sun had set unnoticed by all inside. At first he didn't see him, sitting in his chair by the fireplace, slumped down, looking small in the high-backed club chair. Usually George Defoe sat ramrod straight, and for a fleeting moment Defoe wondered . . .

But his father looked up with a start as his son lightly touched his arm. "Wha—Chase; it's you. Must have dozed off for a moment. Damned long day, and a trying one, too. Not every day you have to plant someone you've known as long as . . ." The elder Defoe noisily refolded the paper that had slipped from his lap to the floor and said, "Fix me a bourbon and water, Chase. And one for yourself."

Defoe poured whiskey in a pair of tumblers and switched on his recorder. "Here you go, Dad." He raised his own drink in his father's direction. "To old soldiers."

"Wha—? Oh, yes, yes. To old soldiers." He waved his glass in the general direction of his son, then took a hefty draught.

Defoe sat on the sofa, at right angles to his father, in the spot his mother usually occupied. "All this history," he said. "Your story of the Elsa, General Kilgallen's tapes, got me thinking about the past. Certain fragments stand out in my mind. All of our minds, I guess. For example, I can remember in minute detail what I was doing when I learned of Kennedy's assassination. The moment of the Challenger disaster. One or two other public events like that. And of course the private ones. Andy's death. My first love affair, the day I graduated from college. High points in our histories."

"Yes. Stands to reason, the highs and lows stand apart from the mundane that makes up the bulk of our lives."

"Uh huh. Of course, you've got more than most of us. Not only because you've lived longer, but you've probably been connected with more of the momentous events of the century than most."

"Oh, I wouldn't say that."

"Well, you at least were *around* for quite a few. Black Friday,

Pearl Harbor, the death of FDR. VE Day." Defoe sat back and sipped his bourbon. "What's your memory of VE Day?"

"VE Day . . . Funny, you know, you're right. Some time in April, damned if I can remember the exact date, and I had to stop for a moment there to think of the year. But I can picture the moment I heard they'd signed, just as sharp as I can see this morning's breakfast. I was in London, just arrived there from Metz. Planned to stop at the embassy, touch base, shave and catch a couple of hours sleep, then head for Switzerland to see Dulles. I never did get to sleep that night. Went out and got gloriously drunk with a crowd from the embassy. London was quite a town that night."

"I can imagine." Defoe tasted his bourbon. "I hear the women over there were pretty grateful, too. Not just on VE Day, but all through the war."

"Oh, sure, Lord, yes. Whatever you've read, it was true. Most of their men off to war, and the few lad's still there not sure if they would be alive the next day." George Defoe snorted. "You young pups in the sixties going on about 'free love.' Hah."

"Yes. Tell me, Dad. While you were over there, that day, how did Mother celebrate?" He watched his father with unblinking intensity across the rim of the heavy cut-crystal tumbler.

The older man's features revealed comprehension of his son's intentions by degrees, the way the shadow of the sun, seen from space, races across the face of the planet, bringing dawn to the sleeping billions below. Puzzlement, recognition, a flicker of fear, then anger, and finally a smile, all in the passage of a blink. "You must have heard the General's account of *his* day in April, eh?" He shook his head, and put his empty glass on the table beside his seat. "I should have realized, earlier today. When you said that his girls came across some tapes over there. I guess it's not so much *what* happened that troubles me, but the fact that he would shout it from the rooftops, for all the world to know."

"Oh, come on, Dad. He hardly did that. I doubt that there are six people alive who could figure out the relationship between the three of you."

"Hell's bells! That old fool. Doing that, to *me*—"

"Dad! General Kilgallen didn't even know you, back then. And from what I gather, it was just that once, never again, in all the years he lived nex—"

"Yes, yes, *yes.* Don't go on with *that* line of reasoning. I've heard it all before. Nothing but, for the past goddamned week, you want to know the truth."

Defoe stood up. "Maybe that's because it *is* the truth. Don't you realize what a blue-nosed hypocrite you are? Stand up, and look me in the eye; tell me that you've not strayed from this ridiculous path of marital fidelity with far greater frequency than my mother ever has. Do that, and then maybe I'll have a little more sympathy for you; you, poor, benighted cuckold!"

George Defoe struggled to his feet and put his face close to his son's, his cheeks blotched scarlet with choler. "Out!" he shouted. "Get *out* of my house!" He pointed at the library door, his hand trembling with rage. "How *dare* you, you bastard whelp—" He turned to the fireplace and snatched a brass-handled poker from the fireset, flailed unseeing at the space around him.

Defoe saw the blind fire of abject rage in his eyes and backed away, knowing that his father was beyond reason. The old man was still cursing as Defoe left the room, the house, and the property.

The pulse was pounding at his temple as he turned in Kit's father's driveway.

The pulse was pounding at her temple as Kit turned in her father's den.

Kronenberger thought she was staring into his eyes as she froze in the center of the room. Nothing to do but burst from the closet and kill her before she spooked and ran.

Defoe pushed the bell and tapped at the glass panes of the front door, then tried the latch. It turned under his grip and he pushed it open, called, "Kit? Whoo-hoo, it's me."

"Chase!" She turned and ran down the hallway toward the front of the house, the towel unwinding as she went, and she grabbed at it, pulling it back up across her chest. "Oh, *my God,"* she sobbed and crushed him to her in the front entryway, hysteria dominating reason.

He put his arms around her and looked over her shoulder,

back to the darkened rear of the house. "Kit! What's the matter?"

She still sobbed, trying to talk, unable, and he brought his hands to her arms, eased her away from him, shook her, said again, "Kit. What's the matter? Tell me. It's okay, now, I'm here."

Kronenberger closed the knife and drew the five-shot revolver from the holster at his ankle, then slipped from the closet and loped across the den to the French door.

As he ran along the side of the house toward the road he extracted a homer from his carryall and paused for five seconds to affix it beneath the Volvo's bumper and activate the transmit switch.

Best laid plans of mice and spooks, he thought, tossing the equipment bag onto the passenger's seat of the Bronco. Too bad there hadn't been time to plant a bug inside the house.

He stopped a quarter mile down the road and removed the handkerchief from his door handle, then lit a Camel. He leaned back in the seat and inhaled, considering the operation. Whatever you do, he thought, *don't violate the Eleventh Commandment: Thou Shalt Not Get Caught.* Exhaling a plume of smoke into the early evening, he smiled and said aloud, "Odin, I wonder if you ever worked the field." Then, to himself, he added, "If you did, then you'll understand why this one is going to cost you extra. And if not, well . . ." He switched the plates again, turned on the headlights, picked up the cellular phone, and put the Bronco in gear. One way or another, Odin was going to pay.

She followed him back along the hall, her one hand clutching the towel to her breast, the other on his back, afraid to break the contact. She took huge, deep breaths, like a diver just risen from the depths of the ocean, and felt the sweet-tasting oxygen replacing the fear that permeated her body.

"Nobody here," he said, turning on the lights as he went, opening doors. His mind was a racing jumble of thoughts and messages, multi-colored lasers crisscrossing the blackness of his cortex. Combat high on adrenaline from her hysteria, and trying to sort out FBI recordings, his father's rage, Jack Brill arranging assignations as he fought off a bookie seeking blood, and overlaying it all, Kit drifting in and out of his day; at Arlington, then here, so tentative about the tape that Sammy found, later, at her Georgetown house, later still back here, listening to the tapes. And now, imagining an intruder. "Are you sure?" he asked, and endured a second attack, swift and sudden, like his father's.

"Sure? *Sure?* God *damn* you, *yes!*" She moved to the desk, turned and pointed to the still-open drawer. "Tell me, what was in that drawer! *Tell* me, Chase!" She began to cry again, bending, holding her face in her hand as she still clutched the towel in the other.

"Hey, okay, okay," he said, moving to her side, putting a tentative arm around her bare shoulder. "I'm on your side." He looked down, saw the drawer, the telephone directory. The tapes were missing.

Kronenberger drove, the cellular receiver at his ear. "The Galleria? Out at Tysons? Sure. But why there? Why can't we meet back at my place. So much more private."

"Think about it, my friend. I can't go prowling around an industrial park in the middle of the night. But if I run into some acquaintance at the mall it will hardly seem notable, let alone noteworthy." Odin drew a deep breath and paused. Millions of little noises, fragmented bits and bytes and microwave sounds that lurk on the edge of audibility filled the brief void. "Don't question and don't argue with me, Eumenides. Not tonight. I've had too much of that these past few days. Just play the game and follow my lead. You were always good at that, don't fail me now. The Galleria Two, forty-five minutes. Lower level, at the elevators." Odin broke the connection and Kronenberger headed up the ramp, goosed the Bronco into the flow of traffic toward Tyson's Corner and the yuppie paradise. Well, he had the tapes, had done what he'd been told. The rest was up to Odin.

"Yes, the tapes are gone. I see that."

Kit sighed, drawing a final deep breath into her lungs, sniffled, wiped her nose with the edge of the towel. "I'm sorry I blew up. It's just that . . . I put the recorder in the drawer, with the tapes, Chase. When I was packing some of

Dad's things. You remember, we left it on the desk. Then Sammy called, while I was in the shower. Oh, *God!*" She moved closer to him, looked around the room. "I ran down here, like *this,* to get a name from Dad's address book, in the drawer. And realized that the tapes and the recorder were gone." She looked up at him. "Chase, I can honestly say that I have never been so terrified in my life. I mean, twenty minutes earlier the tapes were there, and then here I am, practically naked, in this damned house, alone, and I was so sure that someone was . . ."

"Hey, it's over now." He stepped into her and folded her in his arms once again. "Come on, sit down. It's okay, Kit. Whoever it was, he got what he came for."

Defoe led her to the sofa and sat beside her, put his arm around her shoulder as she leaned into him, both staring off into the middle distance, examining separate demons.

"Yukk!" she finally said, easing upright. "My hair feels like a Brillo pad after cleaning the broiler pan. And I'm cold." She stood up and smiled down at Defoe, her eyes red. "I'm okay now. Let me go up and finish my shower." She reached down and took his hand, tugged him up to her level. "Really. Still shook up, but okay, now that you're here. How 'bout helping with the dinner; get Dad's grill out of the basement while I make myself presentable?" She laughed briefly and with little humor. "I bought a dress, at the mall. Thought I'd be glamorous for you. Scratch that idea."

"Kit?" he said, looking at her eyes, "You look terrific." Shook his head. "No, I'm lying, you don't look terrific, not right this minute. But you *are* terrific. Go finish your shower. I'll lock the doors and see about dinner. Then I'll tell you about my day. Not as exciting as yours, but interesting."

He watched her go down the hall and start up the stairs on her tiptoes, bare feet lightly touching the treads. Defoe turned to the French door to check the lock and see that it was secure. *I don't know what I'm going to tell you about my day, but I guess I'll come up with something. I* have *to come up with something, if only for myself.* Disturbing facts, concepts, and suppositions were beginning to coalesce into an explanation of his father's behavior.

THIRTEEN

Kronenberger entered the mall through the same doors that Kit had used a few hours earlier. Unlike Kit he had time to spare; forty-five minutes, Odin had said, and it had taken him less than thirty to reach the Galleria. One of the rules of the game was never hang about, so he went into a brass-and-fern bedecked place called Ruby Tuesday. At least it was dark and crowded and had a bar. He found a seat and ordered a bottle of Beck's, shook his head sadly when he saw how little change he got from a five-dollar bill. In Germany he could buy a case for little more the cost of a bottle in here. The sparkling light, reflected from polished brass and the thousands of glasses suspended in racks overhead, gave the customers an air of glamour and excitement they didn't deserve. *How many of you,* he thought, looking at the pampered women, stopping for a trendy kir after an exhausting day of shopping, *have ever done anything really dangerous? Felt the adrenaline flow, known the sour stink of the sweat that rose from fear?* And the men. Fit from racquetball, tanned from Carribean weekends, lawyers and executives, discussing foreign policy in languid drawls over vodka martinis, well insulated from the men in the field who had to translate their abstract concepts into concrete plans, and then execute them. *How many of you,* he silently asked, *have ever killed a man?* He poured the last of the beer into his glass and signaled the bartender for another. Might as well. Ten more minutes to kill, and he'd earned the second beer.

He walked slowly toward the glass elevator that shuttled shoppers between the three levels of the mall, tuned to the crowd that swirled past him and the shops they wandered in and out of. Cacique was having a sale on French sleep shirts, whatever they were. He read the sign in the plate-glass window as he used its reflection to check his rear. Old habits are the best kind, the ones as automatic as respiration and digestion. He didn't really expect any sort of intrigue, but then the trigger of a disaster was the unexpected. He passed Cignal and Aram, looked across the broad central atrium to the shops on the other side, their names difficult to see through the vegetation that rose toward the clerestory windows forty feet above his head. A place called Gynpes. Pelle Cuir. He couldn't even pronounce their names, let alone guess what they sold. Part of the mystique that justified the ridiculous prices. He went to the railing and looked down at the horseshoe of upholstered seats at the base of the elevator on the lower level. As he watched Odin approached from the opposite direction, passed the seating nook that was edged on either side by lush plantings of tropical greenery. *I see that you, too, are still a careful man,* Kronenberger thought, and smiled. He checked his watch and headed to the escalator, took it to the lower level. Halfway down his eyes met Odin's, rising on the other set of moving stairs. A brief smile flickered across his lips and Kronenberger knew that, yes, his mentor hadn't lost his touch. He had spotted Kronenberger first, and was abandoning the meeting place they had agreed upon. Routine, of course. Either a tap on the phone or a slip by either man could have alerted someone to the prearranged meeting place. He stepped off the escalator, turned, and rode back up to the second level. No need for all of this, of course.

"This is Tyson's Corner, not Moscow," he said, slowing his step to match the other man's.

"Quite true, Randolph. But I am a careful man and like to exercise all available precautions. I assume that you have carried out your assignment?" He stopped and sat on a bench by the Nieman Marcus fountain.

Kronenberger smiled inwardly. Running water is still the surest foil for electronic eavesdropping. *You're a master, Odin,* he thought. "Yes. Was there a doubt?" He reached in his pocket and delivered the three little clear plastic cassettes. "Are you sure this is safe, out here in the open? Wouldn't you rather use a blind drop?"

"Don't toy with me, Randolph. I haven't the time nor the inclination to fence with you. I hope you have something for me to play these things on."

Kronenberger sighed and handed over the recorder. "It was a bit dicey there, at the end. The daughter realized that the tapes were gone and I was trapped in a closet. Luckily the man arrived at the front of the house. She yelled 'Chase' and headed for him while I slipped out the back."

"Don't bore me with details. Go back to your place and wait for me to call. I'm afraid I'm going to have another little chore for you tonight, but I want to listen to these and be absolutely positive that it is necessary. It would be unfortunate to take needless actions." He looked at the tapes resting in the palm of his hand, hefted them as though measuring their worth. "I'll call you in a few hours." He looked at his watch, added, "Let's say ten o'clock." Odin stood up, touched Kronenberger lightly on the arm. "You reek of beer. Stay sober and stay sharp. Any questions?"

"Yes. All these years, I never thought to ask, until today. Eumenides. Who was he?"

"Ah. Study your Greek mythology, Randolph. Not *who,* but *what.* The Furies. The avenging deities that executed curses pronounced on criminals, tortured those with guilty consciences. Carried out the unpleasant sentences handed down. Eumenides means 'the kindly ones,' you know." He smiled. "A euphemism, meant to propitiate, my friend. Expect to hear from me at ten. Eumenides."

Kronenberger watched him disappear in the crowd of shoppers, then turned and headed for his Bronco. He had a stop to make, someone to see. He anticipated, suspecting that he would be asked to perform one more deed before the night was through.

FOURTEEN

Defoe found a salad bowl, large and wooden and roughly carved from some exotic tropical species. A trophy from across the seas. He wiped the dust from it with a damp cloth and put it on the table beside the vegetables.

She'd said the grill was in the basement. He went down the stairs and unlatched the Bilco door and awkwardly carried the contraption up the few steps to the backyard, then wheeled it around to the brick patio outside the den. There was no gauge on the propane tank, but it felt heavy enough to be sufficient for a couple of steaks. He found the switch for the outside light in the den and examined the grill. It had a layer of those things called "lava rocks" where one usually put charcoal briquets and was covered with a patina of dust. A spark lighter and a long fork dangled from the valve on leather thongs. He cracked the valve and lit the gas, stepped back as the dust ignited with a soft poof and a flash of yellow flame. Defoe was a purist and liked his steaks cooked under the broiler of a stove, preferably a stove that was inside a house in a room called a kitchen. However, he had also eaten steaks that had been cooked outside, over charcoal fires, mesquite wood, and once, during an unfortunate camping trip, damp pinecones. Lava rock would be a first, he thought, and turned up the flame. The unexamined life is not worth living. He wondered if Socrates had known about lava rocks when he'd said that, and went back inside.

Time to force both his father and Jack Brill, as well as the tantalizing and conflicting emotions concerning Kit, from his mind and focus on the more immediate question. What was on the tapes that would make either one of the men risk so much to get them?

Kit stood under the rushing water, her face turned up into the stinging blast. It was safe inside the warm cocoon of the shower stall, and she forced herself to relax with slow and measured breaths, letting the hot water flush the tension from her body. She closed her eyes and visualized the stress and fear coursing away, down the drain.

Kit rinsed the shampoo from her hair, properly this time, and wrapped a fresh towel around her head, then dried the rest of her body. Nothing bad could happen, not with Chase downstairs. Whoever stole the tapes had gotten what they wanted, and were gone.

She ran her fingers through her short hair, damp-combing it in front of the mirror, then went into her old bedroom and put on her new clothes. New clothes always cheered her up. The silk slipped and shimmied against her bare skin, feeling sexy as hell, the way it should. She quickly put on the Lancôme foundation, brushed just a touch of gloss on her lips, then concentrated on emphasizing her large, dark eyes.

The three-inch heels would put her at eye level with Chase; not a bad place to be, she thought, coming down the stairs. The terror of a few minutes ago was not gone, but it had been pushed into some small space in her memory, securely shut away. She could hear him in the kitchen, went through the doorway, and found him at the sink, washing potatoes. He turned and took her in, slowly checking the separate parts, nodding in approval at the whole. "You look absolutely ravishing. I'm both flattered and impressed."

"That's the whole idea." She smiled. "Why else would a gal spend eight hundred bucks on a dress?" She laughed and twirled, belling the dress for him, showing a flash of leg before crossing the room and reaching out for the potatoes. "Here, let me do that."

"Done," he said. "Or nearly so. Just have to rub a little of this marvelous olive oil on them. The oven's already heated and waiting." He opened the oven door and quickly put the potatoes inside.

"What was in that pan?"

"Rock salt. I found a bag down in the cellar when I was hunting for the grill. If you bake your spuds on a bed of rock salt, it helps to draw the moisture out. We'll stab 'em with a fork at halftime, to let the steam escape. Makes them nice and fluffy."

"Ah, you seem to know something about cooking, then."

"Learned a few tricks, here and there." He looked at his watch. "I took the Pommard out of the 'fridge and opened it. Should be aerated and at the proper temperature by the time we're ready for it." He washed the oil from his hands and dried them on a dish towel. "When you live alone you either succumb to frozen dinners or learn to cook."

Kit began to mix the salad greens, tearing them into bite-sized pieces. "Living alone. Something I've never, ever done. Even after Dee died I had Sammy with me. What's it like? Don't you get . . . lonely?"

"No. Well, sure, at times. But I spend a good bit of time away on business, and I have a lot of friends." He leaned against the counter and watched her work. "There are times when I miss a steady . . . companion."

"You don't have anybody; a . . . a regular . . ."

"Lover? Not at the moment. There have been a few since my wife and I divorced, but I am currently, as the actors say, 'between engagements.' I turned the grill on, by the way; lit it about fifteen minutes ago. I hope that's the proper thing to do. I'm not checked out to operate one of those things."

"Well then, pour us a couple of Scotches while I toss this salad, and we'll go take a look at it." She draped the dish towel over the bowl, then put it in the refrigerator and got the steaks and dressing out while Defoe turned the potatoes and poked them with a fork.

The rocks glowed red and the gas burned blue in the cool evening, adding a psychological warmth to the outdoors. "Looks fine to me, Chase," she said, forked the meat from the platter to the grill and turned her attention to the sky. "What a night! Look at the stars. That's what I love about it out here. In the city it's so bright that you really can't appreciate the heavens. You live out in the country, don't you?"

"Yes, about fifty miles from Philadelphia. Even more rural

than here. Are you warm enough in that dress? I'd think your bare shoulders would be frozen."

"They are. Let's go inside and sit. We can keep an eye on the steaks from there. I don't know what I was thinking of, earlier today, when I suggested that we do the steaks outside. June, I guess."

They sat on either end of the sofa, turned a few degrees toward each other, and sipped their drinks. "Well," Kit said, "I bought some steaks, bought some clothes, and had the wits scared out of me today." She turned and smiled at Defoe. "What did you do?"

He leaned forward and put his glass on the low table. "Took that tape to the FBI, by way of Doug Winston at the Justice Department. He introduced me to the head of the FBI's ID section, a man who took me down to their lab, where we got a voiceprint of the General's visitor who came through those doors. The technician couldn't do anything to enhance the quality, so we don't know what he said. But he managed to produce a rough voiceprint that we can compare with any suspects we might come up with." Defoe hesitated before he added, "I have to tell you, Kit, that I already had him compare one voice to it."

"Oh? Who?"

"Your husband. I, ah . . . I recorded Jack, at lunch today, Kit. I wasn't going to tell you, but you have the right to know. See, it's a cruel reality that almost all murder victims know their killers. And more often than not, money is the motive. You told me that you and Sammy were the one's who inherit your father's estate, but I couldn't see either one of you doing that to him, so I focused on the next person in line. Not a very nice thing to do, I admit. And futile. The technician couldn't match Jack to the voice on the tape." He looked over at her. "Not too mad, I hope?"

Kit swirled the ice in her glass with a slender finger, not looking at Defoe. After a few moments' reflection she said, "No, I suppose not, Chase." She sighed. "I mean, I guess I'm a little hurt, that . . . No; you don't know Jack, never met him before today, and I suppose that you only did it for me. For me, and Dad's memory. You're trying to help, I can't fault you for that." She looked up and smiled. Stood up and walked to the French doors, looked out at the grill. "Time to flip the steaks."

She came back inside and finished her drink, saying, "Hey, where are we going to eat? I never even gave it a thought. Come on, help me set the table, they'll be done in a couple of minutes."

The General had always eaten his solitary meals in the kitchen, and after looking in at the dark and musty dining room, its heavy Victorian table and chairs cloaked in dust, Kit and Defoe decided to do the same. She found a candle and put it between the two places she had set with Corelle and stainless steel on the scarred and battered wooden tabletop.

He scooped the potatoes from the oven with a hot mitt, then went to the grill and brought the steaks in while Kit tonged salad from the big bowl into a pair of smaller ones. She sat down and surveyed the table as he poured the wine. In Georgetown she had Irish linen and English silver, and when Jack Brill entertained she set their table for twelve with Waterford crystal and Wedgwood china. "Not very romantic," she said, "is it?"

"The hell it ain't," he replied, reaching across to briefly squeeze her hand. "I ate an awful lot of peanut butter sandwiches at this table, drank an awful lot of milk." He raised his wineglass to her, held her eyes. "Romance, after all, is mostly made of memories."

FIFTEEN

Kronenberger took the Beltway north, passed the exit that would take him to Langley and the CIA, past the exit that would take him to his building in the industrial park, and crossed the Potomac into Maryland. He drove past Burning Tree and through Bethesda, drove down dark and dirty streets to an area of tired buildings with tenants that sold used auto parts, janitorial supplies, and wholesale restaurant china. The bar on the corner was a three-story cube, faced with squares of a pink-and-gray artificial stone that had fallen off in several places, revealing the cement block skeleton beneath. Its aluminum triple-track windows had long ago oxidized to a mottled, tubercular gray, and its flat roof sprouted half a dozen different television antennae, external evidence of the rooms for rent above the first-floor saloon.

He parked in the weedy lot behind the building, eased the Bronco into a space between a pickup with ladder racks and a dozen black and chrome Harleys clustered together at the edge of the sidewalk. An illuminated red-and-white plastic Pepsi sign with black stick-on letters proclaiming Nick's Tavern jutted from the building above the door. A red neon Coors sign with a bad transformer buzzed noisily in the window, reminding Kronenberger of summer flies trapped between glass and screen. He bought a long neck Bud and turned, resting his elbows on the bar as he surveyed the room.

The bikers occupied the rear half of the thirty-foot-square barroom, were clustered at half a dozen round Formica tables, the tops a brown forest of empty bottles. He sipped his beer and studied the men. Mostly kids, mid to late twenties, their women five to ten years younger than that. One or two of the men had streaks of gray in their long pony tails, and wisps of white in their beards. He walked across the room to one of them, sitting at the fringe of the noise and action, talking to an overweight girl in a tight black T-shirt with orange Harley wings rolling over the contours of her breasts. She looked up at Kronenberger and smiled, showed a broken tooth. The older man squinted through smoke that rose from the cigarette in the corner of his mouth and lazily scratched beneath his chin. His nose had been broken once and badly set and he had a strip of black leather tied around his head, holding his shoulder-length hair away from his face.

"Hey there," Kronenberger said, easing an empty chair away from the table and putting his foot up on the seat. "Looking for the Clipper. You wouldn't know where he is, would you?"

The biker drew on his cigarette until the coal glowed. He took it from his lips, tapped the ash on the tabletop, and let the smoke slowly drift from his nostrils as he said, "You a cop? Probation?" He examined Kronenberger's tweed hacking jacket, its leather buttons, then picked up a nearly empty bottle of beer and tipped it to his lips, keeping eye contact with the man who stood over him.

"Get serious, chief. Just a friend of Bob's. A friend who wants to do a little business."

The biker chewed the corner of his lip, then stood up. "You got a name, friend?" he asked, pulling a worn trucker's wallet from his hip pocket and zipping it open. It was attached to his wide leather belt by a heavy chrome chain that swung lazily against the leg of his Levi's as he searched inside, then extracted a creased business card. He turned it over, looked at the number scrawled on the back in pencil.

"Kronenberger."

"Sit down a minute." The biker turned and went to the pay phone fastened to the wall beside the doorway to the men's room. A shout and then laughter erupted from a table in the corner, followed by the sound of breaking glass. The bartender looked up from the other side of the room, then went back to his conversation with a man in a plaid shirt and a yellow Caterpillar tractor hat.

"You a Jew?"

"What?"

"Kronenberger," the girl said. "That's a Jew name, ain't it?"

"Do I look like a Jew?"

She picked at the paper label on an empty bottle with a long and deep-red fingernail. "I don't know. What's a Jew look like?"

Kronenberger reached in his pants pocket and took out half a dozen fives, folded once. He peeled one off and said, "Go buy us a beer" as he handed the money across the table to her.

She looked at him for twenty seconds, then got up and walked toward the bar. Kronenberger briefly watched her buttocks rise and fall in the tight jeans before turning his attention to the man on the phone.

The man on the phone watched them as he talked, then let the receiver dangle on its armored cable and walked back to the table. "Wants to talk to you," he said, jerking his head toward the telephone.

"Clipper?"

"Hey, Mr. K., my main man! What's happening?"

"I want to see you, talk a little business."

"Yeah? You looking to deal some crystal?"

"Get serious. I may have something for you, later on."

"Yeah? What you got?"

"Maybe a little field work, just like old times."

"No shit? All *right.*"

"Hey. You're not strung out, are you? This is serious business I'm talking about, Bob."

"No, no, I'm okay. You know I don't use that shit."

"Sure."

"So what's the setup?"

"Stop by my place, the store, in a couple of hours. I should have the details by then."

"Couple of hours? Shit, I got to pick up my old lady, go somewheres. My new old lady. Can this business wait?"

"Hey, Clipper. It's me, Kronenberger. What the fuck do you mean, 'can it wait.' Besides, it's worth a dime. Is whatever else you got planned that important?"

"Ten? No shit! Hey, my man, I'll be there. Okay if I bring my old lady along?"

"On an operation? Come on, son. You know better than that."

"No, no, I mean over to your place."

"Yes, sure, okay. Don't do anything before you get there, Bob. I mean it. I want you straight for this one, you can't go into this operation messed up."

"Yeah, yeah. Hey, Mr. K., I'm straight as a broke dick dog. I ain't no speed freak. I just deal; you know that."

"Sure. You keep telling yourself that, Snips. Two hours, my place." Kronenberger hung up the phone and went back to the table. The biker looked up at him, waiting for an explanation.

"Thanks," Kronenberger said. He picked up the third bottle of beer on the table and took a small sip, put it down. He turned to the blond girl. "You want to know how to lose twenty pounds of that ugly fat? Cut off your head."

He left the bottle of beer on the table, left the bar, and headed back toward his darkened building behind the industrial park. As he drove through the deepening night he swore softly to himself, hoping that the Clipper had not decayed to the point where he was no longer useful. Kronenberger did not want to be the one to execute Odin's instructions.

The CIA employs a great many people with diversified skills, and can call upon them to perform many of the routine tasks that make up the Agency's day-to-day operations. The CIA also maintains a formal list of personnel, whose clearances are kept up to date, for "special services." They are not carried on any government payroll and cannot be connected to the Agency. They work as free-lance contractors and are rumored to have done things that are proscribed by Acts of Congress. There is a third list of individuals, an informal list that is not written anywhere, or even acknowledged by the official world, but which, nonetheless, exists. It is made up of operatives who have been terminated from formal employment because of liabilities that exceed their assets.

In the case of the Clipper, or Snips as he was sometimes known, he became a liability to The Company when he developed too great an enthusiasm for his work, and out of his enthusiasm gained unwanted notoriety in the clandestine community.

He was run by Kronenberger during the later stages of the Vietnamese conflict, moving through South Vietnam, Laos, and Cambodia, doing the bidding of his handler. The Clipper extracted information from the local populace and sent it back up the pipeline to his case officer in Saigon.

Before Kronenberger met him in a whorehouse in Bangkok during a riotous week of R&R, the Marine had been a communications sergeant. Stringing wire through the steaming jungles held little excitement for the twenty-year-old from Baltimore, and Kronenberger, who made it a practice to scout for talent in the bars and brothels of Bangkok, Singapore, and Saigon itself, found him a willing recruit. Long after he had graduated from handling radio traffic for the CIA he continued to wear the leather sheath on his belt that held a lockback lineman's knife and pair of heavy-duty wire cutters. Big enough and sharp enough to cut through an inch-thick telephone cable, the young sergeant quickly found that they could just as easily sever the Achilles' tendon at the base of a man's leg. This operation not only caused a great deal of discomfort, but it removed the ability to walk, and the Clipper was free to either question the man at his leisure or turn his attention to other prisoners, reassured that the ones he had clipped weren't going anywhere faster than a crawl. But it was later, when he started using the lockback with excessive enthusiasm during his interrogations, started taking trophies, that Kronenberger had acceded to higher authorities and terminated his agent, or in the parlance of The Company, "effectuated his disposal."

Disposal by the CIA did not necessarily mean a cessation in contact between Kronenberger and his youthful protégé, and the case officer found occasional "off the books" employment for the ex-Marine after he returned home.

The Clipper returned home with a fondness for both the excitement and the exotic drugs so plentiful in Southeast Asia, and soon discovered that they were equally available stateside, if you knew where to look.

The Pagan's, an outlaw motorcycle club styled after the West Coast Hell's Angels, was formed in 1959 in Prince

George County, Maryland, a county that abuts the eastern edge of the District of Columbia. Other chapters of the club were later chartered along the East Coast and soon there were Pagans from Connecticut to Florida.

The thirteen founding fathers became known as the Mother Club, and its members wear a black number 13 on the back of their sleeveless denim jackets to honor them. While the Pagan membership is involved in a variety of criminal activities, running from dealing in stolen motorcycle parts to homicide, their principal business has been the manufacture, transportation, and marketing of methamphetamines, and their principal diversion has been beating people. Both appealed to Bob the Clipper, and he soon found himself a busy young veteran.

Kronenberger unlocked the back door and put the MacDonald's bag on his desk. The homer on the Volvo was faithfully transmitting its FM signal and Kronenberger readjusted the receiver after carrying it from the showroom to his office in the rear of the building. It was a new piece of equipment; "state of the art" the salesmen always said when touting the latest in high-tech gear. Supposedly you could follow a vehicle without ever having it in your sight; the radio signal was translated, by a computer chip inside the receiver, into a winking light on the cathode tube, moving right or left as the vehicle made its turns. That's what the manufacturer claimed. Be nice to test it out tonight, see just how well it worked. Only, if things went the way they were supposed to, the homer fastened beneath the Volvo's bumper would stay right where it was, until later, when the Clipper shut it down and brought it back.

Kronenberger uncapped a bottle of Beck's and sat down at his desk, took the holster off his ankle and the pistol from the holster. He sipped the beer as he opened the cylinder and ejected the five .32 caliber cartridges. He stuck his thumb in the open breech and squinted down the barrel. The light from the fluorescent tubes overhead reflected off his thumbnail and illuminated the bore, shining brightly, showing the lands and grooves in crisp relief. He took a tube of Rig from the center drawer of the desk and squeezed an inch of the slippery grease onto a piece of old undershirt, worked it into the moving parts of the weapon. Then he wiped the weapon down with a dry rag, reloaded, and put it back under the surface of his desk in the special holder screwed there. Throughout the building there were equally well-concealed weapons at strategic locations. In Korea, as a draftee grunt, he had survived by watching his rear. In Southeast Asia, as a CIA case officer, he had flourished by covering his ass.

He opened the yellow foam clamshell and extracted the Big Mac, then settled down to watch the winking light and wait for Odin's call.

SIXTEEN

Defoe poured the last of the Pommard into their glasses as Kit cleared the table. "Make a deal with you," she said, scraping plates. "I'll clean up in here, do the dishes, if you'll go make a fire in the den." She shook her shoulders, added, "It's chilly in here."

"Not surprising, since you're half naked."

"Ah, you finally noticed! No, seriously, it feels damp."

"Yes. We're supposed to get showers tonight. Where's the firewood?"

"Should be some right there beside the fireplace. There's a stack outside, around the corner. Maybe if it's going to rain, you better bring a couple of more logs in."

"Will do." Defoe found some tinder-dry cedar shingles in a copper coal scuttle and broke them into slivers, then built a rick on a crumpled sheet of newspaper. The logs were split ash and caught in a matter of minutes; he had a cheery fire crackling by the time Kit came through the door with a bottle and two snifters.

She glanced at the fireplace as she put the glasses on the table in front of the sofa. "Nice work, Dan'l Boone. Look what I found, back behind the Scotch." She held up a bottle of Courvoisier and smiled. "Nothing like a little Napoleon brandy to finish off a meal."

"Yes," Defoe answered, shoving a log back from the hearth with his toe. "Candy is dandy, but liquor is quicker." He crossed the room to the sofa. "Before dinner, when I confessed to doing a voiceprint on your husband, you said that I didn't know him. True, but I'd like to. I got the impression he was involved in work similar to mine, although I don't know when. He told me, down in the cellar when we were shooting his pistol, that he'd been a lawyer with the National Security Agency, knew a lot of their agents. I'm just wondering when that was; maybe we have some common acquaintances." He didn't tell her that the NSA, headquartered a few miles away at Fort Meade, was the largest and most secretive of the intelligence agencies, had a budget several times the size of the CIA's, and ran worldwide listening posts, both from the ground and from orbiting satellites. It was on the very frontiers of technology, and had no human agents. Defoe wondered why Brill had lied.

Kit poured a splash of brandy into the snifters and handed one to Defoe. "Oh, I don't think so, Chase. That was before we were married, and he'd been in private law practice for some time by then. I got the impression it was the CIA, though, not the one you said. Or DIA. Is there such a thing?"

"Defense Intelligence Agency. Operates out of the Pentagon."

"Maybe. It was one of those alphabetic spy organizations." She raised the brandy to her nose and inhaled. "But it was a long time ago. He's ten years older than we are, Chase."

"Ah." He swirled the amber liquid and warmed it with his hands. "How did you two meet?"

Kit sat on the sofa, in the center, and put her feet up on the coffee table. "Come and sit down," she said, patting the cushion beside her, "and I'll tell you." She took a swallow of her brandy and watched the flames dance along the surface of the logs. "Dee died in '78, when Sammy was ten. Things were awful, financially. Dee's business had finally taken off, and there was lots of money coming in, but he had borrowed heavily to get it going, even against his life insurance. And without him the business just crumbled to the ground. Luckily our mortgage was insured, so it was paid off with his death. But that's all we had, the house. Jack had handled all the business's start-up papers for Dee, and I didn't know any other lawyers, so I turned to him. I was desperate; I didn't finish college, had never worked a day in my life, and suddenly I was responsible for myself and a ten-year-old child. Well, Jack helped me sell the house, and advised me on what to do with the money from it, checked up on us from time to time. Sammy loved him from the word go. He and I started seeing each other, the three of us at first. The zoo, that sort of thing. He was at the end of a very messy divorce, a horrible custody battle over *his* daughters, and I think we became a substitute family for him. His wife had taken off with the children, he didn't know where . . . It was awful. Anyway, he got me out of my funk over Dee's death, and as I said, Sammy loved him." Kit turned to Defoe and laughed. "Between the two of them, they broke down my resistance, and I said yes. Barely a year after Dee died the three of us honeymooned in Acapulco." She finished her brandy and refilled her glass, offered the bottle to Defoe, who shook her off. "Sammy was very close to Dee, Chase. I told you that, didn't I? Anyway, Jack has been awfully good to her, good *for* her. She's transferred the relationship she had with her father to Jack." She sighed and gazed at the fire. "It was a lucky day for both of us when he came along. I was so naive, in many ways.

"Your mother was an absolute brick. I don't know how we'd have gotten through those first few days, without Aunt Mary. Your father, too. Ever since Mom died Dad was . . . distant. He never really got over her death." She sipped her brandy, swirling it, looking into the glass, at the flickering flames reflected in the liquor. "You said something earlier today, about it being—what? *Warmer* over here? More homey? Funny, I felt the same way about *your* parents. Mom was great, of course, but Aunt Mary was a close second for me. And your dad . . . He treated me more like a daughter than my own father did." Kit shook her head. "Uncle George always had a new penny in his pocket for me, or would send me off to the kitchen with one of his fancy envelopes, sealed with a great glob of red sealing wax, and that cook you had—remember Belinda?—she'd open it up and read the message and give me some treat or other. While Dad was always after me to stand up straight, be a good soldier, children should be seen and not heard, don't speak unless you're spoken to."

Defoe smiled and put his snifter on the table. "Sounds like a perfect description of *my* father. I think it's a just case of the grass being greener on the other side of the fence." He got up and tossed another section of split ash on the fire, sending a cascade of sparks up the chimney, swirling and dancing like a host of fireflies.

"I guess so." Kit sat up, put her feet on the floor, and turned to him as he sat back down beside her. "Something's wrong between them, isn't there, Chase? Aunt Mary and Uncle George, I mean. I can't exactly put my finger on it, but there's a tension there. Sammy noticed it, at the cemetery today."

Defoe drank the last of his brandy, rolled it in his mouth before he swallowed. "Yes." He carefully put the glass on the table. "You remember, Kit, your father's story about being wounded, and the mystery woman he met while he was in the hospital. Madam X, the girl who helped him find and buy this house."

"Yes," she said, leaning back and closing her eyes. "Such a lovely story. And I never thought Dad had a romantic bone in his body."

"Well, bits of it seemed vaguely familiar to me, and when I left here, after we heard the tapes, it all fell into place as I walked back across the fields. Kit, the mystery woman was my mother."

"No!" Kit sat up, wide-eyed, and turned to him. "You're serious, aren't you?"

He nodded. "I asked her about it, this afternoon. It turns out that that's where Sammy's transcript disappeared to. Your dad took it over there, asked her to read it, and give him permission to include it in the book. Very gallant. Anyway, every word of it was true. As seen through the General's eyes, but she confirmed the basic facts."

"Oh, *Chase!* My father, and Aunt Mary, having a wartime romance. It's just too, too wonderful!" She poured a little brandy in her glass, and refilled Defoe's.

"Yes, I suppose it is. Unfortunately, my father got hold of it, and flew into a rage."

"Oh, no!"

"Oh, yes. I, ahh . . . suspected *my* wife of a couple of . . . indiscretions, while I was off in foreign climes, but I never really knew, nor did she confess, so I can't say how I would have reacted. But I'd like to think I would have been more understanding than my father was. It happened, after all, nearly fifty years ago. And he was in Europe, apparently had been for some time, judging from your father's account of the affair. Anyway, I think Dad's being a bit of a bluestocking about the whole thing. Overreacting."

Kit turned to him and put her hand on his arm. "I suppose," she said. "But everybody reacts differently to that sort of thing. Maybe if you don't think of the other person as being capable of something like that it comes as more of a shock." She looked down into her snifter, studying the dark liquid. "I'm hardly an expert on the subject, Chase, but I did . . . *stray* once. I've only known, in the biblical sense, four men. You, and Dee. Jack, of course. And, when Dee was in Vietnam . . ." Kit sighed, and looked up, into Defoe's eyes. "I met a guy, and I was lonely, Dee had been over there for almost a year, and . . . well, we wound up in bed. And every afternoon after that, for about a week. Then one day, we were lying there and heard a report on the radio about some battle or other, maybe it was the Tet Offensive, I don't remember. But I had this awful image of my husband dying as I lay rutting with a stranger." A tear slid out of the corner of Kit's eye and ran down her cheek. She touched it with her finger and brushed it away. "I threw him out. Dee was rotated home about six weeks later, and I agonized for days before I finally told him about it. Turns out, for us, it was the right decision. It made our marriage stronger. But for others? I don't know. Maybe, for your parents . . . They are a different generation, Chase. Different people. But I'm glad I told Dee. Then, and even more, now. It would kill me, now, if I hadn't." She smiled and blinked back the other tears, swallowed some brandy, then laughed at herself. "They say confession is good for the soul."

Defoe raised his snifter to his lips. "Indeed they do. But it's not necessarily such a good idea to put the confession in writing. I hope you didn't enter your indiscretion in a diary for Sammy to read when she grew up."

Kit looked at him, puzzled.

"Apparently she ran across a diary not too long ago, in which you'd reported in rather graphic detail the activities of your sixteenth summer."

Kit flushed, the color spreading from her neck up to her

cheeks, then she laughed. "The little witch! I stopped keeping a diary when I went off to Vassar. I didn't even realize that it still existed. I wonder where she found it. She *told* you about it?"

"Yes, this morning, when we were walking over to my house. Speaking of shocks, it came as a bit of a one for me, realizing that the innocent child I'd corrupted had set it all down blow by blow. A shock, too, to hear about it from her grown daughter. It doesn't seem all that long ago."

"No, it doesn't, does it? Only the way I remember it, I was the one who did most of the corrupting. Not that you weren't a most willing accomplice." Kit raised the snifter to her lips, swallowed, and wriggled against the soft leather cushions. "God, what a little Peyton Place we live in. All this steamy sex. And your father flipped out when he read Dad's account of what happened? That's sad. I mean, I love them both, I don't like to see them squabble."

Defoe laughed, but it was without humor. "It's a bit more than that, I'm afraid. Mom said that when he learned about it he flew into a rage, snatched up his hat and walking stick and stormed out. She said he wanted to *confront* your father. I'm afraid that maybe he did. From the way she described his state of mind, he was perfectly capable of coming over here and . . . killing the General."

"Oh, my God, *no,* Chase. You can't mean it!"

He got up and walked over to the fireplace, stirred the coals with the poker and put the last log on. *The trouble with ash,* he thought, *is that it burns so fast.* He came back to the sofa and took the cassette recorder out of his pocket. "Listen to this," he said as he cued the tape and picked up his snifter. He remained standing, looking down at Kit as she in turn lowered her eyes to the machine.

> Here you go, Dad. To old soldiers.
>
> Who—? Oh, yes, yes. To old soldiers.
>
> All this history, Your story of the Elsa, General Kilgallen's tapes, got me thinking about the past. Certain fragments stand out in my mind. All of our minds, I guess. For example, I can remember in minute detail what I was doing when I learned of Kennedy's assassination. The moment

of the Challenger disaster. One or two other public events like that. And of course the private ones. Andy's death. My first love affair, the day I graduated from college. High points in our histories.

Yes. Stands to reason, the highs and lows stand apart from the mundane that makes up the bulk of our lives.

Uh huh. Of course, you've got more than most of us. Not only because you've lived longer, but you've probably been connected with more of the momentous events of the century than most.

Oh, I wouldn't say that.

Well, you at least were around for quite a few. Black Friday, Pearl Harbor, the death of FDR. VE Day. What's your memory of VE Day?

VE Day . . . Funny, you know, you're right. Some time in April, damned if I can remember the exact date, and I had to stop for a moment there to think of the year. But I can picture the moment I heard they'd signed, just as sharp as I can see this morning's breakfast. I was in London, just arrived there from Metz. Planned to stop at the embassy, touch base, shave and catch a couple of hours sleep, then head for Switzerland to see Dulles. I never did get to sleep that night. Went out and got gloriously drunk with a crowd from the embassy. London was quite a town that night.

I can imagine. I hear the women over there were pretty grateful, too. Not just on VE Day, but all through the war.

Oh, sure, Lord, yes. Whatever you've read, it was true. Most of their men off to war, and the few lad's still there not sure if they would be alive the next day. You young pups in the sixties going on about "free love." Hah.

Yes. Tell me, Dad. While you were over there, that day, how did Mother celebrate?

You must have heard the General's account of his day in April, eh? I should have realized, earlier today. When you said that his girls came across some tapes over there. I guess it's not so much what happened that troubles me, but the fact that he would shout it from the rooftops, for all the world to know.

Oh, come on, Dad. He hardly did that. I doubt that there are six people alive who could figure out the relationship between the three of you.

Hell's bells! That old fool. Doing that, to me—

Dad! General Kilgallen didn't even know you, back then. And from what I gather it was just that once, never again, in all the years he lived nex—

Yes, yes, yes. Don't go on with that line of reasoning. I've heard it all before. Nothing but, for the past goddamned week, you want to know the truth.

Maybe that's because it is the truth. Don't you realize what a blue-nosed hypocrite you are? Stand up, and look me in the eye; tell me that you've not strayed from this ridiculous path of marital fidelity with far greater frequency than my mother ever has. Do that, and then maybe I'll have a little more sympathy for you; you, poor, benighted cuckold!

Out! Get out of my house! How *dare* you, you bastard whelp—

Defoe touched the stop button on the recorder. "Those last sounds were my father grabbing a poker from the fire set and thrashing at me with it. I never understood the expression 'blind with rage' before. I really don't think he could see me, standing there. I don't think he realized that I had turned and left him there, flailing at empty air."

He sat beside Kit on the sofa, picked up the snifter she had refilled, and took a swallow. "You heard the rage in his voice. He could have done it."

"Oh, God; *no,* Chase. Not Uncle George."

"Well, we'll know, tomorrow, one way or the other." He put down his brandy and turned to her, his voice cracking with emotion. "I made that recording with the intention of comparing it to the voiceprint at the FBI."

Kit put her hand on the back of his neck and her head against his cheek. "No, Chase. Not your *father.*"

"I have to know, Kit. I haven't thought about what I'll do if they match, but I have to know."

She raised her face to his, her eyes shining. She put her hand on his cheek. "Poor baby," she said, and kissed him.

SEVENTEEN

The Clipper killed the Harley, flipped the kickstand out with the toe of his boot, and eased the black helmet from his head. After the roar of the engine the silence rang in his ears, a white noise that blocked the voice of the girl on the seat behind him.

"Bob-*bee,*" she said again, shaking her long red hair out as she removed her helmet, "what *is* this place?"

"Huh?" He turned in the saddle. "It's a warehouse, what the fuck does it look like? You never saw an industrial park before?"

"Oh, *sure.*" She dragged out the word, trying for sarcasm. "Only, like, in the *night* time? What; are you going to knock it *over,* or something?"

"Hey, can it. Get off the bike, and can it." He put the ignition key in his pocket and smacked her ass, once, hard. "Just shut up and do what I tell you and maybe Daddy will have a treat for his little girl." He grinned at her. His teeth were blue-white and even and had been made for him in the dental lab at Camp Pendleton. Set, as they were, behind full lips surrounded by a jet-black beard and long, matching hair, they gave him a wild, piratical look. The earring helped.

Kronenberger heard the motorcycle and opened the heavy steel door that looked out on twenty feet of sun-crazed macadam, six feet of weedy gravel, and ten of rusty chain-link fence.

"Mr. K," the biker said, slapping and grabbing the extended hand in a buddy grip. "Long time no see. This here's Willy," he added, nodding at the girl and shouldering his way into the building. She was an even six feet tall in her black engineer boots; four inches shorter and a hundred and thirty pounds lighter than the Clipper. She wore faded jeans and her butt twitched as she sauntered across the concrete floor behind the Clipper. "Wilhelmina. Her old man married some kind of Kraut when he was over there." He took off his leather jacket and dropped it on the desk, then looked around the ten-by-twenty room, its bare block walls unadorned by posters of product and calendars of undraped women. The gray-enameled industrial-strength shelving, stacked high with inventory, was attraction enough for any customer with the credentials to be there. "Same old shit," he said, flopping onto the sofa, one denim-clad leg bouncing up over the arm as he threw his own arms along the back, effectively monopolizing the entire seven feet of its width. "Still got a cold Beck's or two in the box there?"

Kronenberger looked down at the big man sprawled across the dark upholstery. Size twelve engineer boots, greasy jeans, black T-shirt with some biker shit printed across the front, topped by the sleeveless denim jacket with arcane patches sewn across its front and back. "Colors," they called them. An Iron Cross, SS lightning bolts, an enameled death's head on the lapels. The back had PAGANS in six-inch pseudo-Gothic lettering across the shoulders, the number 13 centered on his spine, and just below, targeting his kidneys, MC. "Really into it, aren't you?" he asked, handing him a foil-topped beer.

"Hey, got to have backup, my friend. Since The Company cut me loose, I had to join the B Team." The Clipper twisted the top off the bottle, held the cap between his thumb and forefinger, and sighted, one-eyed, at the metal wastebasket beside the desk for a second before tossing it into the container with a curiously delicate motion. "Doesn't pay as good as the outfit did. But the work is steadier." He blinked and shook his head, the way a club fighter works off a punch he'd failed to slip, then rolled his shoulders and tilted the green bottle above his throat.

"She old enough to drink?" Kronenberger looked at the girl and smiled. She had mismatched eyes, one green, one blue, and smooth freckled skin stretched across high cheekbones, a look more Hibernian than Aryan.

"Oh, she's old enough, yeah, Mr. K. Only she likes candy better than booze. Isn't that right, little girl?" He looked up at her and grinned, eased a small plastic envelope out of his denim jacket, tossed it to Kronenberger. "Give her a beer, Mr. K. If she's a real good girl, maybe she can have a little treat, later on. What's this operation you got for me? I can't sit around all night, you know."

Kronenberger put the envelope in the center drawer of his desk, watched Willy watch him do it, then opened the little refrigerator and handed her a beer. "You've hit the big time, have you, Clipper? A dime isn't enough to get you to sit around all night?"

"Oh, hey, come on, my man. You wasn't serious about the dime." The Clipper sat up, got up, stood on the hard concrete floor between his new lady and his old boss. "You are, aren't you?" He finished the beer and dropped it in the wastebasket, took Willy by the arm and led her into the hall. "That's the pisser, right there," he said, pointing to a door toward the front of the building. "Go do what little girls do, and take your time."

"Bob-*bee,*" she said, wrenching her arm away from his grip, "you can be so uncouth at times. If you want to talk to him, just say so. You don't need to send me off to the ladies' room. Besides, I only just now took a sip of beer. I don't *need* to tinkle."

The Clipper waited until she closed the bathroom door behind her before turning to Kronenberger. "Stupid cunt. Tell me about this operation."

The retired CIA officer looked at his watch, then shook a cigarette out of his pack and into his mouth. "Take it easy, son. Slow down, calm down. Remember what I taught you?"

"Yeah, yeah. 'If you don't have time to do it right, you don't have time to do it over.' Hey, I ever let you down?" He watched the man thumb his Zippo and light his smoke. "Over there, all that time out in the fuckin' jungle, only white man for a hundred miles, I ever let you down? And back here, the shit jobs you handed me. Ever' damn one carried out by the numbers."

"Yes. But don't forget the garbage trucks I had to send

along behind you. Sometimes you left awful messes, Clipper."

"Ahh. Talk's cheap. Action costs. You pay, I act." He walked across the small room, turned, pacing. "How 'bout another frostie?"

"Wait until ten o'clock. If the call comes, you get a job and ten thousand dollars. If it doesn't, you get a beer." He watched his harnessed killer flop back onto the sofa. "Either way," he smiled, "you're ahead of the game." Willy came back into the room.

"I hope you guys are done talking, because that's a really *bor*ing hallway." She turned to Kronenberger. "And your bathroom stinks. You ought to get somebody to clean it or else tell your customers to stop pissing on the floor. *Really!*"

The Clipper grinned.

The telephone rang.

Kronenberger looked at his watch. It was ten. He jerked his head at the doorway, said, "Take your girlfriend out to the showroom, let her hold a pistol." He waited until they left the room, then picked up the receiver. "Kronenberger," he said.

"Obviously. I assume that you know the whereabouts of our two friends?"

Kronenberger looked at the steadily blinking light on the cathode tube. "Yes, sir."

"Good. Well, my friend, I'm afraid it's time to send them to Switzerland without shoes." There was a pause. "You know the expression?"

"A little bit before my time, but yes, I know what it means. Never called a spade a spade, did you?"

"In *those* days it was a game played by gentlemen, on both sides."

"Hey, I've heard all the stories. I may not be a gentleman in your book, but I handled my end of *this* operation."

"Yes, I know you did. I appreciate your planning ahead, for this eventuality."

"Uhm hum. Which brings us to the topic of financing the operation, Odin. I assume you won't be going before Congress to fund this little escapade."

"Humor isn't your strong suit, Eumenides. I think fifteen should take care of it. Since there are two, instead of one."

"Twenty-five."

"Out of the question! You pegged it right, this is an off the books operation. Out of my own pocket. Fifteen thousand dollars, and I shouldn't even give you that."

"Don't, then. Do it yourself, and keep it all."

"How *dare* you! You're asking twenty-five thousand dollars of me, to kill . . ." The voice on the telephone fought for control, and got it. "All right. I haven't got anyone else. And it has to be done, tonight. And done properly. This stupid thing has gone far enough. Those damned *pictures!* You have to stop it, stop it now. I don't want to know the details, but it can't be connected to the General's suicide. Defoe will have made duplicates of the tapes—be sure and get them. And come up with some sort of an accident. On the highway, something like that. You know what I want."

"Yes, sir. That's why I want twenty-five to do it."

"Oh, go to hell! You think I enjoy this sort of thing? Especially, since he; *and* the woman . . ."

"Yes?"

"Never mind. Just get it over with. Call me when it's done. And, and . . . make it a proper job."

The telephone went dead and Kronenberger hung up.

He walked up the dark hallway to the showroom at the front of the building. The lights were on and the Clipper was explaining how to field strip a Brazilian knock-off of the AK 47.

"It's a go," he said.

The Clipper turned to Willy. "Stay here." He followed Kronenberger back to the office, stood inside the door, arms folded, concentration focused.

More like it, Kronenberger thought, sliding into the chair behind his desk. *My old operative; tight, tense, and eager.* "Ten thousand dollars," he said. "Do it right."

The Clipper let out a long, slow breath then inhaled. "Details. All the little details."

Kronenberger opened the center drawer of his desk. "Here's a map. I drew it up a couple of hours ago. The house is an old clapboard farmhouse, blue and white. Utilities enter here, above ground. I'd take out the phone, just in case. The woman is forty something, a nothing, no problem. Say boo and she'll fold up. I was in there today, six feet from her, Bob. A rabbit. The man is something else. An unknown. Same age, was in Naval Intelligence for twenty years. Supposedly a hotshot. Don't take any chances with him—take him out quick. The woman you can fool with, but don't give the man anything. One more thing. I don't know what the details are, but this General was supposed to have shot himself, and this operation can't look like it's connected. It was suggested that we make it look like an accident. Can we get them out on the highway, set something up?"

"We? You got a mouse in your pocket or are you coming along on this thing?"

"Hey, don't get frisky. You're going in solo, I know that's your style. But I'm here to help. Backup. You need some help, just say the word. Like I said, it can't be connected to this General's death."

"No problem. We'll saturate the building with nerve gas, drop a Huey into the backyard, airlift them to Andrews, load the bodies on a C-47, and dump 'em in the ocean. Don't even need me."

Kronenberger shook his head. "Yeah, I hear you. They always think that we've got all the resources of the DOD behind us. Only this is a dirty operation, Bob, you realize that." He shook his head again. "Just go do what you can, make the best of it." He paused, then added, "He said he wanted it to be clean. 'Proper' I think was the word he used. Something Anne Landers would approve of. He talked like he had a personal involvement with these people." Kronenberger looked up at his protégé. "Just do it, son. Slow, and messy if you must, but do it." Kronenberger stood up and stuck his hands in his trouser pockets. "Any hardware you need, just say the word."

"I think I have all the hardware I need, Mr. K. The hardware I took into the jungle seemed to be enough, back then. I don't think this guy is going to be any tougher than some of those little slopes."

"Okay, okay, I remember. I'll get out of the way and let you do the job. Keep it in mind, this is a pro you're going up against. Oh, and I put a homing device on the bumper of the tan Volvo parked in front of the house. When you have finished the assignment, take it off and turn it off. There's a switch on the base. Bring it back here; it's new, it's the only one I have, and it costs three hundred dollars, wholesale. State of the art."

The Clipper looked at him and smiled. "State of the art, eh? That means when the shit hits the fan, it don't work. How we gonna work the payout?"

Kronenberger unlocked the lower left-hand drawer of his desk and took out a steel box, unlocked it, and began counting hundred-dollar bills onto the desk. "There's five," he said, tapping the pile into a neat stack and handing it to the Clipper. "I'll have the other five in a couple of days." He put the cash box back in the desk and locked it.

"Good enough." The Clipper pulled out his trucker's wallet and zipped it open, removed a plastic card holder containing his driver's license and the Harley registration. He put the money in the wallet and handed the identification to Kronenberger. "Keep an eye on Willy for me, Mr. K. Like I said, she's got a candy nose. Dole out some dust to her if she gets out of line." He picked up the hand-drawn map and studied it, tucked it in a zippered pocket of his leather jacket. "See you in a couple of hours." He turned in the doorway and grinned. "He gonna take my word that the job was done or is he gonna want to see scalps?"

"Jesus! No, he's not going to need that kind of proof." Kronenberger put the Clipper's license in the center drawer of the desk. "Just do what I told you to."

"Good." The Clipper grinned and reached for the handle of the back door. "Then I can keep 'em for myself."

EIGHTEEN

Defoe put his hand on Kit's bare shoulder and gently pushed her away. Her lips were soft and warm and the brandy had suffused him with a pleasant feeling of languid detachment from the earlier events of the day, but his father's parting words were nagging at the fringes of his mind. He got up and went to the fireplace where he stood, his eyes fixed on the glowing bed of coals.

After a moment Kit walked across the room and stood beside him. She slipped her fingers through his and asked, "Are you really so much like your father? Is it because I'm a married woman now, Chase?" She turned her head and watched him watch the fire.

"Hmm?" He faced her, saying, "No, no, I suppose not. Yes, I've made it a general rule not to get involved with married women, Kit. But not from any great sense of morality. It's just that there is so much potential for hurt that it never seemed worth it. But that's not why I broke away a moment ago." He disentangled his hand from hers and turned toward the door. "We could use a few more logs in here."

He came back through the French doors, a load of ash cradled against his chest, his face wet. "Starting to rain." He dropped the wood beside the hearth and brushed bits of bark from the front of his shirt. "I'd better get that grill back down in the basement."

"Oh, don't be silly," Kit said, going to the door. Rain was hitting the floor, blown inside by the gusting wind. "You'll get soaked. Just drag it in here for the night."

She came back from the powder room with a hand towel

and gave it to him as he locked the doors. Defoe mopped his face and dried his hands, then put a pair of logs on the fire. Finally he looked at Kit.

"You remember my father's parting words? On the tape? 'Bastard whelp.' Precision with the English language is something that I got from him. I realize that it makes me sound pompous and pedantic at times, but . . ." He shrugged, said, "It's the way I am. Anyway, what he said, coupled with what the whole row was about, the General and my mother, made me think, Kit." He stepped closer to her, took her hands in his, their faces half a foot apart. "I calculated backward, from the date of my birth. And realized that I was born, like a great many other babies, nine months, almost to the day, after the Germans signed the surrender documents. My father was in London on VE Day, you heard him say that on the tape, and going on to see Dulles. I don't know how long he stayed in Switzerland, but I know it took at least a week to sail back to the States by boat." He felt her fingers tighten in his as she realized where his thoughts were leading. He looked into her eyes and said, "The General was my father, Kit. That's what has him in such a frenzy."

She moved against him and kissed him lightly on the lips, pulled back, and breathed, "That's the most ridiculous thing I ever heard," then slid her tongue into his mouth.

The Clipper turned his attention away from the red Ford Ranger with the jacked-up body and watched the right-hand column of numbers repeatedly flicker from zero through nine. When the digit in the center column changed from eight to nine he released the trigger of the nozzle, then squeezed it in short bursts until the numbers on the pump read $5.00. He replaced the gas cap and wheeled the Harley away from the pumps, set the kickstand, and went inside the station.

A kid in his early twenties was making change for the guy with the four-by-four and talking on the phone. The Clipper took off his helmet and waited until the man ahead of him turned away from the counter, stuffing his billfold in his hip pocket. The kid was surrounded by racks of cigarettes and candy and gum and metal trees with bags of chips and pretzels fastened to little clips. A Pyrex carafe of inky black coffee sat quietly evaporating on a hot ring beside a stack of white foam cups, paper packs of sugar, and a jar of powdered creamer. A hand-lettered sign said "50¢ + Tx."

"Yeah? Uh huh. You're shittin' me. Naw, go on. He said that?" He looked up at the Clipper, saw the way he was dressed, and turned to the plate-glass window, spotted the bike. He looked back at its rider. "Number three, right?"

"Fuck if I know." The Clipper jerked his head toward the pump he had used. "Five bucks."

The kid turned to his console and punched a few keys, looked up. "Yeah, five. Cash? Nuh uh. I gotta stay until ten. 'Cause Ronnie says so, that's why. Pete didn't come in today, and I got to cover, until Ronnie gets back from eatin' and can scare up somebody else. How the fuck should I know?"

"Hey, gimme the key to the head, kid." The Clipper pulled his black leather glove off his left hand with his teeth and dug a wad of folded bills from the front pocket of his jeans. He dropped a five on the counter as he looked past the clerk's head at the bathroom keys, wired to foot-long chunks of worn and grease-impregnated pine hanging on cuphooks below a shelf that held cans of 10W30 oil, transmission fluid, and STP gas treatment.

"Hey, babe, soon as I get off here, that's when. I'm telling you, I don't *know.* When Ronnie gets back and says I can, that's when." He turned and flipped the slab of wood that said MEN in black marker off the hook. "Hey, I gotta go." He hung up, handed the key to the Clipper, and smiled out of the side of his mouth. "Fuckin' broads," he said, and turned to the window, watched a man in a topcoat pumping unleaded extra into a BMW. He turned back to the motorcycle rider. "Little cold out there for a scoot, ain't it?"

"Yeah. If you're a pussy." The Clipper took the key and went behind the building. The bathroom was warm and bright and clean. He used the single urinal, washed his hands, and dried them with a pair of paper towels that he pulled from the dispenser. Then he went into the stall that enclosed the toilet, put his helmet on the floor, and latched the door. He took off his leather jacket, his other glove, and sat down on the hopper. He reached inside his helmet and peeled back the hi-density foam liner, extracted his kit.

He wrapped the foot-long section of surgical tubing around his left elbow and snugged it up with his teeth, then tore open a tiny plastic pouch, carefully tapped its contents into the bottle cap and rested it on top of the chrome cover of the toilet-paper roller.

He threw the match on the floor and drew the liquid up into the little syringe. *Lock and load one round of ball ammunition.* He held it in his teeth while he thwacked the bulging vein below his muscle with his right index finger. Blood mixed with the clear contents of the hypo as he pulled the plunger back. *Ready on the right, ready on the left. Ready on the firing line.* The meth hit with a teeth-clicking kick, and he leaned back against the white-tiled wall and closed his eyes as the first rush flooded through his system.

He packed up, got up, felt as though he could tear off the door and walk right out through the green-enameled cement block wall. That feeling was the best part of doing speed. He was ready to execute the mission.

They were in her bedroom, a place they had been many times before, but never with the door open, never with their voices raised above a whisper. She was working at the knot of his tie and he was trying to discuss philosophy and ignore the erection that was straining against the fabric of his trousers. "Kit," he said. "It was different then, thirty years ago. We didn't know . . ." She had untied his tie and was working on the buttons of his shirt, one by one, down from the top.

She stepped back and put her hands on her hips, saying, "How is it different? If you think that Dad is your father *now,* then he was *then,* too. Just because we didn't know—"

"No, Kit. You don't understand. We can hardly feel guilt for something we did then, in innocence, but now, now that we know . . ."

She let the dress fall to her hips, where it caught for a moment, before she freed it with a wriggle. The half-slip quickly followed and she stepped out of the silken pool they made on the floor and, wearing nothing but a teenage fantasy of heels, black stockings, and matching lace panties, put her finger on his lips. Her pale skin was a stark contrast in the dark room as she moved against him and said, having the final word, "Chase. Uncle George is your father. Trust me; a woman knows these things . . ."

Twenty minutes later he leaned over the front fork and read the map a final time in the glare of his headlight. Quarter mile, hang a left, then a couple hundred yards past the new house. He got into top gear and rolled by for a look-see at thirty miles an hour and a thousand RPM's, the engine a low burble. The road was dark and the rain covered any slight sounds he made as he turned the bike and headed back toward the driveway. A few hundred feet from the General's farmhouse he killed the engine, then the headlight, and rolled silently to a stop beside the road. He eased the machine down on its side, below headlight level.

He snipped the telephone wire where it entered the surge protector, slid the side cutters back into the sheath with the lockback, and worked his way around to the rear of the house, checking the windows as he went. The ground floor was dark and he stepped away from the side of the house, looked up at the second floor. A light silhouetted two people, close together. The black figures kissed as he watched. He wiped rain from his eyes and grinned. Give them five minutes, they'd be naked, in bed. So easy! He moved to the rear of the house, where Mr. K. had said to go in. Darker than a jigaboo's asshole back here. He stumbled over a couple of logs that had fallen from a stack of firewood. He picked one up, held it up like a club. The panes of glass in the French doors flickered with the reflection of the flames from the dying fire and he went over his plan a final time.

An accident, something out on the highway, was what the top man wanted. Sure, pal. He wondered how much he was paying Kronenberger. Back when he had been on the books, over in 'Nam, they had planned and executed a few assignments like that. Special drugs that mimicked a coronary, special equipment to deliver the drugs. Only this was a black operation. Even Mr. K. didn't have access to those kinds of pharmaceuticals anymore. Besides, the Clipper's way was more fun.

He'd go in, catch the man, naked in the saddle, put him down and snip him before he knew what was happening. Then do the lady. He'd play with them both a little. The man was Navy Intelligence, probably a fuckin' O; good, good. A little challenge. Make sure there was a phone in the room; let the guy drag himself to it, when he thought the Clipper wasn't looking, was busy with the woman. Surprise the shit out of him when he found out it was dead. Mr. K. said watch out for the man, put him away right off. Yeah, well, bullshit. Half the fun of it was having an audience to appreciate your work. But Kronenberger was right, the guy could be dangerous. Might have a gun somewheres. Clip his wrists, too. Get that tendon at the base of the thumb, the man would be flopping on the floor like a fish while he did the woman.

He'd already worked out the scenario. It was a cult killing, some kind of hoodoo shit, sacrificial stuff. The woman, she'd be naked, that would be good. He'd cut her and run her. Pop the veins in both her wrists and then get her real pumped up, chase her through the house, arms flailing. Scared to death, her little old heart going *whump whump,* pulse up there about a hundred and eighty beats a minute. *Spray* the fucking house, baby! When she was empty he'd put her in the tub and write some shit on the walls with the last of her blood. Crosses and swastikas, crap like that. Maybe he'd gut her out, too. What the hell; play the scene as it unfolded.

The man, he'd take him downstairs, spread him around. Cops would find him, puke their guts, figuring they'd seen everything. And then, upstairs . . . sur-prise, sur-prise!

Mr. K. said the guy was nothing to fool with. Mr. K. knew his business. Bust the glass in the door here, and go in like the Hulk; guy would never know what hit him, no time to grab a gun or nothing. He put his face against the glass and peered into the den. A fire was dying, just a few coals glowed. There was a hallway, lit by a low-wattage bulb. He could see the stairway. Time to do it.

They were standing halfway between the doorway and the bed, illuminated by the soft light filtered through the frilly pink shade of Kit's old bedside lamp. It gave their skin a warm, centerfold glow. Defoe kissed her throat and slipped his thumbs inside the waistband of her panties as she slid her hands between their bodies and wrapped both of them around the erection that was pressed against her belly. The Clipper punched out a pane of glass with the piece of firewood and put his gloved fist through the shattered pane to unlatch the door.

Defoe opened his eyes, cocked his head, said, "Did you hear that?"

"What? All I can hear is the pulse pounding in my ears." She let go of him as he backed away but put her arms around his neck and hung from him. "Put me on the bed, Chase. I don't think I can stand up."

He raised his hand, said, "Shh! It sounded like breaking glass." He broke her grip and said, "Stay here," went through the open bedroom door and flipped on the upper hallway light.

The Clipper looked up, his foot on the first step, and saw the man, naked at the landing, his dick at half mast, and the broad just coming through the bedroom door, both frozen like marble statues under the bare bulb in the ceiling socket above their heads.

"*RAAAAAH,*" he screamed and charged up the stairs, lips purled and canines bared, his hands stretched ahead of him, fingers crooked like claws, knowing that the shock would freeze them for that all-important two or three seconds. After that it would be over, and the fun part could begin.

Defoe read the man coming at them during the fraction of a second the subconscious still devotes to the prehistoric fight-or-flight decision.

A million years of human evolution culminated in the apogee of intellect that occurred during the middle of the second millennium.

About nineteen hundred and fifty years after the birth of the man whom the keepers of the current calendar acknowledge as Christ the Savior, the genetically weak, lame, and halt suddenly began to multiply, began to laugh in the face of Darwin's theory of natural selection as the miraculous discoveries of the medical world were applied to their roiling mass. Those members of the tribe who a scant half century earlier would have died at childbirth suddenly survived to spawn a half dozen fecund offspring of their own, spawn that in turn dropped litters unfit or unwilling to survive without the largess of the few.

The few who, with good conscience, chose to have but one or two children of their own—unless they subscribed to the Zero Population theory and had none.

Defoe was a product of the dwindling genetic pool that shared genes with the Sabre Tooth and Cro-Magnon, ancients who had preyed on the Herbivores and Neanderthals that grazed the ancient plains. A survivor.

Mid- to late thirties, well over six feet, well over two hundred pounds. Mostly black; his beard, his hair, the leather jacket, gloves. Eyes and teeth were white and wild, bared in that feral rictus of attack. This had to be a follow-up on the stolen tapes. Adrenaline kicked in and replaced the wine, the brandy. In less than two seconds the man would be at the top of the stairs; barely time to turn and retreat to the bedroom. Kit was right behind him; they would collide. Even if they made it back into her room they would never be able to shut the door in time. He put a hand on either newel post at the top of the stairs and lifted his feet off the landing as the man's arms reached for him. He launched himself into the stairwell, legs first. His bare feet shot between the man's outstretched arms and hit him in the chest.

The Clipper's left foot was on the third step from the top, and his right was lifted in midair, poised above the second-stair tread. His upward momentum was effectively canceled by the pull of gravity and Defoe's unexpected blow to his chest knocked him over backward.

He landed on his back on the center of the stairs and slid to the bottom, his head crashing into the wall beside the kitchen door. Defoe regained his balance at the top of the stairs and watched the man roll over, shake his head, and, using the wall for support, get back on his feet. *Discretion,* Defoe thought, turning toward the bedroom door, *is the better part of valor.* By the time he had completed the cliché he had pushed Kit into the room and slammed and locked the door. "Help me with the bed," he yelled and turned on the overhead light. He had already shoved the heavy oak dresser against the door. The bed effectively filled the remaining space between the dresser and the wall and would buy them a little time.

The Clipper raised his boot and struck the door with its heel. He'd done it before, and expected the stile to shatter into a cloud of splinters as the latch and strike plate parted company.

He'd done it in motels and rented rooms and postwar tract houses in bedroom communities. The General's house had been built around the turn of the century. Instead of hollow core interior doors, two skins of Philippine mahogany sandwiching a corrugated paper interior, the bedroom door was of frame and panel construction, made up of inch-and-a-half oak rails and panels a full inch thick, floating in deeply rabbited mortices. Three, not two, cast-iron hinges held one side of the door in place, and the lock was technically crude but mechanically sound. He hurt his heel.

"Son of a *bitch!*" he yelled, and tried his shoulder. He bounced back, nearly went over the banister and down the stairs again. He stopped and paused to breathe and think. The element of surprise was lost, now it was time to plan and execute the plan. He ran back down the stairs and got the section of firewood he had dropped when he had first started up after the man.

He used it as a short battering ram, attacking the lock with repeated blows, until the cast iron finally shattered. The door moved in two inches and stopped. He threw his shoulder against it several times, then methodically began to attack the upper panel with the log.

The end of the piece of ash began to mushroom, fray, and splinter against the oak, but the thinner door panel was splitting under the steady pounding, and it was not long before the Clipper had broken through the panel and was assaulting the back of the dresser.

That, too, gave way to his fury, and in less than a minute he was able to reach through the splintered kindling and shove the remainder of the bureau away from the door. He peered through the opening into the darkened room.

As soon as Kit and Defoe had pushed the bed into place he

had killed the light and opened the window. "Quick!" he said, grabbing her hand. "Climb out on the roof and jump down to the ground." He hoped that there wasn't a second man outside, waiting. The asphalt shingles rasped against the bottom of his feet and sanded Kit's stockings to shreds. The rain was cold on their overheated skin. At the edge of the shallow slope of the roof he pulled her to him and said, "Jump out as far as you can, to clear the woodpile. The lawn is soft; land with your feet together and tuck your knees, roll forward. Nothing to it, it's only an eight-foot drop, just like a parachute jump."

She looked into the blackness and the rain. "I never made a parachute jump!"

"Neither did I!" he lied, and launched himself into the night. He planned to use the delay they had gained with their barricade to jump to the lawn and get around to the front of the house, where he would get his spare ignition key from the magnetic box in the fender well. The image of the two of them, he stark naked and Kit in panties and stockings, ringing the doorbell of his parents' house, brought a flicker of a grin to his lips. Kit landed beside him on the wet turf and the plan was canceled.

"Ow!" she yelled, and rolled into him. She reached down and grabbed her ankle. "Oh, Chase, I think it's broken. Oh, shit. Goddamn it." He scooped her off the sodden turf and looked up at the gaping bedroom window. The steady sound of wood smashing above them continued. In a matter of moments their assailant would realize that they were not in the room and he would go back down the stairs, find them outside. Go to plan B.

He carried Kit around to the patio and went into the den through the open door. He felt the broken glass crunch under his bare feet and winced, tried to step lightly. He put her on the sofa and said into her ear, "We've got him now! I'll grab one of your dad's shotguns and ambush the bastard when he comes down the stairs!"

Kit let out a whimper. He could see her, sitting on the sofa, massaging her right ankle.

"Chase!" she whispered, the intensity of her voice turning

him in midstride toward the gun cabinet. "I packed up all the bullets and put them in the trunk of my car this afternoon, along with his pistol!"

"Oh, shit," he said aloud.

NINETEEN

"What's this?"

"A pager."

Willie, Wilhelmina, had begun at the far left-hand shelf in Kronenberger's office and started picking up objects from his inventory. She had gotten into his suppressors, opened the boxes, and pulled them out; the Cieners and the Qual-a-tecs, the shelf devoted to La France and AWC. "Silencers," he'd told her, watching from his desk chair and drinking beer. "James Bond toys."

She poked at the digital radios, the kind used by the FBI, that were secure from eavesdropping, she tried on the Kevlar vests, twenty-two layers thick, backed up with Lexguard scales to prevent bruising, and she pulled a Mac 10 submachine gun off the shelf and pointed it at him. She put it back and opened a small plastic carrying case next to it. It bore the Litton logo and the words Electron Device Division on it. He told her it was the M-845 night sight and for five thousand dollars she could have her very own.

"What's a pager?"

"A beeper? You must have heard of them."

"Yeah, what the little nigger kids carry, sell crack in the schoolyard."

"Uhm hum. Except that one is a little more sophisticated. It doesn't beep, it pulses. The latest model, favorite with congressmen who want to show off. All the Secret Service carry them. It's silent, so nobody knows when you are being paged."

"Yeah? How's it work?"

"Here. I'll show you." He took the pager from her, a black

plastic tube the size and shape of a large fountain pen, right down to the metal pocket clip. He reached for her T-shirt, slipped the barrel of the pager down between her breasts and set the clip on the neckline of her shirt. He crossed to the desk and picked up his cordless phone and dialed a long series of numbers. He carried the phone back to her, gave it to her while he turned on the pager. His hands brushed across her full breasts as he twisted the barrel of the pager, activating it.

"Each one has its own code," he explained. "I just called up the number for the cellular hookup." He pointed to the star button on the telephone. "Push that."

Willie touched the button and a quarter of a second later felt a vibrating pulse between her breasts. "Ooh," she said.

Kronenberger smiled as she did it again, holding the button down longer the second time. "ET, phone home," he said.

She walked around the room, working the buzzer. She went back to the shelves, took the night sight out of the box. "Show me how this works."

Kronenberger took it from her, turned it on. "It amplifies available light. I'll go turn off the light. You hold it up to your eye, you can see just like it was daytime." He hit the switch beside the door. The lights were still on in the showroom at the front of the building, but for someone not equipped with one of the night-vision scopes it was as black as midnight in the room.

Kronenberger quickly moved to the shelves and took a Smith & Wesson Star-Tron out of its field case. Willie was holding the M-845 to her eye and had zeroed in on the center drawer of the desk.

"Naughty, naughty," he said, watching her. She whirled, turned the sight at the sound of his voice. In the blackness she saw him, grinning, holding the little bag of cocaine between the fingers of his right hand as he watched her through the nightsight in his left.

"You bastard!" she said, and put the Litton on the desk. Then she popped the button at the top of the zipper of her jeans. "So. You can see in the dark, too, eh? What am I doing now, old man?"

He put his sight on the desk beside the one she had held, and turned on the desk lamp. She winced at the sudden brightness, and he smiled. "Too much light?" He took off his tweed jacket and dropped it over the lamp, turning it into a pale glow that did little more than define the edges of the desk and sofa.

Willy hooked her thumbs on either side of her zipper and spread them. The metal teeth separated with a ripping sound as she said, "Bobby said if I was a good girl you'd give me some candy. Remember?"

Kronenberger chuckled. "Yes, Willy. I remember."

She came toward him, taking small steps with her jeans dropping toward the floor as she moved. "Well, then, fix my nose for me, old man."

He dropped the packet on the desk. "You shouldn't do that to yourself, young lady. Bad for your sinuses. Eat holes in your septum."

"Hey, what the fuck do you care? You gonna do me or not?"

He reached for the pager and pulled it from her shirt. "Take off your panties," he said, "and sit on the desk." He separated her thighs and worked the black plastic body of the pager into her, held it with one hand while he touched the telephone with the other.

"Ooh," she said.

He wiggled the vibrating pager for a moment, then withdrew it.

"Oh, hey, don't," she said, "Not yet."

Kronenberger smiled. "Just wanted to get it damp, honey." He put it on the desk beside her and tore open the packet of coke with his teeth. It was very fine and he guessed that it was very pure. "You know that coke is absorbed through mucus membranes, don't you? That's why you put it up your nose." He put the tip of the pager into the envelope and rolled it in the powder. "Well, you have mucus membranes in other places besides your nose. Lots of other places." He slid the pager back into her and handed her the telephone. "Play," he said.

Willie pressed the button and rolled her eyes and made

little sounds, said, "oh!" and "What a rush!" She said, "How come there's a delay when I press the button?"

"Because the signal goes to the cellular relay station, and from there to a microwave dish at the AT&T Long Lines Division. They beam it thirty thousand miles up into space, to a satellite in geosynchronous orbit. Then it comes back down here, through more relays, until it gets to an FM transmitter that sends the signal to your pussy. A sixty-thousand-mile trip between your finger and your snatch, Willie." He smiled. "You just set the world record for long-distance masturbation."

She held the button down on the phone and bit her tongue. "Yeah. Guiness book, here I come!" Her breath was rapid and shallow. "Hey, hit me with another line of coke, man. Do my nose this time, I can't take this buzzer out to reload right now, know what I mean?" She tilted her head toward the ceiling and closed her eyes as she squeezed the telephone.

"Hop off, lean on the desk," Kronenberger said. "And I'll fix you up." He took the tube of Rig from the drawer and anointed himself with the slippery lubricant and then shook the remainder of the cocaine over his erection until it resembled a sugar-coated cruller. He eased himself into her from behind and she drew a quick deep breath. A shudder ran through her body as the coke entered her system, and he felt her muscles contract around him, felt the pager tremble within her.

She panted and whimpered and broke out in a sweat, stiffened and screamed and dropped the telephone on the floor, then went limp across the desk.

TWENTY

Defoe turned on the desk lamp and forced himself to take slow, deep breaths while his mind raced. Get a knife from the kitchen, try to ambush the man when he came back down the stairs. No; naked, and giving the guy ten years and a hundred pounds advantage besides seemed a good way to get them both killed. He looked around the room, flicked his eyes across the useless guns in their rack, glanced at the General's big steel filing cabinet. One of the airtight kind, three-hour fire rating. He turned and looked at the gas grill just inside the door. Maybe . . .

He walked over to the fireplace and peed onto the last embers of the fire, sending a hissing cloud of steam up the chimney. "Can't risk an open flame," he explained in a whisper, and squatted, wrapping his arms around the hundred-and-fifty-pound filing cabinet. He stood and carried it to a spot between the French doors and the entrance to the hallway, then unplugged the desk lamp and put it in the bottom drawer of the filing cabinet. He got the fireplace poker and tapped the end carefully against the light bulb until it broke. "Gonna build a bomb," he said.

He ripped the rubber hose from the top of the tank of LP gas and opened the valve until he smelled gas, then put the tank in the second drawer, shut both it and the bottom one, listened as they sealed with a satisfying click. He left the fourth, the top, drawer slightly open, then crawled behind the couch and found the wall receptacle. "Propane is heavier than air," he explained as he picked Kit up and carried her behind the sofa. "So the bottom will fill up with gas first. I don't want to kill us all, so I left the top ajar, to direct the force of the explosion. When he walks into the room, I'll plug the light in and blow him away." *I hope,* he added silently as he put her on the floor behind the sofa and pulled the heavy Oriental carpet over her body. "Keep your head down."

"Chase," she said, her voice muffled from beneath the rug, "is this going to work?"

"Sure," he quickly said and crouched behind the couch, waiting.

The Clipper tore the pieces of the upper panel from the mortices that had held it and crawled into the bedroom, stood unsteadily on the mattress and looked around. The window was open and the room was empty. He looked out at the slanting roof. Fuckers went out the window! He put his leg through the opening and followed. The two of them were out there in the rain and the night, naked. Didn't stand a chance. He reached back on his hip to check the knife and duck-walked across the shingles to the edge of the roof, peering into the night.

Defoe looked up at the sounds above his head, jumped over the sofa, and turned the filing cabinet toward the French doors as the Clipper dropped onto the patio.

They saw each other at the same instant, and the man outside took two quick steps to the doors as Defoe vaulted over the back of the sofa and felt for the plug with one hand and ran his other across the baseboard, searching for the outlet.

The Clipper grabbed the handle and found that they had locked the door on him. He reached through the broken pane and felt for the latch.

Defoe found the outlet and aligned the twin prongs of the plug with the matching openings, and with trembling fingers shoved it in.

The one hundred and ten volts of electricity ignited and burned the tungsten in the light bulb in a flash that lasted less than a thousandth of a second. Nobody saw it. The pool of propane gas that the light bulb's filament ignited burned in an equally short span of time, but everybody saw it. They also heard it and felt it.

Defoe was right, in theory. The slightly open top drawer of the filing cabinet did serve to direct the force of the explosion, so that most of the energy of the blast was concentrated on the French doors.

But he had failed to take into consideration the gas remaining in the tank, a reserve supply that ignited a few milliseconds after the first explosion. Confined to the tank as it was, this explosion, centered in the filing cabinet, tried to go in all directions at once, and largely succeeded. The center of the steel column bulged, separated at the seams, and sent a shock wave radiating from its epicenter throughout the room. The force of the blast knocked the sofa over and upon both Defoe and Kit. It moved the General's massive desk a foot closer to the opposite wall, rearranged the books on the shelves, and sent the ashes in the fireplace swirling through the air.

But the main force of the blast shattered every pane of glass in the French doors and turned the mullions between them into splinters. Both hit the Clipper with the full force of their power. He was wearing his heavy leather jacket and gloves so that his hands and upper body were largely protected from the crystal cloud.

His face was not so fortunate. Bits of glass embedded themselves in his skin and penetrated deeper into his eyeballs. A tiny fraction of a second later the front of the top drawer of the filing cabinet burst through what remained of the doors and struck him in the upper chest and lower face. The force of the impact pushed him back even as the foot square of gray-enameled steel smashed his jaw into a mix of bone, blood, bits of flesh, and shards of dental porcelain.

He screamed and turned and staggered onto the lawn, a red haze descending across his vision. He raised his gloved hands to his face, but could feel nothing. He lay on his back, trying to breathe, desperately trying to suck air into his lungs. His throat began to fill with blood and rain and bits of himself, and a red cloud settled on his mind like a blanket thrown over the sun, blotting out the light.

Defoe pushed the back of the piece of furniture off his legs and got to his knees. "Kit! Are you all right?" He stood up, dizzy, held onto a recently exposed leg of the sofa. "What was it we used to say? 'Ring your chimes.' "

"Ohhh," she said, still wrapped in the rug. She coughed, then peeled the carpet away from her head. "I'm alive. I *think.* What happened? You said something about directing the force of your bomb."

Defoe went over to the door and looked through the blasted opening. He turned on the outside light. "I think I did." He went outside, putting his feet down very carefully on the glass and wood that littered the patio. The man's body lay in the grass a dozen feet away, very dead.

He began to have second thoughts about the attack, now that it was over. The man lying on the grass in the rain seemed much less threatening than the berserk monster who had charged up the stairs a few minutes ago. Had he really been intent on killing them? He bent down and checked the man for weapons. Just a folding knife and a pair of pliers in a leather pouch; the sort of thing an electrician might carry. He stood up and thought about the incident. The dead man didn't look like the kind of operative the CIA would use. Maybe it was just a simple burglary. He picked up the black leather wallet, fastened to the dead man's belt by a chain, and opened it. A half-inch-thick stack of hundred dollar bills. No identification. He checked the pockets, found nothing but a few small bills. No, the man had been sent, been paid, to kill them.

Only the police might not look at it that way. They might say it was a simple burglary, that Defoe had used excess force; hell, he didn't even live there. He turned and looked at the house. This man had obviously been outside when the bomb went off. Was self-defense valid when the intruder broke in, and then went back outside?

He reentered the house and helped Kit to her feet. "Can you walk? We've got to get out of here. I don't know who he was or what is going on, but we have to assume that he wasn't operating alone."

She leaned heavily against him and tested her foot on the floor. "The good news," she said, "is that it isn't broken after all." She took a tentative step, then two, and stood alone.

"The bad news is that it doesn't look like we're going to wind up in bed."

Defoe smiled and eased her down on the sofa, bent, and kissed her briefly. "Hey. The night is young." He straightened and went to the doorway that led into the house. "Stay here. I'll run up and get our clothes."

"Get my navy skirt and sweater, Chase," she called, peeling off her ruined stockings. "And my loafers. I don't much feel like Arnold Scaasi anymore, and I sure as hell won't be able to walk in heels."

While he was upstairs she made her way along the hall and returned herself to the edge of humanity in the powder room. By the time he got back down with their clothes she was sitting at the kitchen table, naked except for black bikini panties, drinking Chablis from the bottle. "Hi, sailor," she said, taking the bottle from her lips and smiling. "You always show your dates such a good time?"

He put her clothes on the table and shook his head with a smile. "Cool under fire, aren't you, Kit? I bet your dad was like that in combat." He paused as he buttoned his shirt. *"Our* dad."

It took her twenty seconds to put on her skirt and sweater, slip into her shoes. She winced as she worked the leather over her arch, then tested her foot again as she came around the table to him. "Hey, you don't know that for a fact, Chase. Besides, what does it really matter which one your father was? You're *you,* no matter what." She handed him the bottle of white wine and he took a swallow.

"I suppose you're right," he said, picking up his address book from the table. "Come on, let's get out of here. The telephone's been cut and I have to make a call."

"Oh? Where are we going? To a hotel, I hope."

"No," he answered. "We're going to the FBI."

"Oh. Why not the local cops?"

"Because they wouldn't offer much in the way of protection. Kit, I'm not quite ready to tell them that I killed a man with your father's gas barbecue. I mean, there's no real proof that he was trying to kill us; in theory he could have been breaking into an empty house, looking for a place to sleep. Do you really want to spend the night in jail while the person who sent that monster after us is planning his next move against us?"

He found a Bic pen in the desk and smashed its plastic barrel on the hearth with the poker, then took half a handful of three-by-five cards out to the corpse on the lawn. Kit watched silently as he stripped off the man's gloves, inked his fingers, and rolled the pads across the sheets of card stock. "Yuk," she said when he had completed the chore and stood up.

The line of showers had passed and the stars were back in the sky. Defoe cranked the Jag without result. Electricity is still considered to be a largely mysterious natural phenomenon by the British, particularly when it comes to applying it to the operation of a motorcar. Defoe looked over at Kit. "She's temperamental when it's wet," he explained. "You would think, as much as it is damp over there, that they would have gotten the hang of it by now, wouldn't you? Well, I guess we'll have to take your car. I'll drive if you want to give your foot a rest." His scrotum tightened as he thought what would have happened if they *had* tried to escape in the Jag. Time to do something about that damned car.

"Why are we going to the FBI?" Kit asked as he turned onto Route 66 and headed for Washington.

"I want to identify our dead friend back there, try to get some handle on who is trying to kill us."

"Ah! Then you've dropped the idea you had earlier, that your father killed Dad."

He drove for a minute in silence. Finally he sighed, said, "I don't know. The guy looked like a biker; motorcycle gangs? The kind of muscle that organized crime keeps on retainer. Besides, I can't see my father sending a killer after us just because the General screwed his wife fifty years ago. Of course . . ." He turned to her and shook his head. "I guess I really don't know him, Kit. Never did. He shocked me, the way he reacted to me tonight; I've never seen him like that. Out of control." He looked at the rearview mirror, reached up and flipped the tab to "night," killing the glare of a following car's headlights. He turned his eyes back to the road ahead, drove fast in the sparse traffic, as they both dealt with that suggestion. Suddenly he said, "Ah, there's a phone."

He got Carlton Jarinko's card out of his wallet and waited for the FBI man to answer.

Kronenberger kept one eye on the cathode tube and its blinking light, the other on the girl, sleeping in a fetal curl. It had been a near thing for a minute there, he'd thought she was OD'ing on the dope. Last thing he needed was for her to cook off, have the Clipper come back from the job and find her stiff. But she got herself back together, and he got her clothes back on, and then she had nodded off, been out for more than an hour now. He sipped a Beck's and watched the blinking light.

Suddenly it changed pitch and moved across the screen. He stood up and adjusted the RDF. "Damn it, Clipper, I told you to shut it off before you brought it back." He watched the receiver for a few minutes, and saw the signal fade as the homer reached the edge of its broadcast range. "Where the hell's he going?" Kronenberger got up, poked the sleeping girl with his foot. "Come on, come on, sweetheart, get up!" He grabbed his black nylon bag and the receiver.

She sat up, rubbing sleep from her eyes. "What? Is Bobby back? What's the hurry?"

He grabbed her arm and dragged her, stumbling, out the back door, shoved her into the passenger's seat of the Bronco. "I don't know," he said. "Something's wrong. He didn't turn off the homer and he isn't headed back here." He hit the headlights and sped out of the industrial park, headed in the direction of the farmhouse, one eye on the receiver that sat between them on the seat. "I hope to Christ I can pick up the signal again."

"Carlton! Chase Defoe here. Sorry to call you in the middle of the night. It's an emergency; I have to get an ID on somebody, right away."

"Defoe. Yes, okay. Only I don't have anybody in there this time of night who can do a voiceprint."

"No, no, I realize that. This is a set of fingerprints."

"Whose?"

"That's what I want to know. A guy tried to kill us, me and

General Kilgallen's daughter, a little while ago. Hired-assassin type."

"Jesus! Okay. Meet me at the Tenth Street entrance to the building. The ramp. Twenty minutes. Doug Winston warned me about you," he added as he broke the connection.

Kronenberger pulled to the side of the Beltway as he approached the heights of Tyson's Corner. He put the receiver on the dash and rotated the carrying handle on top. It acted as a Radio Direction Finder, and oriented the signal to the compass. He switched it to audio and pawed through the glove box for a map.

"What the hell's going on?" Willie asked, listening to the steady beep as the light winked at her.

"Your boyfriend screwed up, is what's going on." He turned the map until it matched with the homer's signal. "Shut up and let me think." The signal was steady, and according to the map was about five miles away, in Arlington. Probably somewhere on Route 66. He cranked the wheel hard right and took the exit onto Chain Bridge Road. He'd shoot back toward McLean, pick up the Dulles Airport access road and take it to 66. Son of a bitch! Somehow the Clipper blew it. No way was that him, on his motorcycle, up ahead. Even fucked up on that damned amphetamine, he was enough of a pro to finish up the assignment by reporting in.

He was so angry he nearly missed the Volvo beside the road. Only the sharp change in the sound of the signal told him he had passed the homer. He looked in his right-hand mirror and saw a man walk from the roadside telephone to the car, get in. Kronenberger pulled to the right lane and slowed to forty miles an hour, waiting for the driver to catch up. Time to get rid of Willie. He let Defoe—had to be him, who else—pass, then picked up speed, stayed a hundred yards behind him. Easy to do a visual tail in the light traffic. Just had to make sure he didn't get off the highway suddenly. At the next exit Kronenberger jammed on the brakes and skidded to a stop on the verge. "Out! Quick, quick!" He leaned across and opened the door, pushed Willie out of the Bronco.

"Hey! What the fuck's going on?" she said, stumbling,

nearly falling to the gravel. By the time she had regained her balance and her composure, the Bronco was a set of taillights. "Shit!" she said, turning and sticking out her thumb. "I've about had it with you, Bobby, *and* your spooky friend."

Defoe crossed the Potomac and headed up Constitution Avenue under a midnight sky filled with stars. He turned left on Tenth between Justice and the IRS, stopped a block later at the ramp that led down to the bowels of the FBI Building. A uniformed guard stood in his armored kiosk above the massive steel plate that jutted up from the roadbed, blocking access to any vehicle smaller and less powerful than a Sherman tank.

Closer to the corner he noticed a huddled mass of cast-off clothing sleeping on a sheet of cardboard over a grate in the sidewalk, wisps of steam rising around the body and condensing in the cool air. What would J. Edgar Hoover have said about street people, homesteading the sidewalk in front of his headquarters?

Defoe looked at his watch. Kit turned on the radio and ran down the FM dial, looking for a soothing station. A metronomic buzz issued from the speaker and Kit said, "What's that?"

Defoe glanced at the radio, flicked his eyes back to the nearly deserted street. "Don't know. If we were in my neighborhood I'd say a farmer has a short in his electric fence. Down here it's anybody's guess; probably some clandestine transmitter." He turned to her and winked. "Russians calling home."

Jarinko pulled beside their car and looked across at Defoe and Kit, then turned right, in front of them, showed his ID to the guard, motioned in their direction as he talked.

The guard glanced at them as Defoe swung off the street and stopped behind the assistant director's plain vanilla Plymouth. Its white government license plates confirmed it as a company car.

The steel plate began to recline on hydraulics hidden beneath the roadbed and Jarinko, then Defoe, clattered over it and disappeared into the garage beneath the Hoover Building.

"Son of a bitch," Kronenberger said softly, watching from the corner of E Street at Tenth. He shook a Camel from the pack to his lips. "I don't like the looks of this."

Jarinko handed a pair of visitor badges to Defoe and Kit, then offered her his hand. "Carlton Jarinko. I gather that you are General Kilgallen's daughter."

"Yes," she said. "Did you know him?"

"No." He gestured with his head toward Defoe, but kept his eyes on her. "Your friend here mentioned you, earlier today. Said that you were the one who found the tape of your father's last moments."

Defoe quickly added, "She is Katherine Brill now, Carl. Married to Jack Brill, the lawyer?"

"Oh, yes. Certainly. I understand. Well, let's get down to the fingerprint section. We only have a skeleton crew in here at night. Emergency stuff that comes in over the telex. The AIDS computer we discussed earlier today is largely automatic; RA's can access directly from their offices, but sometimes we get a hot one from some local police force that needs a quick ID." He stopped in front of a pair of swinging doors and pushed one open, held it as Defoe and Kit went through. "Hey, Brad! You're duty officer tonight, eh? Take care of my friend Mr. Defoe here. Has a set of prints to ID."

A man in his early fifties looked up from a crossword puzzle book and tapped the ash from his cigarette into a foam cup. He was fat for an FBI man, and gray, and needed a shave and some sleep. "Prints," he said, and stood up, dropped the cigarette in the cup, the cup in a wastebasket, and slipped the knot of his tie back up to his fleshy neck. Things had loosened up a little, after Hoover's death.

Jarinko turned to Defoe and said, "I'll leave you in Brad's hands for now. I want to shoot upstairs as long as I'm in here, check things out." He winked at Kit, added, "Isn't every night an AD shows up unannounced. Shake up the troops a bit."

When he had gone through the swinging doors Brad said to nobody in particular, "Who's he kiddin'; the guy in the guard shack spread the word in here before Jarinko hit his parking slot." He looked up at Kit. "We're the FBI. We never sleep." He chuckled, said, "Can I offer you folks a cup of coffee? Best in the building, at least at this time of night it is."

"Yes," Defoe said. "That would be most appreciated."

Brad went over to a Mr. Coffee machine and filled three cups, said, "I don't know what kind of prints you got there, sir, but I hope you don't have high hopes of getting an ID. You must have some clout, getting Jarinko out of the sack at this hour, and nobody's better than I am at lifting latents." He looked up at them. "Cream? Sugar?"

"Please," Kit answered.

"Black for me," Defoe said.

Brad carried the two cups across to his desk and handed them to Defoe and Kit. "You got to realize that only twenty-five percent of latents are good enough to make a match. We need eight points of comparison, and ten is better." He shook his head, and went back for his own coffee. "That stuff they show on the TV all the time, bunch of hooey." He sipped the hot coffee and snorted a mirthless laugh. "Some palooka takes a drink of water, and the detective wraps his handkerchief around the glass, shoves it in his pocket, and next thing you know the killer is behind bars." He put his cup down and stuck his thumbs in the waistband of his slacks, slid them fore and aft, adjusting his body and his trousers. "Afraid it's not quite that easy. Half the time the surface is too rough to take a good print, and the other half they get so smeared they're useless. We've got a lot of tools that can help us, but it's still science, not magic." He paused and picked up his coffee. "Well, now that I've thrown cold water on your expectations, what have you got?"

Defoe reached inside his jacket and took out the index cards he had put in an envelope. "Well, if you're as good as Carl says you are, then these shouldn't give you any trouble at all." He smiled as the FBI man opened the envelope.

Brad put the cards on his desk and looked down at them. "Oh, my, my. Yes indeed." He looked up at Defoe. "You're with a law-enforcement agency, then?" He looked back at the set of prints. "Most professionally rolled."

"No, no, just a citizen. Had my own prints taken a few times, enough to remember how it is done."

Brad looked up at him, raised his eyebrows.

"Naval Intelligence. Retired. Mostly I remember how difficult it was to wash off the damned ink."

"Yes. Must have been a few years ago, then. We've made progress on all fronts since those days. Well, let's get these prints into the system and find out who this fellow is. I assume it's a man. Either that or you've printed the biggest woman I ever saw." He picked up the cards and moved slowly across the room toward a video scanner.

Kit sat down at his desk and held her coffee cup with both hands, looked up at Defoe with tired eyes. "Will you explain to me again just what we are doing, Chase? I mean, what good will it do, will finding out who that man was?"

"Ah. Well, I am assuming that he was hired to, uhm, put us out of the picture. By whoever killed your father. Anyway, his background may indicate who employed him. It's not much, but right now we don't have any other leads to follow." Defoe finished his coffee and put the cup on the desk.

"I don't understand. I guess I must be unusually dense."

"No. I'm tiptoeing around, that's the problem." He pulled a side chair around to face Kit and sat down, their knees touching. "If this man who attacked us has a history of involvement with the government, clandestine involvement, than it stands to reason that my father hired him." Kit looked at him blankly. "The CIA," he said.

"Oh," Kit said. "And if he's not?"

Defoe sighed. "If he seems to be an . . . an underworld character, then I am afraid I have to examine your husband a little more closely."

She shook her head. "Why? I mean, I told you that I think Jack worked for the CIA, too. As a lawyer, not a secret agent, Chase. But still . . . Surely, if you suspect your father, because he was involved God knows how many years ago with government spies, then you have to suspect Jack just as much. I don't understand how, what was it you said, the *underworld?* How do they come into it?"

Defoe reached out and took both her hands. "Kit." He took a breath, held it while his mind raced, then exhaled. "Jack likes to gamble, right? My mother told me today that he got my father interested in pro football, betting on games. Well, I learned today, purely by accident, that the people here were very briefly running a file on Jack. Because of his involvement with a bookie who they had under surveillance. Apparently an organized crime figure." He squeezed her hands, shook them gently. "Jack owes this man two hundred thousand dollars. The Justice Department dropped their wiretap as soon as they realized that he wasn't connected to these people, except as a gambler, Kit. They aren't interested in him anymore. But the thing is, it appears as though he has been having a hard time coming up with the money. Remember what I said, to you and Sammy, when you first asked me to listen to the tape? That it's usually money that is at the bottom of murder?" He let go of her hands, stood up, thrust his own into his trouser pockets. "Since he knows one man involved with organized crime, then I'm afraid that the next step is to assume he knows others. Knows the kind of people who could put him in touch with the kind of people who are . . . like that man tonight." He turned around and looked down at her. "I wish to God I'd never pursued this, Kit. My father, whether he's behind this or not, was right when he said to let it lie, not stir things up!"

Kit got up and put her arms around him, put her cheek against his. She stood that way for a minute, inhaled his scent, then pulled back and looked at him, tears running down her cheeks. "But it's not your fault, Chase." She smiled, more with her eyes than with her lips, and it was a sad smile, one that brought tears to his own eyes. "Maybe the truth hurts; but, somewhere in the Bible; Luke I think, it says 'the truth shall set you free.' "

Defoe blinked and cleared his sinuses, let a choking laugh escape from his lips.

"What's so funny?"

He kissed her forehead, then said, "That's the motto of the CIA." They both turned as Carlton Jarinko came through the swinging doors.

"Well, everything is shipshape topside, how you folks making out down here? Brad?" He walked over to where the lab man was holding one end of a sheet of paper coming out of a thermal printer.

He tore it off and handed it to the director of his division as he said something low in his ear. "Humph!" Jarinko replied, slowly walking across the room and scanning the still-limp sheet of paper. He stopped. Read it again, more carefully, then handed it to Defoe, looked up at his two visitors, and said, "The man is dead."

Defoe met his gaze, studied it for a second, puzzled as to how a set of fingerprints could tell him that. "Yes," he said, "I know. Don't let it bother you too much, though. You told me this afternoon that murder isn't a federal crime. Besides, it was self-defense. Kit will testify to that."

"No," Jarinko said, a serious look on his face, not the lighthearted attitude he had shown earlier in the day when he and Defoe were discussing various charges that could be used to bring someone to justice for the crime of murder. "Read the file. That man has been been dead for twenty years."

Defoe dropped his eyes to the sheet of paper. SPAAR, ROBERT JAMES: Sgt. USMC. B. Baltimore Md. 6/10/1948. Enlisted Marine Corps 5/5/67 SN: USMC130-69-1796 First tour, Vietnam 1968–9. Volunteered second tour of duty, 1969–70. MIA 6/10/70, invasion of Cambodia. Identified KIA 8/5/70 15th Mortuary Co 7th Brigade Bien Hoa. File 8/70-RV 179004 Remains returned to CONUS, released to NOK on 9/24/70. FILE: 33756-896867 GGBN: 43-APPO. Ref. USMC: Q-1971C-400121

Defoe called to the FBI technician who was busy at the coffee machine. "Any chance of a mismatch on the prints I gave you?"

Brad looked at Defoe, then his boss for a moment, while he stirred his new cup of coffee. "None," he said.

"Well then," Defoe replied, turning his attention to Jarinko, "I would say that, like Mark Twain, the reports of his death were greatly exaggerated." He turned to Kit, then back to Jarinko. "The man who has these fingerprints was about the right age to match this Spaar. Interesting coincidence; he was reported missing in action on June sixth. His birthday. Not unusual for a man to get drunked up in celebration and go AWOL. But then his body was identified two months later, at Bien Hoa. Quite a distance from Cambodia. Curious."

The FBI man tried to control the twitch in the muscle at

the right corner of his mouth, and failed. "Sometimes," he said, carefully, "other agencies of the government engineered disappearances, for, ah . . . *strategic* reasons." He took the printout back from Defoe and looked at it again.

"Yes." Defoe peered into his empty foam cup, picked it up, lifted it toward his lips. He stared at some point in the middle distance and drummed his fingers on the side of the cup, making a nervous noise that dominated the silence. "I have to go out to our vehicle for a moment, Carl. Since I'll probably get lost or shot or both on my own, I think that you had better escort me." He headed for the door, turned to Kit, and said, "Be back in a flash. Entertain Brad here with tales of our derring-do in the field tonight."

"Defoe," Jarinko said as they marched double time toward the parking garage, "what the hell are you getting me into here?"

Defoe got his leather-bound notebook out of the Volvo and headed back to the fingerprint lab. "Taking a second step toward tracking the career of Robert Spaar, Carl. I think you may be right. What is the chance of you tracing him through the boys across the river? At Langley?"

Jarinko snorted and said, "CIA? Forget it. I can send over a written request for any data on the individual, wait six weeks, and then get back a 'no agency file exists on the subject.' "

"Thought so." He stopped outside the doors to the fingerprint lab. "Tell me, Carl, you have connections here, into the Net. Can you sit me down in front of a terminal and let me have a few minutes access? I think I can run a back-channel check on our recently departed Mr. Spaar, and clear up some of the mystery surrounding him."

Jarinko looked at Defoe for a few seconds, then said, "What the hell. I suppose if things disintegrate too far I can always drop it on your friend across the street." He smiled. "Besides, I retire in three years, and it will take longer than that to bring any malfeasance charges up through the system." He gestured with his head toward the doors. "Grab your lady friend and let's go do it!"

Defoe, Kit, and the Assistant Director of the FBI, Identification Division, went down the underground hallway to an empty office with a computer link to the outside world. Defoe sat down in the chair and studied the keyboard for a moment, then typed in a series of commands from a page of his notebook and looked up at the screen.

"Ah. You guys subscribe to some of the same data bases that I do. Excellent."

"Defoe," Jarinko said, "we subscribe to *all* of the data bases." He paused. "Even the ones you don't know about."

"Yes." Defoe continued to type, glancing up at the screen from the keyboard. "I imagine that you do. Wake up, Harry." Defoe carefully typed HAWCUBITES and a two digit number, then asked Jarinko to enter the FBI code to complete the interface.

While he was doing that Kit asked, "Who or what is Hawcubites?"

"Band of dissolute young fellows who infested the streets of London in the early seventeen hundreds." He turned his smile to Jarinko and added, "Would have been computer hackers, I'm sure, if there had been such a thing." The screen filled with a series of numbers that swam and rearranged themselves into the shape of a mask, then cleared and were replaced by a large flashing question mark. "Ah! Immediate response. Who was that masked man, anyway? Harry never sleeps. He quickly typed HARRY QUERY ID SPAAR, ROBERT DOB 6-10-48 USMC SN#MC130-69-1796 GO LANGLEY DATABASE TREADSOFTLY DEFOE.

The green-and-black lettering cleared on the screen and was immediately replaced by SOLDOUT DEFOE JEDGAR DATCEN WHATGIVES???

He replied BITE YER TONGUE AND EXECUTE REQUEST. REMEMBER CCNY VIRUS. WARRANT BELIEVED STILL OUTSTANDING. "There," he said, swiveling from the keyboard, "that ought to prompt him into action."

Jarinko was staring at the screen and Kit said, "Would you please tell me what's going on, Chase?"

"Sure. I called a friend in California. Hacker that spends a lot of his spare time poking his nose into places he doesn't belong. He introduced a computer virus into a supposedly secure network a few years ago, and . . . what's the term? 'Wrought havoc.' I was setting up a security system for a company out there, new high-tech outfit with a big defense contract, and stumbled across his trail. Harry had bitten off a bit more than he could chew, got himself involved with some government outfits who have absolutely no sense of humor." He paused and looked at the FBI agent. "I, ah, covered his ass, so to speak." He looked back at the keyboard. "Owes me a couple of favors."

"I should say so, if he can get into the CIA data base."

"Yes; well, it's all relative. Anyone can do anything if they want to badly enough." He looked at the blank screen. "I assume that we can leave this access open for a few minutes this time of night? Harry should be back to us before too long. I have another tape for your man in audio to compare with the voiceprint he ran this afternoon. Can we leave it there for him to try a match as soon as he comes in?"

"What? Oh, sure. Just down the hall." Jarinko got up from his seat beside the computer terminal. "Who is it this time?"

"An old friend of the General's, an old CIA man, as a matter of fact. OSS, really. George, George . . . Phillips." They went next door to the audio lab Defoe had been in earlier in the day and he handed the cassette to Jarinko. "No chance that you could try to match this now?"

Jarinko smiled. "What the hell, we're here. I'll give it a try. Haussman's the expert on this, but I ought to be able to figure out how to run the machine. Joe will be ticked off when he finds out we've been fooling with his equipment, but heck, I'm the boss, right?"

"Sure thing. I recorded about ten minutes of conversation between myself and the suspect. That ought to be enough." They walked over to the bench where the technician had played General Kilgallen's recording and Jarinko snapped the latest cassette into a slot.

"That's more than enough. I don't know if he explained it to you or not, but we just need one word for a voiceprint. A common word, but one that both people used. *And, the,* are both good ones." He began pulling loose-leaf notebooks off the shelf, saying, "The problem is finding out which word Joe used from your tape to make a print, and then finding the darn print!"

She didn't know what they were talking about. Kit wandered over to the racks of tapes at the opposite side of the room and scanned the shelves. Thousands of clear plastic cans held reels of tape, identified with names and numbers written on them in felt-tipped marker. BRILL, JOHN C. was right there at eye level and her heart skipped a beat. She turned and looked at Chase and the FBI man, heads bent over the workbench twenty feet away. She slipped the reel off the shelf and looked for something to play it on. It was reel-to-reel tape, something she hadn't seen since Sammy was a baby. Dee had a tape recorder, back in the days before cassettes. You put the full reel on the left-hand peg, and pulled the tape through the slot, like this . . . Then wind some around the empty reel . . . She looked once more at the men across the room, put the earphones on, and pushed the play button.

Hello?

Daddy Jack! How's it hanging?

Hey doll, I was just thinking about you. You want to spend a couple of days in New York with me?

I can't, I have something to do. Will I see you before you go?

Bet on it, kiddo.

What about her?

I told her I'm taking Amtrak up, like always. So we can spend the night at your place. If you'll make sure I get to the airport for the earlybird shuttle.

Kit felt her face flush, and her ears were on fire beneath the headphones. She leaned against the table that held the tape recorder and watched the reels slowly turn. Their motion made her nauseous; she reached for the controls, but the warm, familiar resonance of their voices transfixed her like a rabbit before a rattlesnake.

Damn, I'm horny. Maybe I'll come over now.

Do that. I'll wrap a lip lock on your root.

Hey, such language.

You love it. Hurry up, Daddy, I'm all wet now.

Okay, I'm coming, I'm coming.

Kit felt her stomach heave and she tore off the earphones, leaned over the table and vomited into a metal wastebasket filled with a brown spaghetti tangle of discarded magnetic tape. She sank to her knees and grasped the rim of the container, cried "Oh, God, *no!*" and vomited again, coughing and gagging through her sobs.

Defoe ran across the room to her and Jarinko arrived a step later. Defoe dropped to his knees beside Kit while the FBI man watched the reel of tape continue to run. His face reddened as he saw the markings on the plastic canister, empty beside the machine, and he angrily rewound the tape and stabbed the off button. "Goddamnit, Defoe, this is confidential information!" He put the tape back in its container and returned the canister to its place on the shelves, then turned and rubbed his hand over his face. "Jesus! What have I gotten myself into?"

Defoe lifted Kit to her feet. She stood with both hands covering her face and cried. Jarinko made a helpless gesture with his hands, then said, "Take her across the hall, Defoe. There's a washroom over there, she can clean herself up." He shook his head and sighed. "And then the two of you get out of here." He looked toward the hallway. "God, if anybody finds out . . ."

The world will come to an end, Defoe thought, and guided Kit across the hall. "Fucking bureaucrats," he said softly as Kit splashed water on her face.

She looked up, said, "What?" and pulled a handful of paper towels out of the dispenser.

"Nothing, just ranting at Jarinko. What happened over there? All this finally catch up with you?"

Kit dampened the towels and sponged the front of her sweater. She stopped and looked up into the mirror at the reflection of Defoe standing behind her. "That tape . . . they —they were talking about . . . Oh, *damn,* Chase. I heard him say he told me he was going up to New York on Amtrak, and they . . . *How long has this been going on?*"

Defoe remembered the Amtrak reference and suddenly realized that she had found the tape of her husband's wiretap. A few hours earlier he had agonized over his inability to tell her about it. Now . . . He put his hand out, touched her shoulder and looked at her face in the mirror. Her eyes were red; bloodshot and rimmed with raw pink flesh where she had worn her makeup away. "I know, Kit. I—I read the transcript of the tapes this afternoon, read about the loanshark, the bookie. And the money he owed him. The real story behind his broken knee. But I also read about his girlfriend, read the transcript of her call, about spending the night with him, catching an early flight. I wanted to tell you, but I—"

"Transcript?" She turned around and shouted at him. *"Girlfriend?* Oh, sweet Jesus Christ! That was *Sammy* on those tapes. My *daughter!"*

Jarinko finally tapped at the door. "Defoe?" he said. "You folks okay in there? There's a—uh . . . answer from your California contact, on the computer. About the dead Marine."

Defoe and Kit had been locked in an asexual embrace, frozen under the bright fluorescent lights in the bathroom a hundred feet below the streets of Washington.

"Okay," he said, easing her away from him. She turned to the mirror.

"Lord, what a mess. I left my purse in the car, didn't I?"

"You look fine," Defoe said, putting an arm around her and leading her to the door. "Be right with you, Carl," he called. To Kit he said, softly, "Ten more minutes, love. Hang in there. Give us a little more General Kilgallen moxie, and then we'll both fall apart, 'kay?" He opened the door.

Jarinko glowered, jerked his head up the hall toward the computer terminal. "Defoe, I guess you are going to owe me one, after tonight. Seems to be the way you work, trading markers back and forth." They headed slowly up the hall, shoes clicking on the polished linoleum tiles.

"I suppose I will, Carl. But that's what really runs this town, isn't it? The quid pro quo that greases the gears of our glorious system?"

The computer screen grinned in bright letters from sunny California in the middle of the Washington night.

SPAAR. ROBERT JAMES; CIA FILE RVN70—544-201 RECRUITED VIETNAM JUNE 1970, PAYROLL DATE OF EMPLOYMENT 6/30/70 THRU 9/30/74. CASE OFFICER BBY-23. SUBJECT COUNTERINTEL OPERATIVE REPUBLIC

VIETNAM/LAOS/CAMBODIA CITED DATES. TERMINATED AUG 74 UNSTABLE AND DEVIATE BEHAVIOR. LAST OFFICIAL CONTACT ON SEVERANCE DATE AT US EMBASSY THAILAND—SEE ABOVE CITED CASE OFFICER FILE FOR DISPOSAL OF AGENT. WHAT THE HECK YOU INTO CHASE???

"An ex-CIA hit man," Defoe said, and concentrated on the keyboard. PURGE MEMORY THIS QUERY. EXPLANATION MAY FOLLOW. HANG TUFF. CHASE DE FOE. He shut down the terminal and stood up. "How did you make out with the voiceprint?" he asked.

"Oh; I couldn't find it. It will have to wait until Joe comes in. Call me around ten o'clock." He folded his arms across his chest and leaned his backside against the desk. "Anything else your FBI can do for you? Since you feel that our entire facilities are at your disposal, twenty-four hours a day."

"Hey, Carl; don't think that I don't appreciate all of your help. I apologize for dragging you down here in the middle of the night." He offered the FBI man his hand. "I'll make it up to you." He paused. "In my line of work I come across . . . interesting bits of information from time to time. Ask Doug."

"I already have." He shook his head and grinned. "He told me that having you for a friend could be a two-edged sword." He took Defoe's hand and then walked them to their car. He retired in three years and would be on the job market. Somehow he thought that Defoe could steer him toward something more lucrative than security chief at a department store.

As they drove up the ramp to the city above, Kit rummaged through her purse and began to repair her makeup in the mirror on the sun visor.

"Now what?" she asked.

"We wait until morning. See if their lab man can match my father to the voice on the tape. Right now I think we ought to get some sleep." He turned and looked at her as he stopped at the top of the ramp, waiting for the guard to release them from the concrete fortress that was the J. Edgar Hoover Building.

Satisfied with her face, she returned her gear to her pocketbook and said, "Well, I'm *not* going back to Dad's, not with a dead man in the backyard. And I guess your place is out of the question. That leaves Georgetown. Jack is either in New York or at my daughter's apartment . . ." She looked over at Defoe as he turned left on Tenth, then right on Pennsylvania and headed west. "I can't believe it. Sammy and Jack. God, that was such a shock, in there. Not his . . . extracurricular activities; I mean, I sort of knew that he . . . no, that's not what hurts." She fished a tissue out of her pocketbook and blew her nose. "I told you, Chase, that he was going through a particularly nasty divorce when I met him. What I didn't say is that his wife made some accusations about child molestation. His daughters." She looked away, out the window at the silent city. "Dear Lord, they must have been true."

Defoe looked over at Kit, then past her, at Lafayette Park, across from the White House. Dark, huddled shapes lay motionless under the sodium lights as they drove by. A nation of extremes, he thought, comparing the slumbering homeless people on his right to the sleeping man who occupied the Oval Office on his left. Aloud, he said, "Don't be too quick to blame it all on your husband, Kit. You told me that Sammy took to him immediately, and that she worshiped her father. Today, at her apartment, she . . . ah . . . indicated that she wouldn't repulse any advances I might make."

Kit turned, looked at him, still holding the damp tissue to her face. "She made a pass at *you?*"

He put his hand out, made a teetering motion with it. "More of an invitation than a pass, but . . . Look, Kit. From what she told me this morning she was hurt pretty badly by Quinn's death; well, you and I talked about that, earlier. Anyway, she has been looking for a father figure, that's what she sees in older men. Unfortunate that your husband had to be one of them. And I can guess how you must feel. What are you going to do?"

She stared through the windshield for a long time. "God knows," she finally said, tossing the tissue into a plastic litter bag that hung from the dash. "Leave Jack, I suppose. My husband is sleeping with my daughter and may have murdered my father, might have hired someone to kill us." She turned back to him. "It's like some soap opera. It's crazy, Chase, but I'm having a hard time really believing all this. Weird."

"No. I think it's a natural reaction. The mind trying to handle it, in its own way. I know I haven't begun to sort out all the ramifications of the possibility that the General was my father."

Kit leaned forward and turned the radio on. "I know that he wasn't." She put her left hand on the inside of his thigh as she tuned the radio with her right. "Because I'm having a terribly difficult time, trying to develop sisterly feelings for you." She turned her attention to the radio. "Funny, that buzzing is only down at the bottom of the dial. There! Some smoky jazz." She leaned back beside him and put her hand back on his leg, closed her eyes. "I wish we'd brought that bottle of brandy with us. Well, there's some just as nice, at the house. Are we there yet?"

"What did you say?"

"I said, Are we—"

"No, about the radio, the bottom of the dial." He pulled over to the side of G Street near Georgetown University and stopped under a streetlight and beside a fire hydrant. He tuned the radio back down to 88MHz. A buzz pulsed from the speaker. "I think we've got a transmitter on board. Most bugs transmit just off either end of the FM band—from 86 to 88 Megahertz on the bottom or 108 to 110 at the top. No stations are assigned a frequency below 88, so anything we hear, like this buzz, is suspicious." He turned off the ignition. "I think someone put a tracker on your car, and has been using it to follow us." He got out and started at the left front fender, began to run his hand underneath the body, feeling for a transmitter. Kit got out and stood in the street beside him, watching.

Five minutes later he had worked his way around the car, and said, "Aha!" as he felt behind the rear bumper. Kronenberger raised his left hand and brought the edge of it down on the right side of Defoe's neck.

He grabbed Kit by the upper arm, twisted it behind her, snapped a handcuff on her right wrist, then took her other arm and cuffed her wrists behind her back. He opened the driver's door and pushed her face down across the seats, took the keys from the ignition and unlocked the trunk. A quick glance at the street and sidewalk satisfied him that they were alone. He put his right forearm under Defoe's throat and his left between his legs, lifted him up, then dumped him in the trunk and shut the lid. "One down, one to go," he said, and walked back to the Bronco.

"No Parking Between the Hours of 7 A.M. and 5 P.M." *I should be back before daybreak,* he thought, and smiled. If not, then Odin could pay the ticket. A slight risk, leaving his vehicle here, but one he had to take. For twenty-five thousand dollars he could afford to take a few. He took his nylon carryall out of the Bronco and locked the doors, tossed the bag on the backseat of the Volvo, and hauled Kit upright.

Kronenberger then got in the passenger seat, took the cuff off her right hand, and refastened it to the steering wheel. He put the key in the ignition and smiled at Kit. "Drive," he said.

TWENTY-ONE

Kronenberger parked behind his business and led Kit, her hands once more cuffed behind her back, to the rear door. He put his carryall down and unlocked the building, led her to his office. "Sit," he said, pointing to the sofa. The windowless building stank of stale air and sex and he went back to the outside door, blocked it open with a brick between the door and jamb, then lit a cigarette and stood for a moment in the hallway as cool air flowed through the narrow opening.

The forty-minute drive from the university had taken them out MacArthur Boulevard, along the river, which they crossed to pick up the George Washington Memorial Parkway on the Virginia side. After passing Langley, Kit had lost track of where they were; the final mile or so had been a series of twists and turns through a commercial world that coexisted but never merged with hers. The last few minutes she drove over empty roads with increasing panic.

She looked around the room at the gray cement-block walls, saw the shelves stacked to the ceiling with cardboard boxes. "What did you do to Chase?" she said.

"Ah, Mr. Defoe. Is that who that was? He, I'm afraid, is a thing of the past. You, I gather, are the daughter, Katherine? Yes, Katherine, we met, earlier this evening." He drew on his cigarette and sat behind the desk, swiveled his chair to face her. "You made a most attractive mermaid, dripping on the floor as you answered the telephone." He smiled as remembrance sent a flicker of fear across her face.

"I was in the closet when your friend Chase showed up. Tell me, what happened to the Clipper? Robert Spaar, the wild and hairy man on the motorcycle?" He got up and went over to his refrigerator, got out a beer. "I suppose he underestimated Mr. Defoe. Well, can't say I didn't warn him." He opened the bottle, took a sip. "Is he dead?"

Kit stared at him from the sofa.

"Cat got your tongue?" He went to the refrigerator again and took out a bottle of vodka. He walked over to the sofa and squeezed her jaws with his left hand as he held the bottle to her lips with his right. "Drink up, darlin'. That's it, couple of big swallows." He forced the neck of the bottle back into her throat, making her gag, then swallow. "Loosen your tongue up, make you talk to old Randolph." He put the bottle on the desk and sat down, listened to her cough. He looked at his watch. "We have an hour or so to kill, until the traffic drops to nothing, up there on the Beltway." He smiled at her, took a swallow of beer. "Be a shame to sit here, not talking to each other. Unless, of course, you can think of something else you'd rather do." He smiled and watched her over the neck of his bottle.

"Who *are* you?" she asked, her eyes filling with tears from the raw liquor and the fear. "Why are you doing this to us?"

He tapped the ash off his cigarette and studied the end of it. "The who is easy to answer, but I won't." He tapped the side of his nose. "Just a reflex from years gone by. Need to know, darlin', need to know. The why is a bit more complex, and a question that I can't really give you a reasonable answer to. I believe your father, the General, was murdered. The man responsible somehow feels that you and your late friend out there acquired information from the tapes that might jeopardize him. 'The damned pictures,' he said. Mean anything to you?" He took another sip of beer. "Well, anyway, now you know as much as I do."

"What are you going do with us?"

"Ah. Now that is a subject I can give you more concrete information about." He stood up and took the vodka back to the sofa and forced another two ounces down her throat. "In about an hour from now, you and your friend out there are going to drive into the Potomac, up where they are repaving the right-hand lane on the Beltway bridge. Nasty spot; just the temporary barriers and the flashing signs. Easy to make a wrong move, especially if you've had a few drinks and don't know the road. Don't worry, you won't feel a thing. You will be strapped in with your seat belt and unconscious when you hit the water." He touched the beer bottle to his temple. "Bump your head against the steering wheel, y'know. They say that drowning's quick, and not all that unpleasant. Relatively speaking." He smiled again and rocked back in his swivel chair. "You don't know how lucky you are, missing the Clipper's attentions."

Kit leaned back and tried to get her wrists into a position where the handcuffs stopped tormenting her flesh. "You're crazy. You'll never get away with this. Someone will see you. We don't know anything. Let us go. Is someone paying you to do this to us? However much it is, I'll double it. My husband's rich, he—"

Kronenberger laughed. "That's it, touch all the bases. You're a tough one, darlin', I underestimated you, back in the house. I told the Clipper that you were a mouse, that you'd fold up if he said boo." He got up and picked up the vodka bottle. "I apologize," he said, shoving it into her mouth once more. "You're a gutsy little gal. Shame we couldn't have met under different circumstances." He put the bottle on the desk and sat down, looked at his watch. "But then I guess you're too good for someone like me, eh? Father a general, husband's a hot-shot mover and shaker. Your pal in the car out there I understand was a big deal, too. Me, I'm just a foot soldier, doing the dirty work for the guys like them." He leaned forward and pointed the neck of his beer bottle at her. "But unlike you and your friend Defoe, I'm a *survivor.*"

There were little explosions of white light, flashes that steadily impinged on his cortex until he regained consciousness. Then a black, whirling vortex that ended in a retching nausea. Unconsciousness was preferable. Just before the night fell he remembered hearing the whine of straight-cut gears and the jolt of the car shifting from reverse into a forward gear. He was in the trunk of a car.

He had been about to remove the transmitter from behind the bumper when something had hit him on the side of his neck. His shoulder was numb and his right arm seemed paralyzed, or at least without feeling. He tried to move it in the dark confines of the trunk and couldn't. He worked his left arm under his body and rubbed his neck, tried to massage some sensation back into his shoulder.

Cardboard boxes dug into his spine and he rolled over, trying to stretch his legs out. It had to be Kit's Volvo. It was very quiet.

He felt around the midnight blackness of his prison, orienting himself. He ran his hands over the smooth interior of the trunk lid above his head, touched the wiring that led to taillights. He swiveled and put his feet against the back of the rear seat, hunched his shoulders against the back of the car, and pushed. Nothing. He turned his body in the cramped space and felt the seat. Steel, an integral part of the frame, blocked him from the springs and upholstery of the rear seat. Damn these super safety cars. He relaxed, let his head sink back against a box, trying to ease the pounding in his brain. What the hell had the guy hit him with, anyway? He tried to wiggle the fingers of his right hand and couldn't. He worked at his neck with the fingers of his left hand and thought.

The corner of the box dug into his neck, and he shifted. The boxes. Kit had said she put her father's pistol and all the ammunition in the trunk. He reached behind his head and tore open the carton, felt through the newspaper for a familiar shape. He found ashtrays and picture frames and dozens of unidentifiable shapes. Then a box of shotgun shells.

He turned over and continued to grope with his one good hand. The right was still without feeling. He found the pistol, a .45 automatic, magazine in place. He located the release and it jumped out of the butt of the weapon. Empty.

He searched through the second carton until he identified a box of ball ammunition, and slowly feeding the cartridges into the magazine with his one good hand, he loaded seven bullets into the weapon. He wedged the gun into his right hand, worked the slide with his left, chambering a round. He needed two hands to lower the hammer on a live round, and with no feeling in the fingers of his right hand he was afraid to try the operation in the dark, so he set the safety and shoved the gun in his waistband. Now what?

He rolled over on his back and stared up at the unseen trunk lid above his head. Where the hell was he? Where was

Kit? Why was it so quiet? Even Georgetown, at one A.M., was noisier than this. He had to get out of the car.

Volvos had to have a decent tool kit, must be something he could use to pry his way out. He felt around the interior of the trunk, felt a leather tab beneath his body, and raised himself up, lifted the hatch that concealed the spare tire. The jack. It took ten minutes to get the various parts out and assemble them in the dark, but he finally managed to get it set up between the floor of the trunk and the lock that held the lid shut. The fingers of his right hand were a mass of pins and needles as feeling began to return to his arm.

There was only enough clearance for him to raise the jack one click before he had to remove the handle and reposition it in the hole, by feel, and raise the jack another click. Thirty-two clicks later the lock snapped with a sound like a gunshot and he dropped the jack handle, groped for the gun and punched the safety off, then lay still, listening.

No reaction from outside. Either nobody was around or the noise had not been as loud as it had seemed inside the insulated trunk. He raised the lid a few inches and peered out.

He could reach out and touch the corrugated siding of the building. On the right side of the car he could see a chain-link fence about twenty feet away; darkness beyond that. To his left a sodium light on the eaves at the front of the building illuminated a steel door a dozen feet from the car. The light stabbed at his retinas and he shut his eyes, seeing a shimmering halo of white afterimage. His pupils were slow to react. He opened his eyes a crack and looked at the light. It kept sliding sideways until there were two spots of white. He looked at the metal door, watched it do the same thing. Whatever he focused on seemed to twin. Great. Double vision; *I must have some kind of nerve damage.* He raised the trunk lid and climbed out. *Even if there's just one of them I'll still be outnumbered.* Dizzy, too, he realized, and leaned against the trunk. At least the nausea had passed. *First Kit, in the FBI lab, now me, in the trunk of her car.*

He stood straight, leaned his back against the car, and breathed the night air. *Where is Kit? Where am I?* He examined his muscles, methodically checking himself. Except for the double vision and a sore neck he seemed to have survived whatever his assailant had done to him. He walked slowly toward the door. He found that by letting his eyes slide past the object of his attention it stayed whole; only when he focused directly on the doorway did it separate into two images. A brick held the self-closing door open a few inches and a bar of yellow light from a naked bulb just inside shone through the gap. He stopped and listened, trying to ignore the pounding of his heart and concentrate on hearing what was happening inside.

He could make out voices, too low to differentiate or understand. He slipped his shoes off and slowly pushed the door open a few more inches. A hallway ran toward the front of the building, disappeared into darkness. A door ten feet ahead was halfway open, spilling white light onto the concrete floor of the hall. That was where the voices were coming from. He held the pistol at port arms and slid along the block wall until he was at the edge of the door.

A man's voice, deep, sure, holding a note of humor. And Kit. He couldn't make out the words, but it was her voice. Carrying tension, fear. Defoe waited and listened, trying to determine if there was more than one man in the room with Kit. As he listened to the sound of fear in her voice he wanted to leap through the door, gun blazing, rescue the damsel. He forced himself to take shallow breaths, forced his pulse to slow. Hardest of all, he forced himself to close his eyes.

Maintain control.

Overt conflict results from inner conflict. A lack of confidence, prejudices, any of the emotions.

Rid the mind of all negative thoughts.

Breathe the way you were taught. The breathing that relaxes the mind, controls it. Inner control must come before outer control is possible.

Knowledge is power, self-knowledge is control of that power.

He opened his eyes and spun on the ball of his left foot through the doorway, the pistol extended in a two-handed combat grip.

No matter how many messages the brain receives it can only concentrate on one at a time.

Except for smell, the rawest and most primitive of the senses, all other data must be processed in the thalamus before going on to the cerebral cortex, otherwise the brain would be overloaded with largely unimportant information. Fortunately the thalamus is able to sort the wheat from the chaff rapidly and efficiently and Defoe was able to ignore the sounds of both Kit and the man's voice, ignore the images of the steel shelving stretched across the wall behind the sofa, the blank wall to his left, the little refrigerator to his right, and concentrate on the man in the swivel chair behind the gray steel desk. The odors of beer, stale tobacco smoke, and sex delivered their messages and got out of the way of the incoming visual data.

The man swung his attention from Kit to Defoe and raised his eyes. He put his hands on the edge of the surface of the desk and pulled his chair closer to it. He began to speak.

"Well, well, Mr. Defoe—"

"Put your hands on top of your hea—"

"What a surprise to—"

"—d and do it slowly."

"—see you in here. You must have an exception—"

"Are there any others, Kit?"

"—ally thick neck, I thought I had broken it."

"Chase! He said he's going to kill us!"

"Keep your hands where I can see them." Defoe reached behind his back and closed the door, closed the possibility of an assault from the rear. The man had put his hands not on top of his head, but had laced his fingers behind his neck and leaned back in his chair, springs squeaking. He casually put his right ankle on his left knee and looked at his captor more as an equal than a prisoner. "Put your gun down, Mr. Defoe. May I call you Chase? You're not going to shoot me. Not in cold blood. You're an officer and a gentleman, and gentlemen don't behave that way. Now someone like me would have walked through that door and put a bullet in the man in this chair without a second's hesitation. That's the difference between you and me, Chase. I'm not burdened with the hangups and baggage your kind have had ingrained from birth. Oh, don't misunderstand me, my friend. I was taught at an early age that 'thou shalt not kill.' And a lot of other

Sunday school nonsense designed to keep children and the lower classes in line. But then I grew up; learned, courtesy of Uncle Sam in Korea that 'thou *shall* kill,' and later was introduced to your Old Boy network when I was recruited by the CIA, learned what *really* makes the world go round. I never became a part of the inner circle, of course. Didn't have the right background and breeding." He turned his head and swung his body on the chair slightly toward Kit, who still sat on the sofa. He dropped his right leg back to the floor and moved the chair a foot to the left so that he was no longer directly in line between Defoe and the daughter. Now if Defoe fired, a miss would hit the woman. "But, as I was just saying to General Kilgallen's daughter, I am a survivor." Defoe would not look directly at him, even though the big automatic was still leveled at his torso. Defoe seemed to be concentrating on a spot somewhere in the middle distance. "I'm amazed that you are still alive, Chase, I really am. You seem to have some trouble, though. Eyes bothering you?" He slowly unlocked his hands and put them on the edge of the desk and began to pull the chair closer once more. "I don't wonder; a blow like that should have crushed the vertebrae in your neck. Well, you have the advantage, my friend. What are you going to do?" Kronenberger raised his left hand in a sharp movement, turning his wrist and looking at his watch.

Lag time is measured in fractions of a second and is caused by internal conflict and external distraction. Sharp, sudden movements can be used to distract and create a short circuit in the cooperation between an adversary's mind and body. Against an armed subject always act when he is talking to you, as that gives you an additional split second's advantage.

Kronenberger fully expected Defoe to respond to his question with some inane demand to put his hands back on his head, and as he turned his gaze from his wristwatch to the man at the door, he was surprised when Defoe shot him in the chest instead.

TWENTY-TWO

The sound of the .45 in the enclosed room overwhelmed the short, scatological exclamation that was Kronenberger's dying declaration.

The sound of the gun was replaced by a high-pitched ping in Defoe's ears and he didn't hear Kit scream, but he saw her roll sideways off the sofa as the man in the desk chair fell forward onto his desk. He saw both images of the man slide from the chair to the floor and lie in a crumpled heap. He saw the little nickel-plated .32 on the floor and the hideout clip beneath the desk as he bent to search for the handcuff key in the dead man's pocket. He touched the side of his neck, searching for a pulse. "I'm no longer an officer," he said softly. "And I'm not even sure what a gentleman is." He found the Peerless key and stood up, put the General's .45 on the desk. "But then neither were you."

Kit had struggled to her feet and Defoe worked the locks on the handcuffs, tossed them and the key on the desk. She looked down at the man on the floor. "Is he dead?"

"Yes. He was about to shoot me with that little gun he had hidden under his desk." He looked around the room. "Who was he? Where are we?" He touched Kit's cheek. "Are you okay? Your lip is bleeding. Did he hurt you?"

She shook her head. "My mouth is kind of sore; he stuffed that bottle of booze down my throat. I've got half a load on, probably why I'm not having hysterics. He said he was going to run us off the Beltway bridge, make it look like I was drunk. I tried to plead, to bargain with him, but it wasn't any use."

Defoe walked over to the shelving and examined the hardware. "Interesting place. Interesting man. He tried to keep control of the situation, right up to the end. Ex CIA. That pretty well tears it, Kit. My father. Let's see if we can find out who this man was." There was a stack of magazines on the shelf. Defoe picked one up and glanced at the cover, then riffled the pile. *The Periscope.* "Journal of the AFIO." He turned to Kit and showed her the cover. "Association of Former Intelligence Officers. Mailing label says Randolph Kronenberger, Federal Supply Company." He looked around the room. "I'd guess that's where we are now." He looked back at the address. "Prospect Industrial Park, Old Georgetown Pike." He bent over the body a second time and extracted Kronenberger's wallet.

"Well, we're in some kind of an industrial park. He made me drive, but after we crossed over the river from MacArthur Boulevard, I was kind of lost." Kit moved closer to Defoe and looked down at the body on the floor. "He said he was going to kill us at the Beltway bridge, and he acted like it was close."

"Yes. I guess we must be out around Langley, somewhere. Not that far from home. Damn! I wish I knew what was going on. Why did they try to kill us? There's something I'm missing, overlooking."

"He said, when I asked him that, why he wanted to kill us, he said that . . ." Kit lowered her head and bit her thumb. "Let me think. He said that Dad was murdered." She looked up at Defoe. "And that there was something on the tapes that . . . that would *jeopardize* him. Not him, the man on the floor there; him, the man who killed my father. And then he, this man, Kronenberger? said 'the damned pictures.' Like he was quoting someone. Then he asked me if it meant anything to *me.*"

"Pictures." Defoe went over to the desk and picked up the .45. "Come on, Kit, let's get out of here. This place gives me the creeps, all this clandestine death machinery. Besides, who knows how many more of these characters are out there, roaming the night." He snapped off the light, then opened the door a crack, looked quickly up and down the hallway.

At the car he said, "Are you okay to drive? My eyes are still a little funny. I was afraid I had a concussion or nerve damage for a while, but it seems to be getting better. Only I'd rather not get behind the wheel just yet."

"Sure. Let's hope we don't get stopped, though. With all that booze he poured down my throat I'm probably over the limit." She watched Defoe fasten her trunk lid down with a wire coathanger he'd taken from the office.

"We're a great pair," he said. "You're over the limit and I'm seeing double." He got in the passenger seat, lowered the hammer on the pistol, and put it in the glove box. "With a loaded, and probably unlicensed gun. Drive carefully, Kit. If we get caught they'll throw away the key." He laughed and leaned across, kissed her. "Let's go find a clean, well-lighted place. With lots of hot coffee and lots of people."

They found both at an all-night truckstop off the Beltway. They both went into the rest rooms and worked on their bodies. Defoe fed quarters into a slot and exchanged them for a towel, soap, and a hot shower, bought a disposable razor and shaved, then spent the last of his change on a shoeshine machine. Kit performed similar ablutions, washed her face with steaming water, then repeatedly rinsed with icy-cold to tone her skin. Her lip was puffy where it had been crushed against her teeth by the vodka bottle. She camouflaged it as best she could with lip gloss, then dusted on a layer of powder and carefully applied eye liner. She damp-combed her hair with her fingers and threw her wedding band in the trash can.

Defoe had two containers of coffee waiting at the restaurant table by the big picture window overlooking the diesel pumps and a paper cup full of ice for her lip. He smiled when she sat down. "You look terrific! I thought we had it all in the men's room; there's even a vending machine that sells everything from combs to condoms, but it looks like the ladies have it beat. Got a beauty shop in there, right? Even found a place to get a quickie divorce."

Kit looked down at her left hand, up at Defoe. "You don't miss a trick, do you?"

He reached across and took the hand in his. "I stayed alive for a number of years by not missing too many." He paused, and gave his head a little shake. "I'll tell you, that ex-Marine out at your father's place was nothing, compared to Kronenberger. Remember, you were handcuffed on the couch, and I asked you if there were any others? And you didn't answer. Instead you said, 'Chase! He said he's going to kill us.' That's when I knew. Knew that he had told you, and convinced you of his intentions. Knew that he considered me already dead, even before he said he thought that he had broken my neck. And that's when I knew that whichever one of us moved first was going to be the one to walk out of that room alive." He let go of her hand and picked up his coffee, sipped it, and looked out the window at the trucks fueling in the night. A man in crisp white coveralls stood on a step ladder and washed the windshield of a crimson-and-chrome Peterbilt with a sponge and squeegee on a stick. "I've never done that, shot a man in cold blood." He turned his attention back to Kit. "It's crazy." He shrugged. "But I don't feel the slightest bit of remorse. No more than if I had shot a stray dog that was chasing my neighbor's cows. I suppose that makes me just as bad as him."

She reached out and put her other hand on his, held it with both of hers. "Don't *say* that, Chase! He was going to kill us, what else could you do?"

Defoe thought for a moment before answering, "What else indeed," he said, peering into her dark eyes.

"Hey," she said, squeezing, tugging his hand. "Remember, when I was agonizing over Dee's death? Because I was the one driving and felt responsible? And you told me not to play 'what if' games. 'Accept the past,' you said, 'and get on with the future,' you said."

"Okay," he said, smiled, and pulled his hand away, picked up his coffee. "Advice given is advice taken. Let's leave the soul-searching for our twilight years and get on with the immediate case at hand. What did the man who killed the General mean by 'damned pictures?' " He tilted the coffee to his lips and closed his eyes. "Pictures. It has to refer to the paintings your father's executive officer found in the bank vault, over in Germany. Remember? There were a couple of big Rubens, and a whole truckload of Italian pictures. I remember your dad saying, 'Caravaggio, Correggio, something like that.' He also said that they were worth ten times the value of the boxes of gold." Defoe got the cassettes out of his suit coat and sorted through them, put them in his recorder, and played them until he found the one he wanted. "Here it is, the last one." He pressed the fast forward button, then stopped, played, repeated the operation until he found the section.

> —Another Rubens. Ah, here's the Italian paintings. Bit smaller than the others. One man can hold them up. Good, clear shots. But I think the first one, the one with the horses, and Jenks, of course, is the one we'll use. Ah. This must be the Roberts man. What was his name? Pierson. Yes, Pierson . . . OSS, I mean, not the Roberts Commission. Hmm . . . No ID on the back. Just First Lt, XX Hq. Of course the photographer wouldn't necessarily know who he was. People coming and going in those days, confusion at the end of the war. We had new faces showing up almost daily. Wait a minute. Here he is, better focus, a smaller painting. Damn. Forty, forty-five years ago. But that looks like . . .

There is the sound of photographic prints rapidly shuffled against one another, and the General says once again

> Damn! It has to be . . . What's he doing . . . never told me he was . . . Son of a bitch!

There is the sound of a desk drawer opening, the ruffle of pages spilling from beneath the General's thumb, then the crisper sound of individual pages turning.

> Call, see what he has to say about this. Queer. I wonder why he never said that he—Hello? Hello! Harmon here; lis—

The tape stopped with a click. Defoe looked up at Kit, sipped his coffee. "That's not the passage I was looking for; there's one earlier, where he has the captain describe the Rubens paintings as being pictures of a bunch of naked broads. But still, I don't see anything about the paintings that would—"

"No, not the *paintings,* Chase," Kit interrupted, excited. "The *pictures,* the photographs themselves! It's that man; Pierson? You said that Dad recognized him, remember?"

"Sure. But he's dead; your father got a copy of his OSS file . . ."

Defoe hit the rewind button and the General's voice squealed at high speed. Two truckers in cowboy boots and tight jeans looked up from the next table at the sound.

> Damn! It has to be . . . What's he doing . . . never told me he was . . . Son of a bitch!

"Son of a bitch is right," Defoe said. " 'What's he doing'; 'never told me he was'—both remarks referring to the *present.*"

> Call, see what he has to say about this. Queer. I wonder why he never said that he—Hello? Hello! Harmon here; lis—

"I think he called this 'Pierson.' " Defoe looked up from the machine into Kit's eyes. "Earlier today I accepted as gospel the OSS file on Pierson, just as your father did. That he died in Greece a couple of months after the incident with the crates of gold." He reached across the table and took Kit's hand. "But you saw the report on that man who tried to kill us. Killed in Vietnam, twenty years ago. Why couldn't the CIA files—OSS, I mean—have been diddled the same way? You're right, Kit. Your father recognized this Pierson, recognized him as someone who was still alive. And called him up."

"And he *killed* Dad, after all these years? Because he made off with some gold?"

"Yes," Defoe said carefully. "If it was someone whose reputation stood to be destroyed if knowledge of what he had done got out. Someone like my father." He looked down into his coffee cup, swirled the dregs that lay in the bottom. "Someone who would refer to *photographs,* not paintings, as 'pictures.' His generation says 'motion pictures', ours calls them 'movies.' 'Pictures' versus 'photos.' We know he was over there, on VE day, Kit. Said so himself. And he told me he was involved with this Roberts Commission. No reason to think that he wasn't there on other occasions. He very easily could have been the one who went to this little town and checked out the stolen paintings in the bank vault." Defoe drank the last of the coffee.

"Chase! Your *father,* stealing gold bars? Come on; he was rich, even then, wasn't he?"

"Yes, but . . . who knows what motivated him? Say he found himself away from his dull and cosy Research and Analysis desk in Washington, thrust into the action with the Special Ops boys, and lost his head. Anyway, I just realized how we can answer the question, once and for all." He ejected the cassette and put another one in, played a brief selection, said, "Yes, I think this is the one . . ." and began to search for the passage about the photographs.

> —the Office of War Information released a lot of Signal Corps photos for general media use during the war. All that material is now at the National Archives, in the still-picture collection. We had the sergeant's name, his unit, and the date the photos were taken, so I called the director of the Archives, who put me in touch with the proper person, and I ordered a set of prints, everything the photographer shot that day. He assured me that I'd get the photographs in a day or two, so I am expecting them tomorrow or the next day. I look forward to seeing them; from the way Jenks described the scene there should be some rather dramatic pictures of the large Rubens—

"There! The name, unit, and date this sergeant took the pictures. That's all the General needed to find them, and that's all we'll need."

"Where did he say he got the sergeant's name? Someplace in Maryland, wasn't it? Find the place on the tape."

"Not necessary. The photographs are at the National Archives, and they must have some kind of a record of what your father, *our* father, ordered. It was sometime last week. How many requests for that sort of thing can they get?"

"So we wait until they open, waltz in, and tell them to drag out the box of pictures for us to look at."

Defoe closed one eye and looked at her. "How long have you lived in this town, dear? Long enough to know that one doesn't *waltz* anywhere, not without a great deal more clout than we have." He stood up, said, "Get us a couple more cups of coffee, would you? I have to pop out to the car for my bible."

Kit got up and accepted the dollar he handed her. "Who is it this time, Chase? The Librarian of Congress?"

"Nope." He smiled. "The guy who offered to help us in this exact situation. Senator Kinship."

The horizon was outlined with a thin orange line and the sky above it was turning to a paler blue, but the stars still sparkled overhead when Defoe went back into the truckstop with his book. "Good morning, Senator. I'd apologize for waking you, but you're a notoriously early riser, so I thought that six would not be too soon to call."

"Not at all, son. Surprised to hear your voice, though. My house boy said 'Mr. Defoe,' and I naturally assumed that it was your father calling."

"Afraid not, although he may figure into the equation. You remember you asked me to let you know what was going on with this mess concerning General Kilgallen's notes and tapes? And that you offered to help."

"That I did, Chase. What can I do for you?"

"Well, we—Kit and I—have discovered that the whole thing hinges on some photos, old Signal Corps pictures, in the National Archives. We would greatly appreciate it if you could cut through whatever red tape they have in place to delay the great unwashed, and get us in to have a look at the photographs in question. The General ordered copies, and we have him receiving them the day he died on one of the tapes, so I'm sure that the archive people will have a record there of what he ordered. Sometime last week."

"Certainly; no problem. Let me give the director a call. I'll catch him at home and tell him what we need. I'm sure that he will have the materials available for you by the time they open up."

"Wonderful! We appreciate your help. Oh, do you happen to know what time they open?"

"Probably nine. Use the Pennsylvania Avenue entrance, not the one around on the Constitution Avenue side. That's where the tourists go in, to gawk at the Declaration and the Bill of Rights. You want the Central Research facilities. Just ask the guards at the desk inside, they'll direct you upstairs. Son? You promised to keep me up to speed on this. What's it all about?"

Defoe looked across the room at Kit. A tall man with a weathered face under a Stetson and a breakfast tray in his hands paused and leaned slightly toward her, said something. She looked up and smiled, shook her head, mouthed a sentence. The man touched the brim of his hat with two fingers and moved to an empty table where he could enjoy breakfast with a view. The rising sun sent a shaft of gold across the universe and illuminated her face. "I think, Senator Kinship, that General Kilgallen recognized the man who killed him. A bit difficult to explain; it all revolves around things that happened long ago. Once I see the photographs I'll know for sure. Let me get back to you when I have something definite."

"Fair enough, son. I'll be in my office on The Hill all morning."

"Thank you, Senator."

Defoe put the receiver on the hook and stood, watching Kit, until a man stopped at the pay phone, waiting for him to leave. "All set," he said, sitting across from her. He looked at his watch. "How 'bout some breakfast? We've got a couple of hours to kill until the Archives open."

"I don't usually eat like this in the morning," he said, cutting a sausage link with his fork. "Piece of toast or an English muffin and a cup of tea is about it. Maybe a piece of fresh fruit." He had ordered, in addition to the sausages, a three-egg omelet, a glass of orange juice, and another cup of coffee. Kit had replicated his order, substituting bacon for the sausage. "But then I lost my dinner, or most of it." He looked up and cocked his head at Kit. "In the trunk of your Volvo, I'm afraid. I guess I'll have to rent one of those carpet shampoo machines later today and clean your car."

She put her hand to her mouth, tried to chew, swallow, and stifle a laugh simultaneously, wound up choking. "God! At least I didn't have to clean mine up. Oh, Chase, I was so embarrassed, back at the FBI. What must your friend think of me?"

"He needed something like that, to loosen him up. That must have been a nightmare for you, Kit. At least Jack isn't the one who killed your father. He was about ten when the OSS man was making off with the boxes of gold." He finished his juice and looked at her. "Are you sure that you are making the right move?" He gestured toward her ringless hand with his eyes. "Taking off your wedding ring?"

"Taking it *off?* Chase, I threw it in the trash can, in the ladies' room." She put her fork down across her plate. "I thought about it, when that man had me handcuffed in his office back at that industrial park. He . . . he didn't come right out and *say* it, Chase, but the couple of times he mentioned you it was in such a final, 'used-to-be' way, I just knew you were dead. And I thought that was where I was headed. He was so . . . I don't know—*evil,* I suppose. There was a certainty to the things he said . . . Anyway, I had time to think about my life, in between the shots of vodka he poured down my throat. I realized that I never loved Jack, that I had married him for the pure and simple, selfish reason that I needed someone to take care of me and Sammy. Support us." She looked down at her plate and pushed bits of her omelet around it with her fork. "I must have known, on some level, that the charges his wife were making about child molesting had *some* basis in fact." She sighed, sniffed back tears that were verging on escape. "Am I. . . . responsible for Jack and Sammy—"

"Hey. Remember 'no looking back'? Maybe that's not a good way of putting it. Studying the past can prepare us for the future." He reached across and took her hand. *I've been doing this a lot today,* he thought. *Touching her.* "I have this friend, her favorite phrase is 'no blame.' She's ah . . . a witch."

Kit looked up, startled.

"Yeah, I knew you'd say that." He grinned. "Not hocus-pocus, black cats, and brooms. She's more into dancing naked at certain times of the year. Seriously Kit, witchcraft, the real thing, is a terribly ancient religion. Predates Christianity by a couple of millennium. Christianity in fact absorbed quite a few traditions and celebrations from the 'old way.' Never mind Halloween; there are more basic tenets than that involved, but that's beside the point. What I'm saying is they believe that there is a cause and effect relationship in everything. The pop expression 'what goes 'round, comes 'round.' Only with a negative twist. That is where Good and Evil, with a capitol G and E, enter into it. The witches break the loop of evil by saying 'no blame.' They aren't *excusing* behavior, no way. Because they believe every act, good or evil, is returned threefold. Pretty strong motivation for the old 'do unto others' homily. No, they are just saying accept something that didn't work out so well. The car wrecked, Quinn was killed. You married Jack; never mind the *reason.* The accident happened, you and Jack Brill got married. So? They were *occurrences,* but they don't have to have negative *values* assigned to the participants. Because that negativity carries forward, creating more negativity, in an endless cycle. Blame-guilt, blame-guilt. It's okay, Kit, to see a cause and effect in something, but stay away from assigning blame. My witch friend would say, about marrying Jack, 'Yes, I did it, it was wrong, I shouldn't have done it, and I will never do it again. Now, let's get on with life.' Am I making any sense?" He let go of her hand and sat back, picked up his coffee cup. "I'm ranting, aren't I?"

She looked across at him and smiled. "I love you," she said.

TWENTY-THREE

They found a place to park on Constitution Avenue near the IRS Building and walked past the Justice Department to the National Archives.

A broad sweep of steps soar up to Corinthian columns supporting the classic portico and sheltering the forty-foot-tall bronze doors that lead to the holy and historic documents of the nation.

Defoe and Kit glanced at a sign on a stanchion. It said that the Archives were on winter hours until the thirty-first of March, and that the building was open from ten in the morning until five-thirty in the afternoon.

They ignored both the sign and the entrance, continued past, turned left at Seventh Street, and walked up the east side of the building. The ramp that led to underground parking and a loading dock was secured by a simple bar across the roadway and tended by a man in a little glass kiosk. No steel plates in the roadbed and bulletproof guard house here, across the street from the FBI Building. A sign said "Delivery hours 9:30AM–4:30PM ONLY." At the bottom of the ramp "CLEARANCE 13′6″ was stenciled overhead.

They turned left again at Pennsylvania Avenue and approached the doorway that is flanked by a pair of massive statues. On the right a toga-draped man sits with a closed book on his lap and a bemused expression on his face. "Study The Past" is chiseled into the plinth below his seat. Across from him, to the left of the doors, a similarly dressed woman also sits, with an open book on her lap and "What is Past is Prologue" carved in the stone beneath her feet. Defoe and Kit paused at the edge of the fountain between the two figures and read the inscriptions before heading for the entrance. A small sign on the door announces that hours are 8:45AM to 10PM Mondays thru Fridays, and that the research rooms close at 5:15 on Saturdays.

Defoe looked at his watch. "Five of nine, but it looks as though we can go on in. Senator Kinship said that he thought they weren't open until nine." Defoe held the bronze-framed glass door for Kit and they walked side by side to the circular information desk presided over by two uniformed guards. A clipboard with a sign-in sheet already bore a half dozen names and signatures. Defoe spoke to the senior of the two.

"Good morning. Chase Defoe and Katherine Brill. I believe that your director is expecting us."

The woman, thirty, black, wearing glasses and a nameplate that said Edith Coyne, looked at her partner; white, early twenties, sparse mustache, and a nameplate that said Jeff Newman.

"What?" he said.

"Chase Defoe. Your director is expecting us. We've come to see some photographs."

"Mr. Prescott?"

"I don't know his name. Senator Kinship was to have arranged this."

"You know anything about this, Edie?"

"Nuh uh. Nobody said nothin' to me about it." She cocked her head, looked under the counter, then at Defoe. "Don't have nothin' here about nothin' like that." She looked at Jeff. "Mr. Prescott say anything to you about these people?"

"No."

"Well," Defoe said, "how do we go about seeing Mr. Prescott?"

"He ain't here."

"Doesn't come in until later."

"I see. Is there someone else we could talk to about looking at some photographs?"

Edie looked at him over the tops of her glasses. "Yeah. Upstairs, second floor."

"Ah, thank you." Defoe took Kit's arm and started to circle the structure to the elevator behind it.

"Whoa! Can't go up there, sir."

"No? Why not?"

"You got to sign in." She pushed the clipboard half an inch closer to the edge of the counter. Defoe wrote his name and address below the last entry, then signed on the appropriate space.

"Lady, too," Edie said.

Jeff leaned over the counter and looked down at their feet. "Any cameras or computers?"

"No," Defoe said.

"If you have any cameras or computers you have to sign them in, with the serial numbers."

"Fine," Defoe said as Kit filled out her line on the form. "I'll remember that."

"Second floor," Edie said.

"Thank you. I'll remember that, too."

The elevator dated from the time that the building was completed, in 1935, two years after President Hoover laid the cornerstone. It was lavishly appointed with bronze Art Nouveau castings and had mover's quilts covering the three walls. Defoe wondered aloud if they were to protect the elevator or the objects it carried. It was a large freight elevator, capable of carrying a full-sized automobile. At the second floor they stepped into a marble-floored lobby with a fifteen-foot ceiling, glanced at a display of archival photographs and documents, and went into room 207.

"Got to sign in," a guard told them.

"We did that, downstairs," Defoe told him.

"Yessir. That was for downstairs." He turned a clipboard to face them. "Sign here, please."

While Defoe filled out his name and address he asked, "Who do we see to look at some photographs?"

"Ah. Photographs. Still Picture Collection. 18-N."

"Eighteen? As in floor?"

"Yessir."

"Then why are we signing in here?" Kit had already begun to fill out the line below Defoe's.

"Got to get your R-I-D card before you go up there."

"R-I-D?"

"Your research identification card." The man indicated a desk across the room. "Over there."

Defoe took a tentative step in that direction, fully expecting to be halted because he had not completed some unknown intermediary step required before one could proceed.

Getting an R-I-D card involved a long series of easily answered questions, embroidering the truth to save explaining that they were looking for a murderer, then showing sufficient identification, and took less than ten minutes. They took the elevator to 18-N. "It gets worse," Defoe said, during the trip. "Next comes the strip-search."

"Oh, goody," Kit said.

Facing them as they got off the elevator was a display of World War Two photographs under glass and a doorway to their left that was the office of the Still Picture Collection. A man occupied the first desk and a young woman the second.

"Good morning," Defoe said, smiling and showing his R-I-D card. "We'd like to see some photographs."

"Certainly, sir," the man said, and handed them each a two-page document entitled Research Room Procedures. "Read the regulations and then fill out the form on the back and sign the document." He waved his hand toward a door to their right. "Then you may proceed to the Research Room."

Defoe gritted his teeth as he read the document, muttered to Kit as he filled out his form. "Now you see why I wanted to have Senator Kinship run interference for us. Wonder what happened to him, anyway." He handed his completed form to the man and turned toward the door.

"Sir! You'll have to sign in first." He offered Defoe another clipboard and a smile.

The Research Room was twenty-five feet square and windowless. Library tables were illuminated by fluorescent lights and surrounded by chairs. As Defoe and Kit entered from the office a door at the other side of the room opened and a woman carrying a stack of boxes came through. Behind her they could see steel shelving stretching off into the distance. "Hi!" she said, putting the boxes on the table nearest the door to the stacks. "Can I help you?"

"Don't you want us to fill out a form first?" Defoe asked.

"What? Haven't you gotten your Research Room Procedures?"

"Yes, we have. Just thought there was another step before we could actually look at some photos."

"No. Well, yes, there is. You have to tell me what photographs you want."

Defoe waved his hand at the door behind her. "Can't just go back and poke around, eh?"

The woman blanched. "Are you serious? Staff only, sir. Howard or I will bring the archival materials in question to you. Except it will have to be me, because Howard isn't in yet. Something happened to his car. Again." She leaned closer and lowered her voice. "Confidentially, I think the problem is with his alarm clock." She stood back and gave them a knowing look.

"Yes. Well, Miss ah . . . how do we go about seeing some photos, then?"

"Alyce. Alyce Carpenter. Alyce with a 'Y.' You just give me the document number and I go get the box for you." She pointed to the boxes on the table, gray containers five inches wide and twice as tall and deep. "We have five million photographs back there. Just tell me what you want and I'll get it for you."

"Yes. Well, we don't know what we want. That's the problem. General Kilgallen ordered some photographs last week. Those are the ones we would like to see."

"General Kilgallen?"

"Lieutenant General Harmon Kilgallen. US Army, Retired. He called and ordered a set of photographs. You people sent copies to him, via Federal Express."

"Oh. What photos were those?"

"That is what we would like to find out. And then look at. Alyce; there must be a record here of what people order from you."

"Yes, sir. But it's confidential. I mean, we can't go giving out—"

"Alyce! Have you heard of General Kilgallen? On the news? He died last week. The funeral was yesterday; he was buried at Arlington. This is his daughter, Katherine. His next of kin? Surely you could let her see the photos that he was looking at just before his death."

"Oh." Alyce looked at Kit, then back at Defoe. "Well yes,

we have that information on file. But I'll have to get permission from the curator to release it to you. Wait here, please."

She went out to the office and Defoe opened the door to the stacks, peered in. The steel shelves stretched for a city block under dim, filtered light in temperature and humidity controlled air. Five million photographs, silently waiting, documenting the past.

"Hey! You can't go in there!" Defoe turned as Alyce came back into the room behind a middle-aged man in a tweed jacket with baggy pockets. "Authorized staff only, sir!"

"Sorry," Defoe said. "Thought I saw a silverfish." He held out his hand. "Chase Defoe."

The man took it, shook it with a two finger grip. "Mr. Aubrey."

"How do you do, Mr. Aubrey. Katherine and I would like to see the photographs that the General ordered copies of last week. Alyce seems to feel that would be a breach of security."

"Yes. Well, ordinarily we don't give out that sort of information." The curator took off his glasses and wiped them with a lens-polishing tissue he pulled from a packet he produced from the side pocket of his jacket.

"Is there a reason for that or is it just a government regulation?"

"What? Sir, the world of academic research is a cutthroat one. Dog eat dog out there. They'll steal a march on one another at the drop of a hat."

"Quite so. And you are to be commended on your security. However, the General is deceased, and his daughter is contemplating carrying on his research. So any assistance that you might be able to render would be greatly appreciated."

"Yes." The curator replaced his glasses and studied both Defoe and Kit through them. "I suppose, as next of kin, we could make an exception, just this once . . . What General was this?"

"Didn't Alyce tell you? General Kilgallen. Harmon Kilgallen."

"*Kilgallen?* Hmph! Popular set of photographs."

"What do you mean?"

"Well, you're the second ones to ask about those photographs this morning, and it's not ten o'clock yet."

"Oh? Who else asked about them?"

"I guess there's no harm in giving out *that* information. Senator Kinship. He was here when we opened, at quarter to nine." The curator looked at his watch. "He left, about fifteen minutes ago. It's a wonder you didn't pass him on the way up."

"Alyce, would you get the photographs for us, right *now?*" Defoe switched to his authoritarian voice, the one that commanded rather than asked. It was a voice that did not invite discussion. "Mr. Aubrey, I'll need to use your telephone." He turned the curator with a firm grip on the man's elbow and led him toward the office. Defoe picked up a phone and dialed.

"Dad! It's Chase. Quick question."

"Chase. You didn't come in last night. Your mother was concerned."

"Yes. I'll explain, later. Senator Kinship. Was he involved with you, during the war? The OSS?"

"Billy? No, of course not. Foolish question."

"Are you sure?"

"Certainly I'm sure. He was with the Roberts Commission. I recruited him. Had his master's in art history; was teaching at Yale. What the hell's this all about?"

"I'll explain that later, too. G'bye." Defoe replaced the receiver and went back into the Research Room. He opened the box and spilled the photographs across the table and turned to Kit. "Look for shots of paintings by Correggio or Caravaggio. You, too, Alyce."

"What do they look like?"

"Good point. Italian Renaissance, but never mind. Those are just the artists that General Kilgallen mentioned. If there were two entire truckloads of paintings there had to be others. Yes, I think this is a Raphael. Never mind the paintings, look for Senator Kinship."

Five minutes later he had nearly fifty photos spread across the table and was frustrated. "Damn! I was sure that Kinship was the man. Dad just told me that he was with the Roberts Commission during the war, Kit. But none of these men even remotely resemble him. No way your dad could have spotted him." He looked up at the archivist. "Alyce. Would it be possible to swipe a couple of these pictures?"

"What? No, certainly not!"

"Why?"

"Well . . . because we have a count of the photos in each file, and we check to make sure that they are all there, after the researcher is finished with them."

"Even someone as . . . *important* as Senator Kinship?"

"Well, I can't answer for the other archivists, but I would count the documents. We don't *lose* the materials entrusted to our care, sir. It's a sacred trust!"

"Yes, very nice. Did you, in fact, count these pictures after the senator was finished with them?"

"No. I brought the box from the stacks when Mr. Aubrey told me to. But then I went down to Two, to pick up the day's mail requests. I suppose Mr. Aubrey must have put the file back."

Defoe went to the curator's office and asked him if that was in fact what he had done.

"Yes. Alyce was downstairs and the other assistant hadn't come in yet." Aubrey looked at his watch. "Still hasn't, for that matter."

"Did you count the photographs? Make sure they were all there?"

"Yes. Certainly. It's standard procedure. These materials are entrusted to our care, Mr. Defoe."

"I understand. So everything was there?"

"Yes. I remember; it was forty-seven photographs."

Defoe went back into the room with Kit and Alyce and the forty-seven photographs. He put his foot on the seat of a chair and stared at the glossy eight-by-ten shots of two-and-three-century-old paintings being held by two and three decade old GI's. He leaned forward and pulled one of them closer. "Wait a minute, what's this?" It was a black-and-white photograph of Saint Sebastian, tied to a tree and full of arrows. Just the canvas; no frame, no grinning soldier supporting it for the Signal Corps sergeant. He found another similar shot of a naked woman holding a baby with a halo. "Look," he said, pointing to the lower left-hand corner of a print. Crossed flags in a circle were surrounded by the words "SIGNAL CORPS." "The logo is on all the other prints, except these two." He looked at Alyce. "Isn't that unusual?"

"Yes. That logo is like a watermark; it's on the negatives. It was on the film that they used. If these are all Signal Corps photographs, then they should all have it."

"Clever, clever. Senator Kinship switched photos on us. Removed the ones with him in them. Probably grabbed a handful from his own collection this morning, shortly after I called him, hustled down here ahead of us, and switched the prints." He looked up from the photographs spread across the table. "Nobody gave *him* the third degree about looking at the file General Kilgallen had requested, so he assumed that we would be treated the same way. Alyce here would fetch the box and leave us alone. No reason for his name to ever be mentioned. Probably cruised in senatorial splendor past all those sign-in sheets that delayed us. Where would the negatives you mentioned be now, Alyce?"

"Gee, I don't know. We have some here. But they could be out at Suitland. Of course lots of them are gone; I mean, we never had them to begin with. That's the case with most of the pictures from the war."

"So he figures that he's home free. No evidence to put him at the scene of the crime, fifty years ago. Unless we can come up with the negatives it's a dead end, Kit." He turned to Alyce. "You can put these away where they belong." He reached out to Kit for her hand, said to her as they walked out of the Still Picture Collection on the eighteenth floor, "Even with a photograph showing Bill Kinship holding an Italian Renaissance painting forty-odd years ago, what would it prove? Not that he killed your father."

Defoe pushed the bell for the elevator. "But he did, didn't he?" Kit asked. "It all fits together, Dad recognizing him from the photos, calling him up. And the senator came through those French doors into the den and . . ."

"Yes. That must be pretty much what happened." The heavy doors closed behind them and Defoe pressed the button marked G.

"What about the thing you did with the tapes, over at the FBI building?"

"The voiceprints. Yes, I was just thinking about that. I'm afraid, Kit, that Jarinko wouldn't touch it with a ten-foot pole. Not unless the request came directly from the Justice Department. And I doubt that I can convince Doug to start an investigation, not with the evidence we have. A voiceprint that might or might not be the senator. A forty-five-year old picture that might be the senator. Your father's supposition that he made off with a couple of boxes of gold. The whole thing is too chimerical, too circumstantial. Without a strong possibility for a conviction, no prosecutor would touch a case like this. Certainly not when it involved a United States senator."

"Well, look at the bright side of it. Your father didn't do it." They stepped out of the elevator and left the building through the doors they had entered an hour earlier.

"Yes, I suppose you're right, Kit. Doesn't mean he *is* my father, though. The dates are still the same; he was off on the other side of the Atlantic when I was being conceived."

A figure with a shock of white hair and a black overcoat sat on the edge of the empty fountain, facing the entrance to the building.

"Senator Kinship," Defoe said.

"Good morning, son, Katherine." He stood up and took Kit's arm, dwarfing her with his bulk, and gestured toward the curb with his cane. "Keys are in the ignition, Chase. You drive. Help an old man with a bum hip, child." He kept a firm grip on Kit's arm and followed Defoe to the black Lincoln that sat facing east on Pennsylvania Avenue. "One of the more tangible perquisites of office," he said, opening the rear door and pushing Kit in, then quickly getting in behind her. "You can park anyplace you damn well please in this town. Around the block, young fella, and head out Constitution, back across the river."

Defoe started the car and looked up at the senator's reflection in the rearview mirror. "Where are we going?"

"Going? Going home, son. To Fairfax County. To George's house."

TWENTY-FOUR

Defoe crossed the river and picked up 66. "Why did you do it?" he asked.

The senator paused for a moment, then expelled a short, mirthless laugh. "You couldn't understand. I know that George was worth a couple of million bucks when you were born, and I suppose a great deal more than that by the time you went off to college. You've never known what it was like to be poor. Poor and living in a rich man's world.

"I *worked* my way through Yale, son. Waited tables for people like your father. Tutored rich men's sons too dumb to make it through on merit. Worked on the docks during the summer, loading freight. All so I could get an education, study art. Be surrounded every day by the beautiful things I could never hope to own.

"And then one day I found myself in the middle of a war, in the middle of a stream, with a jeep full of gold and one lone buck private between me and a fortune. The temptation was too great and I performed a rash act. Buried the boxes, disposed of the jeep and driver, disappeared back into the confusion that was the spring of '45.

"In 1947 the CIA was chartered and I signed on soon after. Knew it was my ticket back to Europe, back to my gold. That was the year the Marshall Plan went into effect, and billions started pouring in to help rebuild the Continent. Of course the unspoken, but equally important part of the Plan was Soviet containment. Hence the CIA involvement. I retrieved my gold, smuggled it to Switzerland, and converted it into cash. Started buying art from impoverished refugees. I sold

George that Monet he has in the dining room, did you know that?

"Anyway, I spent the next couple of decades in the CIA, running operations and dabbling in the international art market. Until Schlesinger came along, in '73. He was appointed DCI in February and started cleaning house. Got rid of anybody who had been with the Agency for more than twenty years. Better than a thousand CIA officers went out the door, over a hundred from the DDO, and I was one of them. Son of a bitch didn't know it at the time, but it was the best thing that he could have done for me. I was out of work, had a few million bucks of my own, squirreled away here and there, too old to find another job, so the logical thing to do was run for the Senate. With some help from a few old friends, and George was one of them, I won. I find being a rich and powerful senator vastly more rewarding than being either an underpaid clandestine bureaucrat or an impoverished art historian. Does that answer your question?"

Defoe looked up in the mirror at the senator. "An interesting history, but no. I had already assumed that you stole the gold because of plain old-fashioned greed. What I wanted to know was why you killed General Kilgallen."

"*Harmon?* I didn't kill Harmon!"

"Senator. He recognized you in the photographs as this 'Pierson' from the OSS. It's on the tape. Are you denying that it was you who he called right afterward?"

"Of course not. I'd be a damned fool to do that. Federal Express will have a time and date they delivered the pictures. The radio in the kitchen mentioned the time, and if that isn't enough, my telephone number and the time of day will be on his bill." The senator watched Defoe react in the mirror. "Missed that, didn't you, son? Sloppy detective work, young fellow."

"Okay. I should have thought to call the phone company, to find out who he called. Then if you didn't kill the General, who did?"

"Ah, now there's the question, isn't it? I suggest we wait, and ask George Defoe to answer it for us." The senator leaned back and closed his eyes, but kept his arm linked through Kit's.

Strange, Defoe thought, flicking his eyes from the road to the mirror, watching the old man beside Kit. *He keeps saying George Defoe, not "your father." I wonder if he suspects the truth. It is an awful,* naked *sensation, having your paternity, your ancestry stripped from you. I don't know who I am anymore—everything I always knew as* me *is gone. The portraits of my ancestors, all those dead Defoes—all a bunch of strangers. I'm a* Kilgallen *and I don't know who they were. I've always had this strong identity as a Defoe—they go back three hundred years and more, back to England before the pilgrims. It's a shock, to suddenly find out that you are not who you thought you were. And now we are going to confront the man I considered my father for nearly fifty years, confront him and accuse him of murder. Accuse him of murdering my father.*

Defoe sighed and turned off the narrow country road, drove slowly up the driveway to the house. Senator Kinship opened his eyes and held onto Kit's arm as they got out of the back of the car. "Open up, son," the senator said, waving his cane at the front door. "And lead us to George." He chuckled. "We'll beard the dragon in his den."

The hall was the same cool and quiet oasis that it had always been, but instead of imbuing him with a familiar sense of place it suddenly was foreign to Defoe and he hurried through it, leading Kit and the senator to the library doors. The entire house seemed still, as though it were waiting, holding its breath as these intruders crossed the threshold. George Defoe was at his desk with *The New York Times* and a cup of coffee. He looked up at them across the top of his reading glasses.

"Bad penny or tomcat, which is it? Hello, Kit. I hope *you* haven't been keeping company with this rake. Billy, good morning. Are the three of you arriving together?"

"Hello, George. Yes, yes, we are." The senator looked around the room, led Kit to the sofa, and eased both of them down on the cushions simultaneously. "Where's the rest of your household?"

"Butterfield drove Anna to the bus terminal. Something the matter with a relative, down where her people are from. Mary went out to replenish the larder. Apparently she'll be cooking for the next few days. Made a pot of coffee before she left. Want some?"

"Good, good. We'll have some time alone, then. To sort things out." The senator looked up at the younger man. "Yes, coffee would be just the thing, don't you think, son? For all of us. I'd send missy here to tend to us, but I need her right here. Besides, it's not her house. Chase, you know where everything is. Don't suppose there are any of those delicious scones that we had . . . My God, it was just yesterday, wasn't it?" He turned to Kit and spoke to her directly for the first time that day. "Time passes quicker the older you get, doesn't it, child?"

Defoe turned and went to the kitchen. He closed his eyes and breathed slowly and deeply, picturing the number on the screen behind his eyes. He punched it on the wall telephone, said, "Chase Defoe again. Is he in? Thank you." While he waited he walked across the room and picked up a silver tray, put three cups and saucers on it, unplugged the coffeepot. "Doug! G'morning. Listen, I need a big favor and I need it fast. No, don't interrupt, I'll explain all the FBI nonsense later. This is vital. I need you to check some local telephone calls. Do it back channel, there's no time to play it by the numbers. I know you have hotshots there with their sources. Use 'em. I need the information in ten minutes, Less if you can do it. I'm serious, friend."

He opened the refrigerator and got out a carton of milk, gave his old roommate the details, and put the sugar bowl on the tray. "Call me back, at this number, when you have the data." As he hung up the phone he grabbed a couple of spoons out of the dishwasher and carried the tray into the library.

"That's a hell of a mess you have there," George Defoe said, looking at the tray. "Milk in a paper carton? And you should have put the coffee in a proper pot, not dragged the electric percolator in here."

Defoe put the tray on the table beside the sofa. "Help yourselves," he said to Kit and the senator, then turned and looked at the elder Defoe behind his desk. "You want a refill, then get up and get it yourself." He walked over to the wall and brought a straight-backed chair to the fireplace, sat so he could see them all without turning his head. "Your service, Senator. The ball is in your court."

"What the hell's the matter with you?" George Defoe asked. "Forgotten your manners?"

"Now, now, George," the senator said, pouring coffee for himself and Kit, "calm down. You'll have to excuse the boy. He's been having a bit of excitement lately. See, he and the General's daughter have been listening to the tapes friend Harmon made. Seems that Harmon got hold of some old Signal Corps photos, taken way back in '45. And young Chase and missy here tracked the originals down, at the Archives, a few hours ago. Photos that point a finger in my direction as an impecunious and somewhat, I'm afraid, impetuous young man. I made off with a small portion of the Nazi gold you R&A boys pointed us to. Tucked it away over there, then came back for it a few years later. Remember the legacy your grandfather left you? The money you came into when you were twenty-one? I do. A hundred thousand dollars. Got you off on the right foot, didn't it, George? God, how I envied you! Well, that's neither here nor there. The point is, I finally got my nest egg. Had to wait until I was thirty years old, but it couldn't have come along at a better time. The war was over, I knew my subject, and there was a whole continent full of art, most of it for sale. Unfortunately, I cut a corner here and there, making my fortune. Daresay I'm not alone in that respect, eh? But the boy here thinks that makes me a killer. Thinks that I killed Harmon last week. And we both know that's not true, don't we? No, that was a crime of passion, wasn't it George? Eh? Harmon put the horns on you, didn't he, back there on VE Day. And when you found out, after all these years, you went over there, confronted him with it, didn't you? Crime of passion, George. I understand. What I need your help with is convincing these two young people. Convince them to let it be." The senator looked first at Chase, then at Kit. "No court is going to convict him of this. There's no evidence. George saw to that, when he had the technical boys clean the place over there. And as for punishment . . . Katherine, don't you think he's suffered enough, the humiliation of knowing that his friend of nearly fifty years had seduced his wife so long ago? Suffered enough, knowing he killed a man he call his friend for all those years? No, child, some things are best left lay. Our motto at The Company was 'The truth shall set you free.' But some secrets are best kept." He turned to the young Defoe and said, "Right, son?"

"What the hell are you talking about?" George Defoe said, rising from behind his desk.

"Hello all," Mary Defoe said, coming into the room with two bags of groceries in her arms and a flush on her cheeks, "I *thought* that was Kit's Volvo. Billy! What a surprise. Chase, darling, there's another pair of bags in the car, would you get them for me?"

TWENTY-FIVE

"Sure," Defoe said, looking at Kit. "Give me a hand, will you?"

Kit tried to disentangle her arm from the senator's, but he held on, saying, "Never mind that right now. Sit down, Mary. Maybe you can help us with these youngsters."

"Goddamn it!" George Defoe said, and came around in front of his desk.

"George!" Mary said, looking at him.

Defoe turned, said to his mother, "Senator Kinship says that your husband killed Harmon Kilgallen, the day he discovered the General's transcript. You remember how you told me that he stormed out of here, wanted to go over and confront the General? Well, according to the senator, he did. And Senator Kinship thinks we should . . . I don't know . . . *overlook* it I guess. Write it off as a crime of passion. Says he's suffered enough, what with the embarrassment of it all. What do you think?"

The telephone rang. "Ah!" Defoe said. "I'll get it." He went to the oval table between the sofa and his father's usual seat by the fireplace and picked up the receiver. "Chase Defoe here. Hi. Uhm hum. Right. What about the other one? Okay. Let you know shortly. G'bye." He cradled the receiver and stood with his back to the fireplace, facing the two men and the two women. He chewed the edge of his lower lip, scratched the back of his right hand with his left, then thrust both of them in his pockets. "Dad?" he said. "Did you tell your old pal Billy about Harmon Kilgallen putting the horns on you?"

"What?" The elder Defoe took a step toward his son, said, "You impudent damned—"

The younger Defoe pulled his hands from his pockets and extended his left, palm toward his father, traffic-cop style. "Mother! How about you? Billy's an old pal. You call him up, bare your soul? The day Dad found the transcript? Or, for that matter, any time in the last forty five years?"

"God*damn* it—"

"No, certainly not, Chase. That was between Harmon, your father, and me. I only told *you* because you came to me and directly asked me about it. Of course you learned of it from the tapes. I knew you would, you and Kit, after you said that she and Samantha had found—"

"Exactly, Mother. Senator Kinship? How did you find out about my mother's little indiscretion? Hear it on a tape, perhaps?"

"Don't know what you're talking about."

"How about the name Kronenberger? Randolph Kronenberger? That ring any bells?" Defoe turned to his father. "Dad?"

"What kind of nonsense—"

"A few minutes ago, in the kitchen, I called . . . well, never mind who. I had someone check the phone calls of the three of you. Defoe, Kinship, and Kronenberger. No record that Kronenberger called Defoe or vice versa. And Senator, with your background in the CIA I'm not surprised that you used pay phones to call him. Unfortunately, Mr. Kronenberger wasn't quite so careful. The few minutes I spent in his company he struck me as a little too sure of himself. Anyway, he made a call to your private line in the Senate office building, from the cellular telephone in his car. Spoke to you at six fifty-one, P.M. I can't prove that he was on one end and you were on the other." He turned to Kit, said, "But that was not too many minutes after you discovered that someone had broken into your father's house and taken the tapes, was it, Kit?"

"Yes," she said, nodding her head, speaking for the first time since the senator had intercepted them outside the National Archives. Her voice cracked and she swallowed, cleared her throat. "He, that man, Kronenberger, said that he was hiding in the closet, while I was on the telephone with Sammy. He told me he was watching me when you came in the front door, Chase. I never even thought about it, until now. He had to have been the one who stole the tapes."

"You're excused, Kit. Had a lot of other things on your mind, right? Yes, Kronenberger stole the tapes. And called Senator Kinship, then delivered the tapes to him. How else could the senator have learned about the General and my mother, on VE Day? And it had to be someone who knew both Mother and General Kilgallen to figure it out. What was it I said earlier today, Dad? Maybe there were half a dozen people alive who would make the connection? Well, Senator Kinship made the connection. You gave it away in the car, Senator, when you twitted me about the general's phone bill. Because you also mentioned the Federal Express delivery and the disc jockey giving the time on the radio. The only way you could know about either of those things was to have listened to the tapes. And when you heard the tapes you also realized that you had been identified by General Kilgallen as the mysterious 'Pierson' who stole the gold and murdered the GI driving the jeep." Defoe paused while he studied the senator. "I suppose you consider murder just another . . . 'rash act?' Impetuous, you called yourself. I'll give you the benefit of the doubt, Senator. Won't call it premeditated murder. However, I won't be so charitable about the two men I killed last night. Spaar, your killer, too unstable, too— what did the report we saw at the FBI say, Kit? Spaar was released from the CIA for 'deviate behavior,' wasn't it? Have to be pretty bad for the *CIA* to drop you. And you sent him after us, Senator. And later, Kronenberger. Premeditated murder, Senator. Murder by contract."

George Defoe said, "What in the name of heaven—"

"I can see why you're having trouble following this, Dad. But try to keep up, will you? This is the speed we moved at, out in the field. Don't have the luxury of taking things under advisement, drafting position papers. Tell me, Senator. What did you hope to gain, by murdering me and Kit? Were you going to kill her daughter Samantha, too? My mother? Where was it going to stop?"

"Shut up!" The senator struggled to his feet and pulled a

small automatic from the pocket of his overcoat, thumbed the safety off, and held the weapon close to his side. "That damn fool! Kronenberger; he knew better than to call me on a traceable phone." He turned to Defoe. "As for this other CIA man, I know nothing about that, I swear to you. That must have been Kronenberger's doing. He . . . he was supposed to do it himself, make it look like an accident. Oh, don't look so surprised, George. Butter wouldn't melt in your mouth. You knew what kind of black operations we ran. Daresay you had a hand in planning one or two." He turned back to the younger Defoe. "Things weren't supposed to ever go as far as they did." He glanced at Kit, said, "I never meant to kill your father, child. It was an accident. He recognized me from the photographs, called me for an explanation. I went over there, and he started ranting as I came in the door." The senator paused and laughed once, almost a cough. "It wasn't that I made off with the damned boxes of gold that upset him so much, it was his not *knowing* all these years that I had been right there in Ohrduf, missed running into him by fifteen minutes or so. Well, the reasons aren't important, not now. I hit him with my cane. Swung it at him, in a moment of temper. The tip connected with his temple, killed him deader than a doornail. So I burned the photographs; had to burn all the other papers, of course. And rigged up the suicide thing." He made a little gesture toward Kit with his free hand. "I'm sorry, child." He turned back to Chase, the man he felt he had to explain it all to. "At the funeral I learned about Samantha's copies of his notes, and I called Randolph, had him break into her apartment, destroy the carbons. And then a few hours later George called me, told me about the tapes. Asked me to urge you not to pursue the General's death. You're a fool, George. A self-centered old fool. Putting your fear of being exposed as a cuckold, half a century after the fact, over the murder of one of your oldest friends. You should be ashamed of yourself.

"Anyway, son, it just kept accelerating. First the carbons, then the tapes. When I sent Randolph for them I told him not to involve you or Katherine, not to make contact." The senator looked down at the gun for a moment, then back up at Defoe. "And then I listened to them, on that little machine. I couldn't face the exposure, son. The humiliation, not after all these years. I'm just like George, aren't I? Filled with self-importance." The senator fumbled behind him for his cane, keeping his eyes on the only person in the room who was any threat to him. He edged around the sofa and backed out of the room, keeping the gun close to his side. "Another mess for you to clean up, George," he said, and they heard the front door open a moment later.

They were still standing as they had been when they heard a car door slam, and a second later a similar sound, as though he had shut the door again. The four of them looked at each other and started for the library door.

"Wait," Defoe said, and his parents and Kit stopped. He went into the hallway, went out the front door, then came back into the room a moment later. "Senator Kinship," he said, "got into the backseat of his car and shot himself. Dad?"

TWENTY-SIX

"I suppose this is what he meant by cleaning up another mess." George Defoe looked down at the senator's body, slumped on the seat of his car. A dark crimson spot, no bigger than a thumbtack, marked the entry wound.

Mary and Kit stood beneath the portico of the house, a few feet away, watching the two men at the car.

"There is a lot more than this to be cleaned up," the younger man answered. "There is a dead body in the backyard over at General Kilgallen's house. I killed him, last night, when he broke into the house to kill Kit and me. And then there is Randolph Kronenberger. Out in an industrial park, near the Beltway. I killed him, too, shot him with the General's .45. Looks like I'm going to have some explaining to do. Can you recommend a good lawyer? Someone other than Jack Brill, please."

"Lawyer? Don't be ridiculous, son. I'll take care of this. Without any publicity. Can't have your name dragged in the mud." He put his hand on his son's shoulder. "Blood's thicker than water, y'know."

"Oh, *can* it, will you? I figured it out. I know what's got you so worked up about Mother and the General."

"What are you talking about?"

"He was my *father,* damn it! You were off in Europe when I was conceived."

"Mary? What the hell's he talking about?"

"Chase, darling—"

"Come on, Mother! I told you, I figured it out. Calculated backward. I was born nine months after VE Day. The day George Defoe was raising hell in London. And from there he went to Switzerland for who knows how long. Finally followed by a week-long boat ride back to the states! *I know!*"

"Darling, a mother knows who is the father of her children." She looked at the younger woman beside her. "And a couple of weeks on either side of nine months is perfectly normal, isn't that right, Kit? As a matter of fact, Chase, *you* were a week *early.* Besides, your father didn't go on to Switzerland. Did you, George?"

"No, of course not. What was the point? The war was over. I bullied and bribed my way onto an Army Air Corps plane; was home in my own bed the next day. In bed with my wife, I might add." He looked, first at his wife, then at his son, and smiled.

His son smiled, too, then laughed, and walked to Kit and kissed her. "Told ya so," she said.

He put his arm around her waist and they turned and went into the house. He stopped at the bottom of the stairs and said to George and Mary Defoe, "Kit and I have been up all night. We've been assaulted, beaten, kidnapped, lied to, and subjected to sustained bureaucratic abuse. We're going upstairs, to bed."

She took his arm and leaned against him, favoring her ankle as they went slowly up the broad staircase.

Defoe no longer knew if anything he'd heard that day was true or not. And he didn't care.

Deforest Day was born in 1941 in Greenwich, Connecticut, and attended Yale College. He lives with his wife and son near Reading, Pennsylvania. *Fatal Recall* is his third Defoe novel.